Archie® as THE MAN FROM R.I.V.E.R.D.A.L.E.

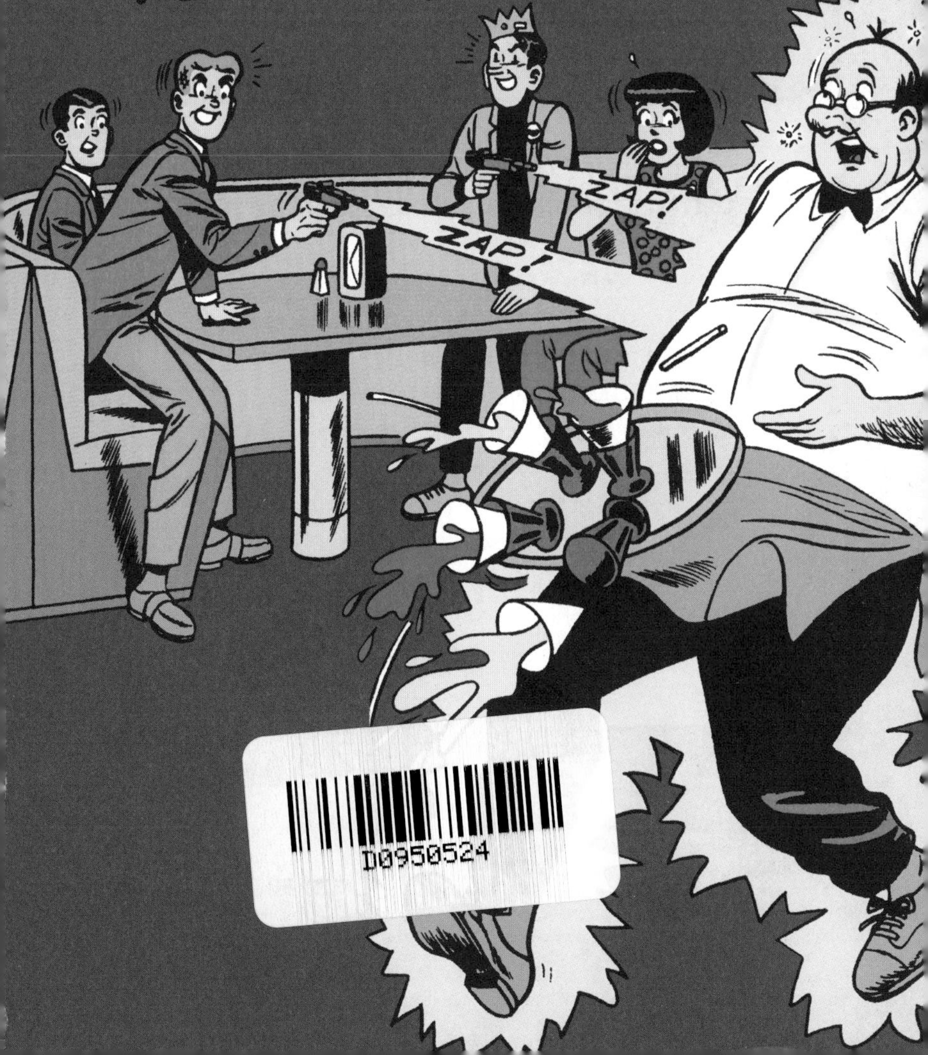
ZAP!
ZAP!

Archie. as THE MAN FROM R.I.V.E.R.D.A.L.E.

Publisher / Co-CEO: Jon Goldwater

Co-President / Editor-In-Chief: Victor Gorelick

Co-President: Mike Pellerito

Co-President: Alex Segura

Chief Creative Officer: Roberto Aguirre-Sacasa

Chief Operating Officer: William Mooar

Chief Financial Officer: Robert Wintle

Director of Book Sales & Operations: Jonathan Betancourt

Art Director: Vincent Lovallo

Production Manager: Stephen Oswald

Lead Designer: Kari McLachlan

Associate Editor: Carlos Antunes

Editor: Jamie Lee Rotante

Co-CEO: Nancy Silberkleit

Printed in USA. First Printing. March, 2019. ISBN: 978-1-68255-845-4

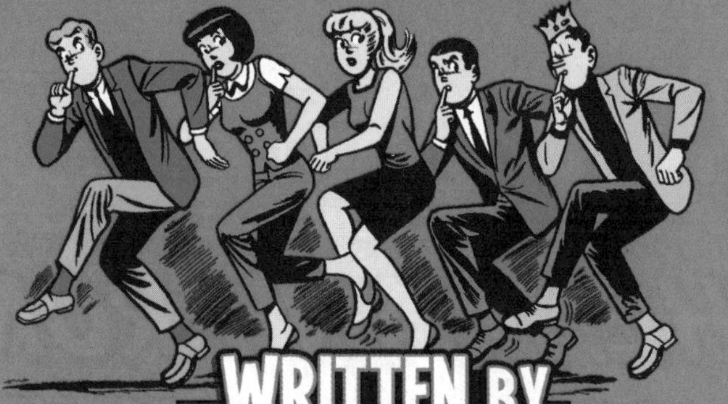

WRITTEN BY

Frank Doyle

ART BY

Bob White, Bill Vigoda, Dan DeCarlo,
Vince DeCarlo, Marty Epp, Mario Acquaviva,
Victor Gorelick & Jon D'Agostino

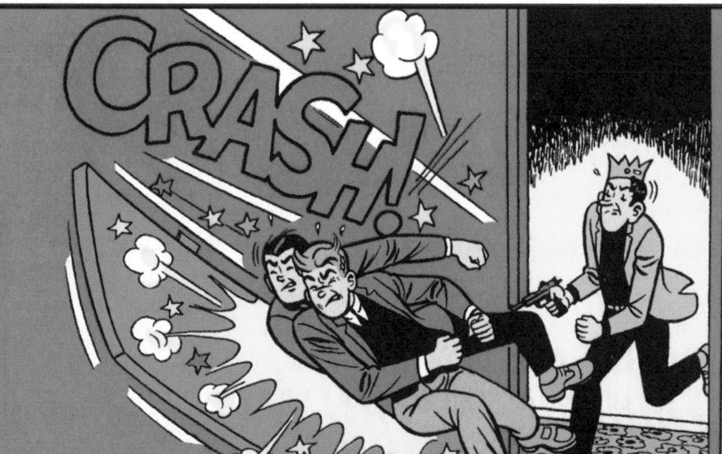
CRASH!

This book contains some material that was originally created in a less socially sensitive time in our society and reflects attitudes that may be interpreted as being unacceptable today. The stories are reprinted here without alteration for historical reference.

Archie® as THE MAN FROM R.I.V.E.R.D.A.L.E.

TABLE OF CONTENTS

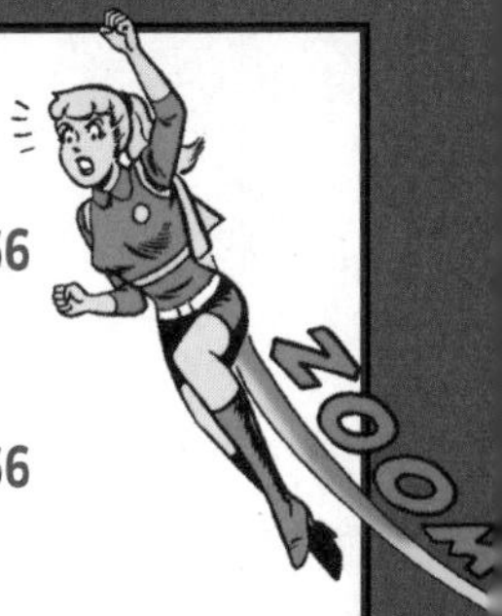
ZOOM

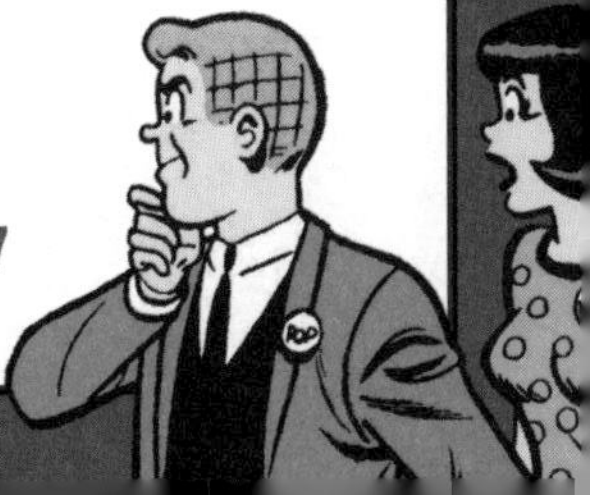

Archie® as THE MAN FROM R.I.V.E.R.D.A.L.E.

The *Man from R.I.V.E.R.D.A.L.E.* was a subseries of Archie stories in an alternate universe that ran from 1966–1967, spanning a number of titles include *Life with Archie* and the *Archie Giant Series*. Parodying spy shows of the time (most famously, *The Man from U.N.C.L.E.*), this alternate take on the gang portrays Archie and his friends as a group of low-key, high-tech spies, who are a part of the world defense organization Protect our Planet—known better as P.O.P. Their main enemies are part of a counter group known as C.R.U.S.H. (a spoof on enemy group T.H.R.U.S.H. from *The Man from U.N.C.L.E.* television series). All the

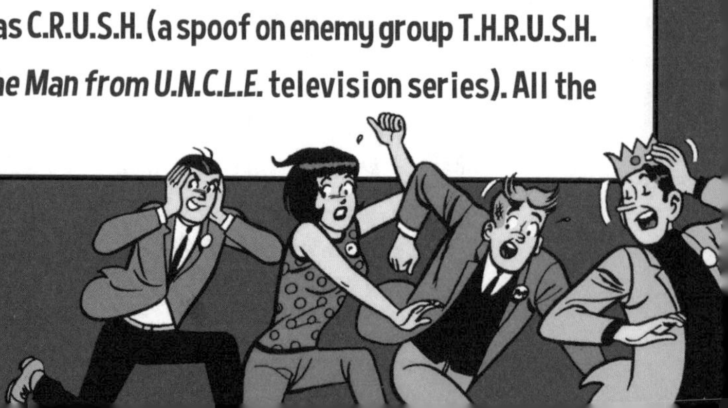

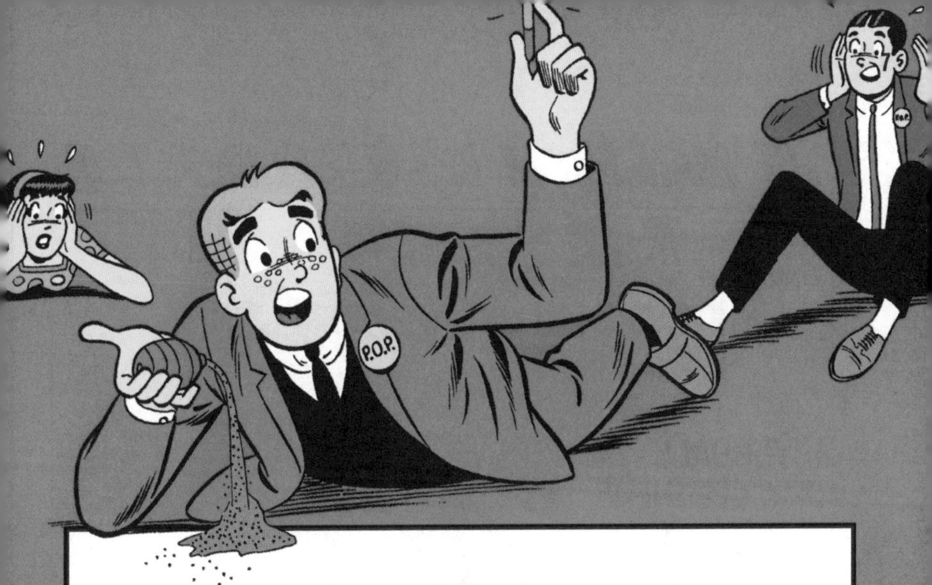
P.O.P.

characters also have undefined acronyms for names (A.R.C.H.I.E., B.E.T.T.Y., etc.). R.I.V.E.R.D.A.L.E. stands for Really Impressive Vast Enterprise for Routing Dangerous Adversaries, Louts, Etc.

Though the original series only ran over the course of a little more than a year, the *Man from R.I.V.E.R.D.A.L.E.* series made a cameo in a 2008 issue of Archie and was revived for a four-part series in the same title in 2010. The *Man from R.I.V.E.R.D.A.L.E.* then returned a second time in Jughead #3,
released in February, 2016.

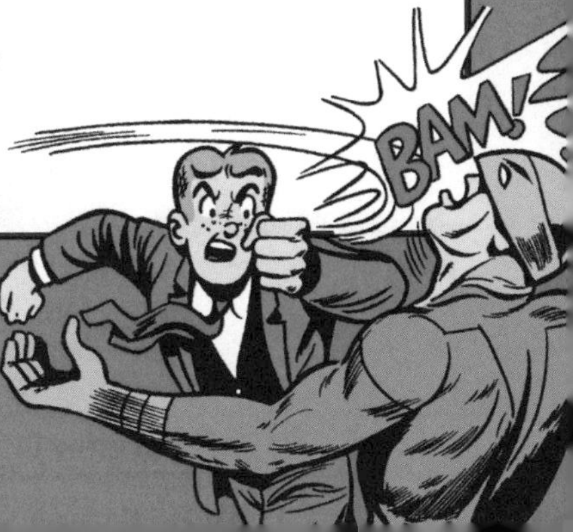
BAM!

THE MAN FROM R.I.V.E.R.D.A.L.E.

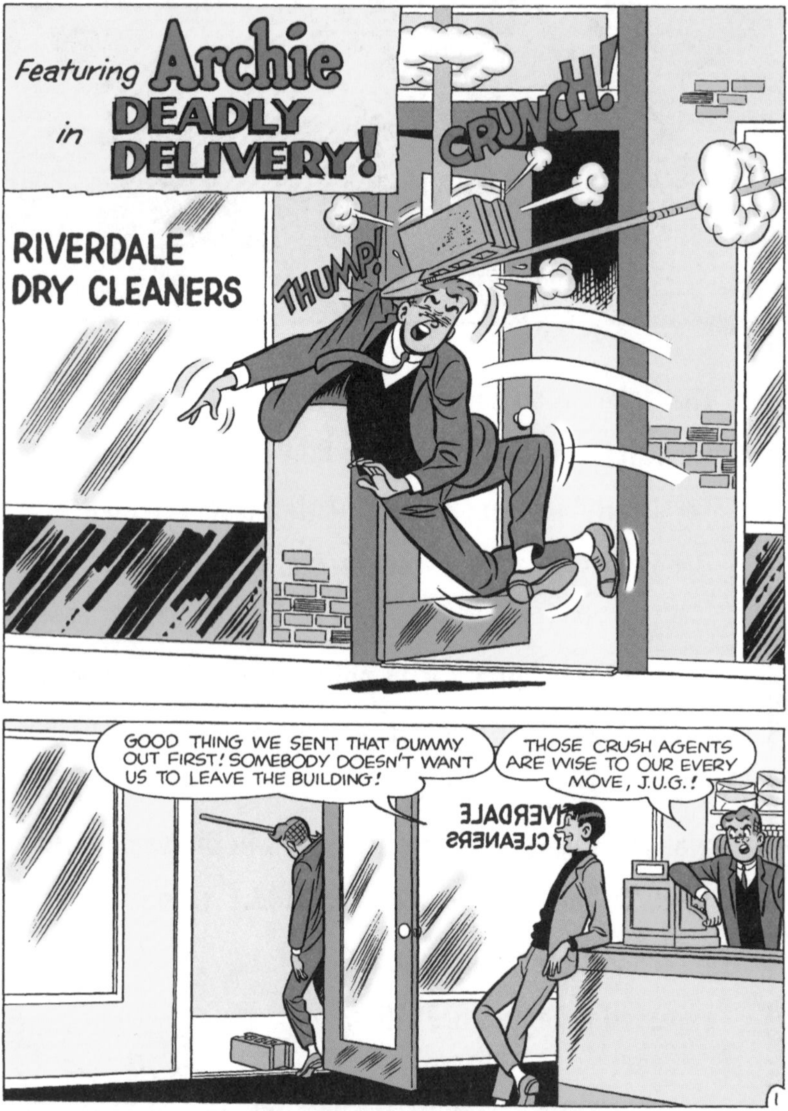
Featuring Archie
in DEADLY DELIVERY!
RIVERDALE DRY CLEANERS
CRUNCH!
THUMP!
GOOD THING WE SENT THAT DUMMY OUT FIRST! SOMEBODY DOESN'T WANT US TO LEAVE THE BUILDING!
THOSE CRUSH AGENTS ARE WISE TO OUR EVERY MOVE, J.U.G.!

Story: Frank Doyle   Pencils: Bob White
Inks & Letters: Marty Epp

Originally printed in LIFE WITH ARCHIE #47, MARCH 1966

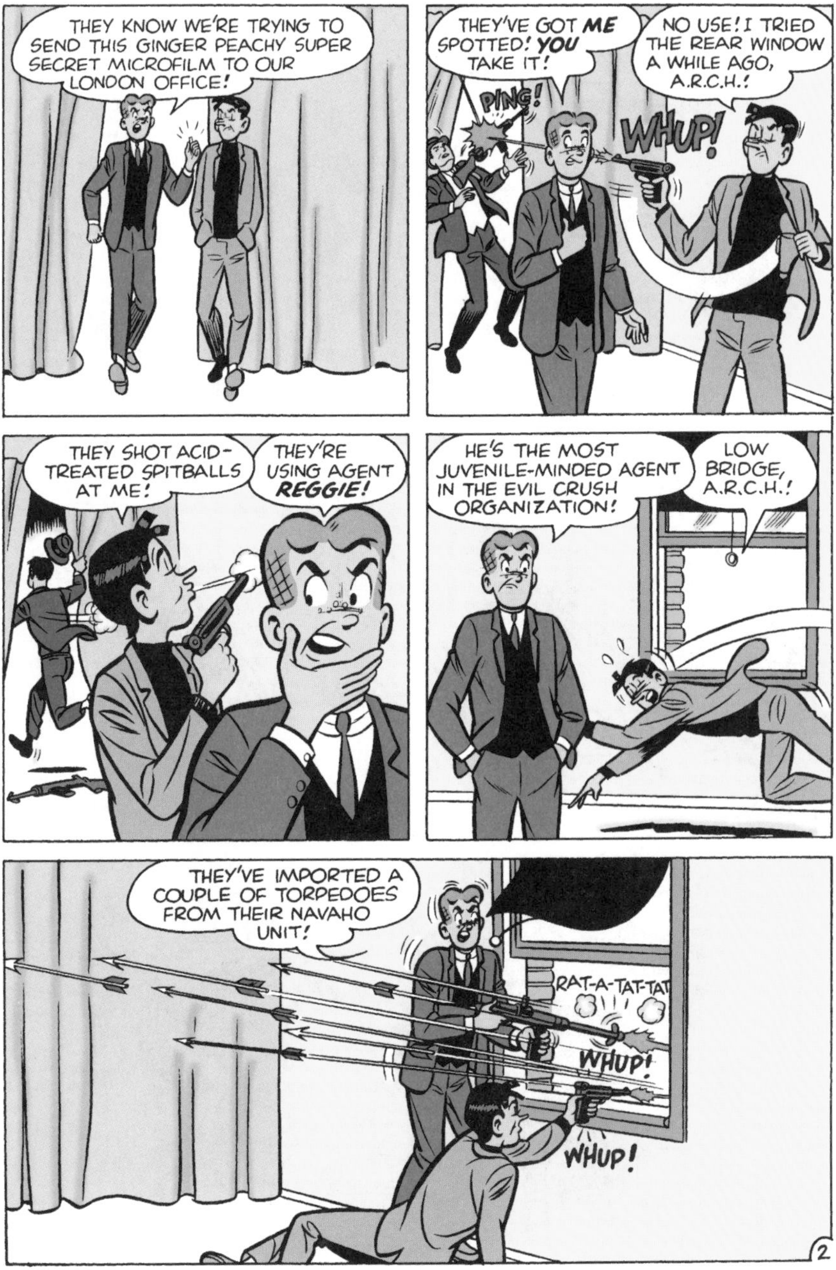
THEY KNOW WE'RE TRYING TO SEND THIS GINGER PEACHY SUPER SECRET MICROFILM TO OUR LONDON OFFICE!
THEY'VE GOT ME SPOTTED! YOU TAKE IT!
NO USE! I TRIED THE REAR WINDOW A WHILE AGO, A.R.C.H.!
PING!
WHUP!
THEY SHOT ACID-TREATED SPITBALLS AT ME!
THEY'RE USING AGENT REGGIE!
HE'S THE MOST JUVENILE-MINDED AGENT IN THE EVIL CRUSH ORGANIZATION!
LOW BRIDGE, A.R.C.H.!
THEY'VE IMPORTED A COUPLE OF TORPEDOES FROM THEIR NAVAHO UNIT!
RAT-A-TAT-TAT
WHUP!
WHUP!
2

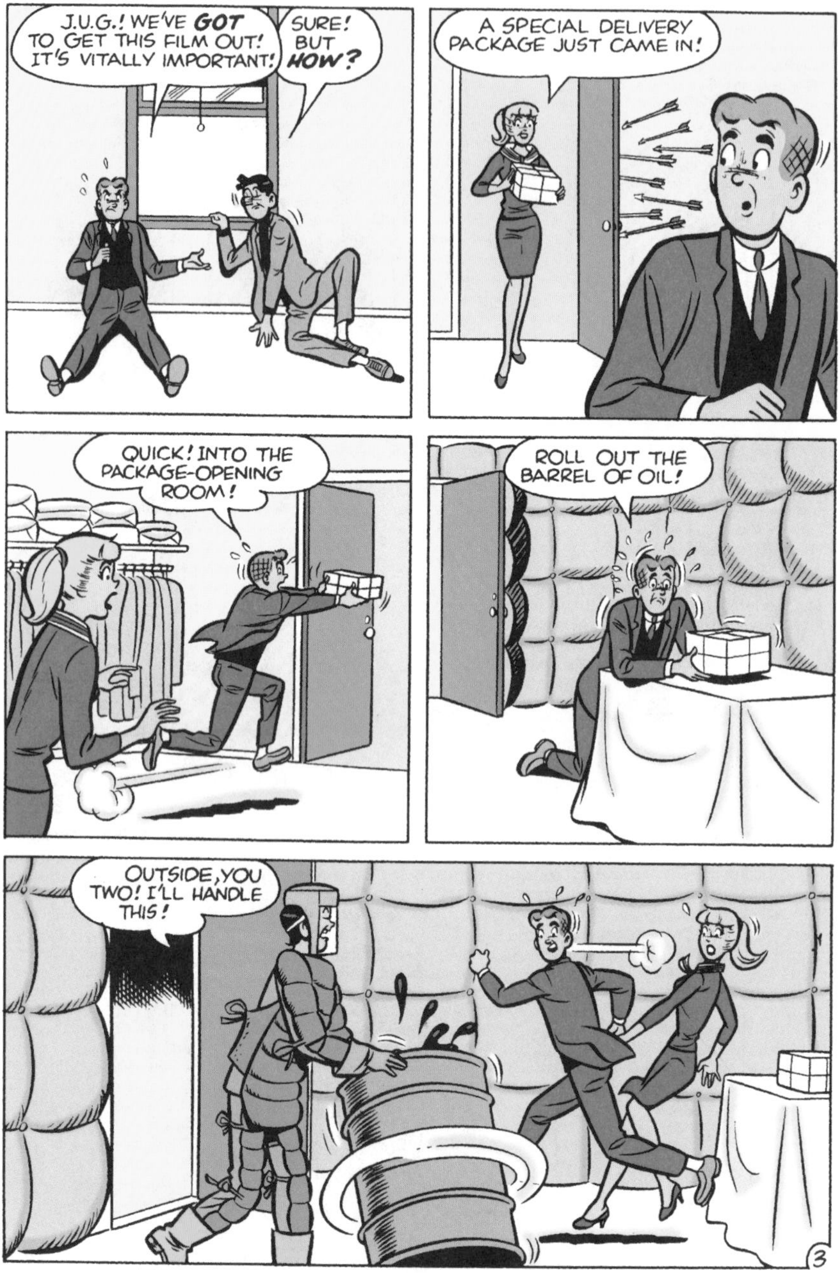
J.U.G.! WE'VE GOT TO GET THIS FILM OUT! IT'S VITALLY IMPORTANT!
SURE! BUT HOW?
A SPECIAL DELIVERY PACKAGE JUST CAME IN!
QUICK! INTO THE PACKAGE-OPENING ROOM!
ROLL OUT THE BARREL OF OIL!
OUTSIDE, YOU TWO! I'LL HANDLE THIS!
3

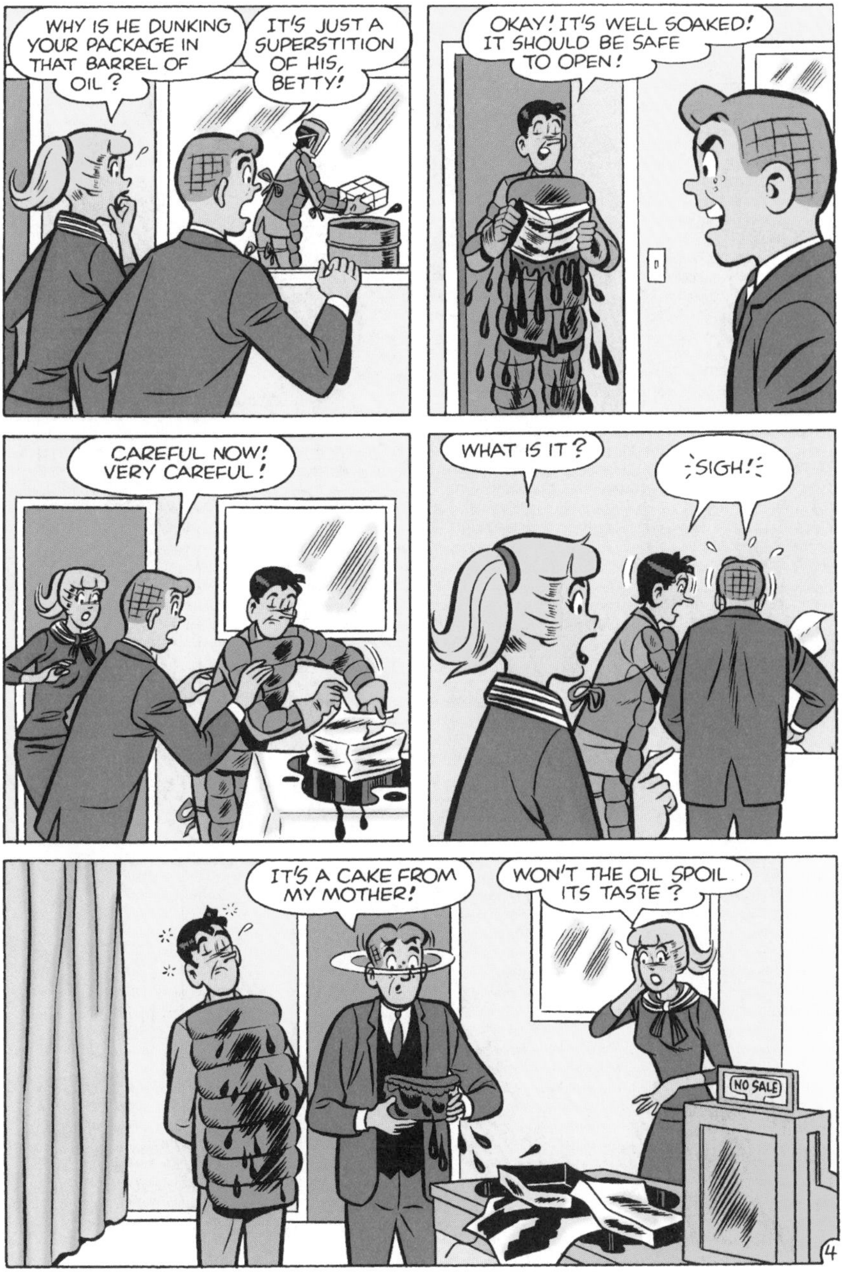
WHY IS HE DUNKING YOUR PACKAGE IN THAT BARREL OF OIL?
IT'S JUST A SUPERSTITION OF HIS, BETTY!
OKAY! IT'S WELL SOAKED! IT SHOULD BE SAFE TO OPEN!
CAREFUL NOW! VERY CAREFUL!
WHAT IS IT?
SIGH!
IT'S A CAKE FROM MY MOTHER!
WON'T THE OIL SPOIL ITS TASTE?
NO SALE
4

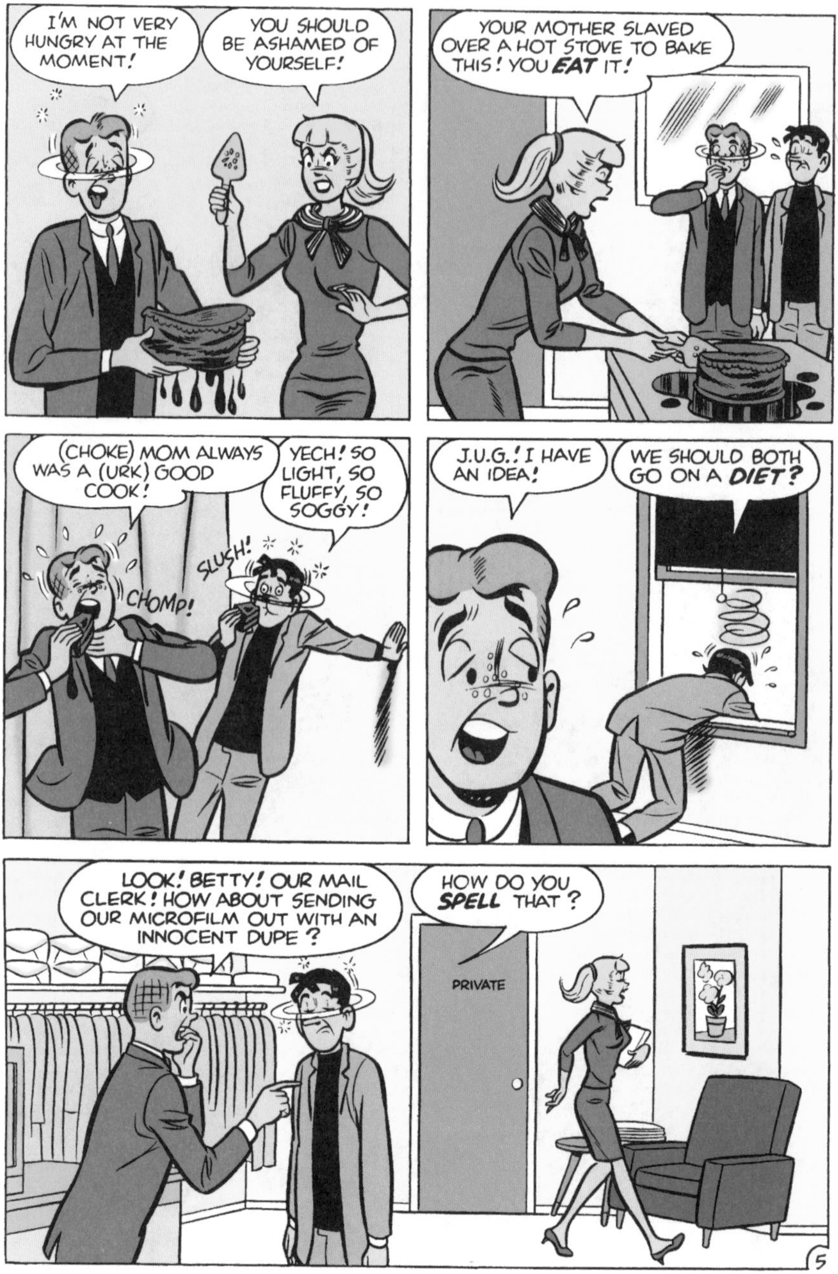
I'M NOT VERY HUNGRY AT THE MOMENT!
YOU SHOULD BE ASHAMED OF YOURSELF!
YOUR MOTHER SLAVED OVER A HOT STOVE TO BAKE THIS! YOU EAT IT!
(CHOKE) MOM ALWAYS WAS A (URK) GOOD COOK!
CHOMP!
SLUSH!
YECH! SO LIGHT, SO FLUFFY, SO SOGGY!
J.U.G.! I HAVE AN IDEA!
WE SHOULD BOTH GO ON A DIET?
LOOK! BETTY! OUR MAIL CLERK! HOW ABOUT SENDING OUR MICROFILM OUT WITH AN INNOCENT DUPE?
HOW DO YOU SPELL THAT?
PRIVATE
5

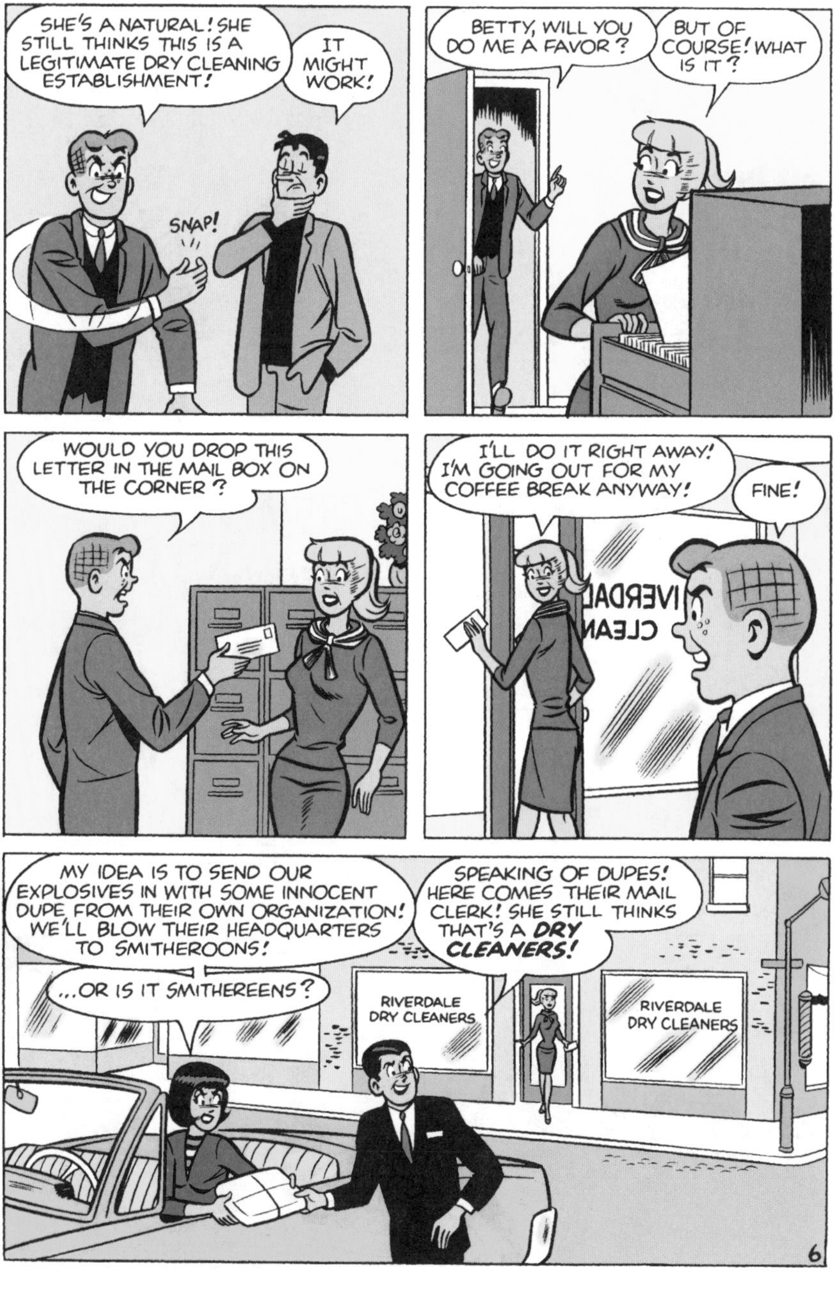
SHE'S A NATURAL! SHE STILL THINKS THIS IS A LEGITIMATE DRY CLEANING ESTABLISHMENT!
IT MIGHT WORK!
SNAP!
BETTY, WILL YOU DO ME A FAVOR?
BUT OF COURSE! WHAT IS IT?
WOULD YOU DROP THIS LETTER IN THE MAIL BOX ON THE CORNER?
I'LL DO IT RIGHT AWAY! I'M GOING OUT FOR MY COFFEE BREAK ANYWAY!
FINE!
MY IDEA IS TO SEND OUR EXPLOSIVES IN WITH SOME INNOCENT DUPE FROM THEIR OWN ORGANIZATION! WE'LL BLOW THEIR HEADQUARTERS TO SMITHEROONS!
...OR IS IT SMITHEREENS?
SPEAKING OF DUPES! HERE COMES THEIR MAIL CLERK! SHE STILL THINKS THAT'S A DRY CLEANERS!
RIVERDALE DRY CLEANERS
RIVERDALE DRY CLEANERS
6

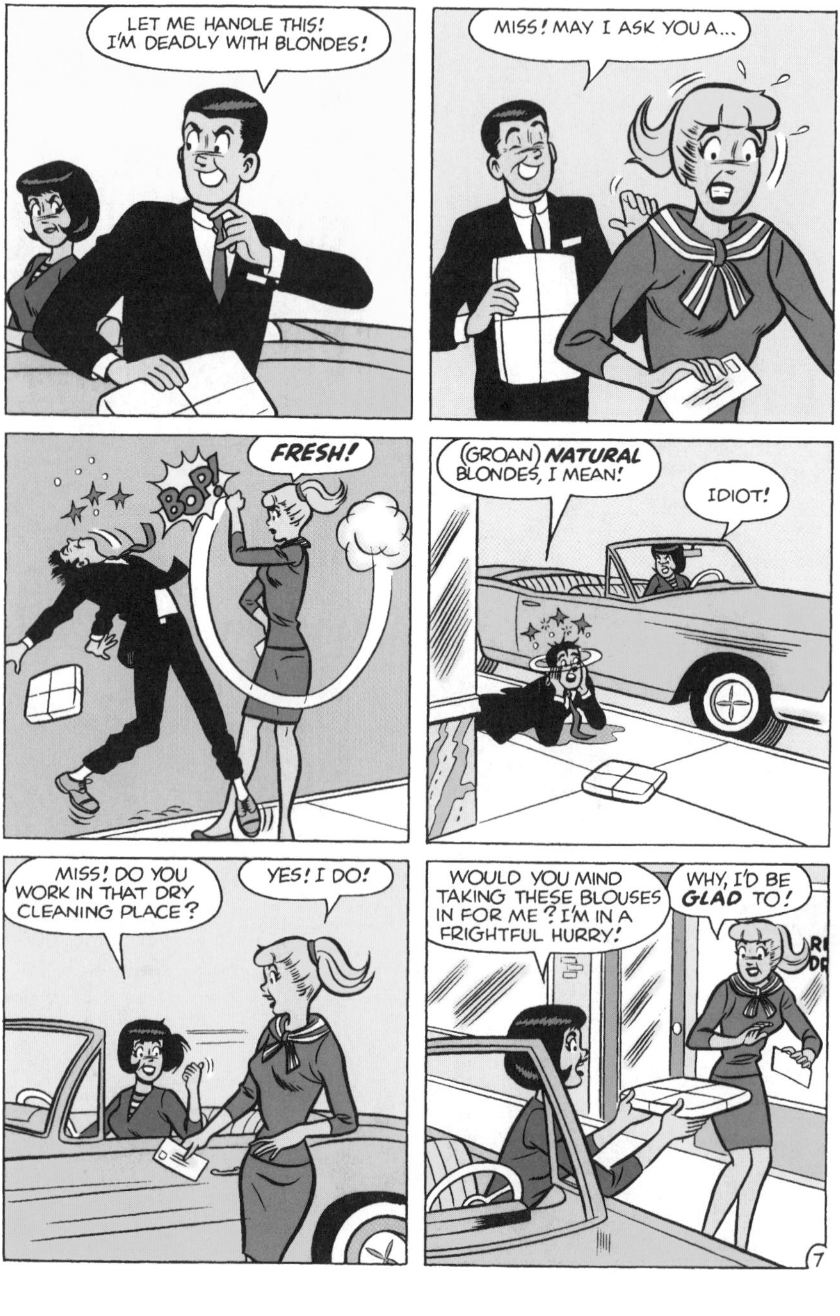
LET ME HANDLE THIS! I'M DEADLY WITH BLONDES!
MISS! MAY I ASK YOU A...
FRESH!
BOP!
(GROAN) NATURAL BLONDES, I MEAN!
IDIOT!
MISS! DO YOU WORK IN THAT DRY CLEANING PLACE?
YES! I DO!
WOULD YOU MIND TAKING THESE BLOUSES IN FOR ME? I'M IN A FRIGHTFUL HURRY!
WHY, I'D BE GLAD TO!
7

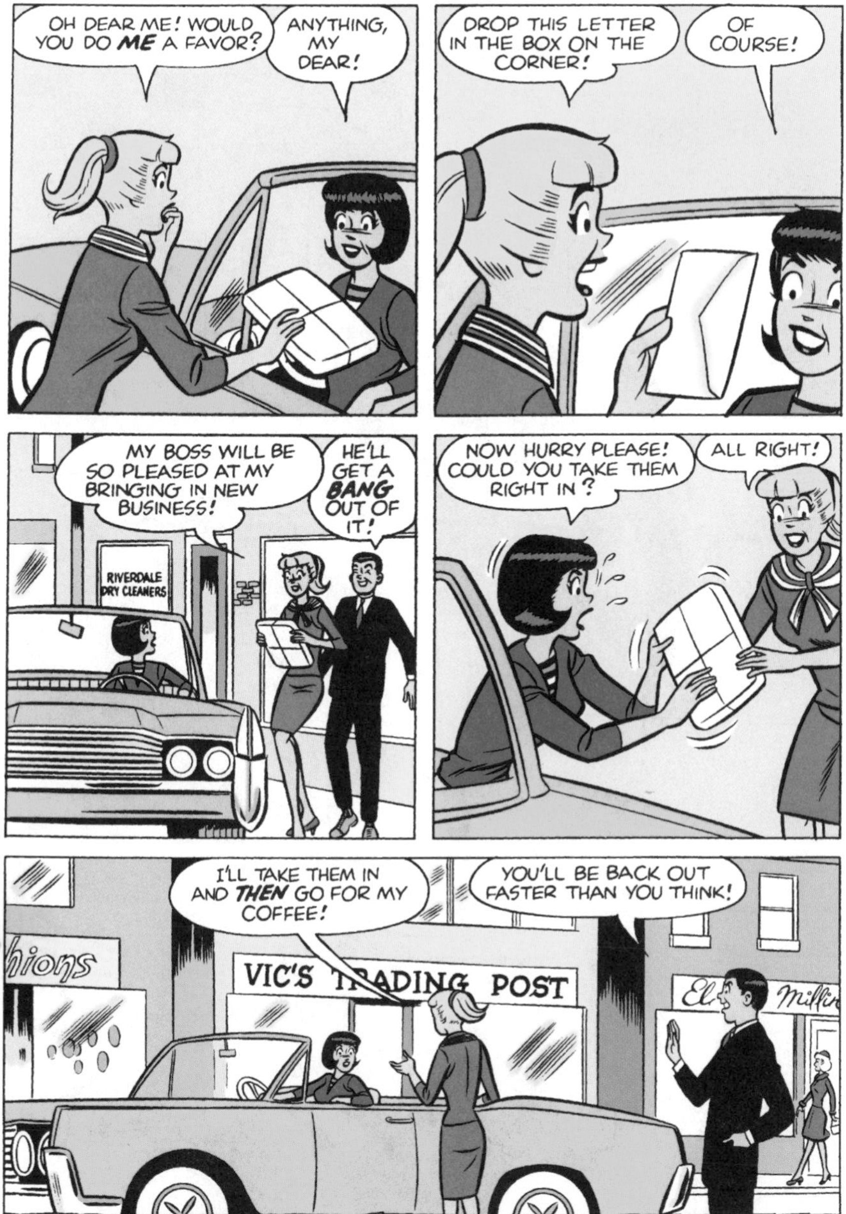
OH DEAR ME! WOULD YOU DO ME A FAVOR?
ANYTHING, MY DEAR!
DROP THIS LETTER IN THE BOX ON THE CORNER!
OF COURSE!
MY BOSS WILL BE SO PLEASED AT MY BRINGING IN NEW BUSINESS!
HE'LL GET A BANG OUT OF IT!
RIVERDALE DRY CLEANERS
NOW HURRY PLEASE! COULD YOU TAKE THEM RIGHT IN?
ALL RIGHT!
I'LL TAKE THEM IN AND THEN GO FOR MY COFFEE!
YOU'LL BE BACK OUT FASTER THAN YOU THINK!
VIC'S TRADING POST
IS THIS THE END OF THE GOOD GUYS? WILL THE MAN FROM R.I.V.E.R.D.A.L.E. AND HIS COHORTS BE BLOWN TO SMITHEREENS?...OR IS IT SMITHEROONS?
8

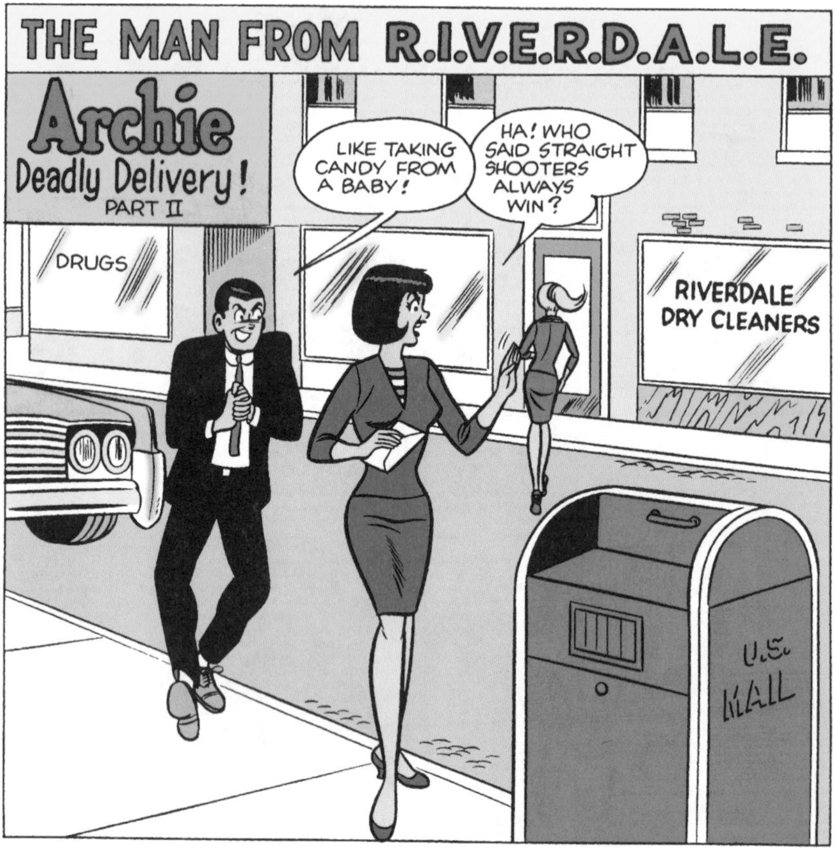
THE MAN FROM R.I.V.E.R.D.A.L.E.
Archie
Deadly Delivery!
PART II
LIKE TAKING CANDY FROM A BABY!
HA! WHO SAID STRAIGHT SHOOTERS ALWAYS WIN?
DRUGS
RIVERDALE DRY CLEANERS
U.S. MAIL

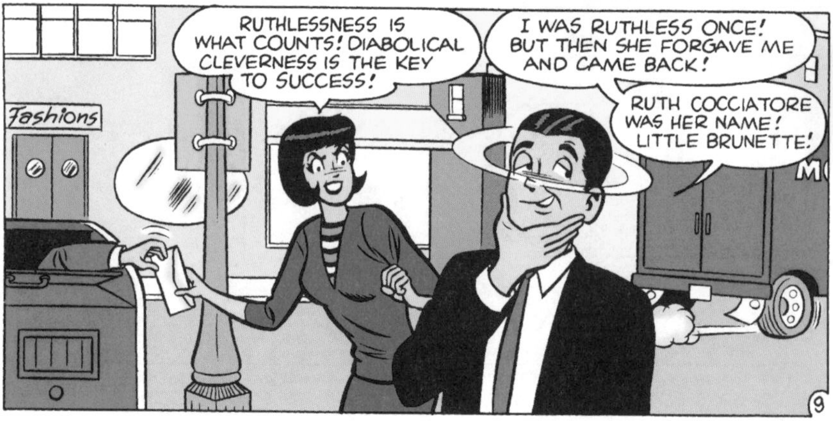
RUTHLESSNESS IS WHAT COUNTS! DIABOLICAL CLEVERNESS IS THE KEY TO SUCCESS!
I WAS RUTHLESS ONCE! BUT THEN SHE FORGAVE ME AND CAME BACK!
RUTH COCCIATORE WAS HER NAME! LITTLE BRUNETTE!
Fashions
9

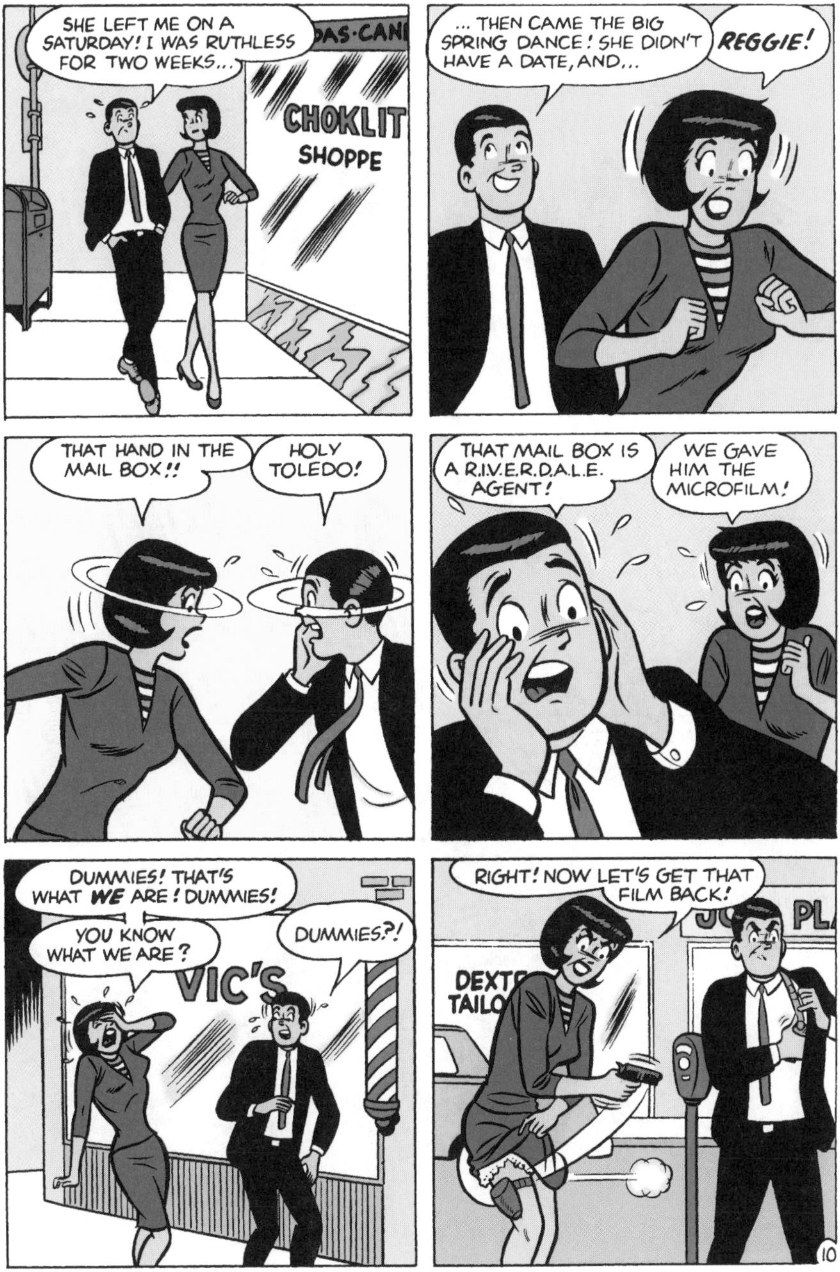
SHE LEFT ME ON A SATURDAY! I WAS RUTHLESS FOR TWO WEEKS...
DAS·CAN
CHOKLIT SHOPPE
... THEN CAME THE BIG SPRING DANCE! SHE DIDN'T HAVE A DATE, AND...
REGGIE!
THAT HAND IN THE MAIL BOX!!
HOLY TOLEDO!
THAT MAIL BOX IS A R.I.V.E.R.D.A.L.E. AGENT!
WE GAVE HIM THE MICROFILM!
YOU KNOW WHAT WE ARE?
DUMMIES?!
DUMMIES! THAT'S WHAT WE ARE! DUMMIES!
VIC'S
RIGHT! NOW LET'S GET THAT FILM BACK!
DEXT
TAILO
10

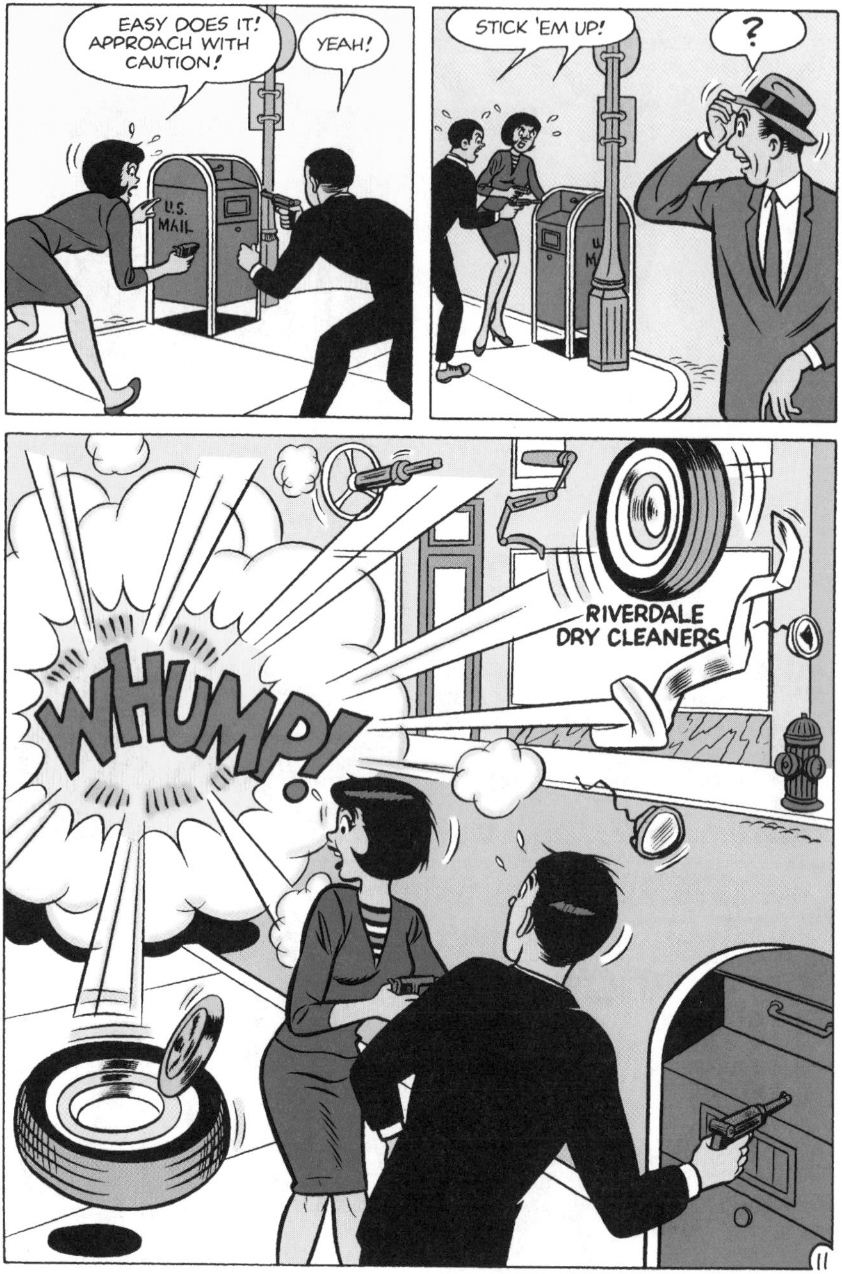
EASY DOES IT! APPROACH WITH CAUTION!
YEAH!
U.S. MAIL
STICK 'EM UP!
?
WHUMP!
RIVERDALE DRY CLEANERS
11

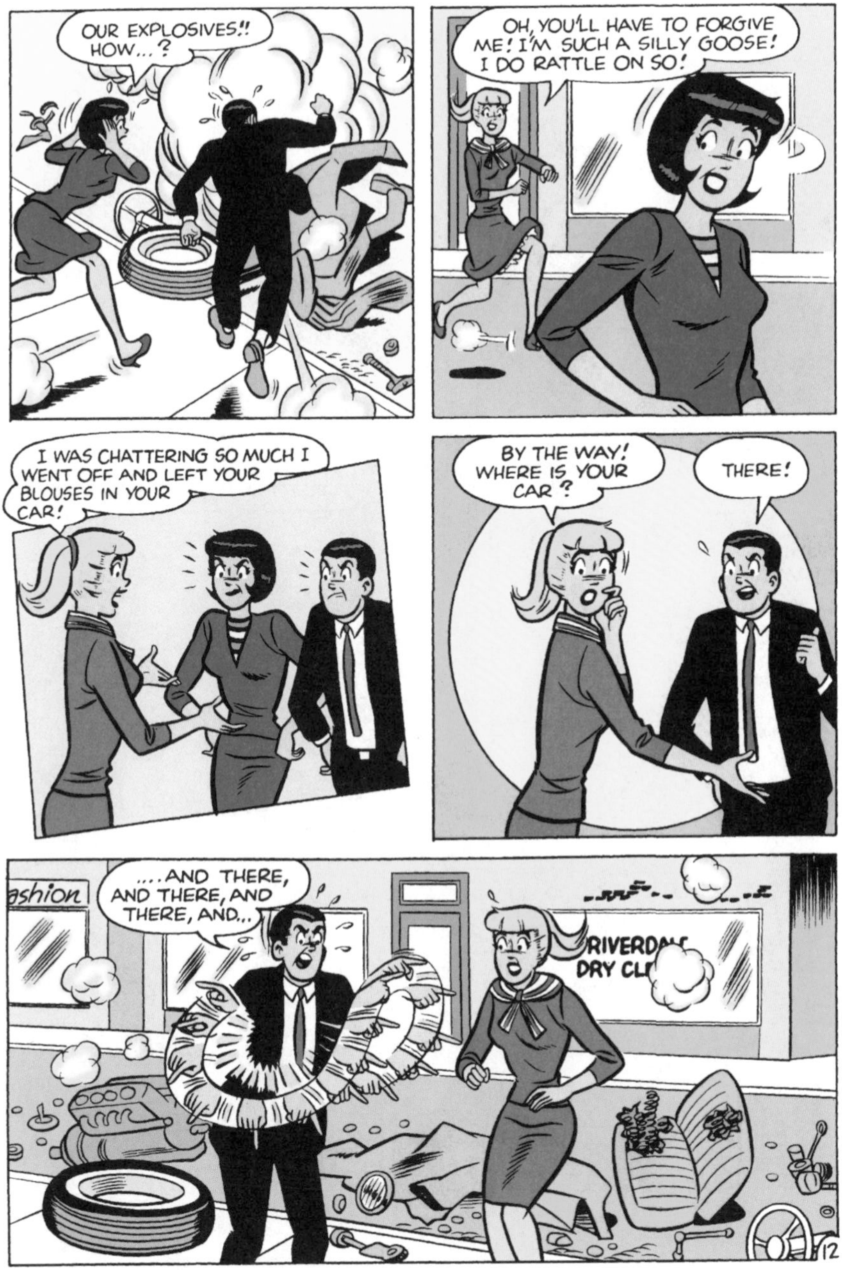
OUR EXPLOSIVES!! HOW...?
OH, YOU'LL HAVE TO FORGIVE ME! I'M SUCH A SILLY GOOSE! I DO RATTLE ON SO!
I WAS CHATTERING SO MUCH I WENT OFF AND LEFT YOUR BLOUSES IN YOUR CAR!
BY THE WAY! WHERE IS YOUR CAR?
THERE!
....AND THERE, AND THERE, AND THERE, AND...
ashion
RIVERDA
DRY CL
12

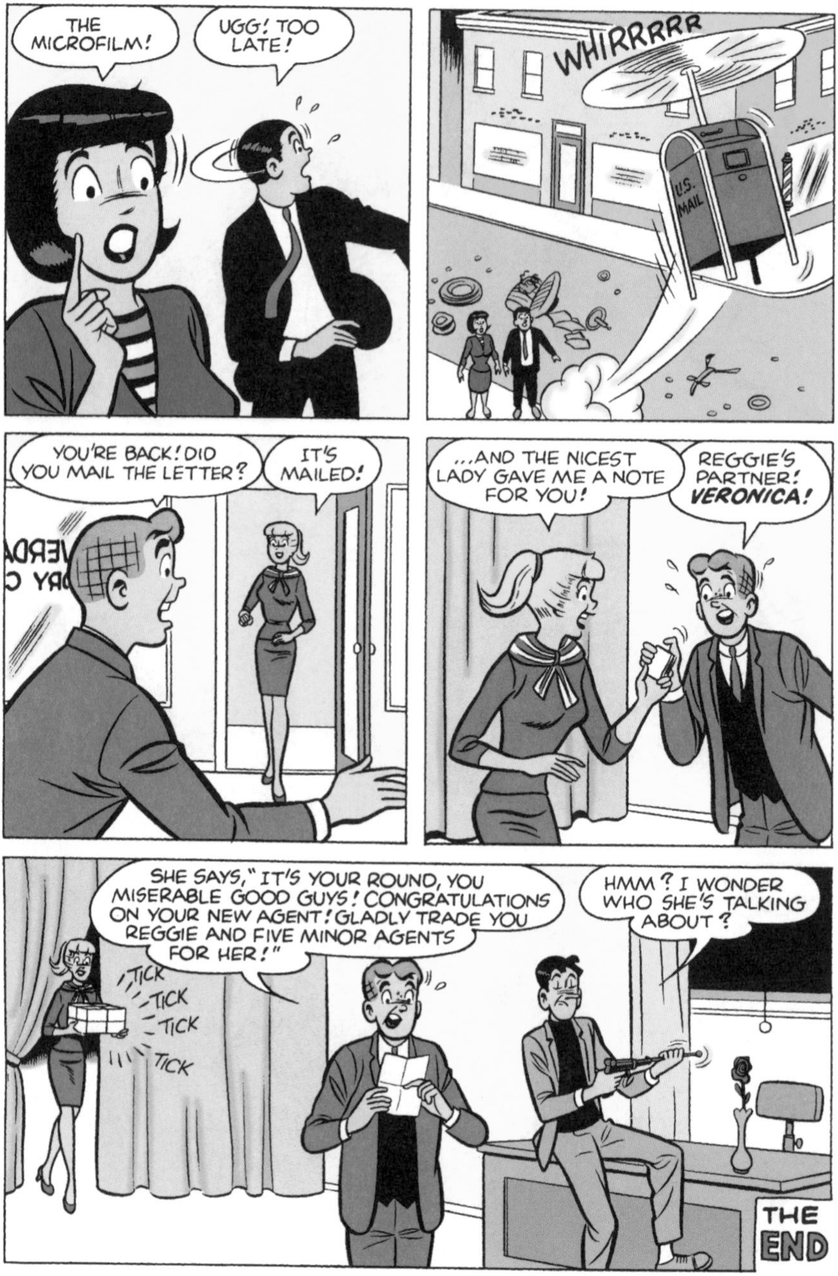
THE MICROFILM!
UGG! TOO LATE!
WHIRRRRR
U.S. MAIL
YOU'RE BACK! DID YOU MAIL THE LETTER?
IT'S MAILED!
...AND THE NICEST LADY GAVE ME A NOTE FOR YOU!
REGGIE'S PARTNER! VERONICA!
SHE SAYS," IT'S YOUR ROUND, YOU MISERABLE GOOD GUYS! CONGRATULATIONS ON YOUR NEW AGENT! GLADLY TRADE YOU REGGIE AND FIVE MINOR AGENTS FOR HER!"
TICK
TICK
TICK
TICK
HMM? I WONDER WHO SHE'S TALKING ABOUT?
THE END

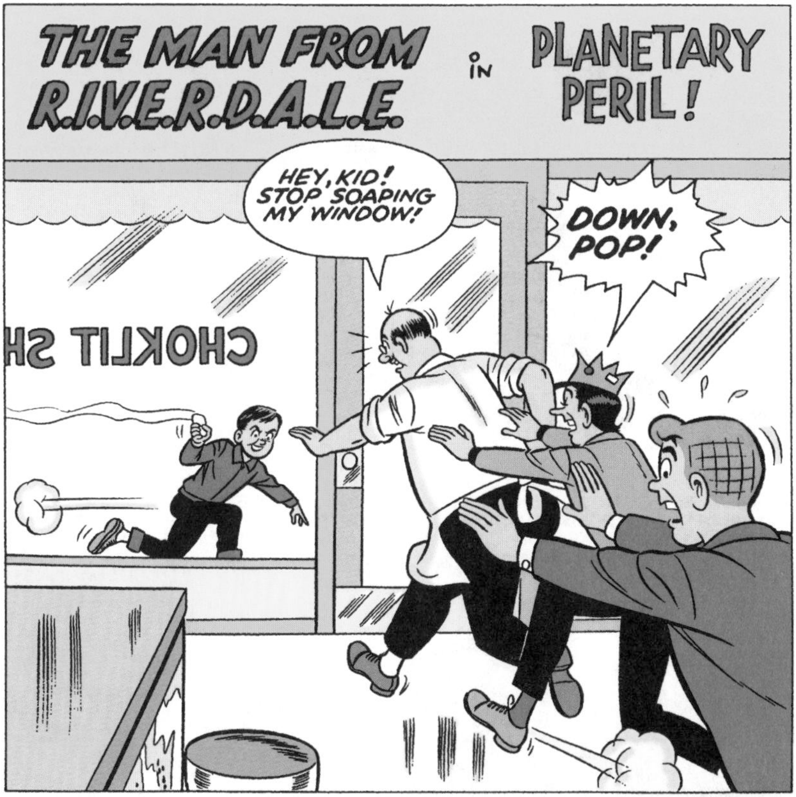
THE MAN FROM R.I.V.E.R.D.A.L.E. in PLANETARY PERIL!
HEY, KID! STOP SOAPING MY WINDOW!
DOWN, POP!

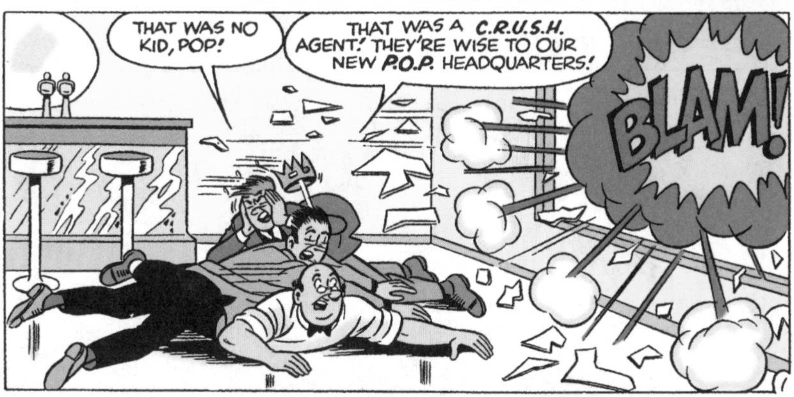
THAT WAS NO KID, POP!
THAT WAS A C.R.U.S.H. AGENT! THEY'RE WISE TO OUR NEW P.O.P. HEADQUARTERS!
BLAM!

Story: Frank Doyle   Pencils: Bob White
Inks & Letters: Marty Epp

Originally printed in LIFE WITH ARCHIE #49, MAY 1966

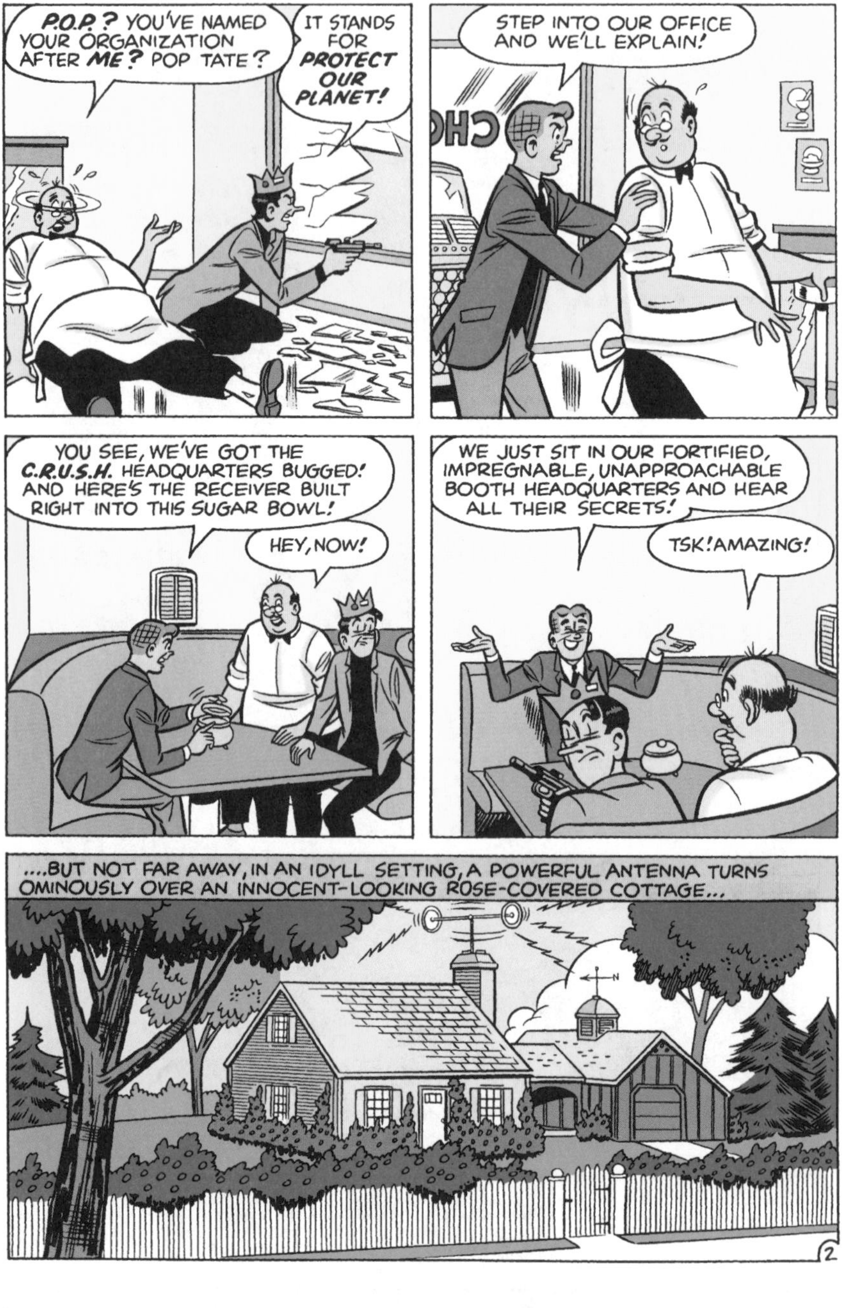
P.O.P.? YOU'VE NAMED YOUR ORGANIZATION AFTER ME? POP TATE?
IT STANDS FOR PROTECT OUR PLANET!
STEP INTO OUR OFFICE AND WE'LL EXPLAIN!
YOU SEE, WE'VE GOT THE C.R.U.S.H. HEADQUARTERS BUGGED! AND HERE'S THE RECEIVER BUILT RIGHT INTO THIS SUGAR BOWL!
HEY, NOW!
WE JUST SIT IN OUR FORTIFIED, IMPREGNABLE, UNAPPROACHABLE BOOTH HEADQUARTERS AND HEAR ALL THEIR SECRETS!
TSK! AMAZING!
....BUT NOT FAR AWAY, IN AN IDYLL SETTING, A POWERFUL ANTENNA TURNS OMINOUSLY OVER AN INNOCENT-LOOKING ROSE-COVERED COTTAGE...
2

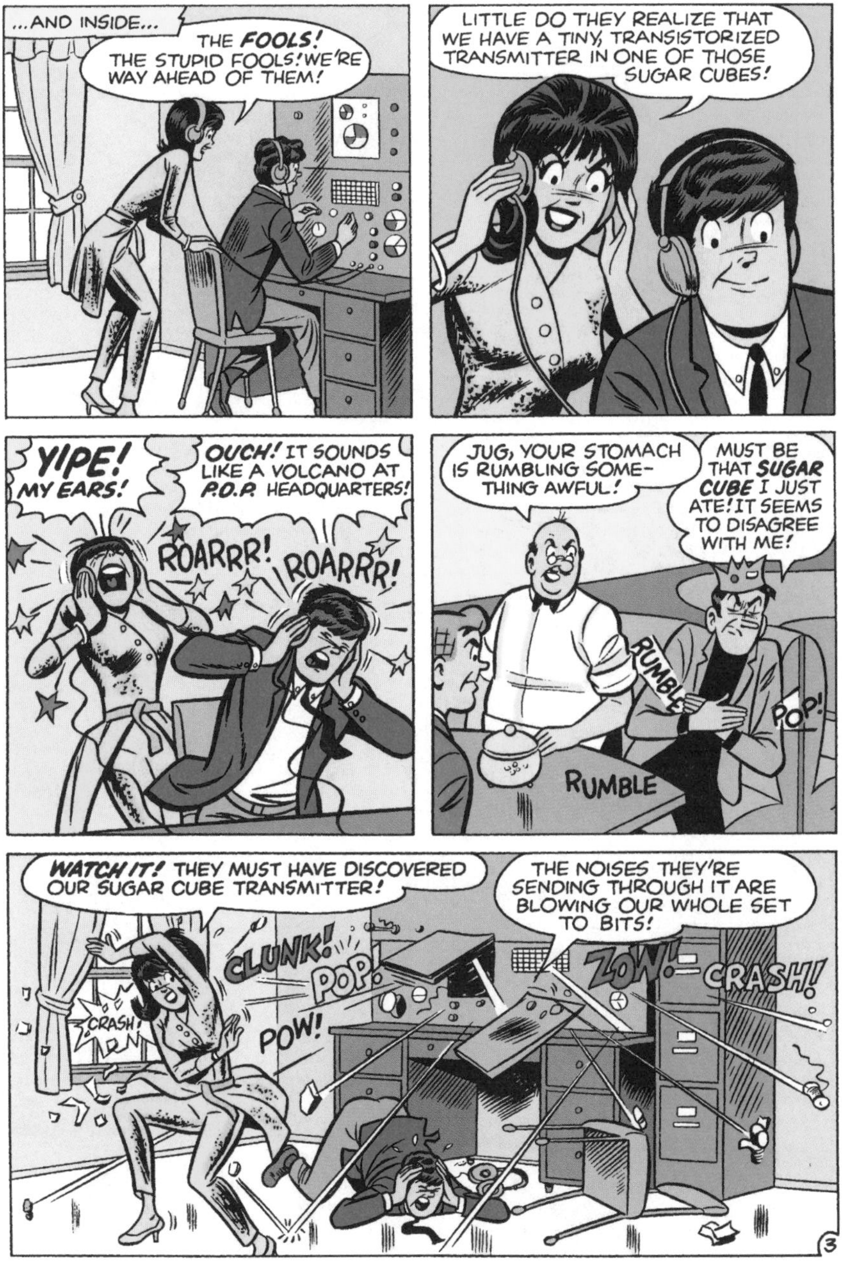
...AND INSIDE...
THE FOOLS! THE STUPID FOOLS! WE'RE WAY AHEAD OF THEM!
LITTLE DO THEY REALIZE THAT WE HAVE A TINY, TRANSISTORIZED TRANSMITTER IN ONE OF THOSE SUGAR CUBES!
YIPE! MY EARS!
OUCH! IT SOUNDS LIKE A VOLCANO AT P.O.P. HEADQUARTERS!
ROARRR!
ROARRRR!
JUG, YOUR STOMACH IS RUMBLING SOME-THING AWFUL!
MUST BE THAT SUGAR CUBE I JUST ATE! IT SEEMS TO DISAGREE WITH ME!
RUMBLE
POP!
RUMBLE
WATCH IT! THEY MUST HAVE DISCOVERED OUR SUGAR CUBE TRANSMITTER!
THE NOISES THEY'RE SENDING THROUGH IT ARE BLOWING OUR WHOLE SET TO BITS!
CLUNK!
POP!
POW!
ZOW!
CRASH!
CRASH!
3

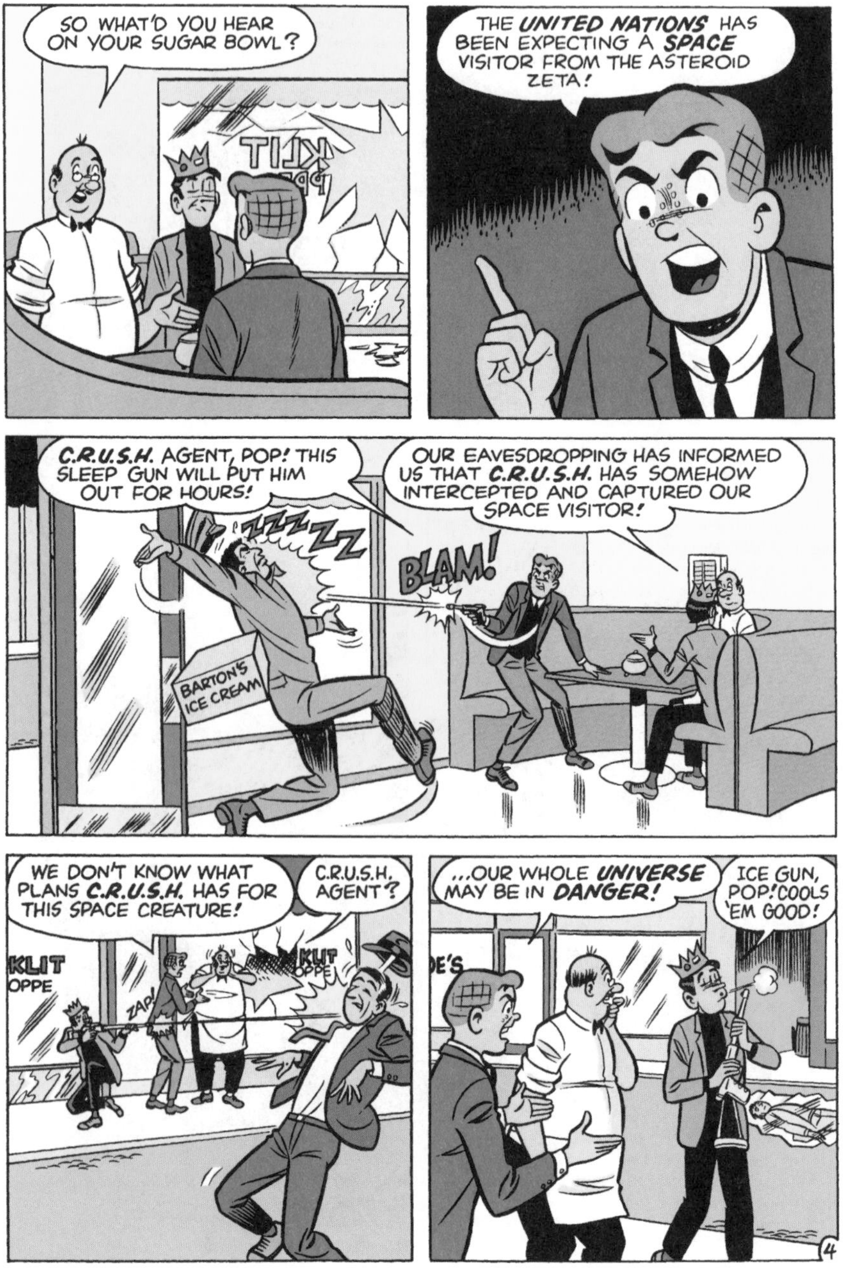
SO WHAT'D YOU HEAR ON YOUR SUGAR BOWL?
THE UNITED NATIONS HAS BEEN EXPECTING A SPACE VISITOR FROM THE ASTEROID ZETA!
C.R.U.S.H. AGENT, POP! THIS SLEEP GUN WILL PUT HIM OUT FOR HOURS!
ZZZZZ
BLAM!
BARTON'S ICE CREAM
OUR EAVESDROPPING HAS INFORMED US THAT C.R.U.S.H. HAS SOMEHOW INTERCEPTED AND CAPTURED OUR SPACE VISITOR!
WE DON'T KNOW WHAT PLANS C.R.U.S.H. HAS FOR THIS SPACE CREATURE!
C.R.U.S.H. AGENT?
KLIT
OPPE
ZAP!
...OUR WHOLE UNIVERSE MAY BE IN DANGER!
ICE GUN, POP! COOLS 'EM GOOD!
4

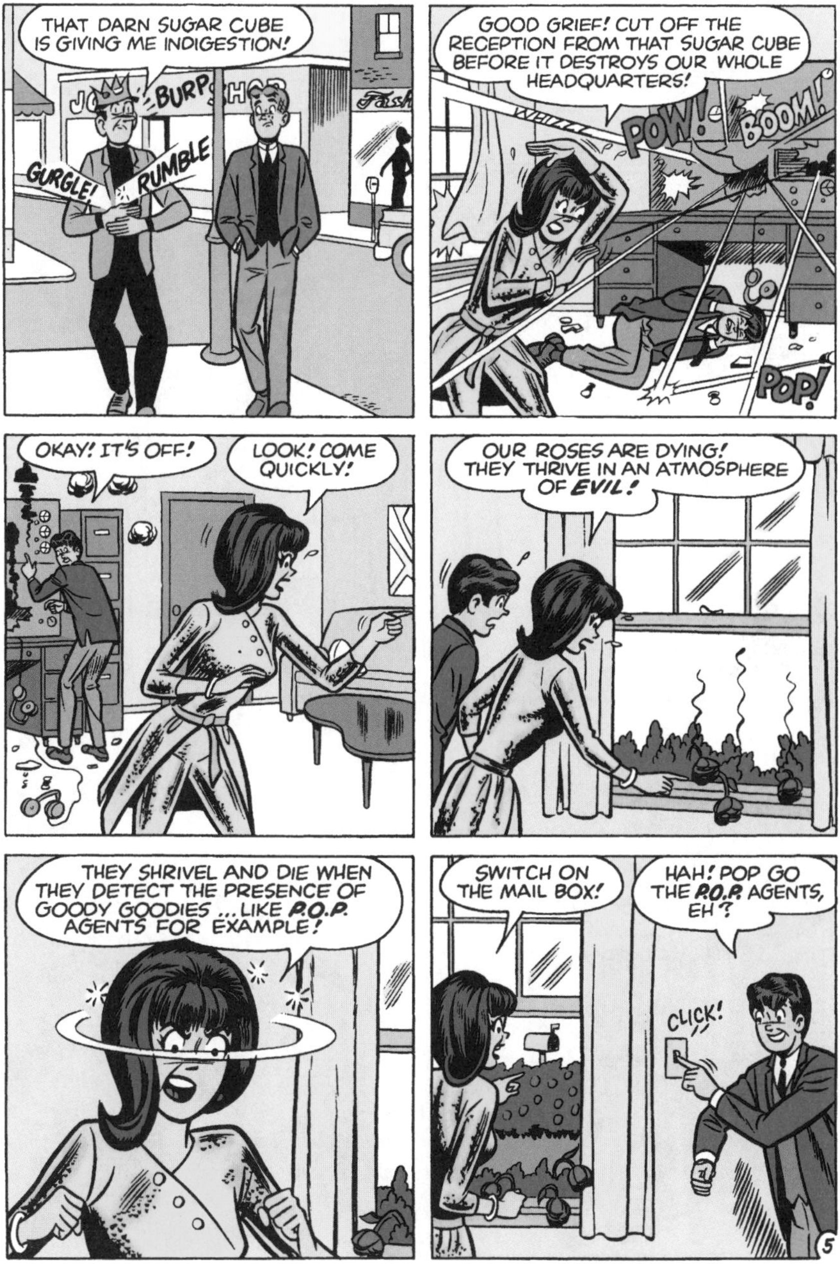
THAT DARN SUGAR CUBE IS GIVING ME INDIGESTION!
BURP
GURGLE!
RUMBLE
GOOD GRIEF! CUT OFF THE RECEPTION FROM THAT SUGAR CUBE BEFORE IT DESTROYS OUR WHOLE HEADQUARTERS!
POW!
BOOM!
POP!
OKAY! IT'S OFF!
LOOK! COME QUICKLY!
OUR ROSES ARE DYING! THEY THRIVE IN AN ATMOSPHERE OF EVIL!
THEY SHRIVEL AND DIE WHEN THEY DETECT THE PRESENCE OF GOODY GOODIES ... LIKE P.O.P. AGENTS FOR EXAMPLE!
SWITCH ON THE MAIL BOX!
HAH! POP GO THE P.O.P. AGENTS, EH?
CLICK!
5

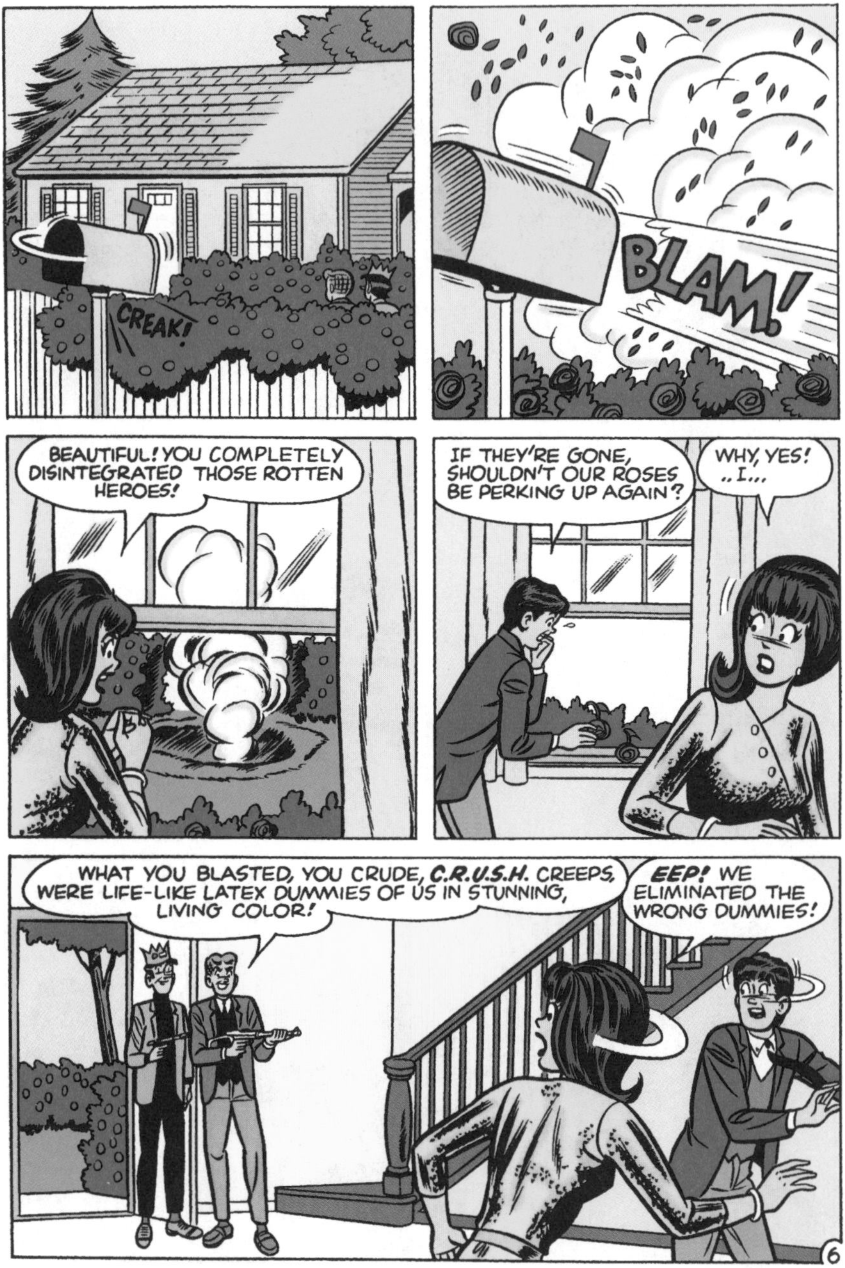
CREAK!
BLAM!
BEAUTIFUL! YOU COMPLETELY DISINTEGRATED THOSE ROTTEN HEROES!
IF THEY'RE GONE, SHOULDN'T OUR ROSES BE PERKING UP AGAIN?
WHY, YES! .. I...
WHAT YOU BLASTED, YOU CRUDE, C.R.U.S.H. CREEPS, WERE LIFE-LIKE LATEX DUMMIES OF US IN STUNNING, LIVING COLOR!
EEP! WE ELIMINATED THE WRONG DUMMIES!
6

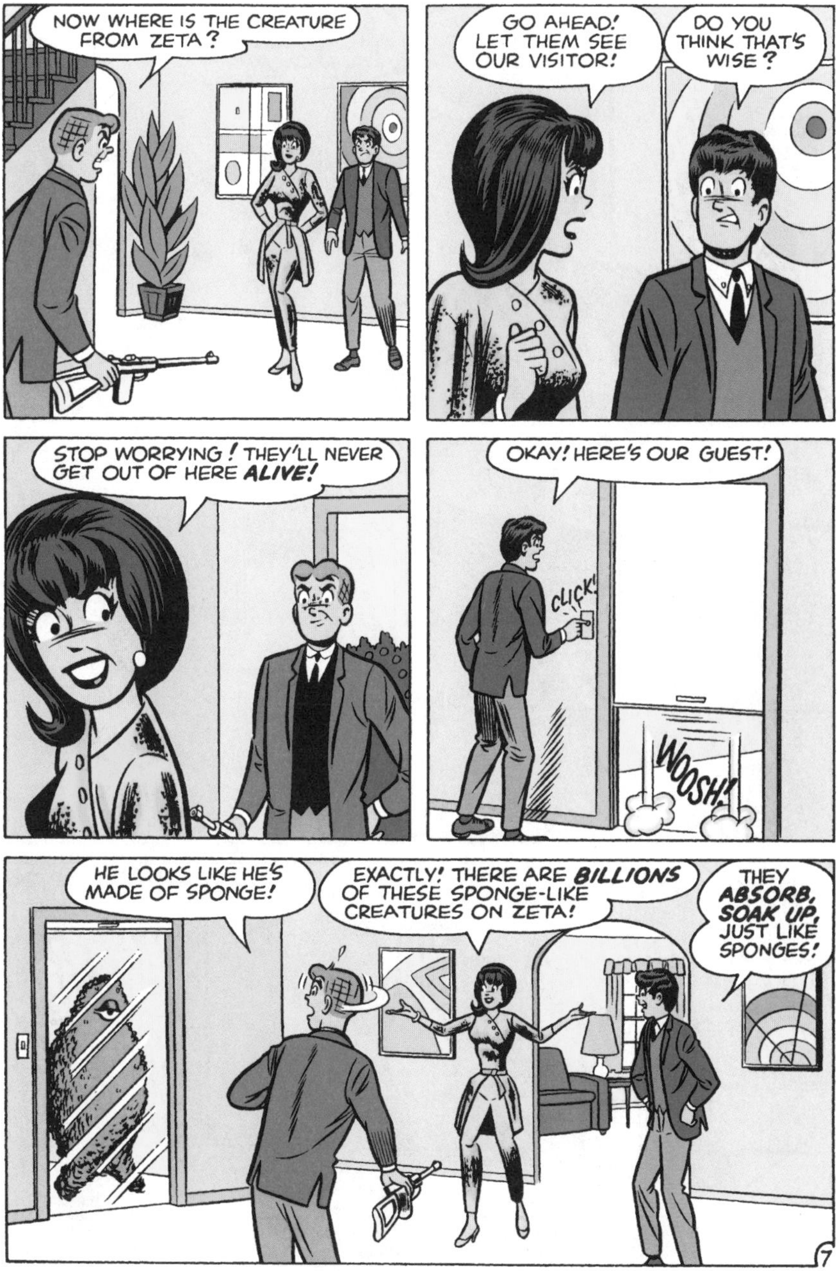
NOW WHERE IS THE CREATURE FROM ZETA?
GO AHEAD! LET THEM SEE OUR VISITOR!
DO YOU THINK THAT'S WISE?
STOP WORRYING! THEY'LL NEVER GET OUT OF HERE ALIVE!
OKAY! HERE'S OUR GUEST!
CLICK!
WOOSH!
HE LOOKS LIKE HE'S MADE OF SPONGE!
EXACTLY! THERE ARE BILLIONS OF THESE SPONGE-LIKE CREATURES ON ZETA!
THEY ABSORB, SOAK UP, JUST LIKE SPONGES!
7

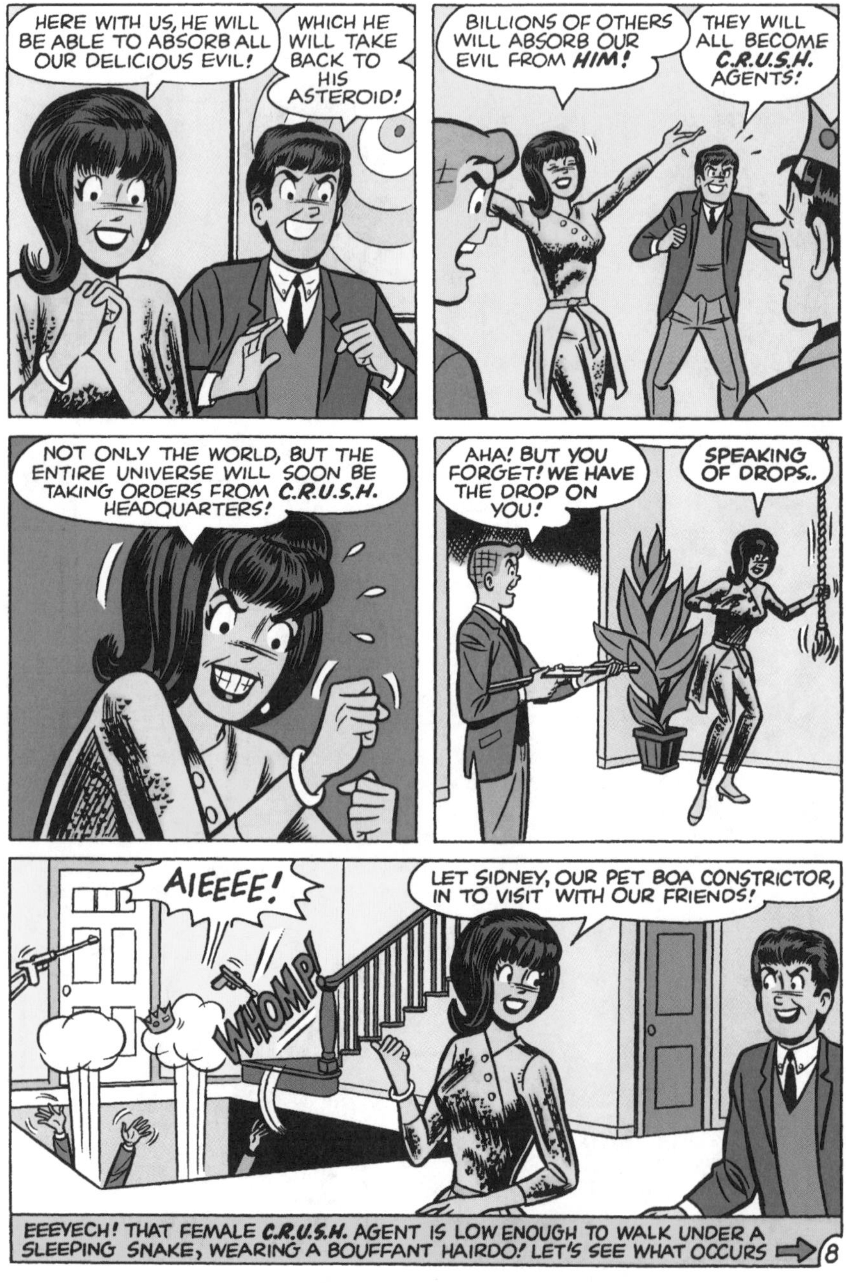
HERE WITH US, HE WILL BE ABLE TO ABSORB ALL OUR DELICIOUS EVIL!
WHICH HE WILL TAKE BACK TO HIS ASTEROID!
BILLIONS OF OTHERS WILL ABSORB OUR EVIL FROM HIM!
THEY WILL ALL BECOME C.R.U.S.H. AGENTS!
NOT ONLY THE WORLD, BUT THE ENTIRE UNIVERSE WILL SOON BE TAKING ORDERS FROM C.R.U.S.H. HEADQUARTERS!
AHA! BUT YOU FORGET! WE HAVE THE DROP ON YOU!
SPEAKING OF DROPS..
AIEEEE!
WHOMP!
LET SIDNEY, OUR PET BOA CONSTRICTOR, IN TO VISIT WITH OUR FRIENDS!
EEEYECH! THAT FEMALE C.R.U.S.H. AGENT IS LOW ENOUGH TO WALK UNDER A SLEEPING SNAKE, WEARING A BOUFFANT HAIRDO! LET'S SEE WHAT OCCURS
8

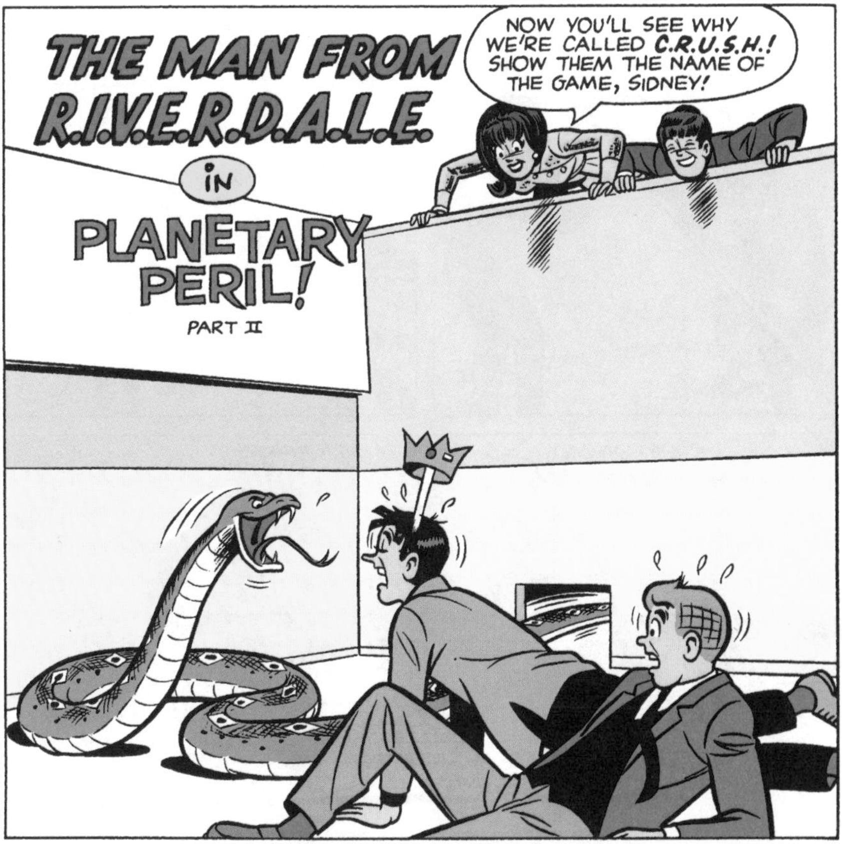
THE MAN FROM R.I.V.E.R.D.A.L.E.
IN
PLANETARY PERIL!
PART II
NOW YOU'LL SEE WHY WE'RE CALLED C.R.U.S.H.! SHOW THEM THE NAME OF THE GAME, SIDNEY!

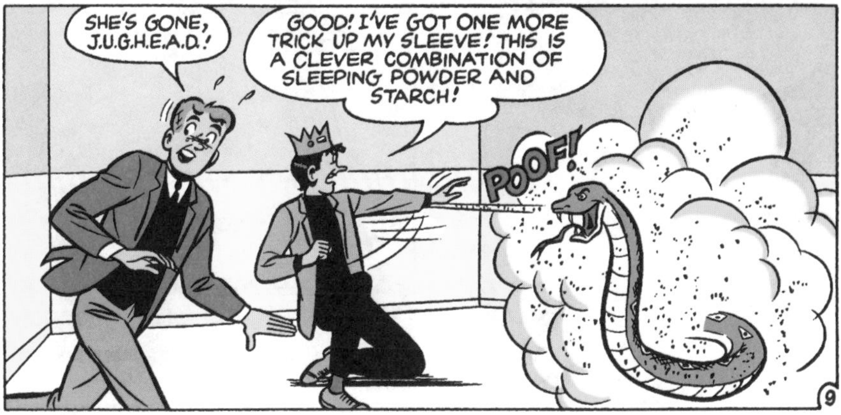
SHE'S GONE, J.U.G.H.E.A.D.!
GOOD! I'VE GOT ONE MORE TRICK UP MY SLEEVE! THIS IS A CLEVER COMBINATION OF SLEEPING POWDER AND STARCH!
POOF!
9

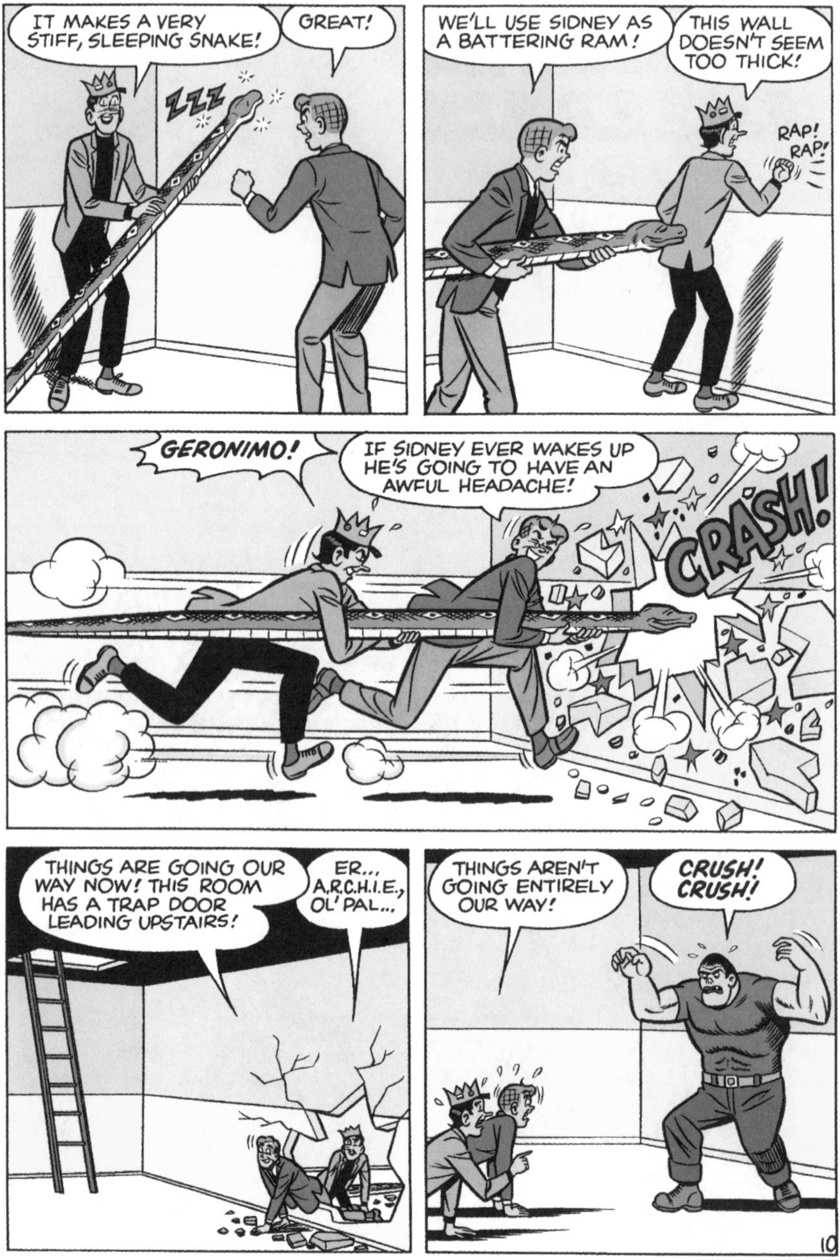
IT MAKES A VERY STIFF, SLEEPING SNAKE!
GREAT!
ZZZ
WE'LL USE SIDNEY AS A BATTERING RAM!
THIS WALL DOESN'T SEEM TOO THICK!
RAP! RAP!
GERONIMO!
IF SIDNEY EVER WAKES UP HE'S GOING TO HAVE AN AWFUL HEADACHE!
CRASH!
THINGS ARE GOING OUR WAY NOW! THIS ROOM HAS A TRAP DOOR LEADING UPSTAIRS!
ER..., A.R.C.H.I.E., OL' PAL...
THINGS AREN'T GOING ENTIRELY OUR WAY!
CRUSH! CRUSH!
10

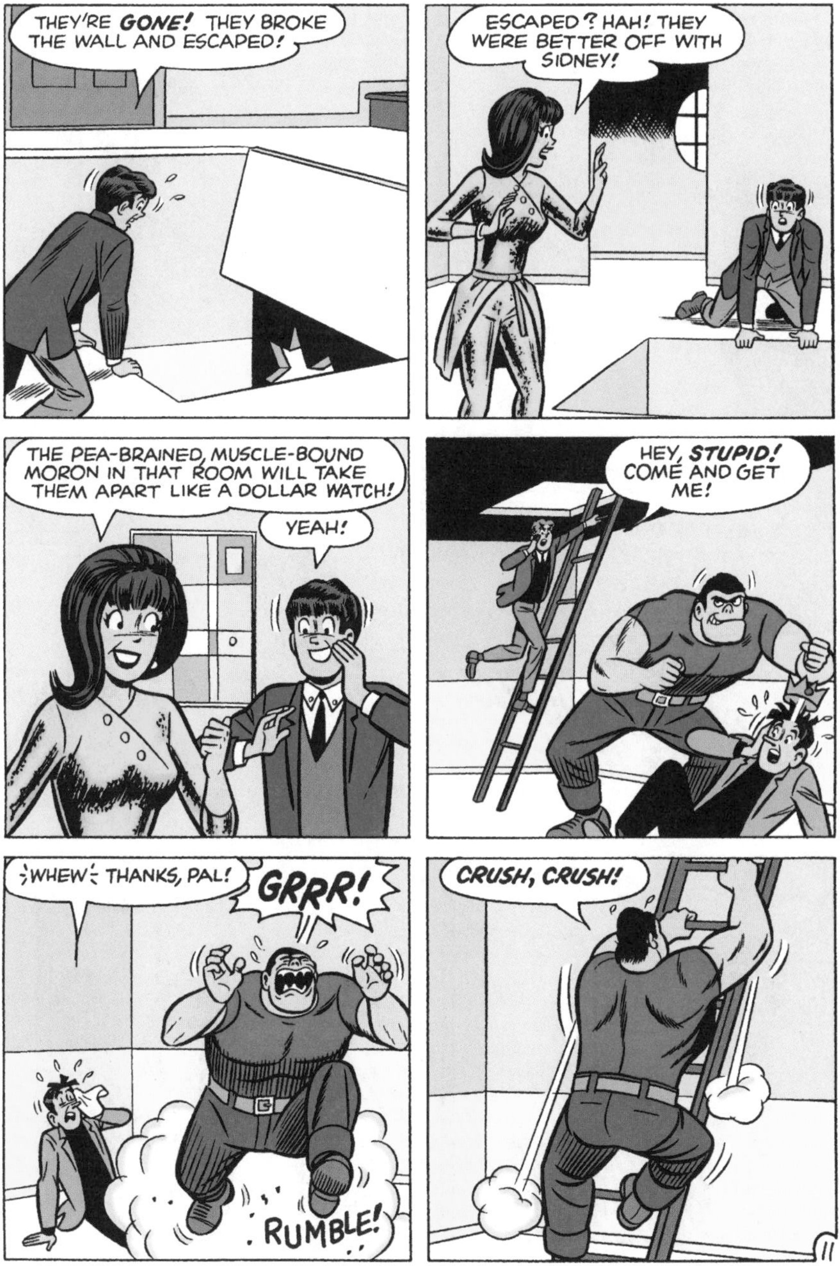
THEY'RE **GONE!** THEY BROKE THE WALL AND ESCAPED!
ESCAPED? HAH! THEY WERE BETTER OFF WITH SIDNEY!
THE PEA-BRAINED, MUSCLE-BOUND MORON IN THAT ROOM WILL TAKE THEM APART LIKE A DOLLAR WATCH!
YEAH!
HEY, **STUPID!** COME AND GET ME!
-WHEW- THANKS, PAL!
GRRR!
RUMBLE!
CRUSH, CRUSH!

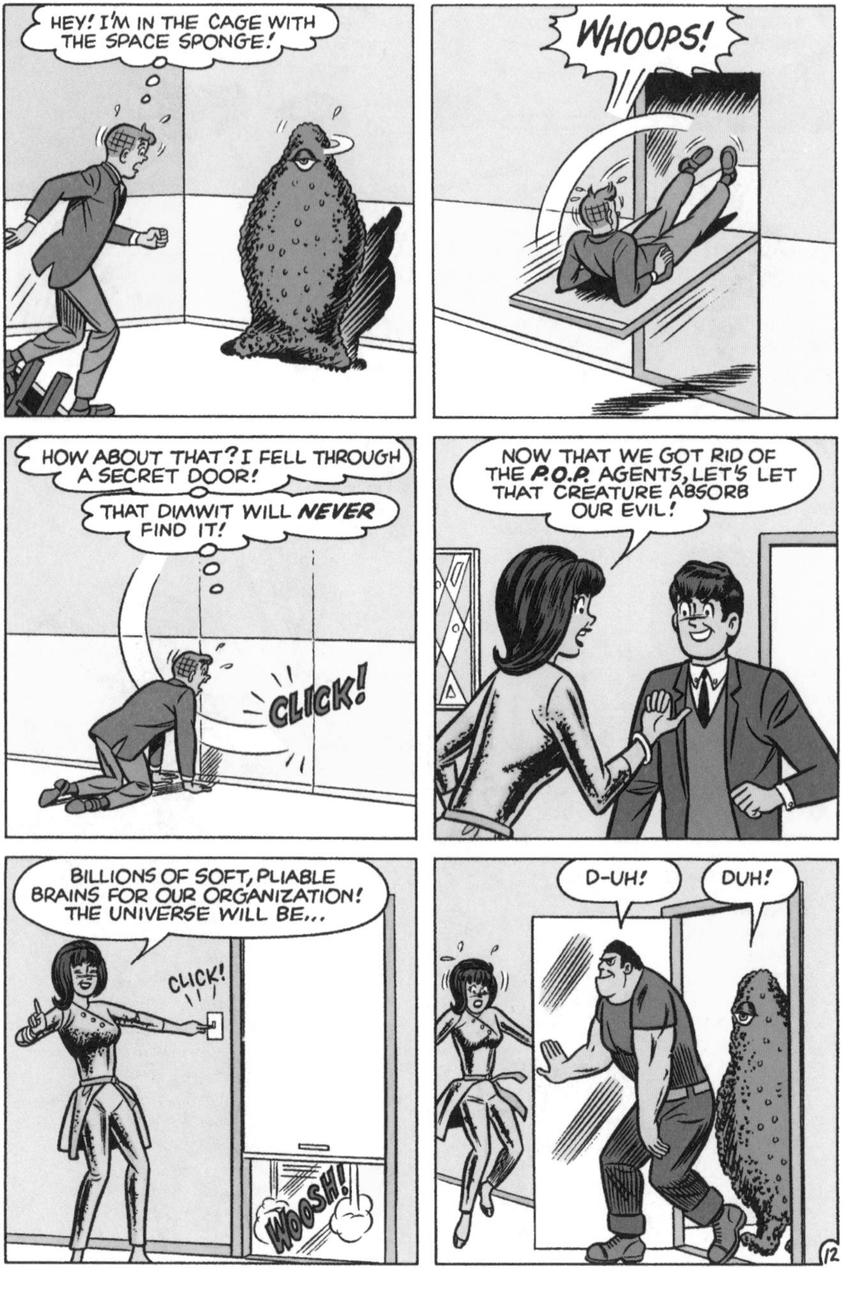
HEY! I'M IN THE CAGE WITH THE SPACE SPONGE!
WHOOPS!
HOW ABOUT THAT? I FELL THROUGH A SECRET DOOR!
THAT DIMWIT WILL NEVER FIND IT!
CLICK!
NOW THAT WE GOT RID OF THE P.O.P. AGENTS, LET'S LET THAT CREATURE ABSORB OUR EVIL!
BILLIONS OF SOFT, PLIABLE BRAINS FOR OUR ORGANIZATION! THE UNIVERSE WILL BE...
CLICK!
WOOSH!
D-UH!
DUH!
12

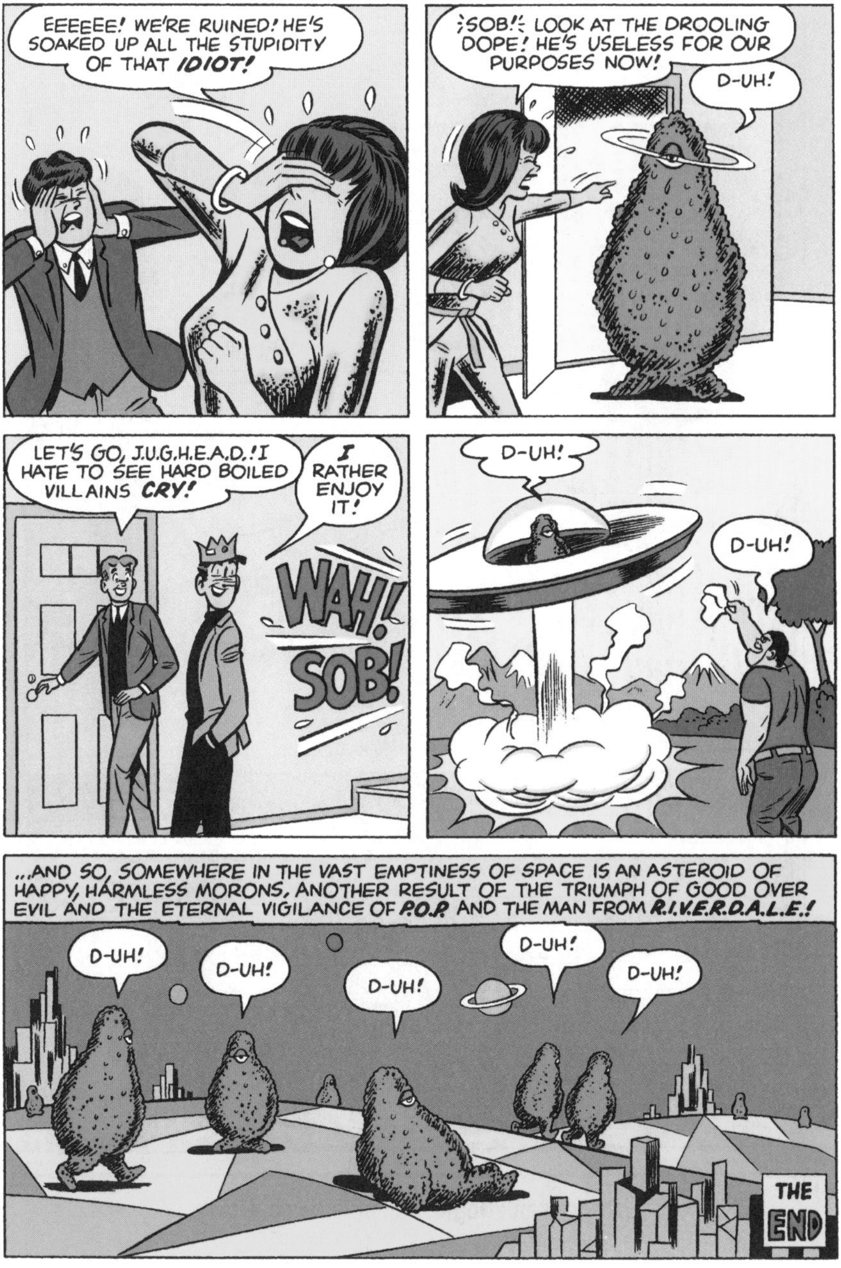
EEEEEE! WE'RE RUINED! HE'S SOAKED UP ALL THE STUPIDITY OF THAT IDIOT!
;SOB!; LOOK AT THE DROOLING DOPE! HE'S USELESS FOR OUR PURPOSES NOW!
D-UH!
LET'S GO, J.U.G.H.E.A.D.! I HATE TO SEE HARD BOILED VILLAINS CRY!
I RATHER ENJOY IT!
WAH!
SOB!
D-UH!
D-UH!
...AND SO, SOMEWHERE IN THE VAST EMPTINESS OF SPACE IS AN ASTEROID OF HAPPY, HARMLESS MORONS, ANOTHER RESULT OF THE TRIUMPH OF GOOD OVER EVIL AND THE ETERNAL VIGILANCE OF P.O.P. AND THE MAN FROM R.I.V.E.R.D.A.L.E.!
D-UH!
D-UH!
D-UH!
D-UH!
D-UH!
THE END

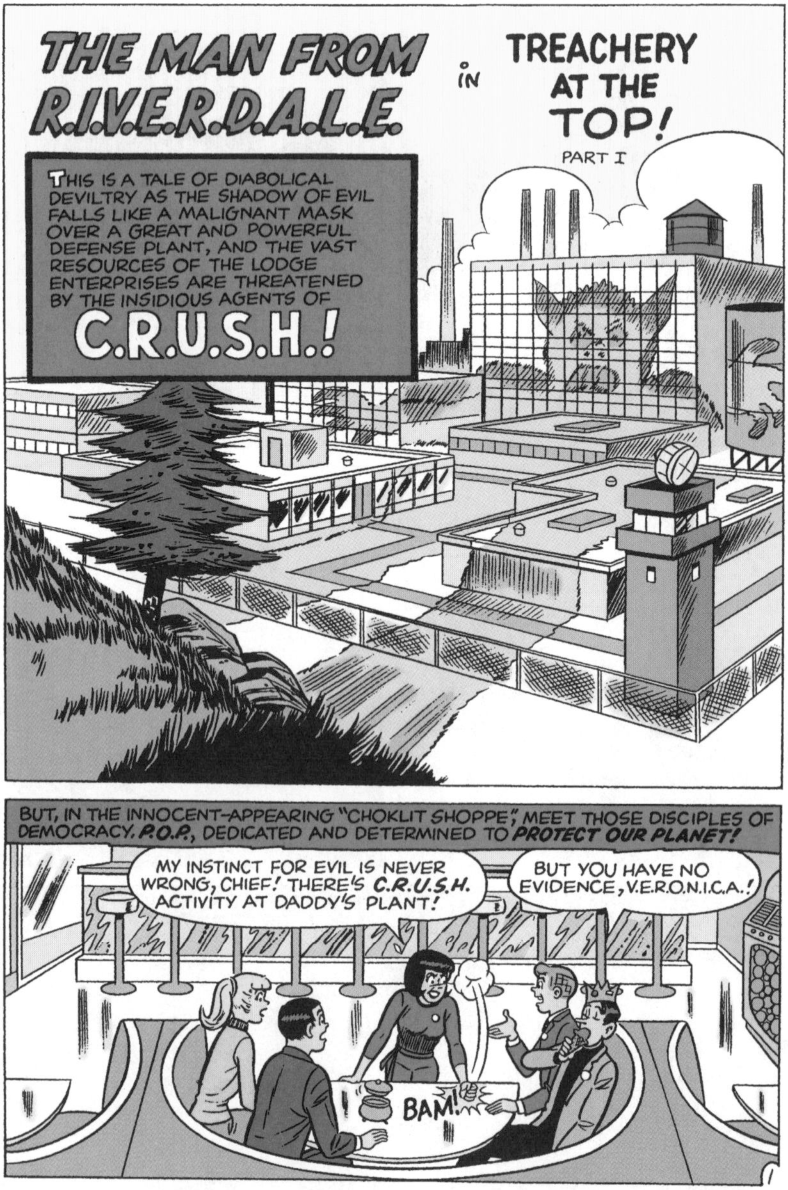
THE MAN FROM R.I.V.E.R.D.A.L.E.
IN
TREACHERY AT THE TOP!
PART I
THIS IS A TALE OF DIABOLICAL DEVILTRY AS THE SHADOW OF EVIL FALLS LIKE A MALIGNANT MASK OVER A GREAT AND POWERFUL DEFENSE PLANT, AND THE VAST RESOURCES OF THE LODGE ENTERPRISES ARE THREATENED BY THE INSIDIOUS AGENTS OF
C.R.U.S.H.!
BUT, IN THE INNOCENT-APPEARING "CHOKLIT SHOPPE," MEET THOSE DISCIPLES OF DEMOCRACY. P.O.P., DEDICATED AND DETERMINED TO PROTECT OUR PLANET!
MY INSTINCT FOR EVIL IS NEVER WRONG, CHIEF! THERE'S C.R.U.S.H. ACTIVITY AT DADDY'S PLANT!
BUT YOU HAVE NO EVIDENCE, V.E.R.O.N.I.C.A.!
BAM!
1

Story: Frank Doyle Pencils: Bob White
Inks & Letters: Marty Epp

Originally printed in LIFE WITH ARCHIE #49, MAY 1966

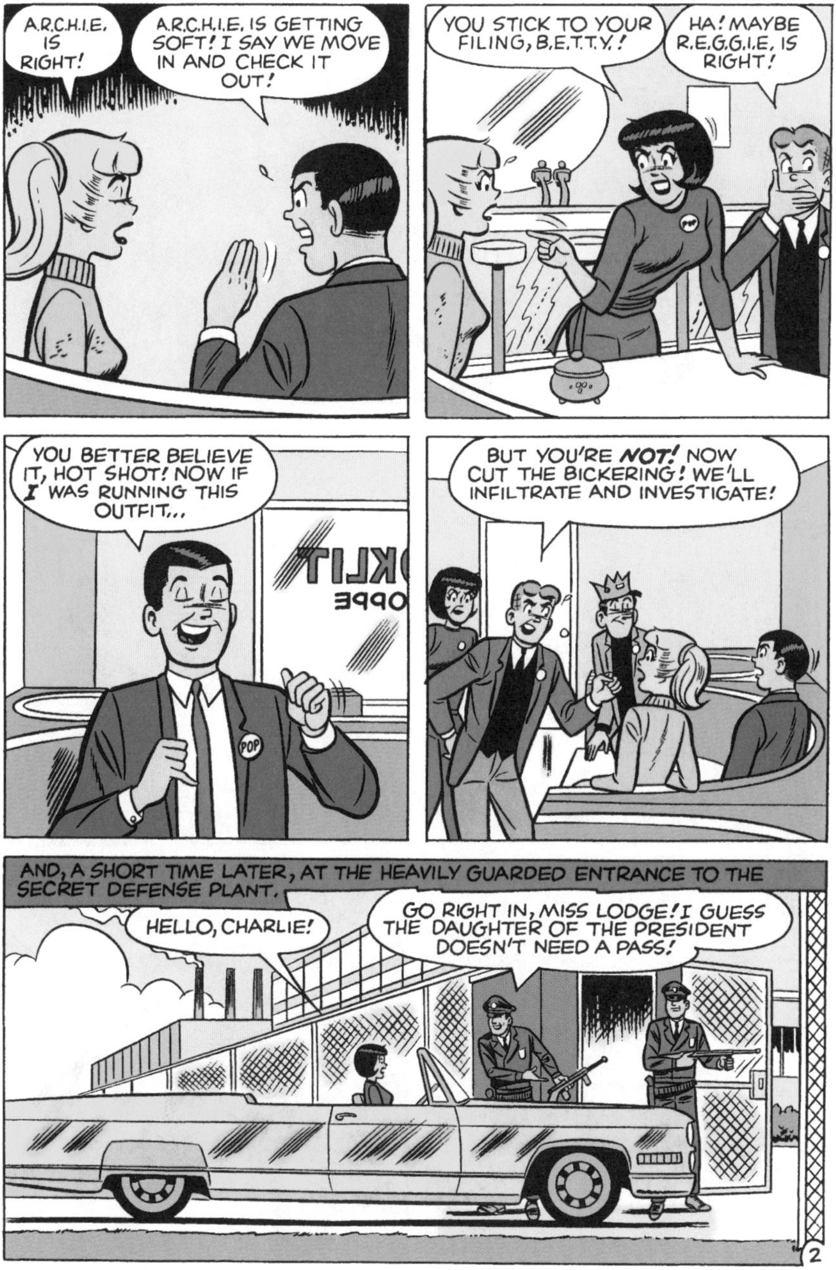
A.R.C.H.I.E. IS RIGHT!
A.R.C.H.I.E. IS GETTING SOFT! I SAY WE MOVE IN AND CHECK IT OUT!
YOU STICK TO YOUR FILING, B.E.T.T.Y.!
HA! MAYBE R.E.G.G.I.E. IS RIGHT!
YOU BETTER BELIEVE IT, HOT SHOT! NOW IF *I* WAS RUNNING THIS OUTFIT...
BUT YOU'RE ***NOT!*** NOW CUT THE BICKERING! WE'LL INFILTRATE AND INVESTIGATE!
AND, A SHORT TIME LATER, AT THE HEAVILY GUARDED ENTRANCE TO THE SECRET DEFENSE PLANT.
HELLO, CHARLIE!
GO RIGHT IN, MISS LODGE! I GUESS THE DAUGHTER OF THE PRESIDENT DOESN'T NEED A PASS!
2

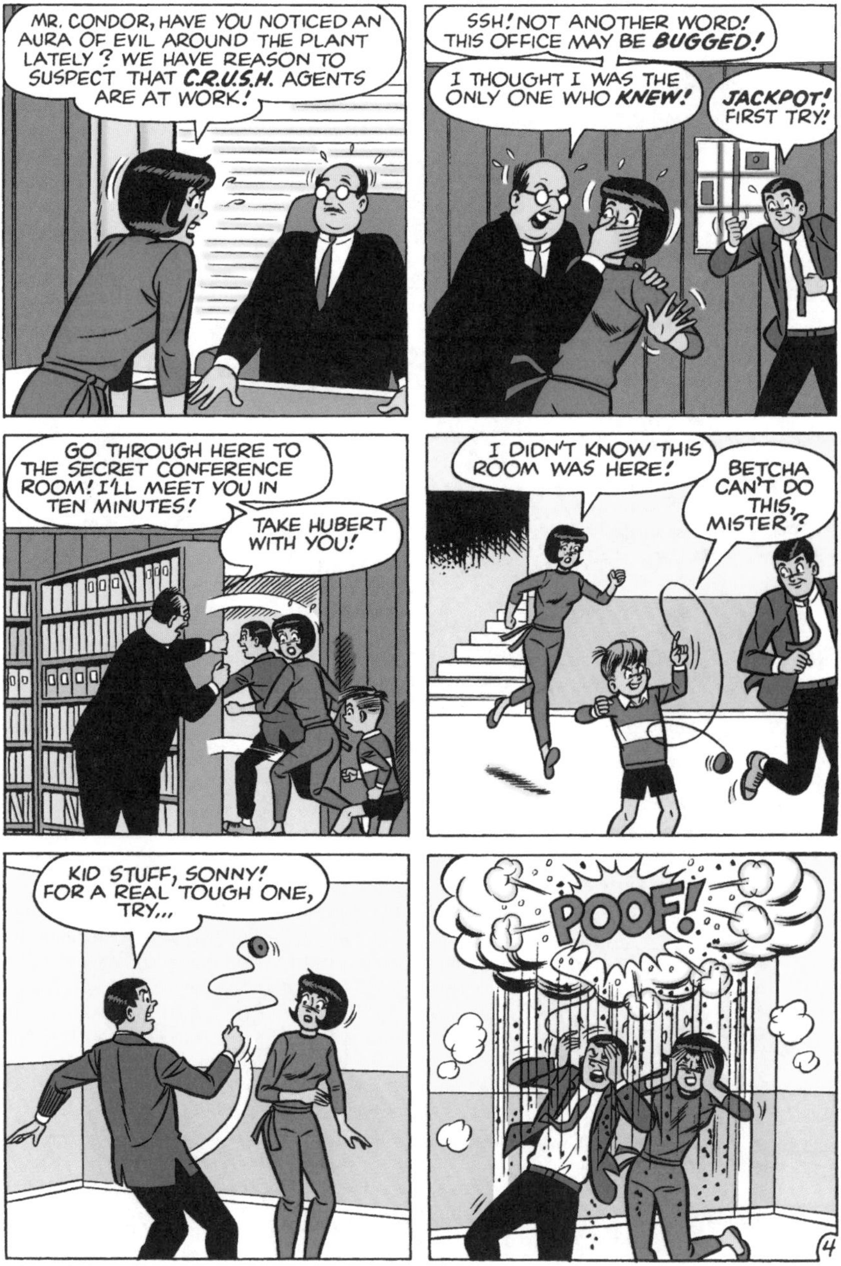
MR. CONDOR, HAVE YOU NOTICED AN AURA OF EVIL AROUND THE PLANT LATELY? WE HAVE REASON TO SUSPECT THAT C.R.U.S.H. AGENTS ARE AT WORK!
SSH! NOT ANOTHER WORD! THIS OFFICE MAY BE BUGGED!
I THOUGHT I WAS THE ONLY ONE WHO KNEW!
JACKPOT! FIRST TRY!
GO THROUGH HERE TO THE SECRET CONFERENCE ROOM! I'LL MEET YOU IN TEN MINUTES!
TAKE HUBERT WITH YOU!
I DIDN'T KNOW THIS ROOM WAS HERE!
BETCHA CAN'T DO THIS, MISTER?
KID STUFF, SONNY! FOR A REAL TOUGH ONE, TRY...
POOF!
4

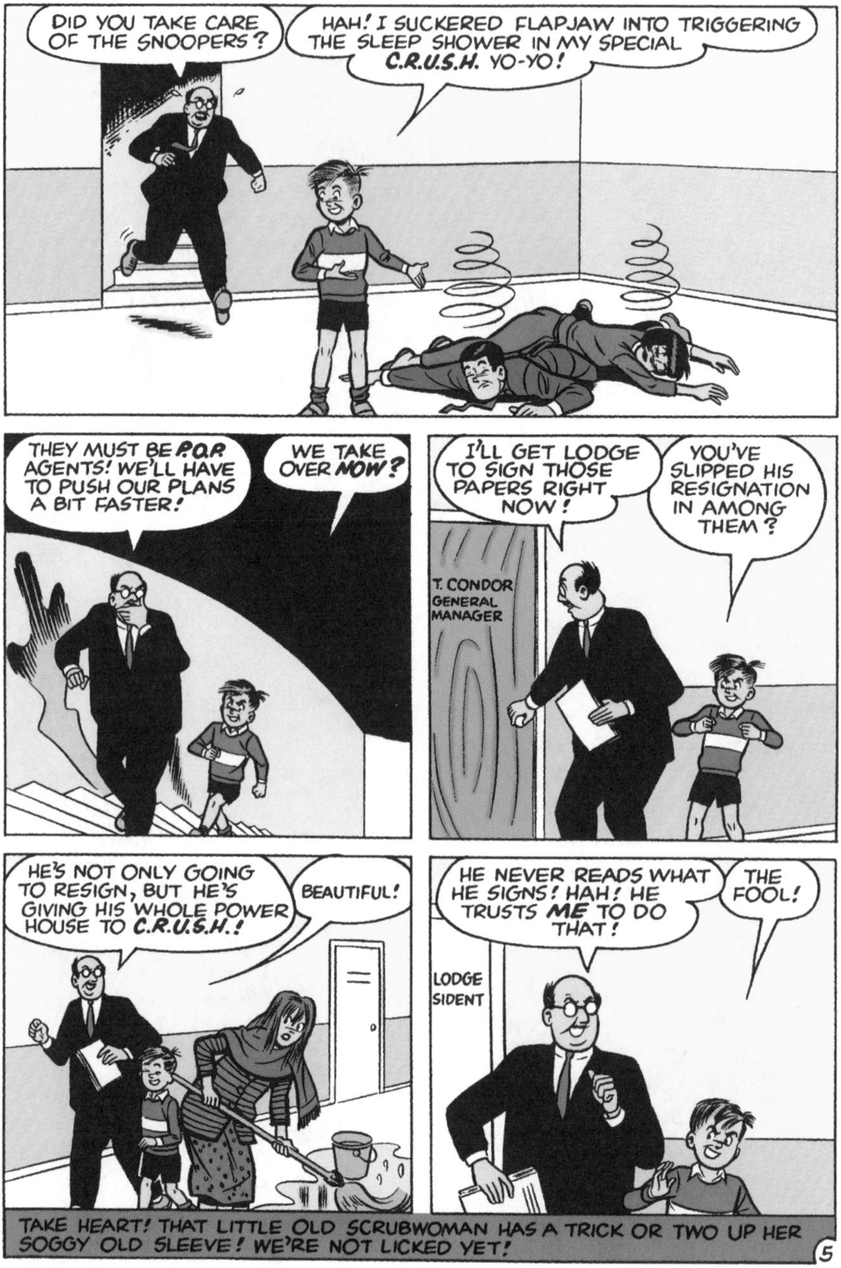
DID YOU TAKE CARE OF THE SNOOPERS?
HAH! I SUCKERED FLAPJAW INTO TRIGGERING THE SLEEP SHOWER IN MY SPECIAL C.R.U.S.H. YO-YO!
THEY MUST BE P.O.R AGENTS! WE'LL HAVE TO PUSH OUR PLANS A BIT FASTER!
WE TAKE OVER NOW?
I'LL GET LODGE TO SIGN THOSE PAPERS RIGHT NOW!
YOU'VE SLIPPED HIS RESIGNATION IN AMONG THEM?
T. CONDOR GENERAL MANAGER
HE'S NOT ONLY GOING TO RESIGN, BUT HE'S GIVING HIS WHOLE POWER HOUSE TO C.R.U.S.H.!
BEAUTIFUL!
HE NEVER READS WHAT HE SIGNS! HAH! HE TRUSTS ME TO DO THAT!
THE FOOL!
LODGE
SIDENT
TAKE HEART! THAT LITTLE OLD SCRUBWOMAN HAS A TRICK OR TWO UP HER SOGGY OLD SLEEVE! WE'RE NOT LICKED YET!
5

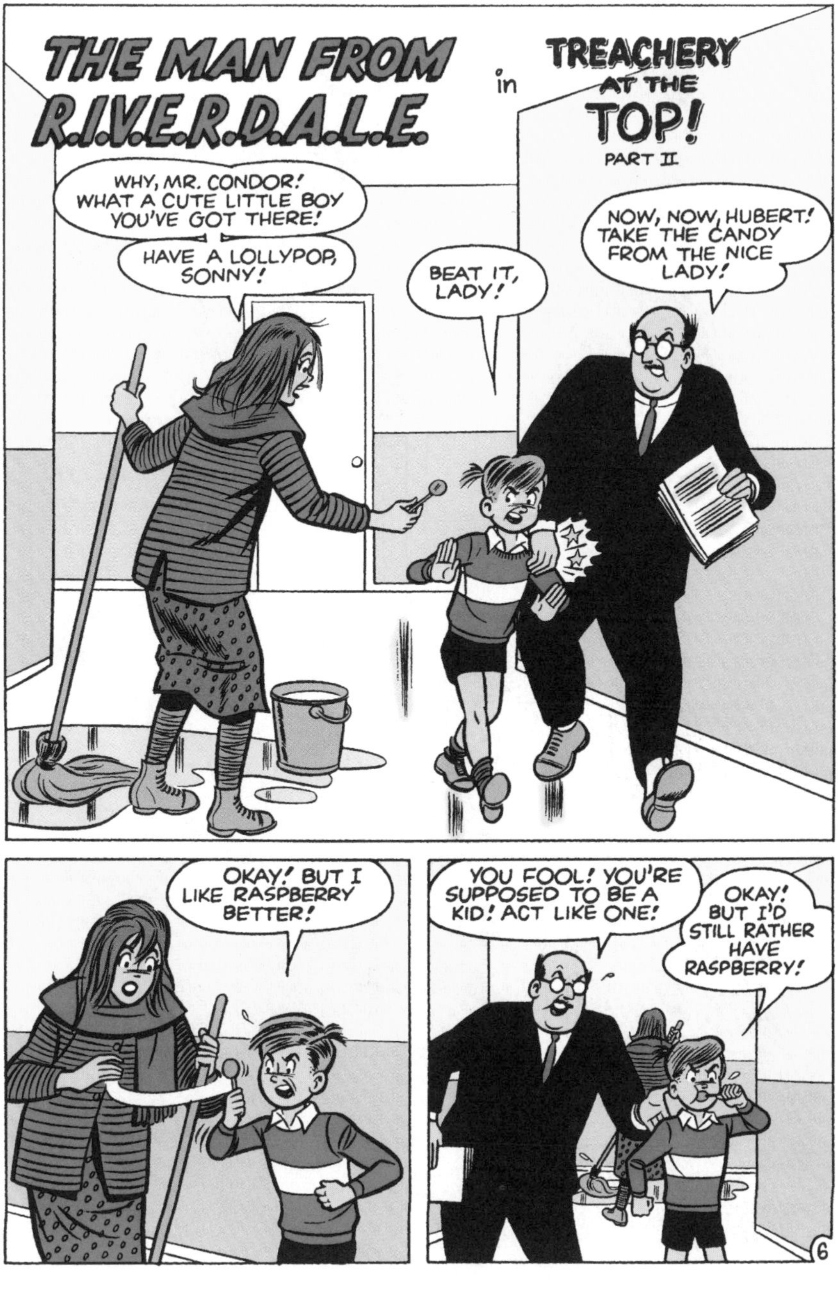
THE MAN FROM R.I.V.E.R.D.A.L.E.
in
TREACHERY AT THE TOP!
PART II
WHY, MR. CONDOR! WHAT A CUTE LITTLE BOY YOU'VE GOT THERE!
HAVE A LOLLYPOP, SONNY!
BEAT IT, LADY!
NOW, NOW, HUBERT! TAKE THE CANDY FROM THE NICE LADY!
OKAY! BUT I LIKE RASPBERRY BETTER!
YOU FOOL! YOU'RE SUPPOSED TO BE A KID! ACT LIKE ONE!
OKAY! BUT I'D STILL RATHER HAVE RASPBERRY!
6

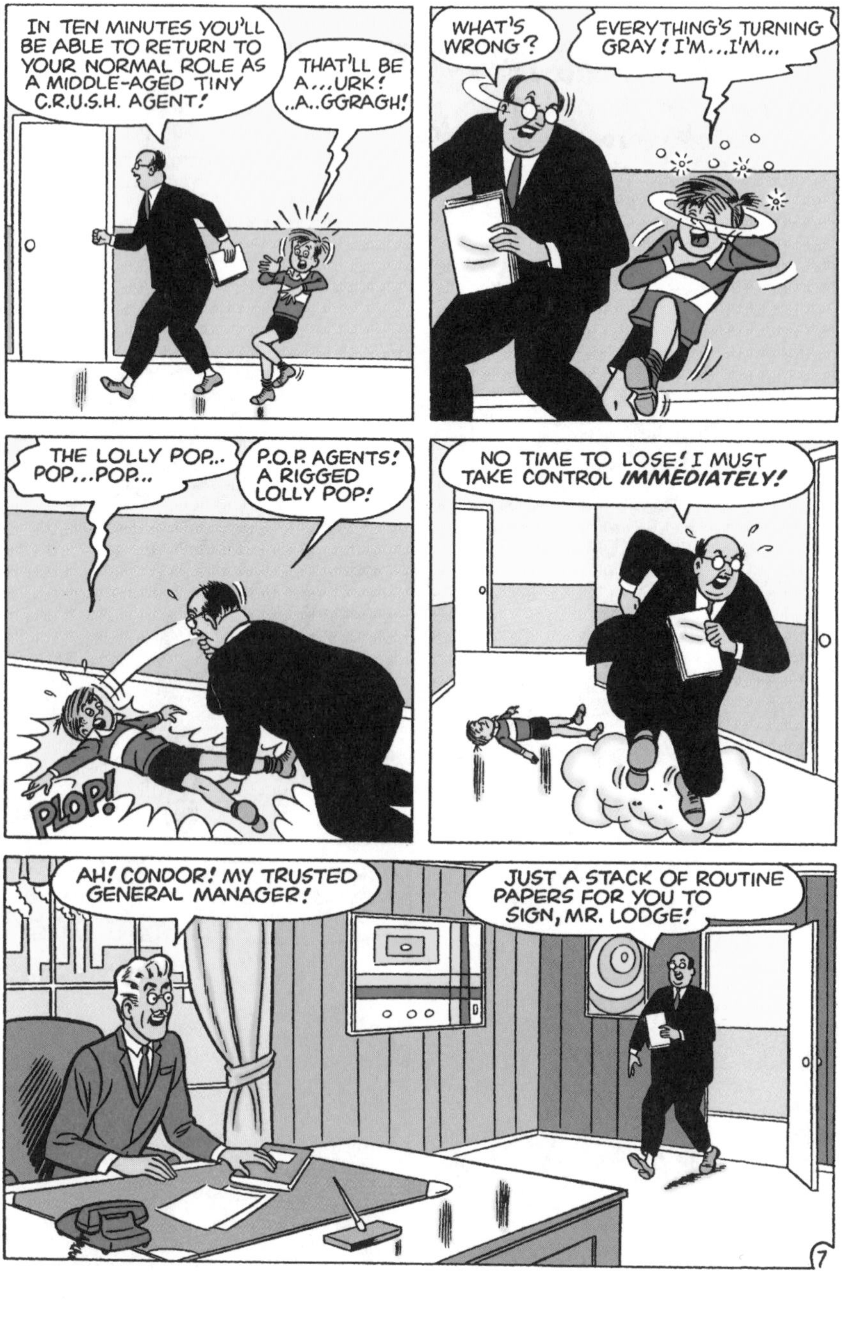
IN TEN MINUTES YOU'LL BE ABLE TO RETURN TO YOUR NORMAL ROLE AS A MIDDLE-AGED TINY C.R.U.S.H. AGENT!
THAT'LL BE A...URK! ..A..GGRAGH!
WHAT'S WRONG?
EVERYTHING'S TURNING GRAY! I'M...I'M...
THE LOLLY POP.. POP...POP...
P.O.P. AGENTS! A RIGGED LOLLY POP!
PLOP!
NO TIME TO LOSE! I MUST TAKE CONTROL IMMEDIATELY!
AH! CONDOR! MY TRUSTED GENERAL MANAGER!
JUST A STACK OF ROUTINE PAPERS FOR YOU TO SIGN, MR. LODGE!
7

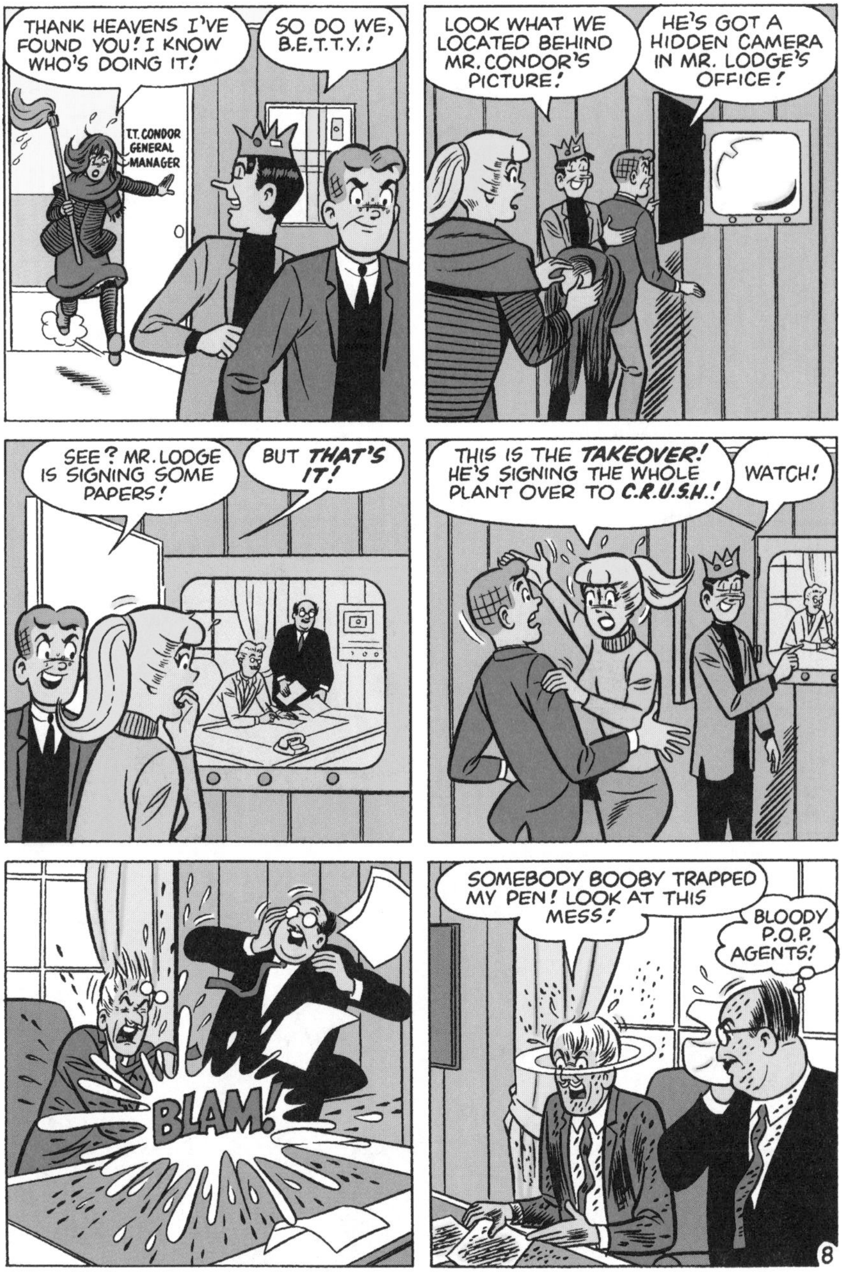
THANK HEAVENS I'VE FOUND YOU! I KNOW WHO'S DOING IT!
T.T. CONDOR GENERAL MANAGER
SO DO WE, B.E.T.T.Y.!
LOOK WHAT WE LOCATED BEHIND MR. CONDOR'S PICTURE!
HE'S GOT A HIDDEN CAMERA IN MR. LODGE'S OFFICE!
SEE? MR. LODGE IS SIGNING SOME PAPERS!
BUT THAT'S IT!
THIS IS THE TAKEOVER! HE'S SIGNING THE WHOLE PLANT OVER TO C.R.U.S.H.!
WATCH!
BLAM!
SOMEBODY BOOBY TRAPPED MY PEN! LOOK AT THIS MESS!
BLOODY P.O.P. AGENTS!
8

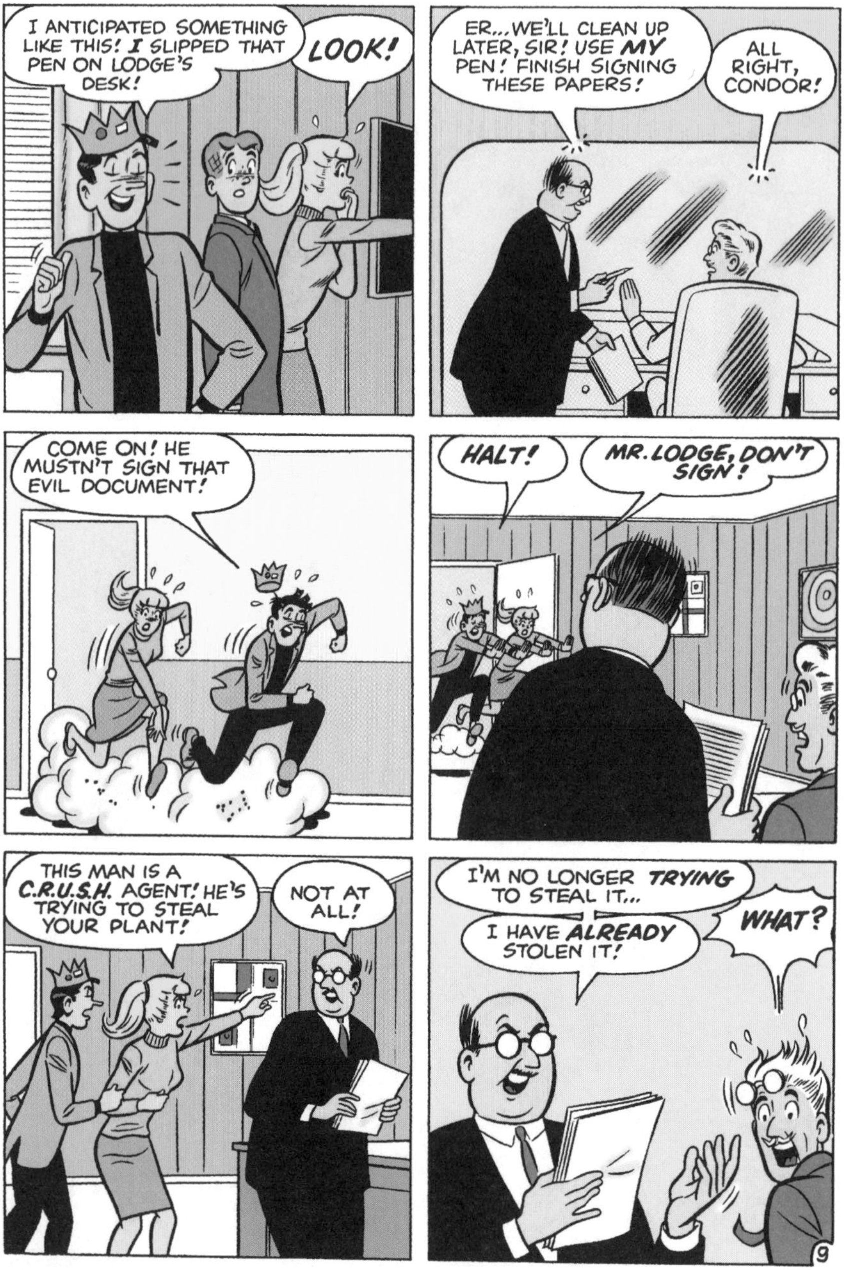
I ANTICIPATED SOMETHING LIKE THIS! I SLIPPED THAT PEN ON LODGE'S DESK!
LOOK!
ER...WE'LL CLEAN UP LATER, SIR! USE MY PEN! FINISH SIGNING THESE PAPERS!
ALL RIGHT, CONDOR!
COME ON! HE MUSTN'T SIGN THAT EVIL DOCUMENT!
HALT!
MR. LODGE, DON'T SIGN!
THIS MAN IS A C.R.U.S.H. AGENT! HE'S TRYING TO STEAL YOUR PLANT!
NOT AT ALL!
I'M NO LONGER TRYING TO STEAL IT...
I HAVE ALREADY STOLEN IT!
WHAT?
9

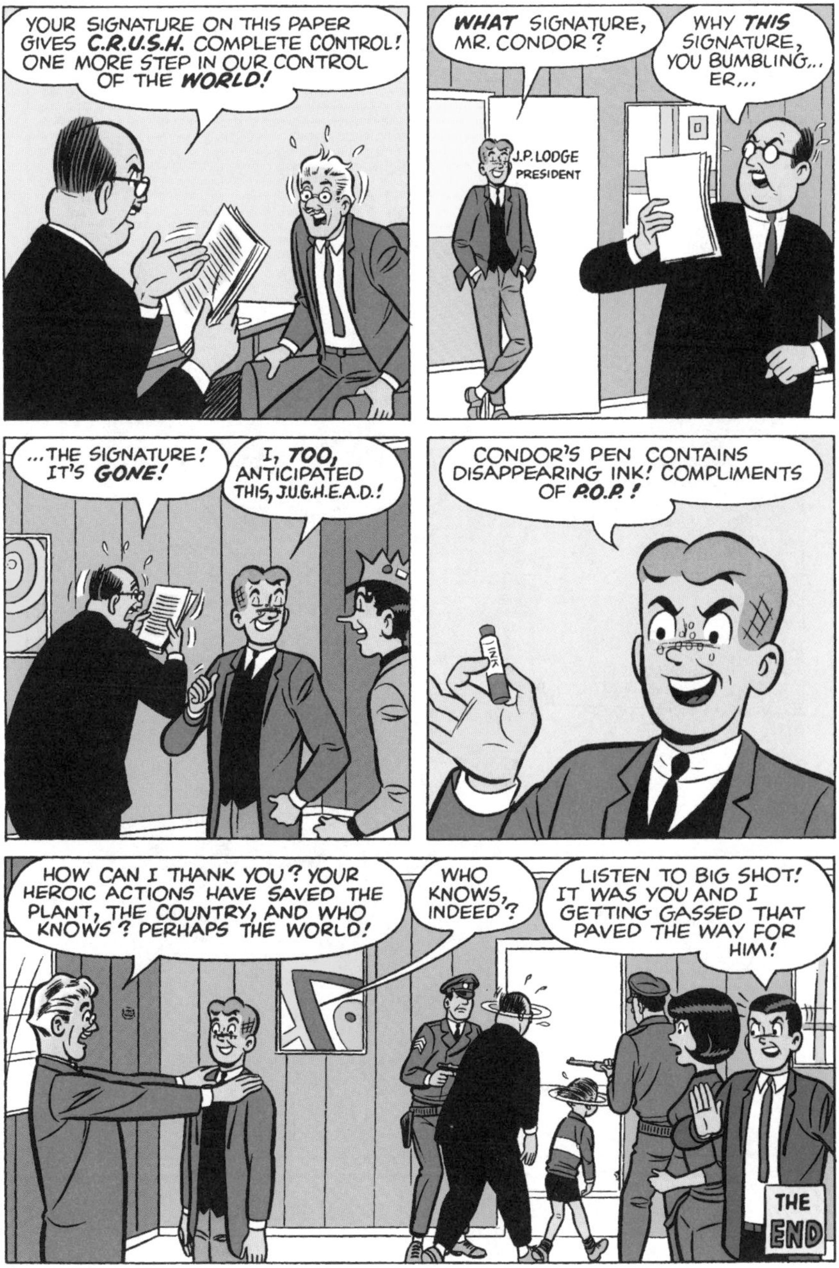
YOUR SIGNATURE ON THIS PAPER GIVES C.R.U.S.H. COMPLETE CONTROL! ONE MORE STEP IN OUR CONTROL OF THE WORLD!
WHAT SIGNATURE, MR. CONDOR?
WHY THIS SIGNATURE, YOU BUMBLING... ER,..
J.P. LODGE PRESIDENT
...THE SIGNATURE! IT'S GONE!
I, TOO, ANTICIPATED THIS, J.U.G.H.E.A.D.!
CONDOR'S PEN CONTAINS DISAPPEARING INK! COMPLIMENTS OF P.O.P.!
INK
HOW CAN I THANK YOU? YOUR HEROIC ACTIONS HAVE SAVED THE PLANT, THE COUNTRY, AND WHO KNOWS? PERHAPS THE WORLD!
WHO KNOWS, INDEED?
LISTEN TO BIG SHOT! IT WAS YOU AND I GETTING GASSED THAT PAVED THE WAY FOR HIM!
THE END

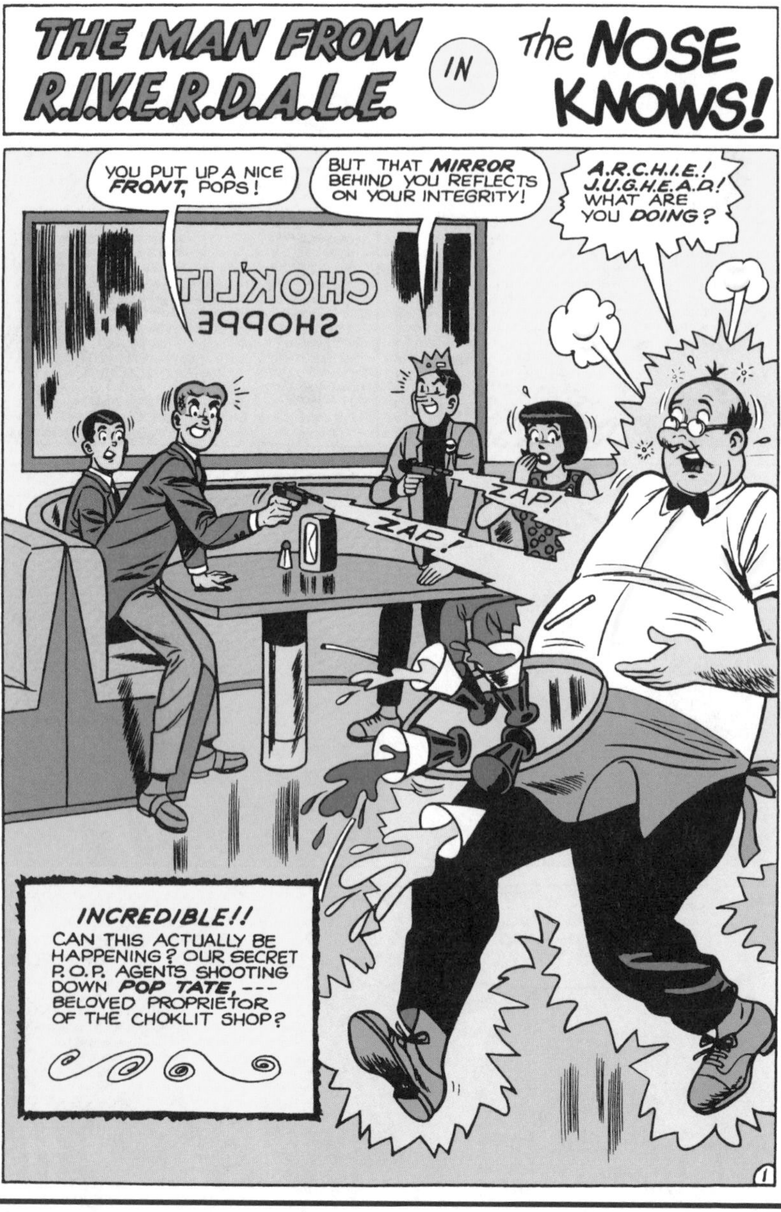
THE MAN FROM R.I.V.E.R.D.A.L.E.
IN
The NOSE KNOWS!
YOU PUT UP A NICE FRONT, POPS!
BUT THAT MIRROR BEHIND YOU REFLECTS ON YOUR INTEGRITY!
A.R.C.H.I.E.! J.U.G.H.E.A.D.! WHAT ARE YOU DOING?
ZAP!
ZAP!
INCREDIBLE!! CAN THIS ACTUALLY BE HAPPENING? OUR SECRET P.O.P. AGENTS SHOOTING DOWN POP TATE, --- BELOVED PROPRIETOR OF THE CHOKLIT SHOP?
1

Story: Frank Doyle Pencils: Bob White
Inks & Letters: Mario Acquaviva

Originally printed in LIFE WITH ARCHIE #51, JULY 1966

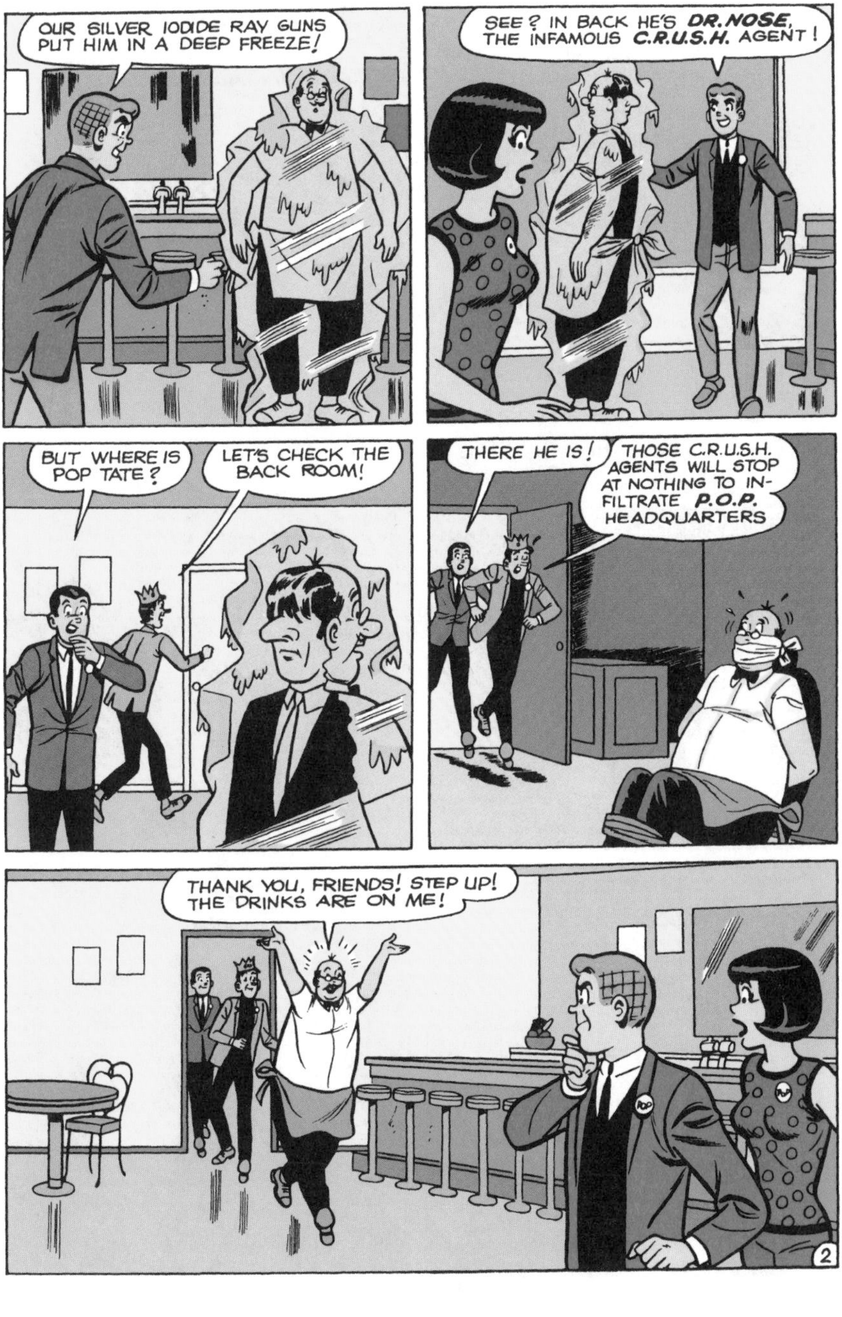
OUR SILVER IODIDE RAY GUNS PUT HIM IN A DEEP FREEZE!
SEE? IN BACK HE'S **DR. NOSE**, THE INFAMOUS **C.R.U.S.H.** AGENT!
BUT WHERE IS POP TATE?
LET'S CHECK THE BACK ROOM!
THERE HE IS!
THOSE C.R.U.S.H. AGENTS WILL STOP AT NOTHING TO INFILTRATE **P.O.P.** HEADQUARTERS
THANK YOU, FRIENDS! STEP UP! THE DRINKS ARE ON ME!
2

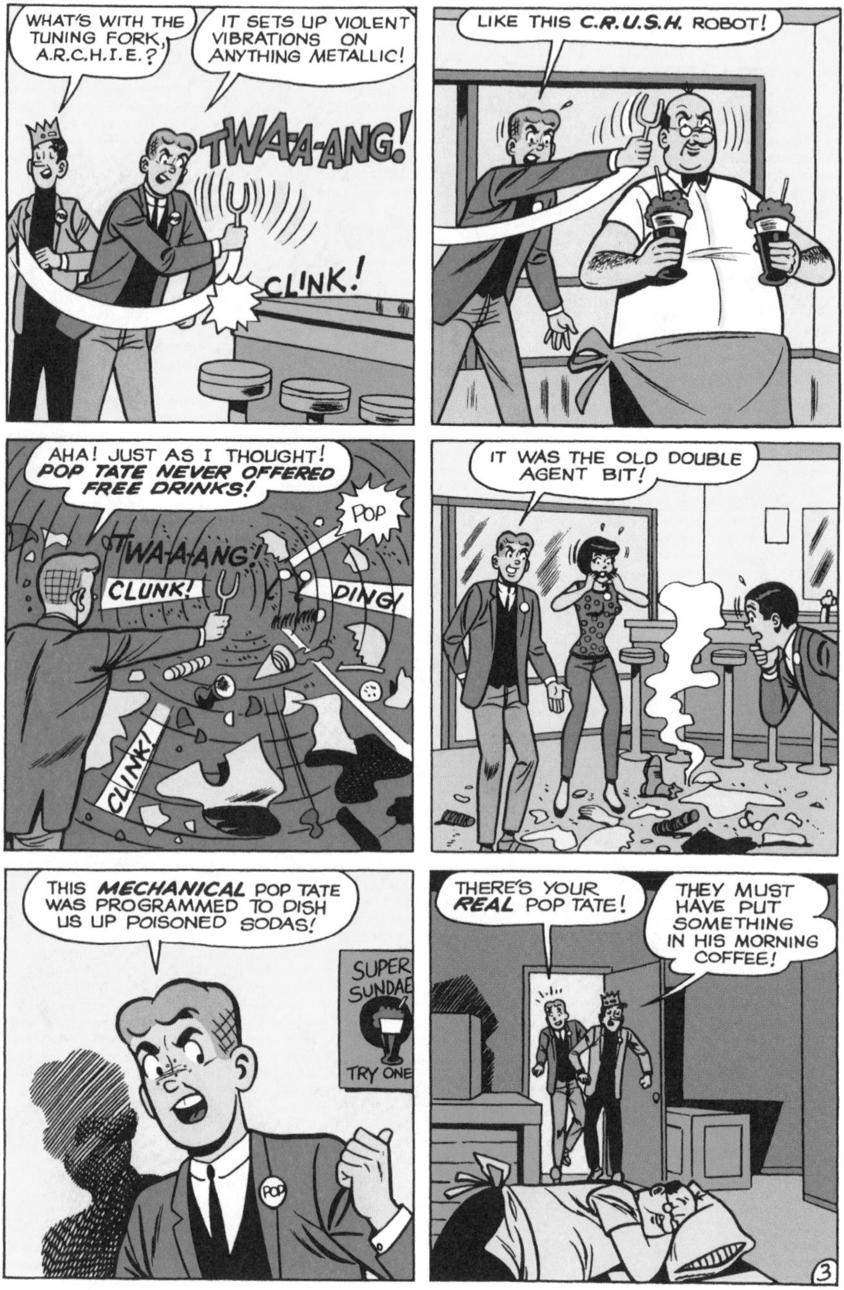
WHAT'S WITH THE TUNING FORK, A.R.C.H.I.E.?
IT SETS UP VIOLENT VIBRATIONS ON ANYTHING METALLIC!
TWA-A-ANG!
CLINK!
LIKE THIS C.R.U.S.H. ROBOT!
AHA! JUST AS I THOUGHT! POP TATE NEVER OFFERED FREE DRINKS!
POP
TWA-A-ANG!
CLUNK!
DING!
CLINK!
IT WAS THE OLD DOUBLE AGENT BIT!
THIS MECHANICAL POP TATE WAS PROGRAMMED TO DISH US UP POISONED SODAS!
SUPER SUNDAE
TRY ONE
THERE'S YOUR REAL POP TATE!
THEY MUST HAVE PUT SOMETHING IN HIS MORNING COFFEE!
3

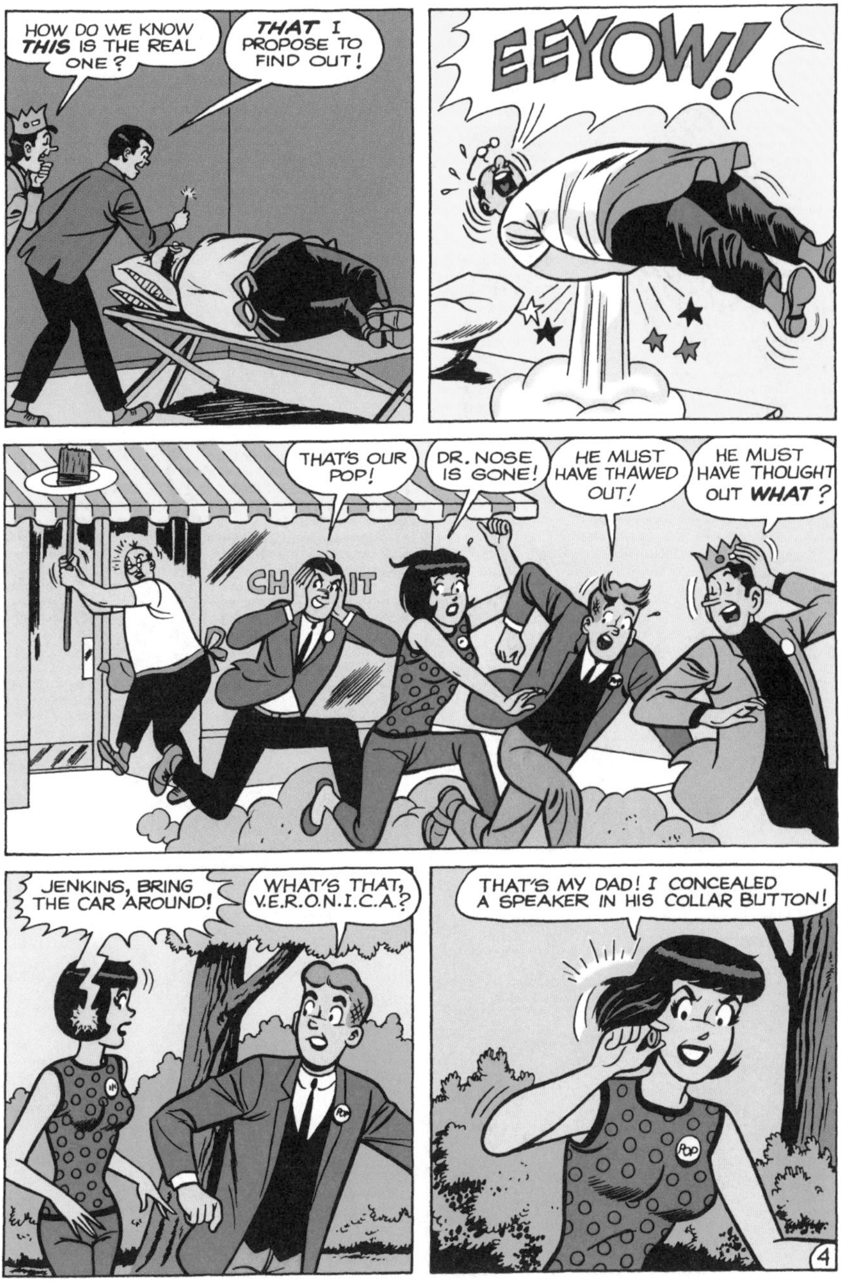
HOW DO WE KNOW THIS IS THE REAL ONE?
THAT I PROPOSE TO FIND OUT!
EEYOW!
THAT'S OUR POP!
DR. NOSE IS GONE!
HE MUST HAVE THAWED OUT!
HE MUST HAVE THOUGHT OUT WHAT?
CH IT
JENKINS, BRING THE CAR AROUND!
WHAT'S THAT, V.E.R.O.N.I.C.A.?
THAT'S MY DAD! I CONCEALED A SPEAKER IN HIS COLLAR BUTTON!
POP
4

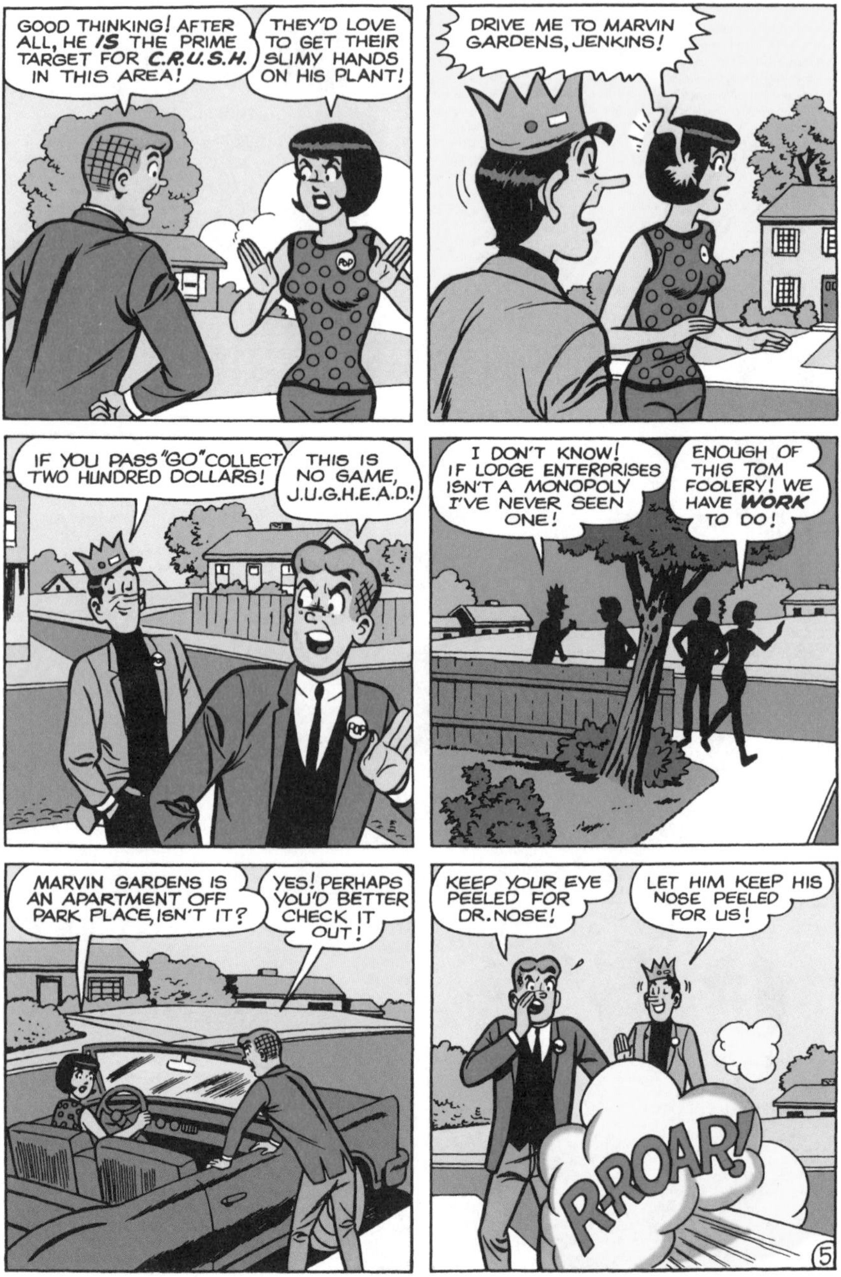
GOOD THINKING! AFTER ALL, HE IS THE PRIME TARGET FOR C.R.U.S.H. IN THIS AREA!
THEY'D LOVE TO GET THEIR SLIMY HANDS ON HIS PLANT!
DRIVE ME TO MARVIN GARDENS, JENKINS!
IF YOU PASS "GO" COLLECT TWO HUNDRED DOLLARS!
THIS IS NO GAME, J.U.G.H.E.A.D.!
I DON'T KNOW! IF LODGE ENTERPRISES ISN'T A MONOPOLY I'VE NEVER SEEN ONE!
ENOUGH OF THIS TOM FOOLERY! WE HAVE WORK TO DO!
MARVIN GARDENS IS AN APARTMENT OFF PARK PLACE, ISN'T IT?
YES! PERHAPS YOU'D BETTER CHECK IT OUT!
KEEP YOUR EYE PEELED FOR DR. NOSE!
LET HIM KEEP HIS NOSE PEELED FOR US!
R-ROAR!
5

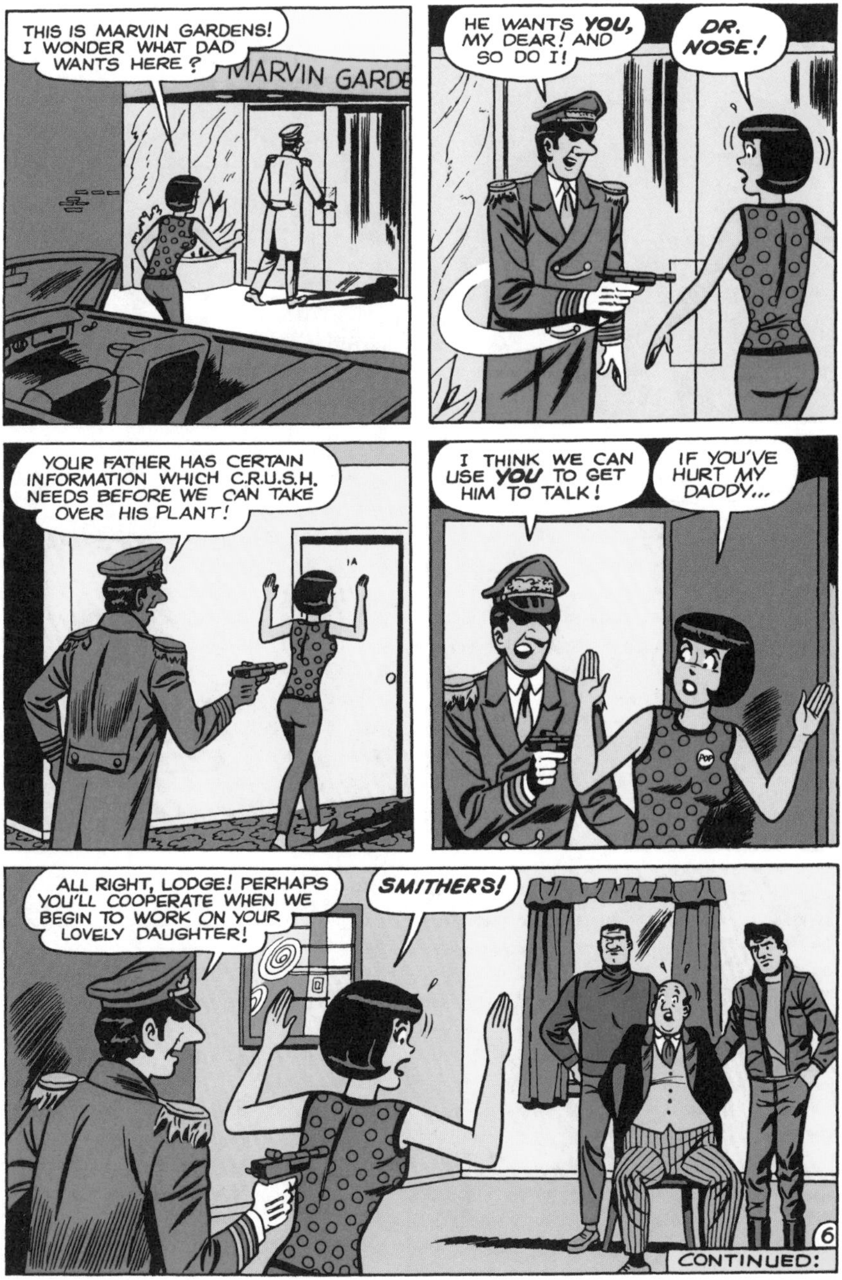
THIS IS MARVIN GARDENS! I WONDER WHAT DAD WANTS HERE?
MARVIN GARDE
HE WANTS YOU, MY DEAR! AND SO DO I!
DR. NOSE!
YOUR FATHER HAS CERTAIN INFORMATION WHICH C.R.U.S.H. NEEDS BEFORE WE CAN TAKE OVER HIS PLANT!
1A
I THINK WE CAN USE YOU TO GET HIM TO TALK!
IF YOU'VE HURT MY DADDY...
POP
ALL RIGHT, LODGE! PERHAPS YOU'LL COOPERATE WHEN WE BEGIN TO WORK ON YOUR LOVELY DAUGHTER!
SMITHERS!
6
CONTINUED:

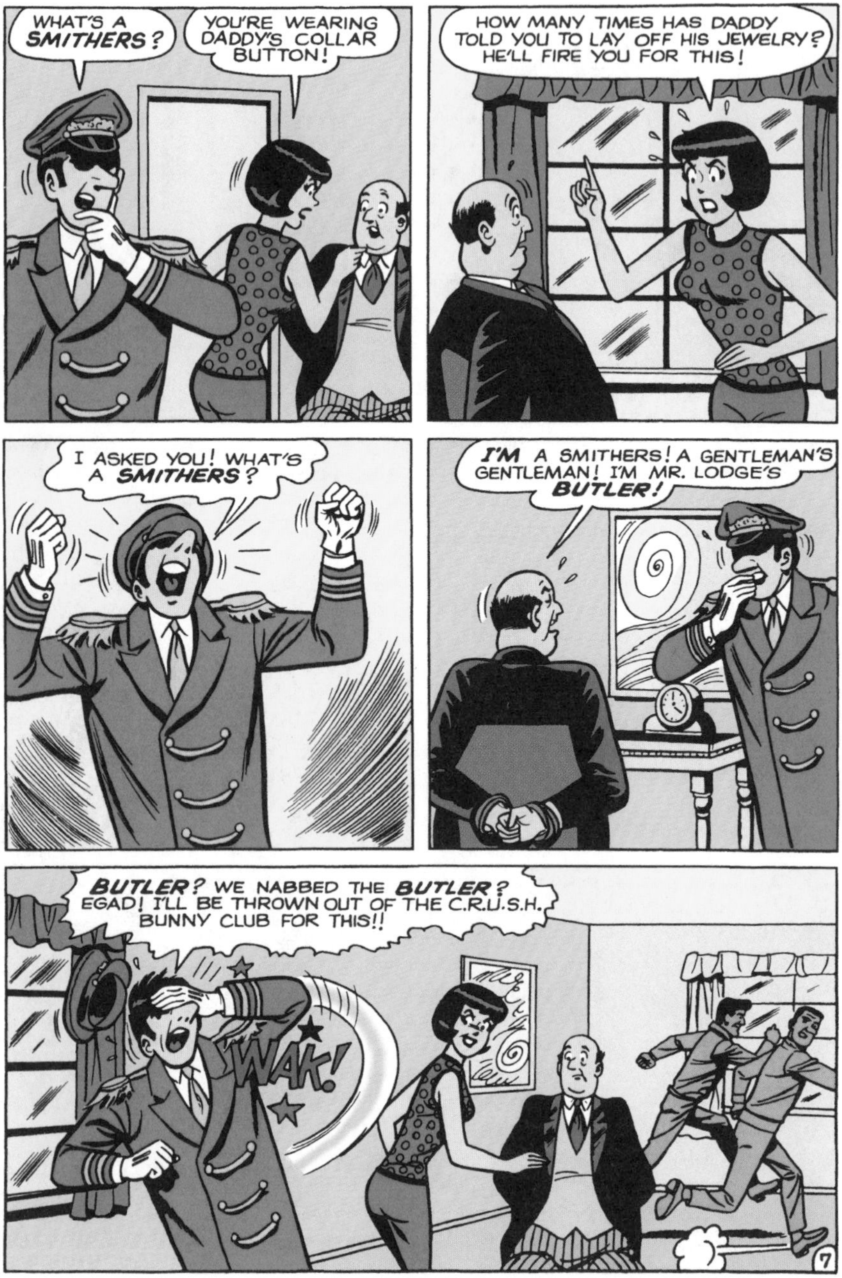
WHAT'S A SMITHERS?
YOU'RE WEARING DADDY'S COLLAR BUTTON!
HOW MANY TIMES HAS DADDY TOLD YOU TO LAY OFF HIS JEWELRY? HE'LL FIRE YOU FOR THIS!
I ASKED YOU! WHAT'S A SMITHERS?
I'M A SMITHERS! A GENTLEMAN'S GENTLEMAN! I'M MR. LODGE'S BUTLER!
BUTLER? WE NABBED THE BUTLER? EGAD! I'LL BE THROWN OUT OF THE C.R.U.S.H. BUNNY CLUB FOR THIS!!
WAK!
7

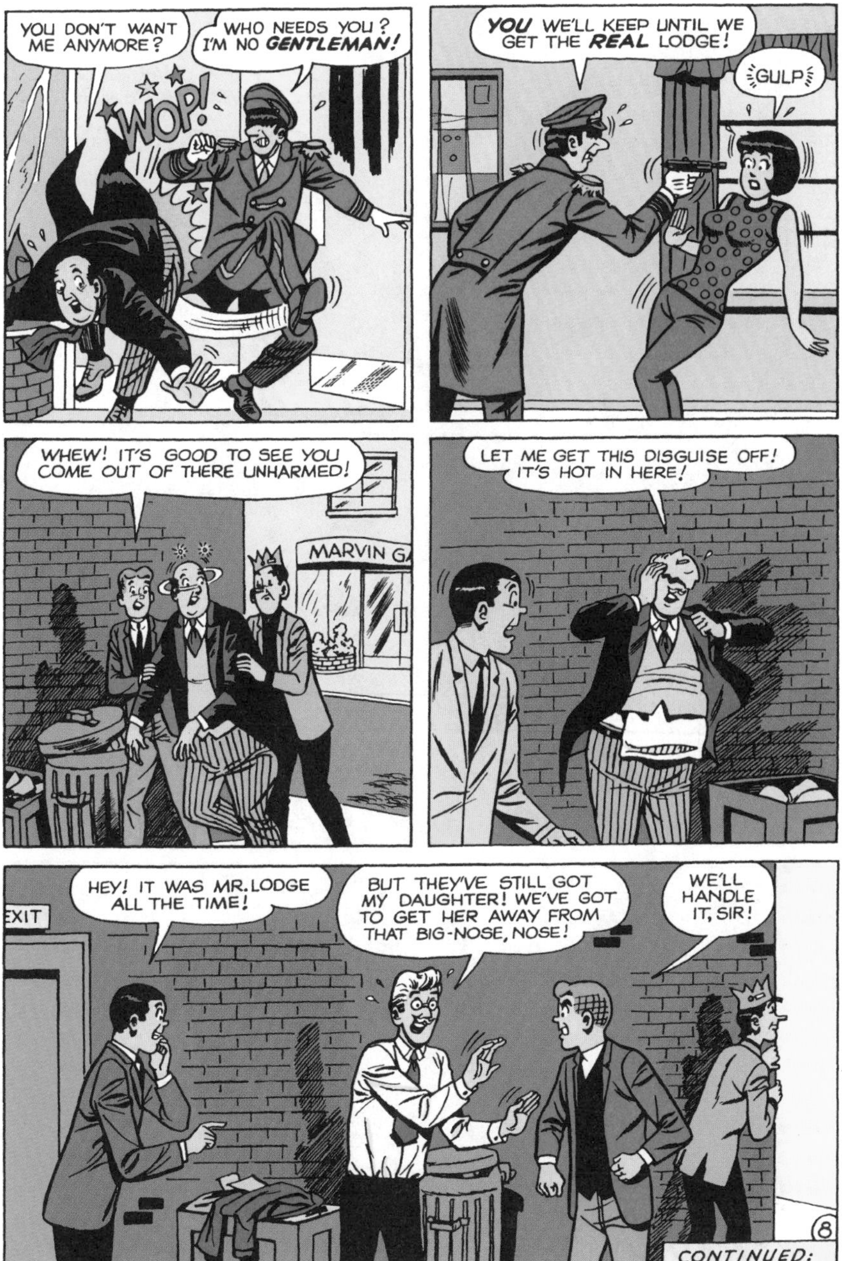
YOU DON'T WANT ME ANYMORE?
WHO NEEDS YOU? I'M NO GENTLEMAN!
WOP!
YOU WE'LL KEEP UNTIL WE GET THE REAL LODGE!
GULP
WHEW! IT'S GOOD TO SEE YOU COME OUT OF THERE UNHARMED!
MARVIN GA
LET ME GET THIS DISGUISE OFF! IT'S HOT IN HERE!
EXIT
HEY! IT WAS MR. LODGE ALL THE TIME!
BUT THEY'VE STILL GOT MY DAUGHTER! WE'VE GOT TO GET HER AWAY FROM THAT BIG-NOSE, NOSE!
WE'LL HANDLE IT, SIR!
8
CONTINUED:

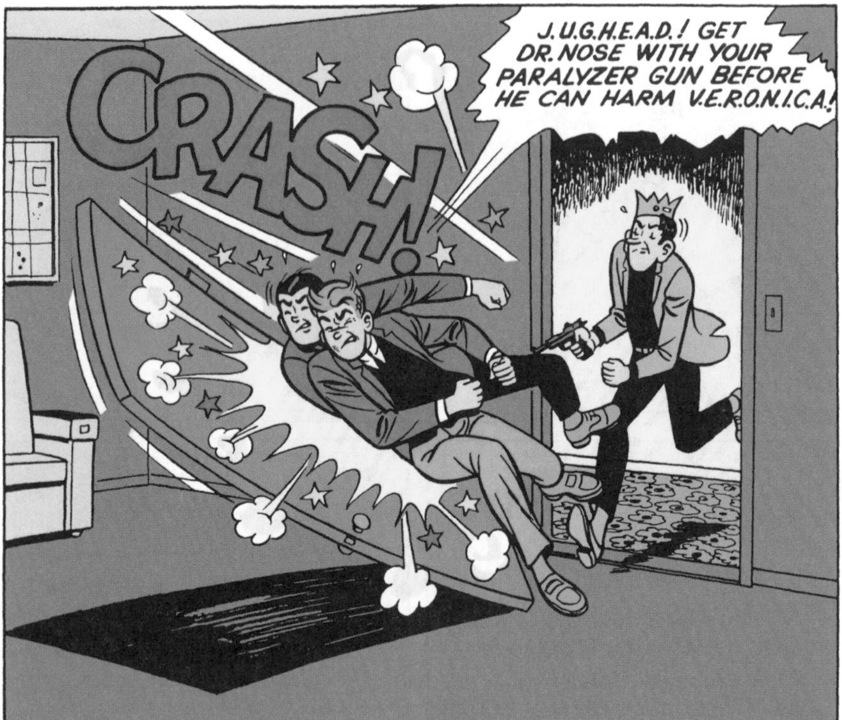
J.U.G.H.E.A.D.! GET DR. NOSE WITH YOUR PARALYZER GUN BEFORE HE CAN HARM V.E.R.O.N.I.C.A.!
CRASH!

PART II the NOSE KNOWS

THE MAN FROM R.I.V.E.R.D.A.L.E.

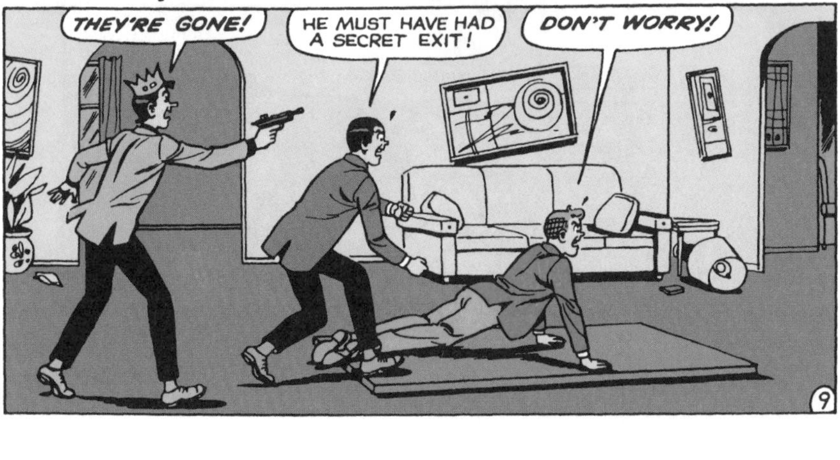
THEY'RE GONE!
HE MUST HAVE HAD A SECRET EXIT!
DON'T WORRY!
9

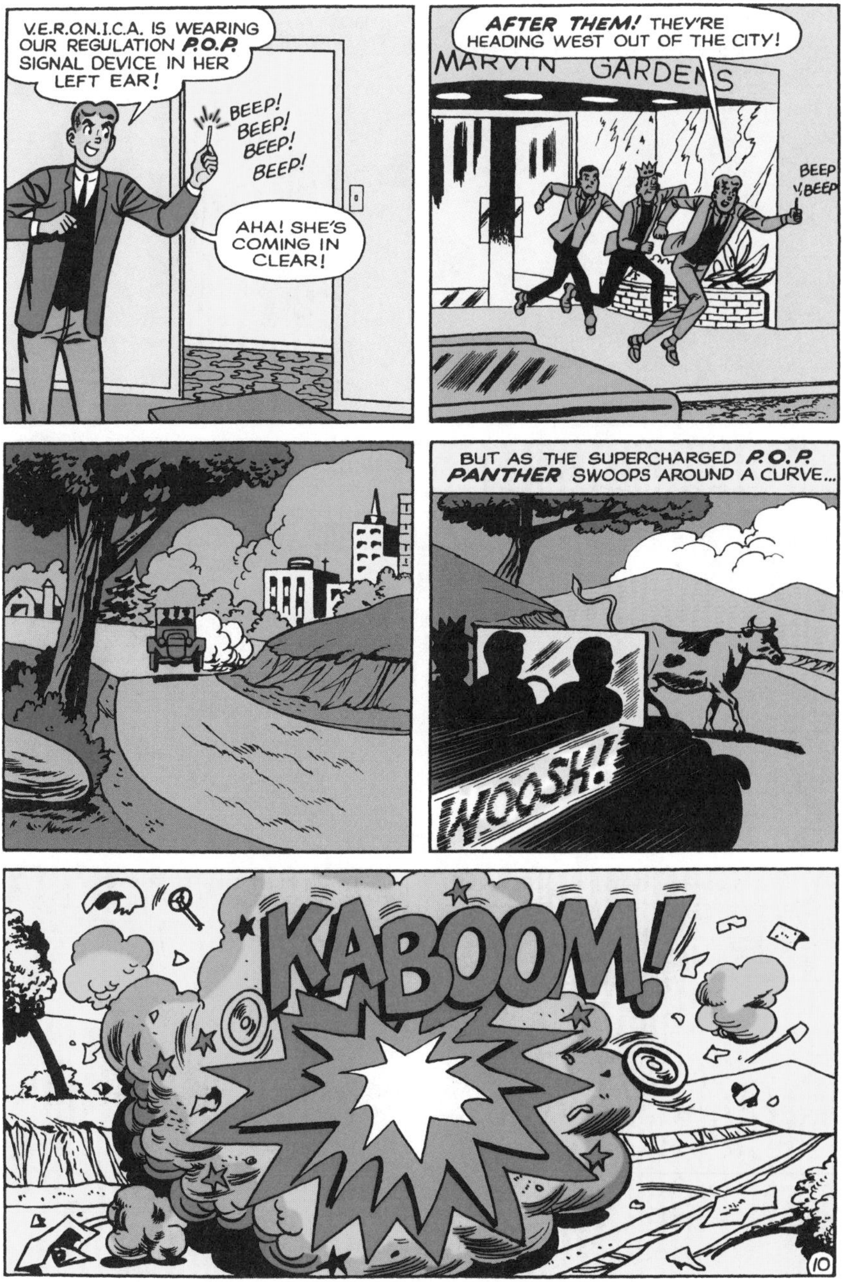
V.E.R.O.N.I.C.A. IS WEARING OUR REGULATION P.O.P. SIGNAL DEVICE IN HER LEFT EAR!
BEEP! BEEP! BEEP! BEEP!
AHA! SHE'S COMING IN CLEAR!
AFTER THEM! THEY'RE HEADING WEST OUT OF THE CITY!
MARVIN GARDENS
BEEP BEEP
BUT AS THE SUPERCHARGED P.O.P. PANTHER SWOOPS AROUND A CURVE...
WOOSH!
KABOOM!
10

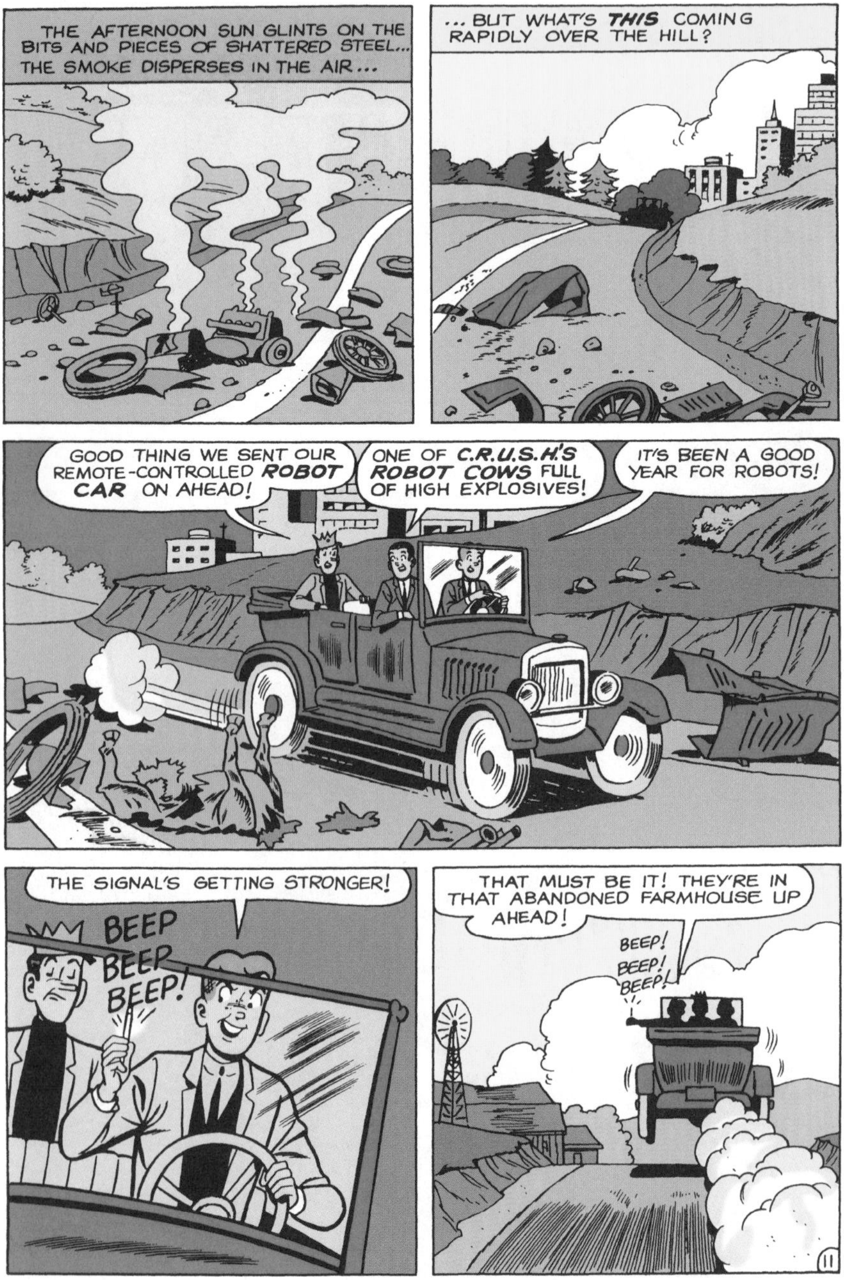
THE AFTERNOON SUN GLINTS ON THE BITS AND PIECES OF SHATTERED STEEL... THE SMOKE DISPERSES IN THE AIR...
... BUT WHAT'S THIS COMING RAPIDLY OVER THE HILL?
GOOD THING WE SENT OUR REMOTE-CONTROLLED ROBOT CAR ON AHEAD!
ONE OF C.R.U.S.H.'S ROBOT COWS FULL OF HIGH EXPLOSIVES!
IT'S BEEN A GOOD YEAR FOR ROBOTS!
THE SIGNAL'S GETTING STRONGER!
BEEP BEEP BEEP!
THAT MUST BE IT! THEY'RE IN THAT ABANDONED FARMHOUSE UP AHEAD!
BEEP! BEEP! BEEP!
11

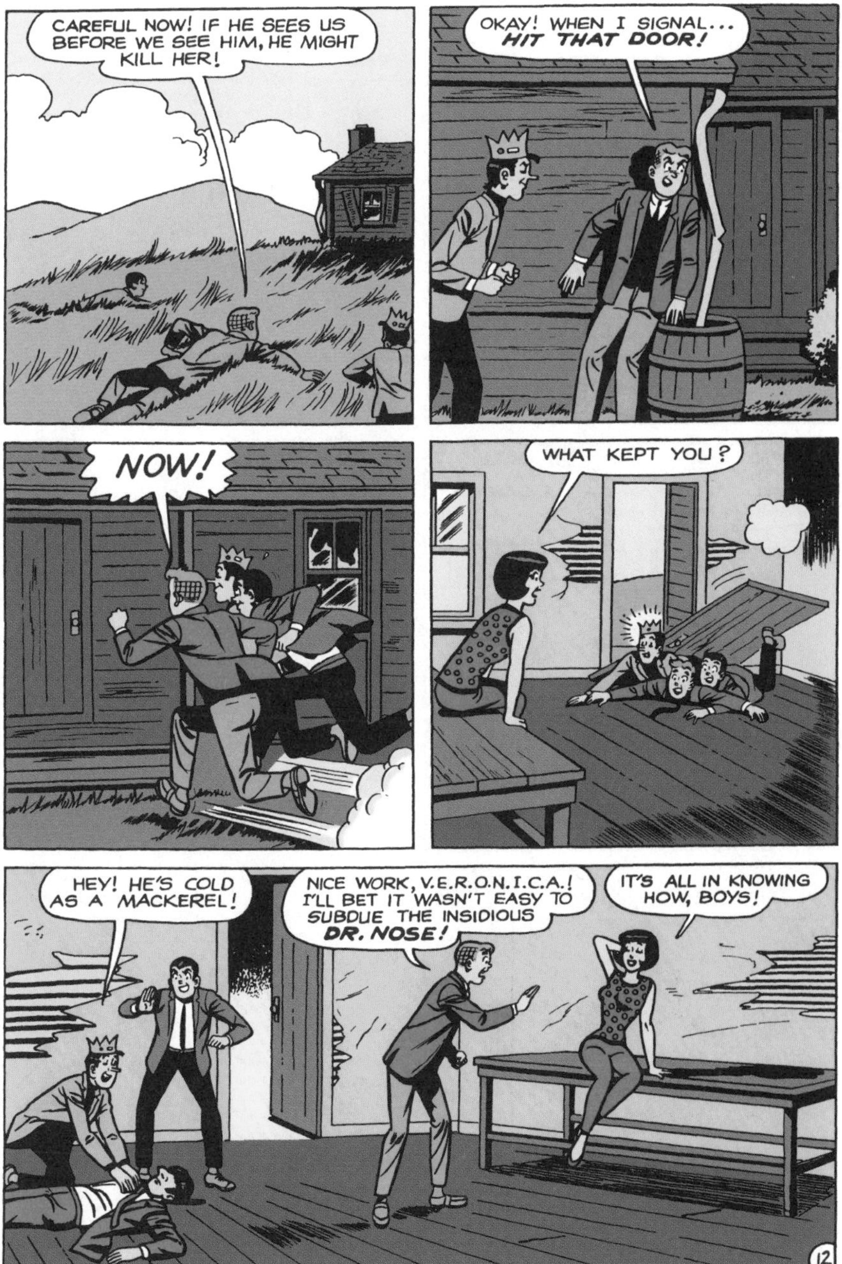
CAREFUL NOW! IF HE SEES US BEFORE WE SEE HIM, HE MIGHT KILL HER!
OKAY! WHEN I SIGNAL... HIT THAT DOOR!
NOW!
WHAT KEPT YOU?
HEY! HE'S COLD AS A MACKEREL!
NICE WORK, V.E.R.O.N.I.C.A.! I'LL BET IT WASN'T EASY TO SUBDUE THE INSIDIOUS DR. NOSE!
IT'S ALL IN KNOWING HOW, BOYS!
12

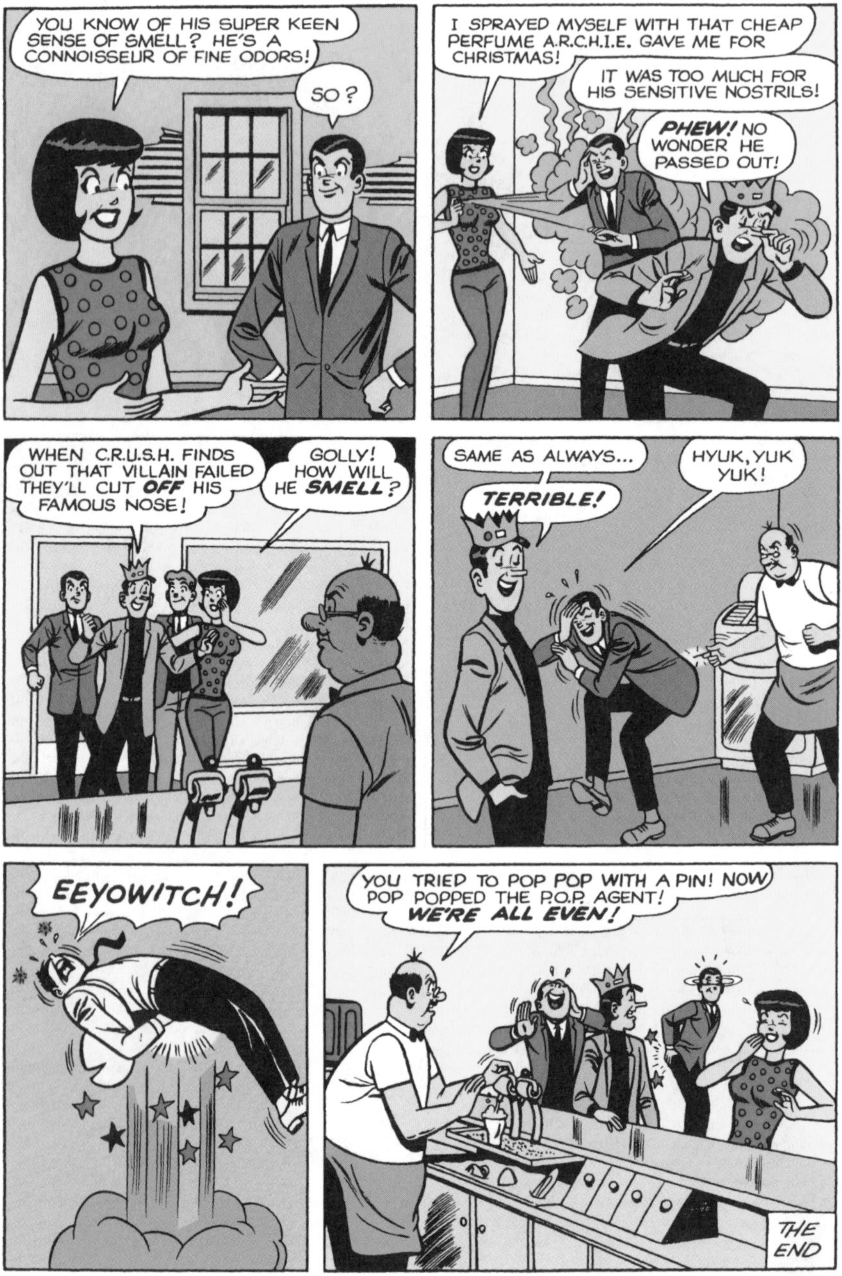
YOU KNOW OF HIS SUPER KEEN SENSE OF SMELL? HE'S A CONNOISSEUR OF FINE ODORS!
SO?
I SPRAYED MYSELF WITH THAT CHEAP PERFUME A.R.C.H.I.E. GAVE ME FOR CHRISTMAS!
IT WAS TOO MUCH FOR HIS SENSITIVE NOSTRILS!
PHEW! NO WONDER HE PASSED OUT!
WHEN C.R.U.S.H. FINDS OUT THAT VILLAIN FAILED THEY'LL CUT OFF HIS FAMOUS NOSE!
GOLLY! HOW WILL HE SMELL?
SAME AS ALWAYS...
TERRIBLE!
HYUK, YUK YUK!
EEYOWITCH!
YOU TRIED TO POP POP WITH A PIN! NOW POP POPPED THE P.O.P. AGENT! WE'RE ALL EVEN!
THE END

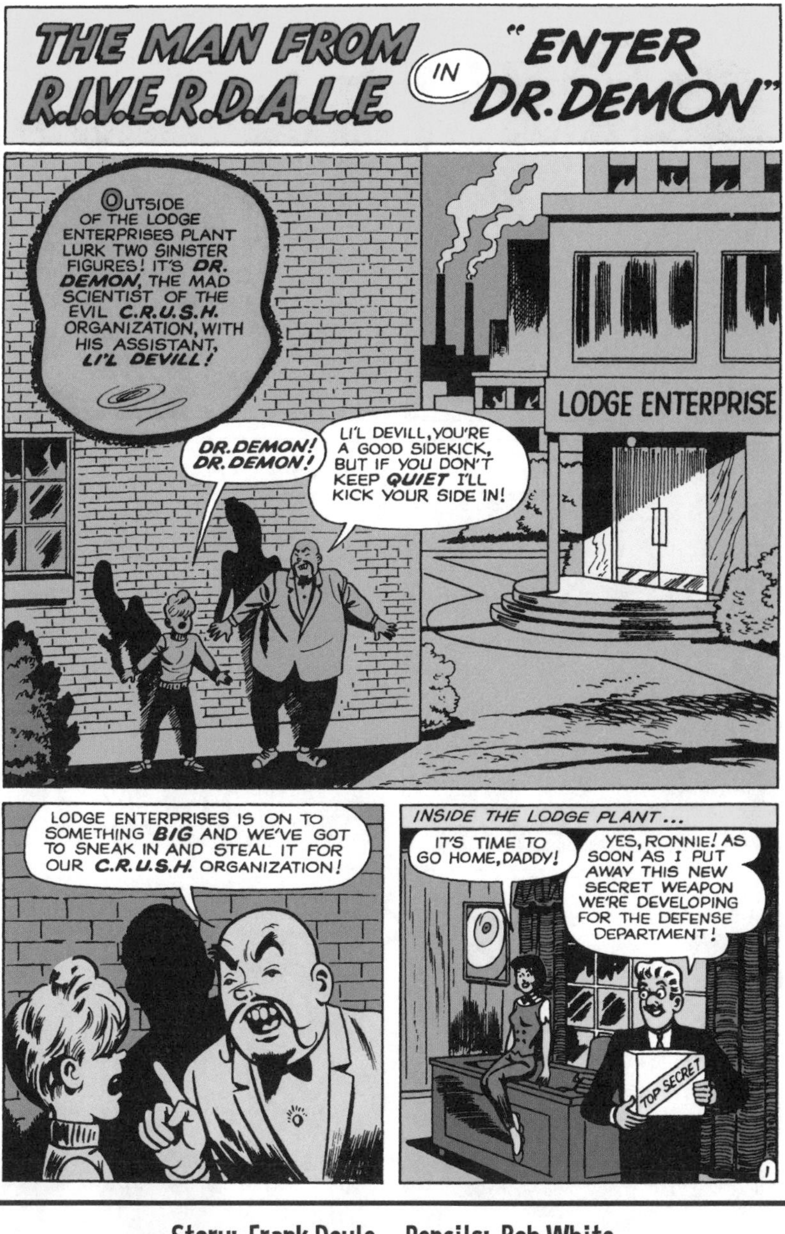
THE MAN FROM R.I.V.E.R.D.A.L.E.
IN
"ENTER DR. DEMON"
OUTSIDE OF THE LODGE ENTERPRISES PLANT LURK TWO SINISTER FIGURES! IT'S DR. DEMON, THE MAD SCIENTIST OF THE EVIL C.R.U.S.H. ORGANIZATION, WITH HIS ASSISTANT, LI'L DEVILL!
LODGE ENTERPRISE
DR. DEMON! DR. DEMON!
LI'L DEVILL, YOU'RE A GOOD SIDEKICK, BUT IF YOU DON'T KEEP QUIET I'LL KICK YOUR SIDE IN!
LODGE ENTERPRISES IS ON TO SOMETHING BIG AND WE'VE GOT TO SNEAK IN AND STEAL IT FOR OUR C.R.U.S.H. ORGANIZATION!
INSIDE THE LODGE PLANT...
IT'S TIME TO GO HOME, DADDY!
YES, RONNIE! AS SOON AS I PUT AWAY THIS NEW SECRET WEAPON WE'RE DEVELOPING FOR THE DEFENSE DEPARTMENT!
TOP SECRET
1

Story: Frank Doyle Pencils: Bob White
Inks & Letters: Mario Acquaviva

Originally printed in LIFE WITH ARCHIE #51, JULY 1966

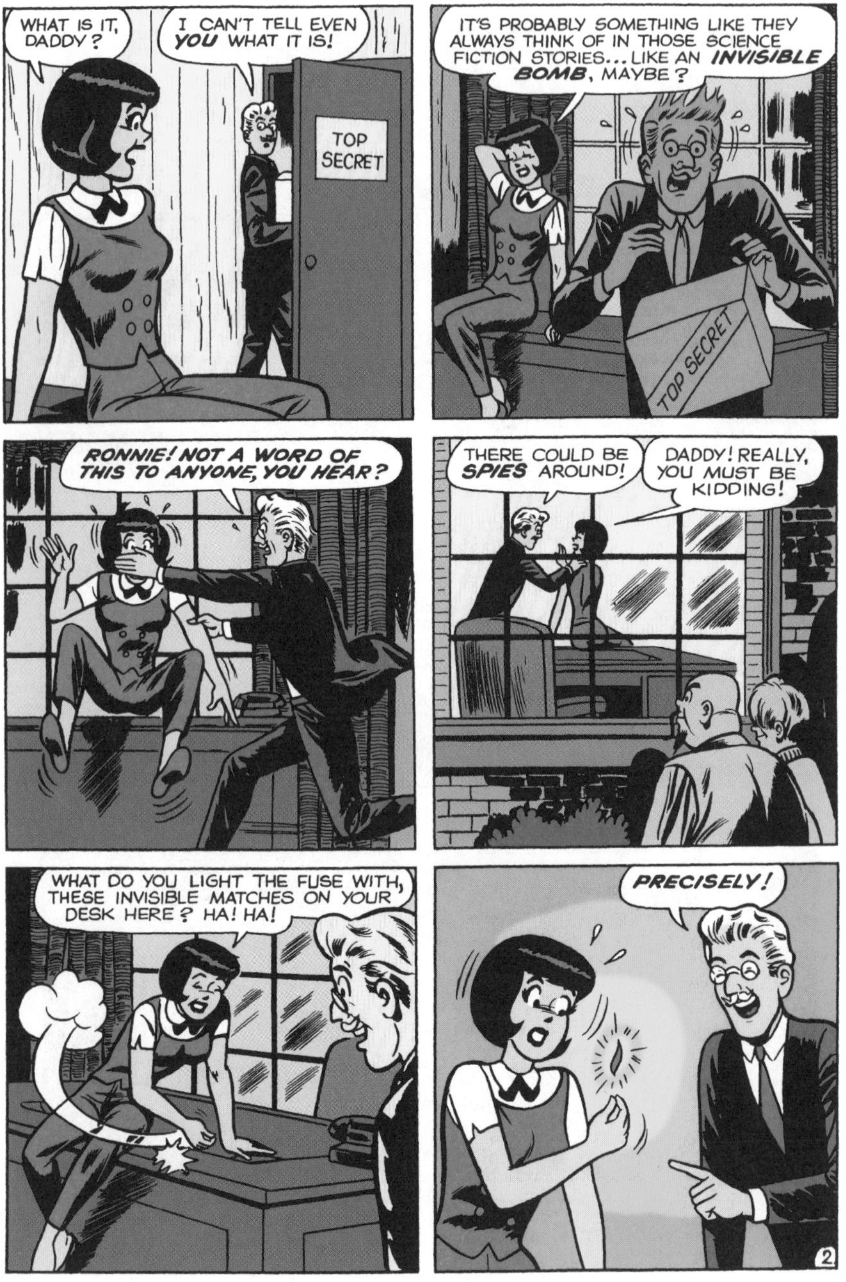
WHAT IS IT, DADDY?
I CAN'T TELL EVEN YOU WHAT IT IS!
TOP SECRET
IT'S PROBABLY SOMETHING LIKE THEY ALWAYS THINK OF IN THOSE SCIENCE FICTION STORIES... LIKE AN INVISIBLE BOMB, MAYBE?
TOP SECRET
RONNIE! NOT A WORD OF THIS TO ANYONE, YOU HEAR?
THERE COULD BE SPIES AROUND!
DADDY! REALLY, YOU MUST BE KIDDING!
WHAT DO YOU LIGHT THE FUSE WITH, THESE INVISIBLE MATCHES ON YOUR DESK HERE? HA! HA!
PRECISELY!
2

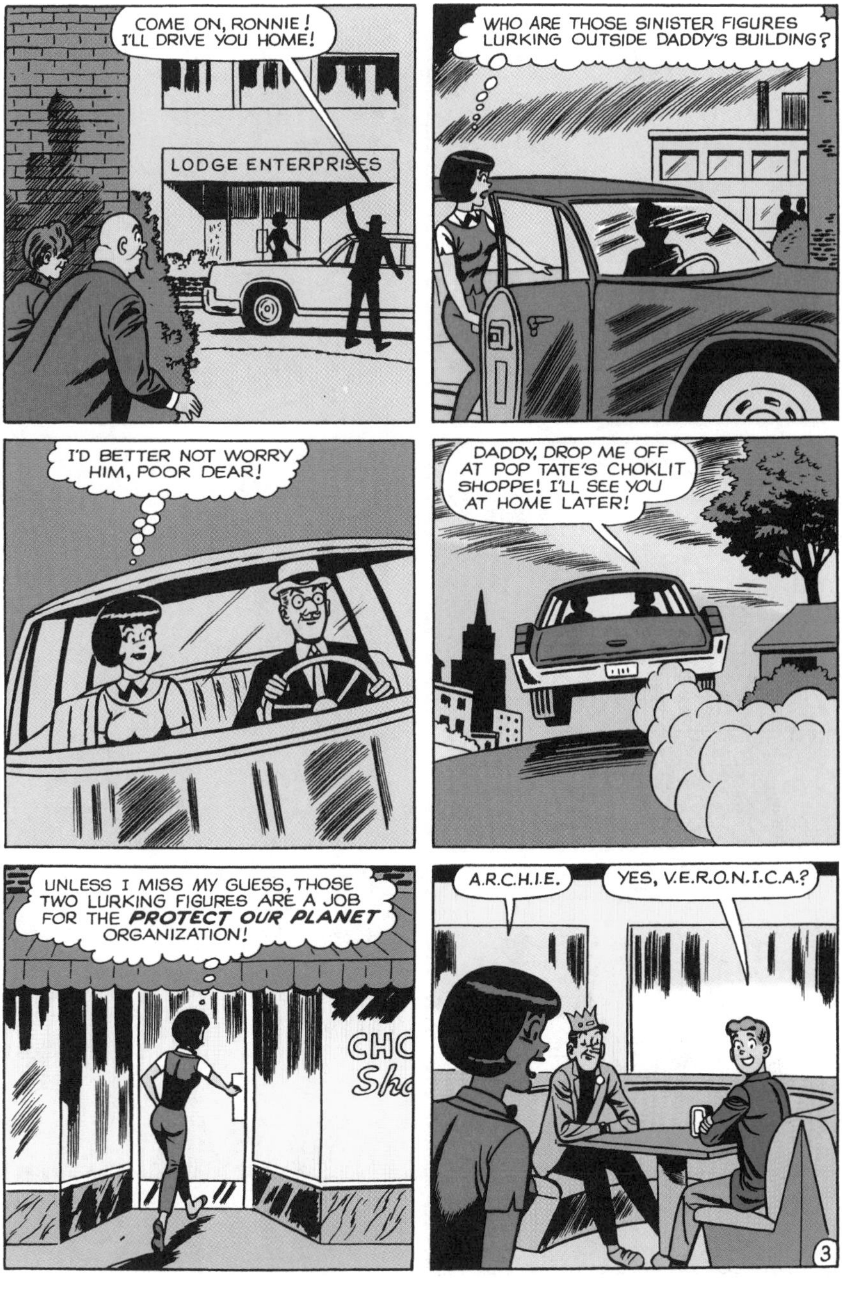
COME ON, RONNIE! I'LL DRIVE YOU HOME!
LODGE ENTERPRISES
WHO ARE THOSE SINISTER FIGURES LURKING OUTSIDE DADDY'S BUILDING?
I'D BETTER NOT WORRY HIM, POOR DEAR!
DADDY, DROP ME OFF AT POP TATE'S CHOKLIT SHOPPE! I'LL SEE YOU AT HOME LATER!
UNLESS I MISS MY GUESS, THOSE TWO LURKING FIGURES ARE A JOB FOR THE **PROTECT OUR PLANET** ORGANIZATION!
A.R.C.H.I.E.
YES, V.E.R.O.N.I.C.A.?
3

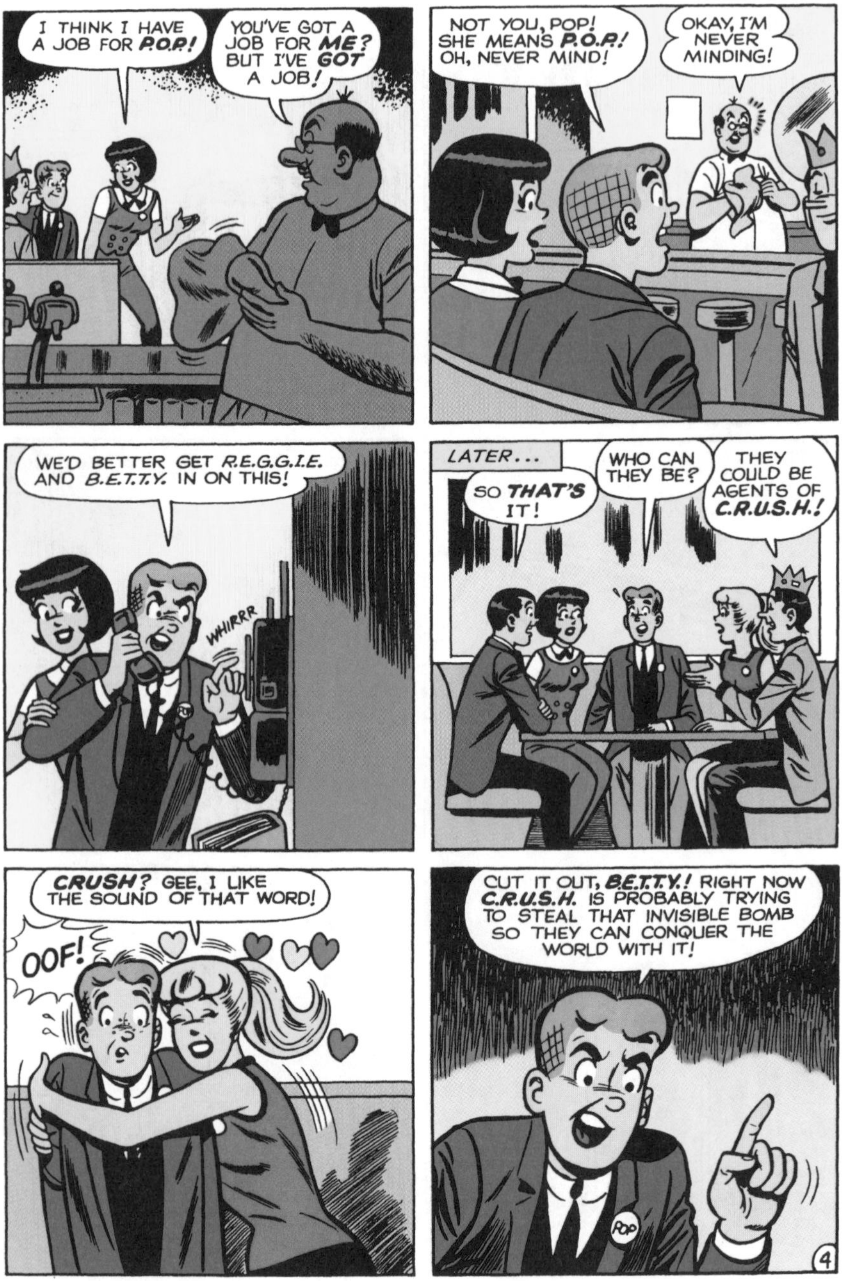
I THINK I HAVE A JOB FOR P.O.P.!
YOU'VE GOT A JOB FOR ME? BUT I'VE GOT A JOB!
NOT YOU, POP! SHE MEANS P.O.P.! OH, NEVER MIND!
OKAY, I'M NEVER MINDING!
WE'D BETTER GET R.E.G.G.I.E. AND B.E.T.T.Y. IN ON THIS!
WHIRRR
LATER...
SO THAT'S IT!
WHO CAN THEY BE?
THEY COULD BE AGENTS OF C.R.U.S.H.!
CRUSH? GEE, I LIKE THE SOUND OF THAT WORD!
OOF!
CUT IT OUT, B.E.T.T.Y.! RIGHT NOW C.R.U.S.H. IS PROBABLY TRYING TO STEAL THAT INVISIBLE BOMB SO THEY CAN CONQUER THE WORLD WITH IT!
POP
4

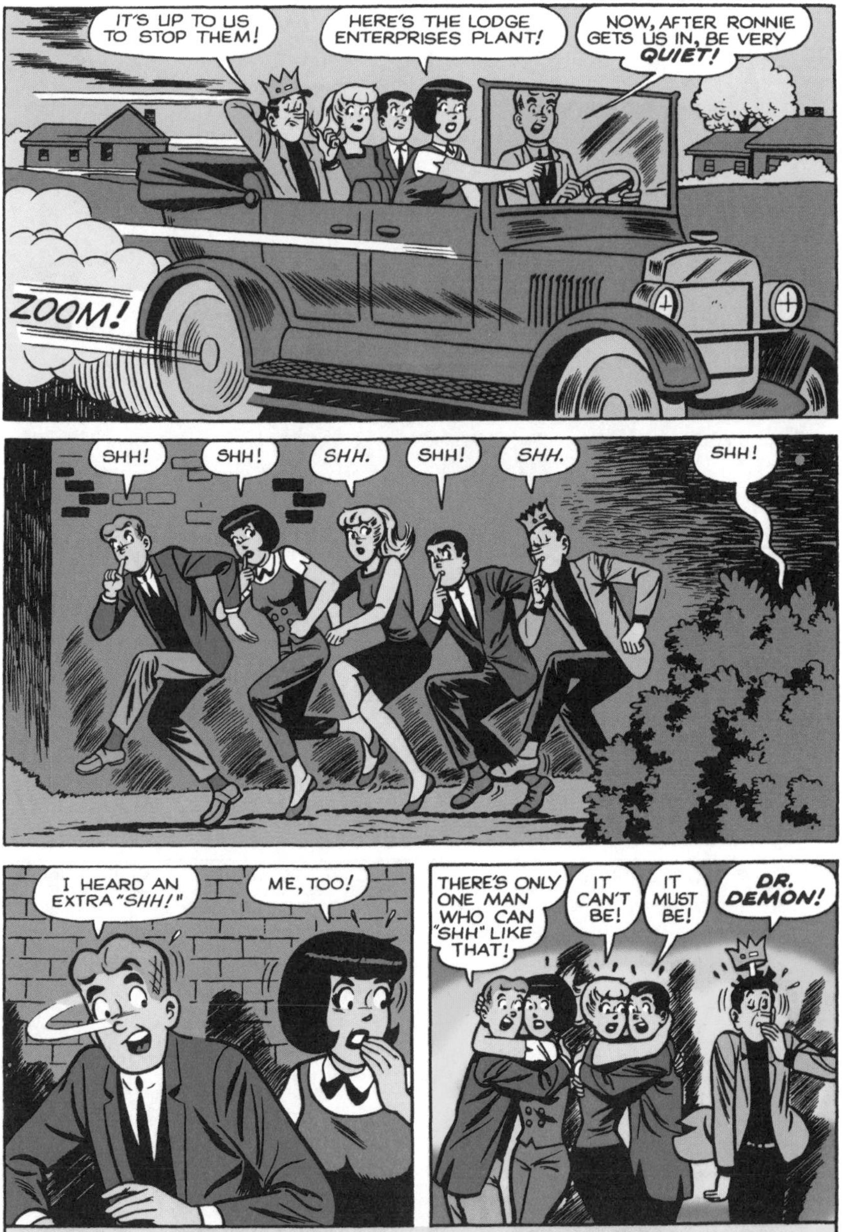
IT'S UP TO US TO STOP THEM!
HERE'S THE LODGE ENTERPRISES PLANT!
NOW, AFTER RONNIE GETS US IN, BE VERY QUIET!
ZOOM!
SHH!
SHH!
SHH.
SHH!
SHH.
SHH!
I HEARD AN EXTRA "SHH!"
ME, TOO!
THERE'S ONLY ONE MAN WHO CAN "SHH" LIKE THAT!
IT CAN'T BE!
IT MUST BE!
DR. DEMON!
HOW DO OUR FRIENDS FROM P.O.P. DEAL WITH DR. DEMON AND PREVENT HIM FROM STEALING THE INVISIBLE BOMB? OR DO THEY? (CONTINUED:)

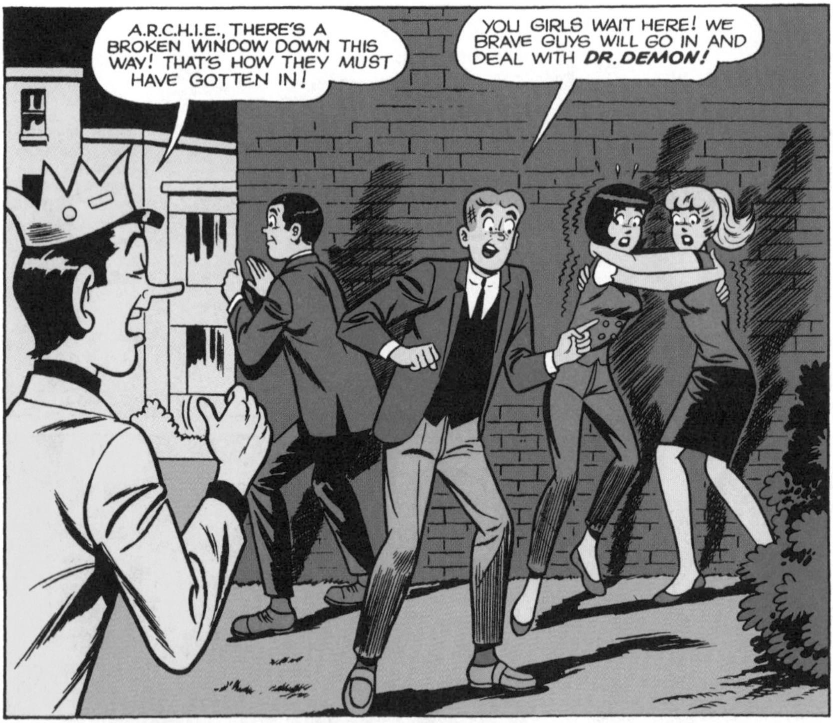
A.R.C.H.I.E., THERE'S A BROKEN WINDOW DOWN THIS WAY! THAT'S HOW THEY MUST HAVE GOTTEN IN!
YOU GIRLS WAIT HERE! WE BRAVE GUYS WILL GO IN AND DEAL WITH DR. DEMON!

PART II

THE MAN FROM R.I.V.E.R.D.A.L.E. in "ENTER DR. DEMON!"

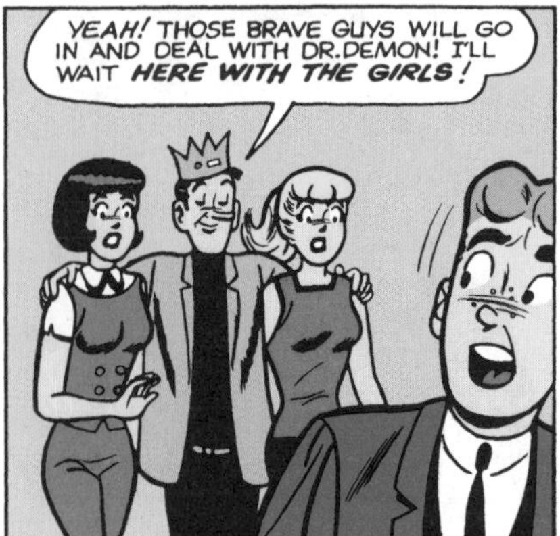
YEAH! THOSE BRAVE GUYS WILL GO IN AND DEAL WITH DR. DEMON! I'LL WAIT HERE WITH THE GIRLS!

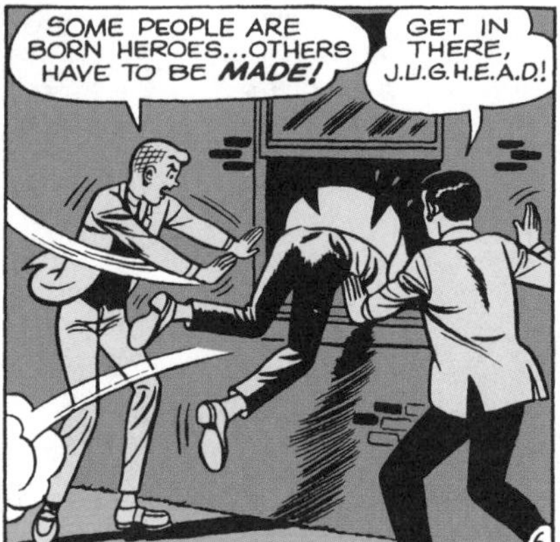
SOME PEOPLE ARE BORN HEROES...OTHERS HAVE TO BE MADE!
GET IN THERE, J.U.G.H.E.A.D.!
6

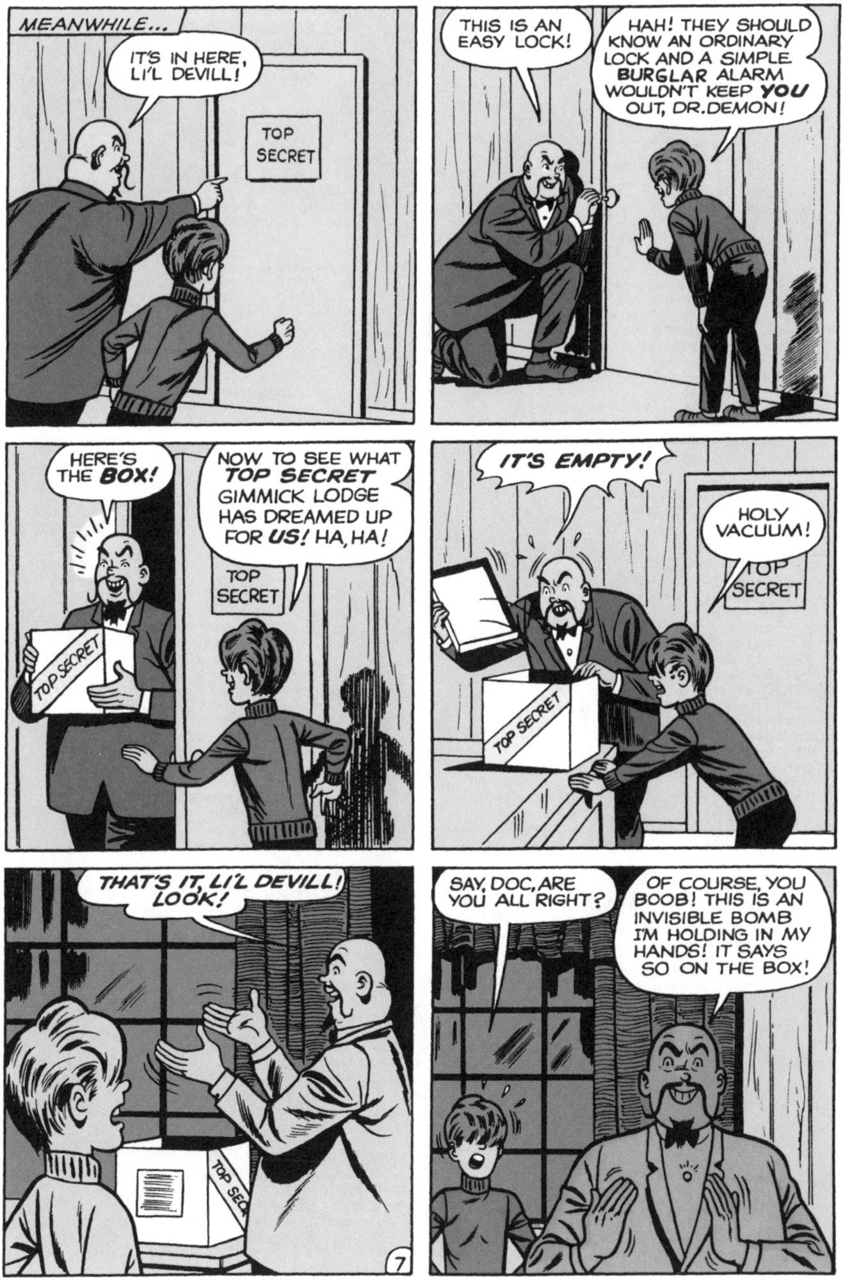
MEANWHILE...
IT'S IN HERE, LI'L DEVILL!
TOP SECRET
THIS IS AN EASY LOCK!
HAH! THEY SHOULD KNOW AN ORDINARY LOCK AND A SIMPLE BURGLAR ALARM WOULDN'T KEEP YOU OUT, DR. DEMON!
HERE'S THE BOX!
NOW TO SEE WHAT TOP SECRET GIMMICK LODGE HAS DREAMED UP FOR US! HA, HA!
TOP SECRET
TOP SECRET
IT'S EMPTY!
HOLY VACUUM!
TOP SECRET
TOP SECRET
THAT'S IT, LI'L DEVILL! LOOK!
7
SAY, DOC, ARE YOU ALL RIGHT?
OF COURSE, YOU BOOB! THIS IS AN INVISIBLE BOMB I'M HOLDING IN MY HANDS! IT SAYS SO ON THE BOX!

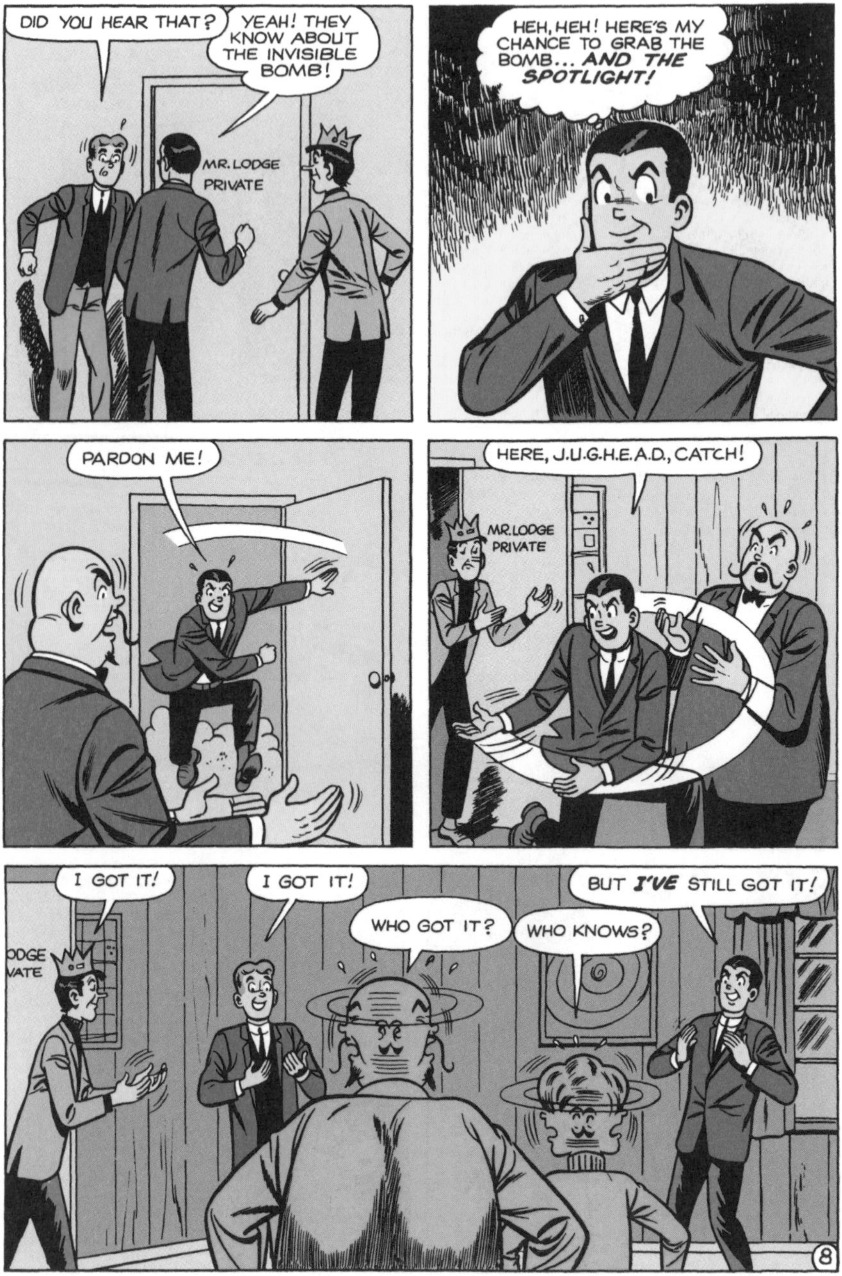
DID YOU HEAR THAT?
YEAH! THEY KNOW ABOUT THE INVISIBLE BOMB!
MR. LODGE PRIVATE
HEH, HEH! HERE'S MY CHANCE TO GRAB THE BOMB... AND THE SPOTLIGHT!
PARDON ME!
HERE, J.U.G.H.E.A.D., CATCH!
MR. LODGE PRIVATE
I GOT IT!
I GOT IT!
WHO GOT IT?
WHO KNOWS?
BUT I'VE STILL GOT IT!
8

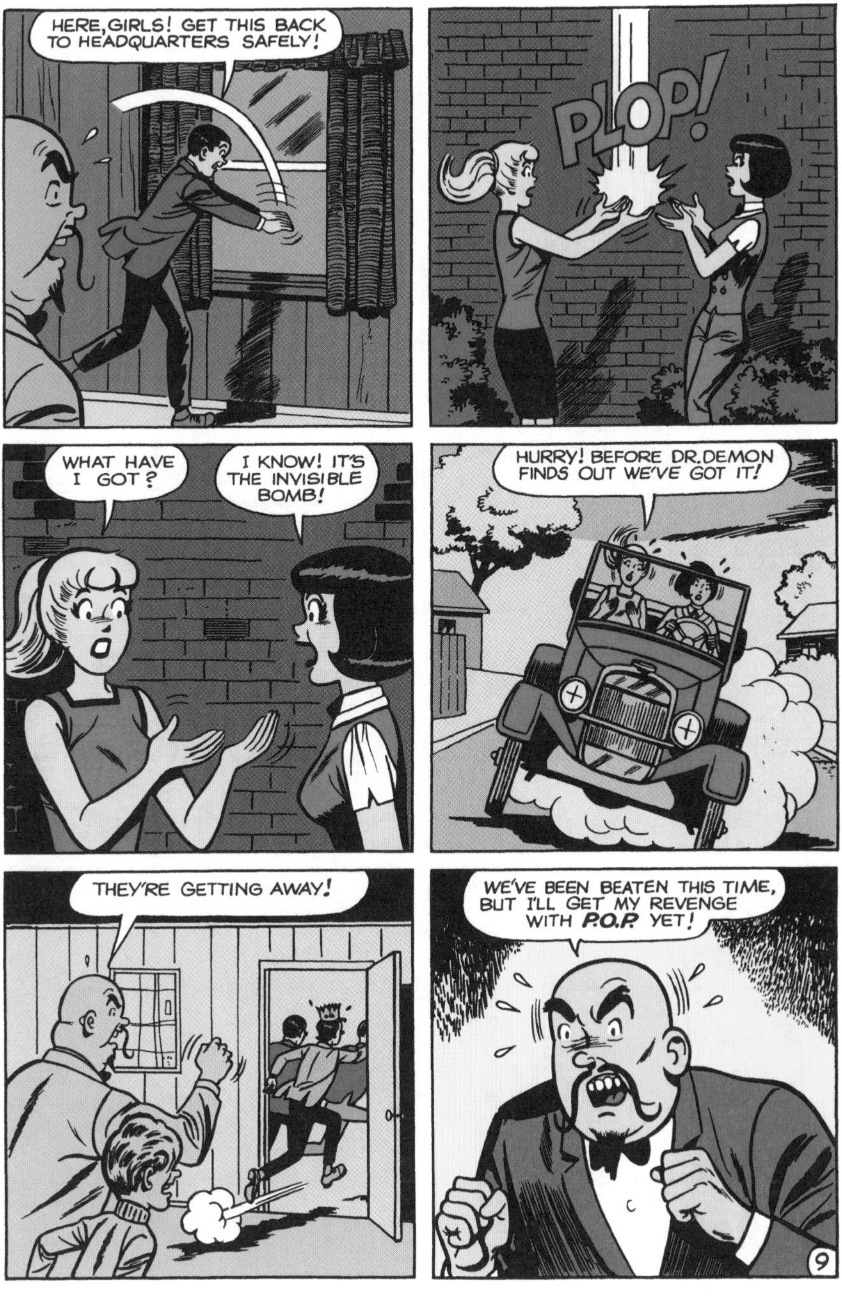
HERE, GIRLS! GET THIS BACK TO HEADQUARTERS SAFELY!
PLOP!
WHAT HAVE I GOT?
I KNOW! IT'S THE INVISIBLE BOMB!
HURRY! BEFORE DR. DEMON FINDS OUT WE'VE GOT IT!
THEY'RE GETTING AWAY!
WE'VE BEEN BEATEN THIS TIME, BUT I'LL GET MY REVENGE WITH P.O.P. YET!
9

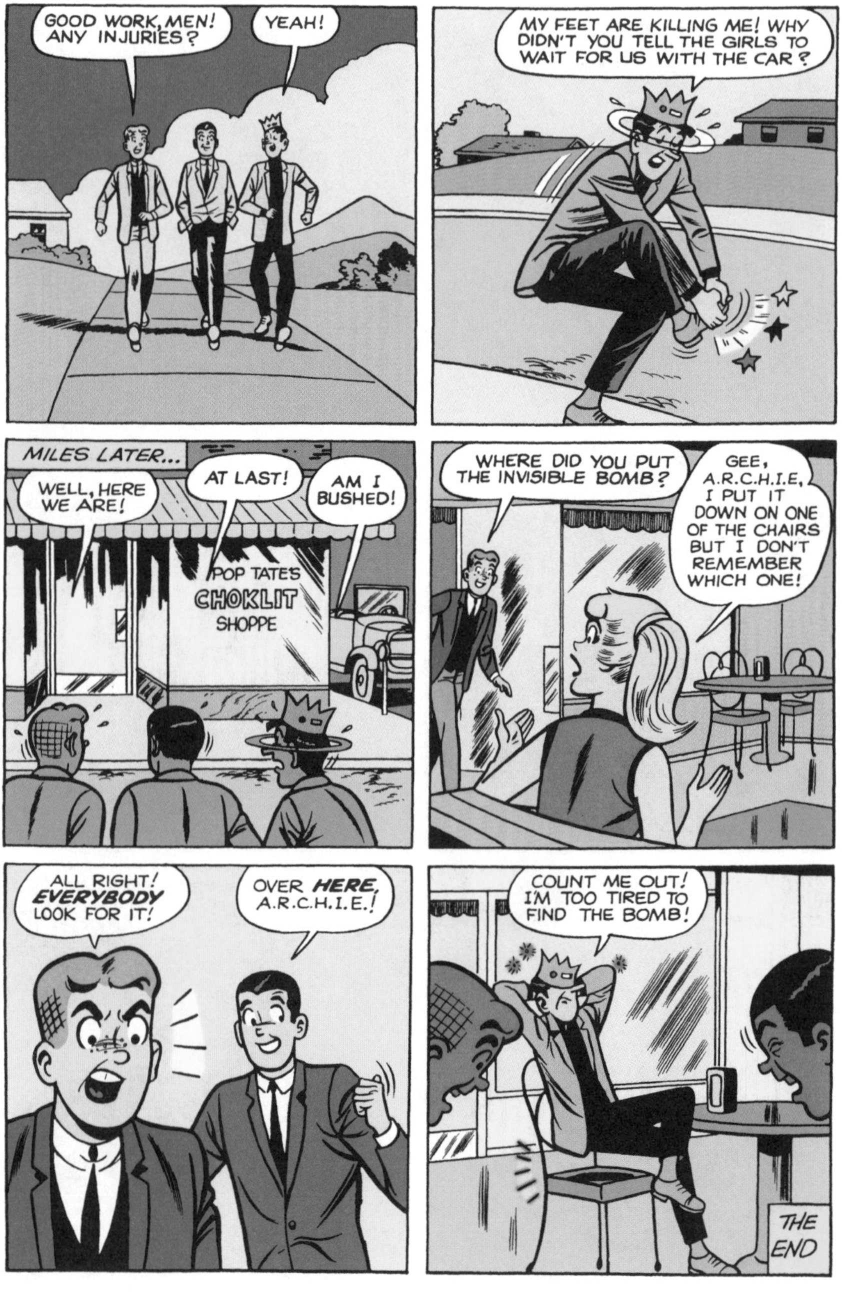
GOOD WORK, MEN! ANY INJURIES?
YEAH!
MY FEET ARE KILLING ME! WHY DIDN'T YOU TELL THE GIRLS TO WAIT FOR US WITH THE CAR?
MILES LATER...
WELL, HERE WE ARE!
AT LAST!
AM I BUSHED!
POP TATE'S
CHOKLIT
SHOPPE
WHERE DID YOU PUT THE INVISIBLE BOMB?
GEE, A.R.C.H.I.E., I PUT IT DOWN ON ONE OF THE CHAIRS BUT I DON'T REMEMBER WHICH ONE!
ALL RIGHT! EVERYBODY LOOK FOR IT!
OVER HERE, A.R.C.H.I.E.!
COUNT ME OUT! I'M TOO TIRED TO FIND THE BOMB!
THE END

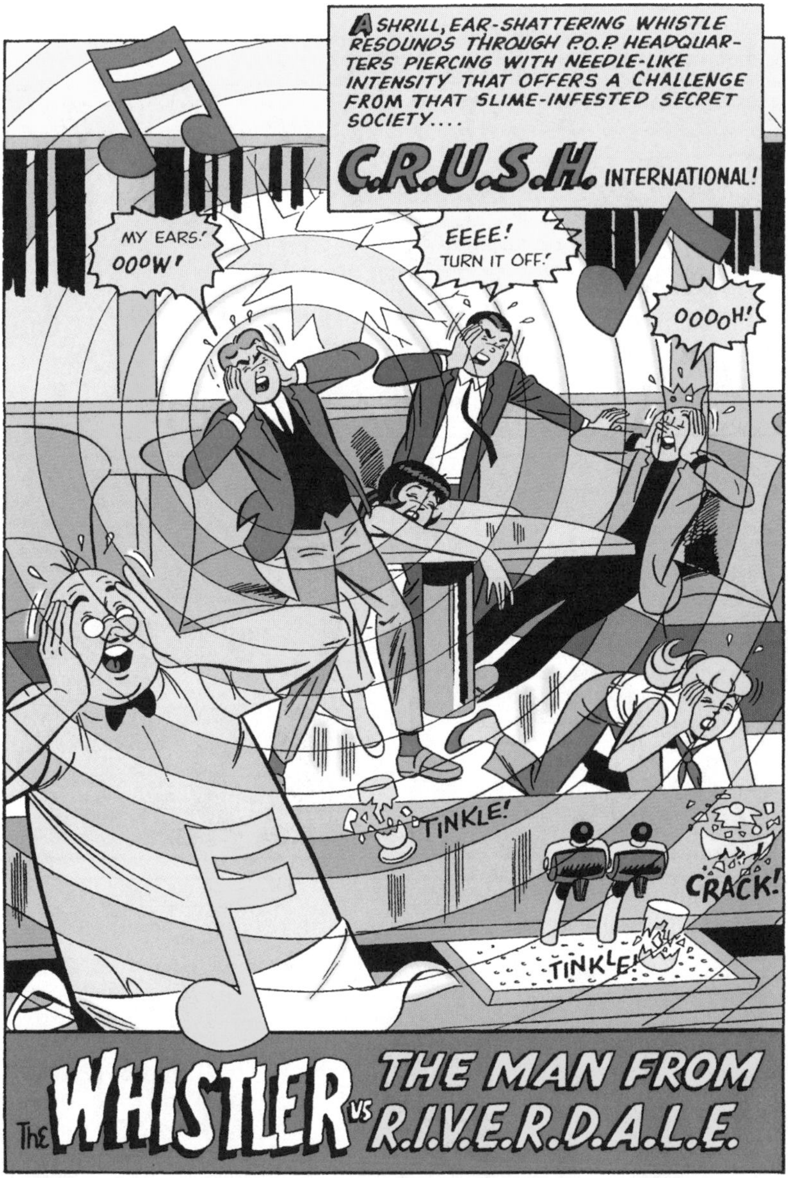
A SHRILL, EAR-SHATTERING WHISTLE RESOUNDS THROUGH P.O.P. HEADQUARTERS PIERCING WITH NEEDLE-LIKE INTENSITY THAT OFFERS A CHALLENGE FROM THAT SLIME-INFESTED SECRET SOCIETY....
C.R.U.S.H. INTERNATIONAL!
MY EARS! OOOW!
EEEE! TURN IT OFF!
OOOOH!
TINKLE!
CRACK!
TINKLE!
THE WHISTLER VS THE MAN FROM R.I.V.E.R.D.A.L.E.

Story: Frank Doyle Art: Bob White
Letters: Victor Gorelick

Originally printed in LIFE WITH ARCHIE #52, AUGUST 1966

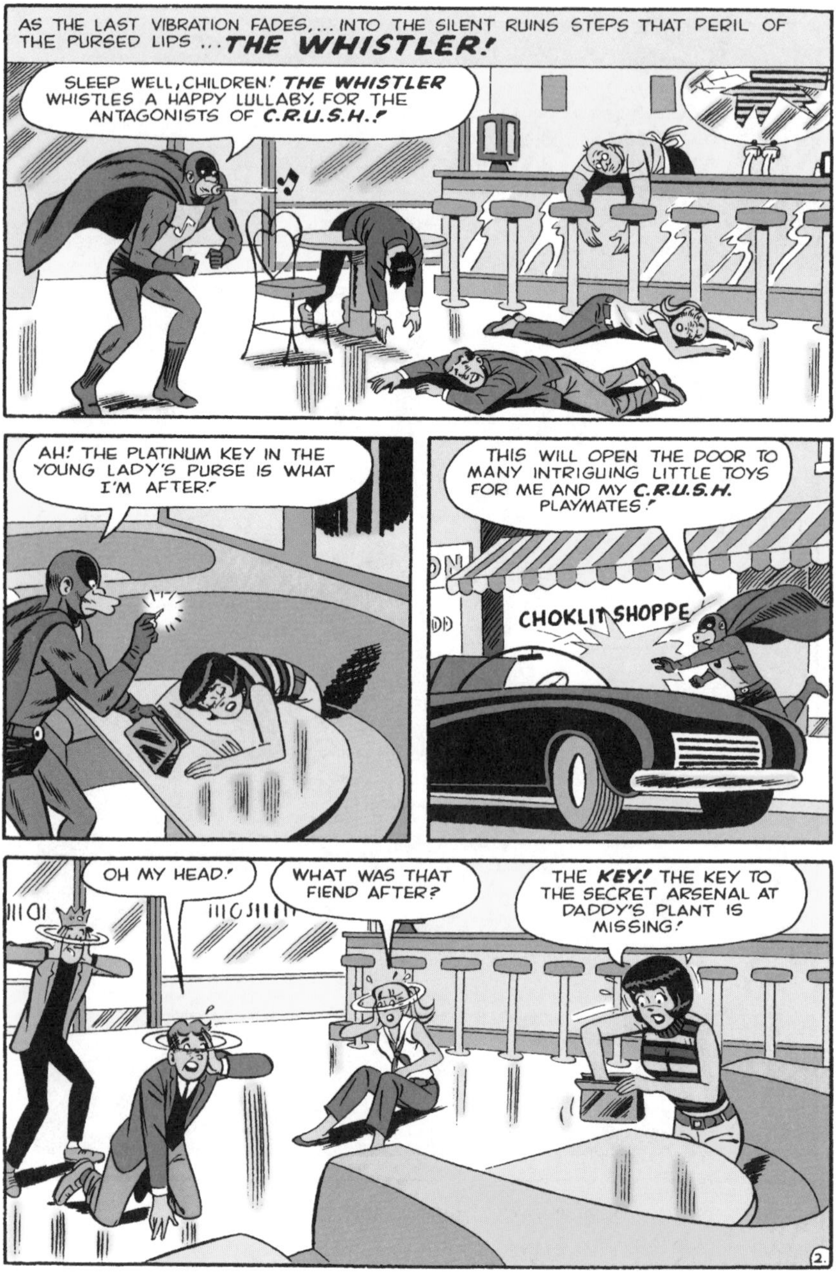
AS THE LAST VIBRATION FADES,... INTO THE SILENT RUINS STEPS THAT PERIL OF THE PURSED LIPS ... THE WHISTLER!
SLEEP WELL, CHILDREN! THE WHISTLER WHISTLES A HAPPY LULLABY, FOR THE ANTAGONISTS OF C.R.U.S.H.!
AH! THE PLATINUM KEY IN THE YOUNG LADY'S PURSE IS WHAT I'M AFTER!
THIS WILL OPEN THE DOOR TO MANY INTRIGUING LITTLE TOYS FOR ME AND MY C.R.U.S.H. PLAYMATES!
CHOKLIT SHOPPE
OH MY HEAD!
WHAT WAS THAT FIEND AFTER?
THE KEY! THE KEY TO THE SECRET ARSENAL AT DADDY'S PLANT IS MISSING!
2.

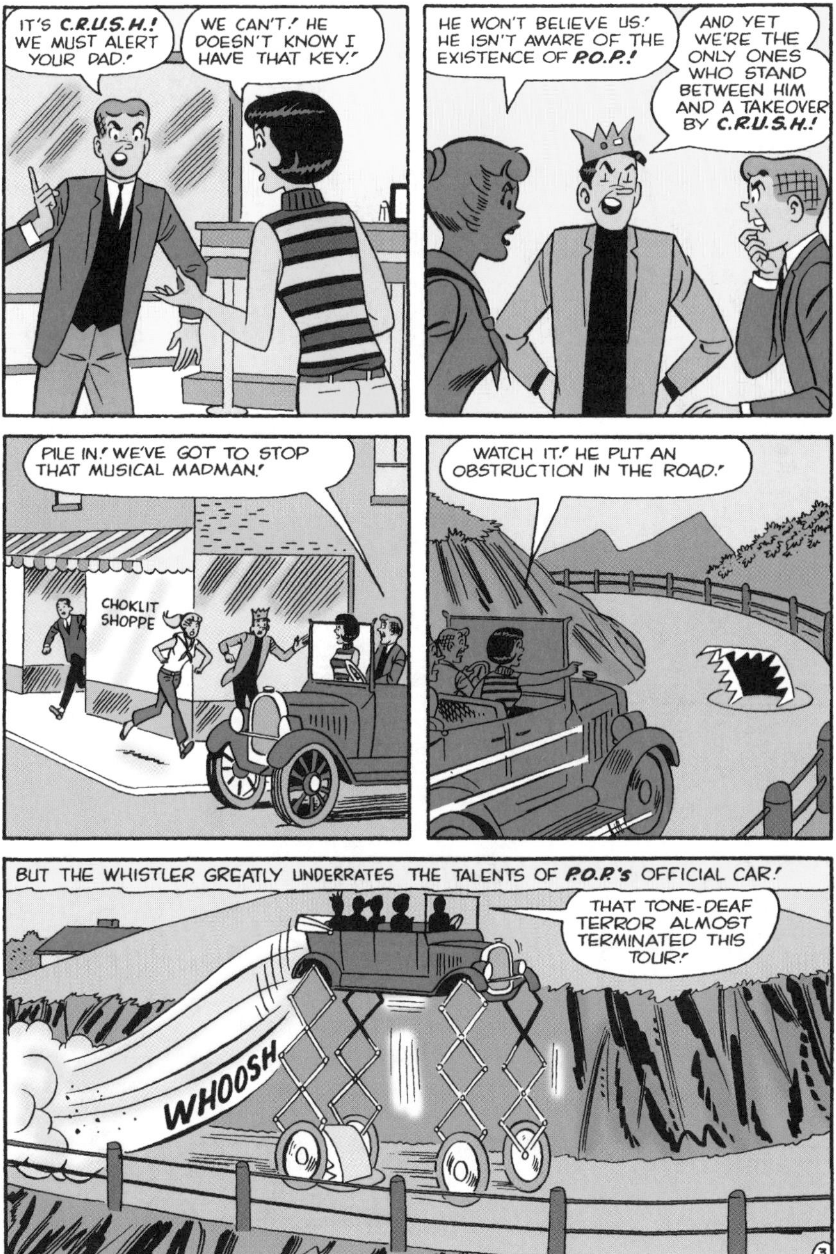
IT'S C.R.U.S.H.! WE MUST ALERT YOUR DAD!
WE CAN'T! HE DOESN'T KNOW I HAVE THAT KEY!
HE WON'T BELIEVE US! HE ISN'T AWARE OF THE EXISTENCE OF P.O.P.!
AND YET WE'RE THE ONLY ONES WHO STAND BETWEEN HIM AND A TAKEOVER BY C.R.U.S.H.!
PILE IN! WE'VE GOT TO STOP THAT MUSICAL MADMAN!
CHOKLIT SHOPPE
WATCH IT! HE PUT AN OBSTRUCTION IN THE ROAD!
BUT THE WHISTLER GREATLY UNDERRATES THE TALENTS OF P.O.P.'s OFFICIAL CAR!
THAT TONE-DEAF TERROR ALMOST TERMINATED THIS TOUR!
WHOOSH
3.

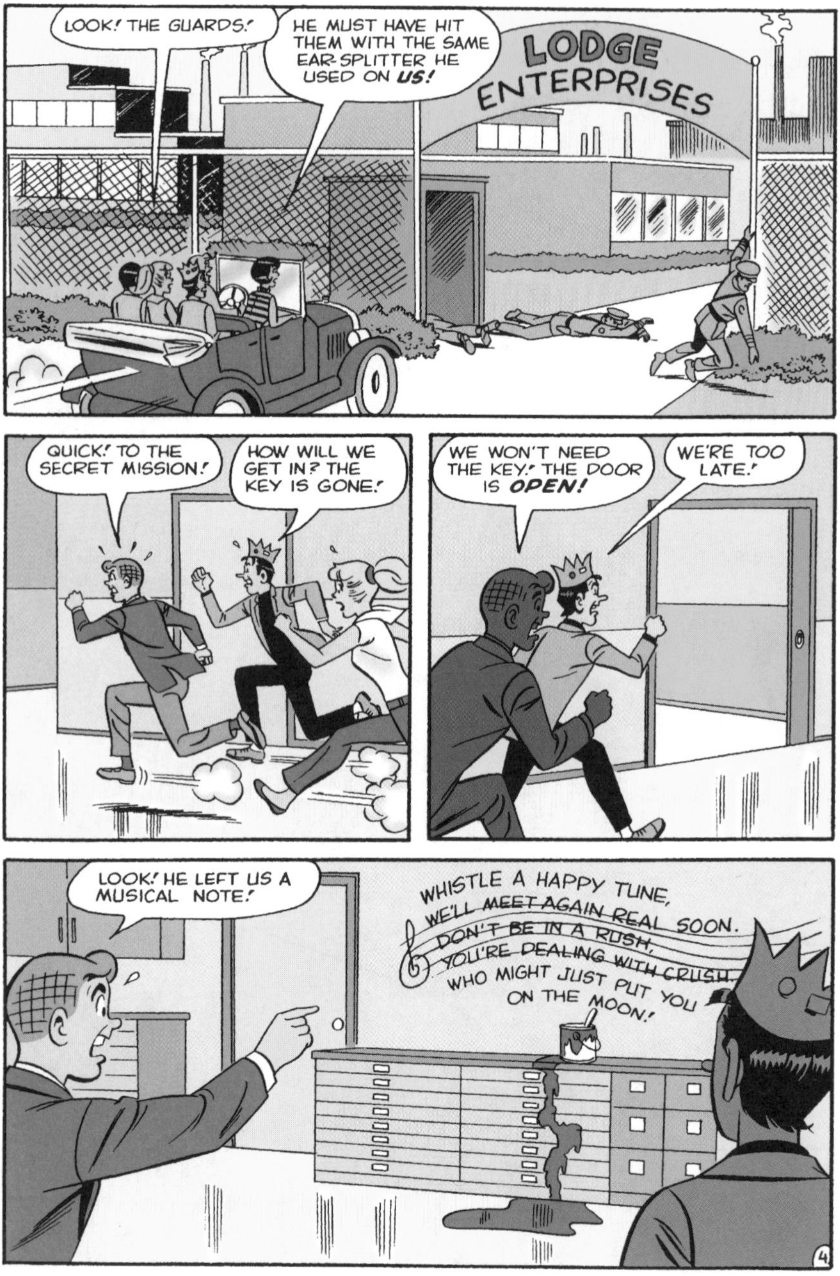
LOOK! THE GUARDS!
HE MUST HAVE HIT THEM WITH THE SAME EAR-SPLITTER HE USED ON US!
LODGE ENTERPRISES
QUICK! TO THE SECRET MISSION!
HOW WILL WE GET IN? THE KEY IS GONE!
WE WON'T NEED THE KEY! THE DOOR IS OPEN!
WE'RE TOO LATE!
LOOK! HE LEFT US A MUSICAL NOTE!
WHISTLE A HAPPY TUNE, WE'LL MEET AGAIN REAL SOON. DON'T BE IN A RUSH, YOU'RE DEALING WITH CRUSH, WHO MIGHT JUST PUT YOU ON THE MOON!
4

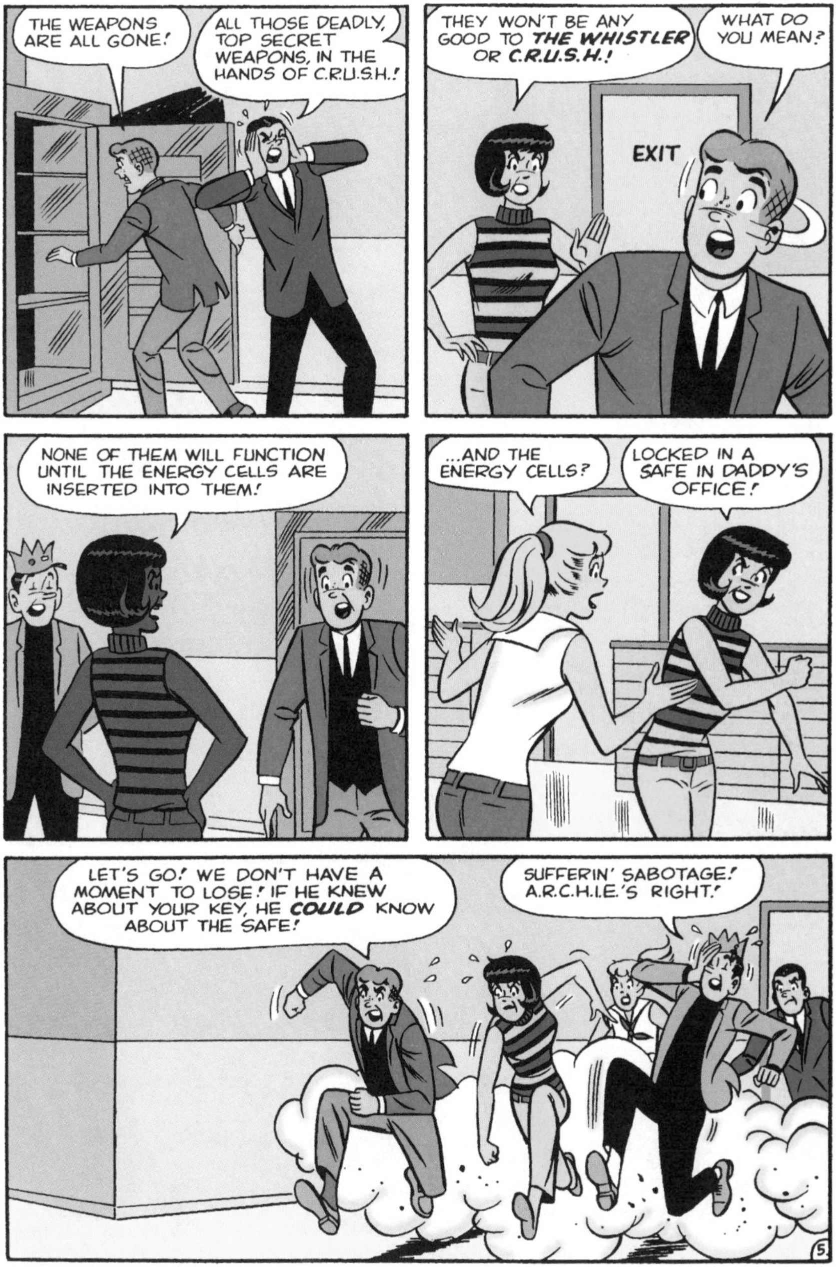
THE WEAPONS ARE ALL GONE!
ALL THOSE DEADLY, TOP SECRET WEAPONS, IN THE HANDS OF C.R.U.S.H.!
THEY WON'T BE ANY GOOD TO THE WHISTLER OR C.R.U.S.H.!
WHAT DO YOU MEAN?
EXIT
NONE OF THEM WILL FUNCTION UNTIL THE ENERGY CELLS ARE INSERTED INTO THEM!
...AND THE ENERGY CELLS?
LOCKED IN A SAFE IN DADDY'S OFFICE!
LET'S GO! WE DON'T HAVE A MOMENT TO LOSE! IF HE KNEW ABOUT YOUR KEY, HE COULD KNOW ABOUT THE SAFE!
SUFFERIN' SABOTAGE! A.R.C.H.I.E.'S RIGHT!
5

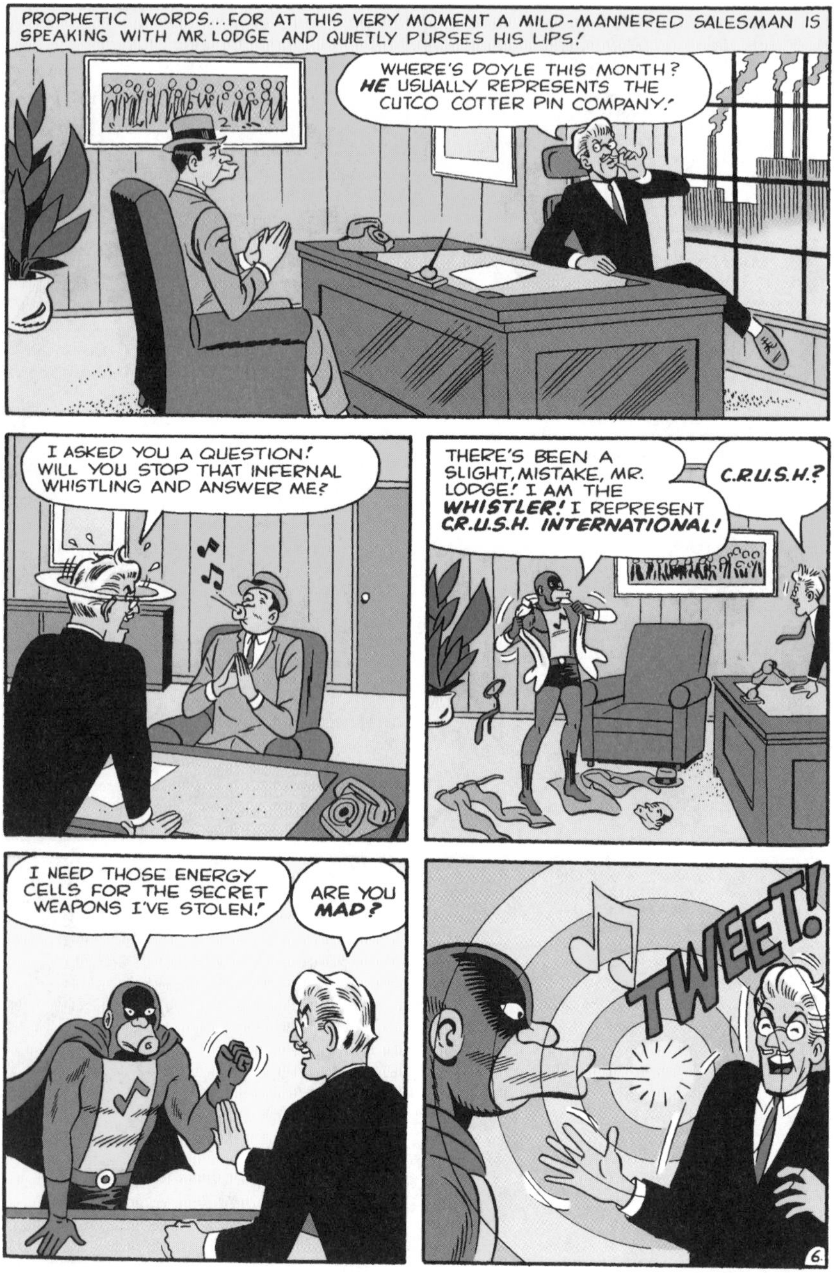
PROPHETIC WORDS...FOR AT THIS VERY MOMENT A MILD-MANNERED SALESMAN IS SPEAKING WITH MR. LODGE AND QUIETLY PURSES HIS LIPS!
WHERE'S DOYLE THIS MONTH? **HE** USUALLY REPRESENTS THE CUTCO COTTER PIN COMPANY!
I ASKED YOU A QUESTION! WILL YOU STOP THAT INFERNAL WHISTLING AND ANSWER ME?
THERE'S BEEN A SLIGHT, MISTAKE, MR. LODGE! I AM THE **WHISTLER!** I REPRESENT **C.R.U.S.H. INTERNATIONAL!**
C.R.U.S.H.?
I NEED THOSE ENERGY CELLS FOR THE SECRET WEAPONS I'VE STOLEN!
ARE YOU **MAD?**
TWEET!
6.

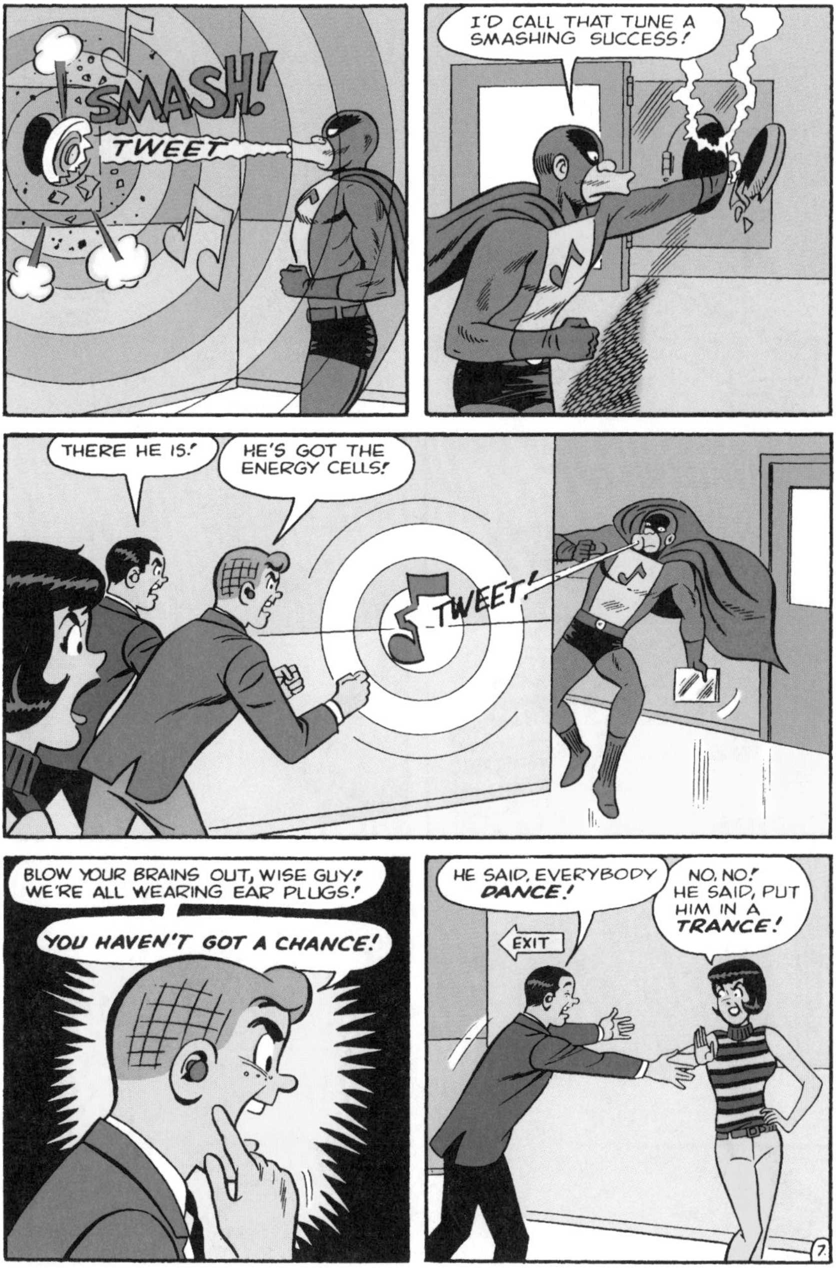
SMASH!
TWEET
I'D CALL THAT TUNE A SMASHING SUCCESS!
THERE HE IS!
HE'S GOT THE ENERGY CELLS!
TWEET!
BLOW YOUR BRAINS OUT, WISE GUY! WE'RE ALL WEARING EAR PLUGS!
YOU HAVEN'T GOT A CHANCE!
HE SAID, EVERYBODY DANCE!
NO, NO! HE SAID, PUT HIM IN A TRANCE!
EXIT
7.

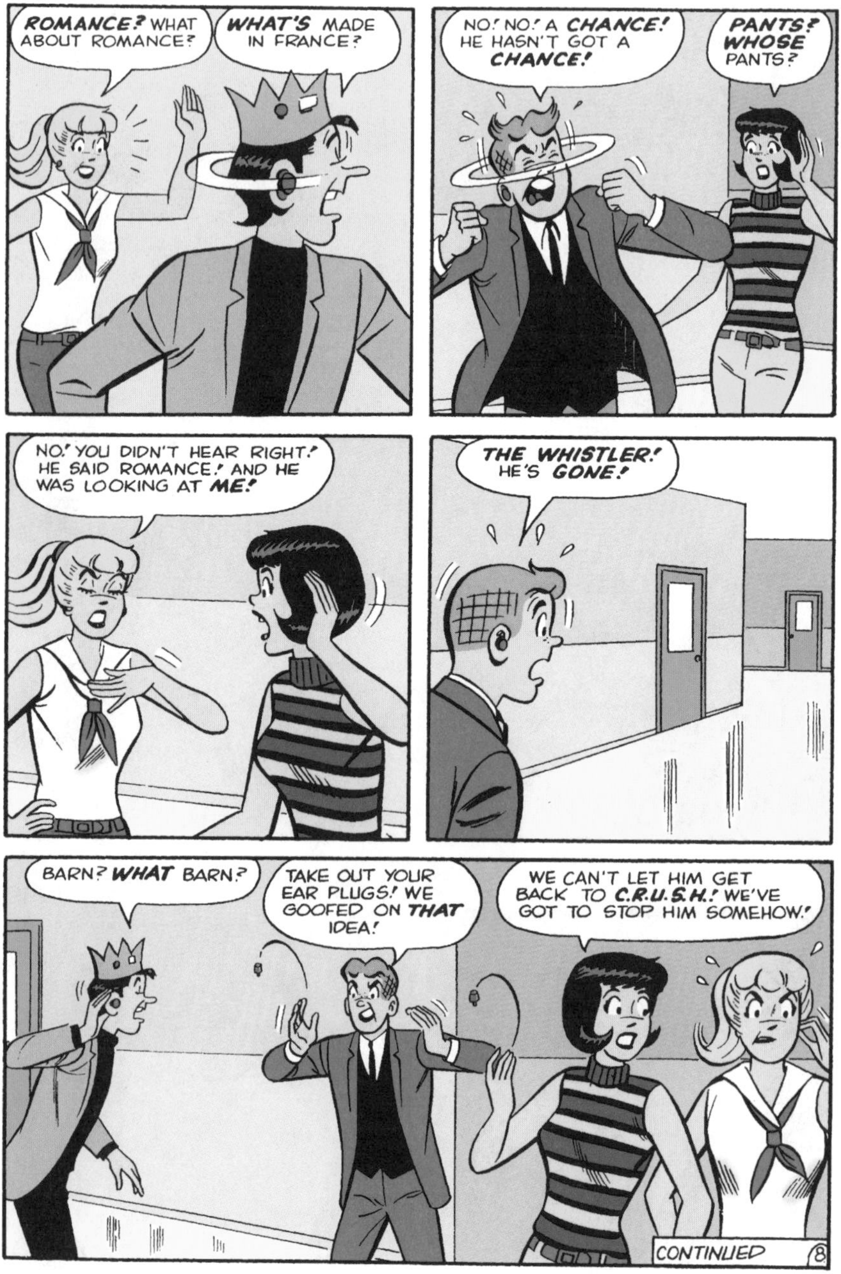
ROMANCE? WHAT ABOUT ROMANCE?
WHAT'S MADE IN FRANCE?
NO! NO! A CHANCE! HE HASN'T GOT A CHANCE!
PANTS? WHOSE PANTS?
NO! YOU DIDN'T HEAR RIGHT! HE SAID ROMANCE! AND HE WAS LOOKING AT ME!
THE WHISTLER! HE'S GONE!
BARN? WHAT BARN?
TAKE OUT YOUR EAR PLUGS! WE GOOFED ON THAT IDEA!
WE CAN'T LET HIM GET BACK TO C.R.U.S.H.! WE'VE GOT TO STOP HIM SOMEHOW!
CONTINUED
8

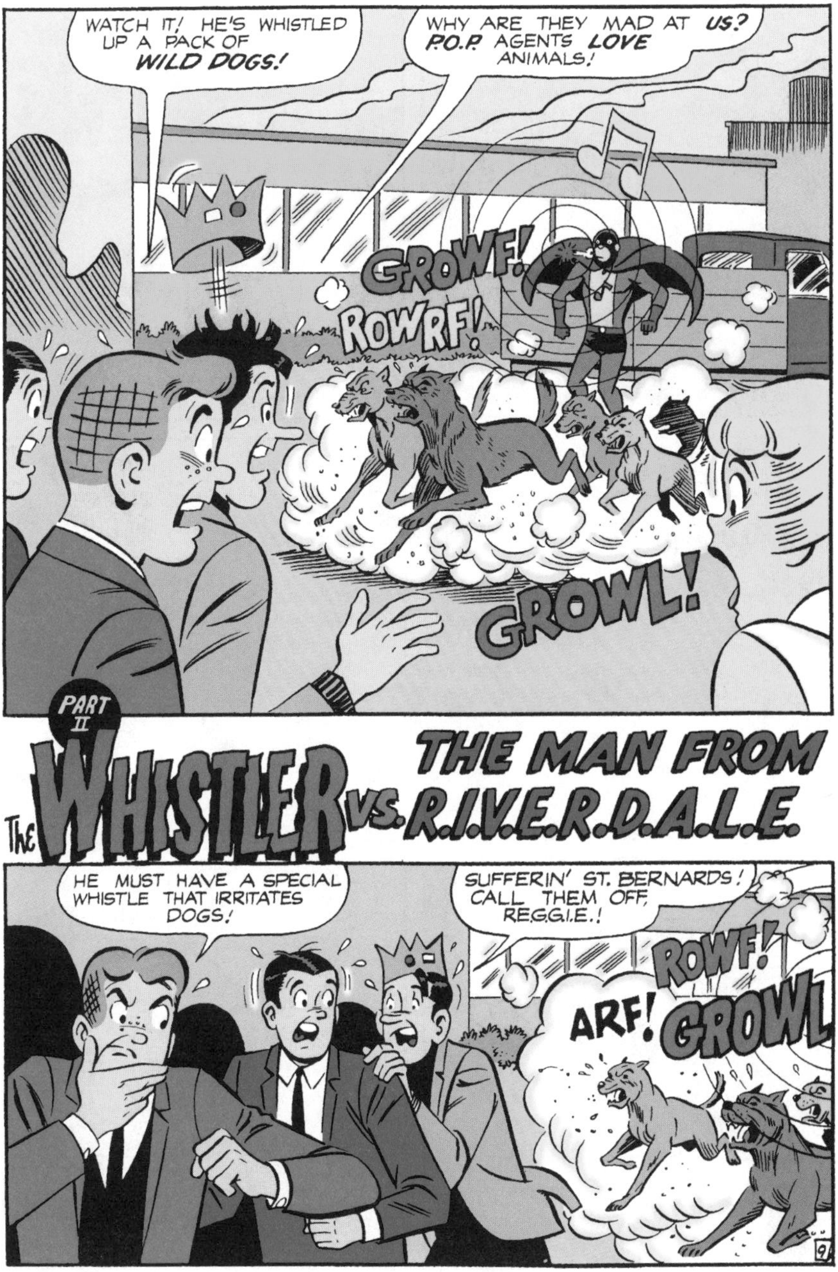
WATCH IT! HE'S WHISTLED UP A PACK OF WILD DOGS!
WHY ARE THEY MAD AT US? P.O.P. AGENTS LOVE ANIMALS!
GROWF!
ROWRF!
GROWL!
PART II
THE WHISTLER VS. THE MAN FROM R.I.V.E.R.D.A.L.E.
HE MUST HAVE A SPECIAL WHISTLE THAT IRRITATES DOGS!
SUFFERIN' ST. BERNARDS! CALL THEM OFF, REG.G.I.E.!
ROWF!
ARF!
GROWL
9

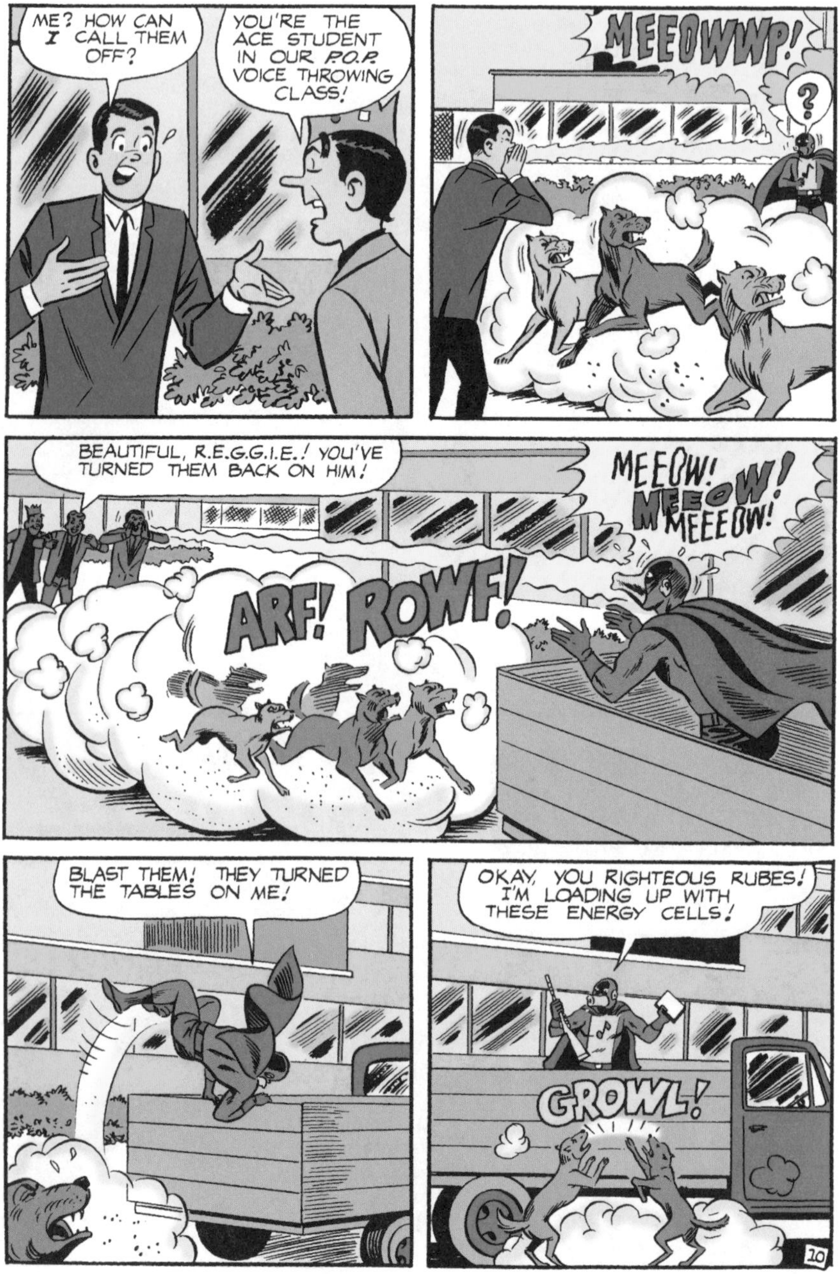
ME? HOW CAN I CALL THEM OFF?
YOU'RE THE ACE STUDENT IN OUR P.O.P. VOICE THROWING CLASS!
MEEOWWP!
?
BEAUTIFUL, R.E.G.G.I.E.! YOU'VE TURNED THEM BACK ON HIM!
MEEOW! MEEOW! MEEEOW!
ARF! ROWF!
BLAST THEM! THEY TURNED THE TABLES ON ME!
OKAY, YOU RIGHTEOUS RUBES! I'M LOADING UP WITH THESE ENERGY CELLS!
GROWL!
10

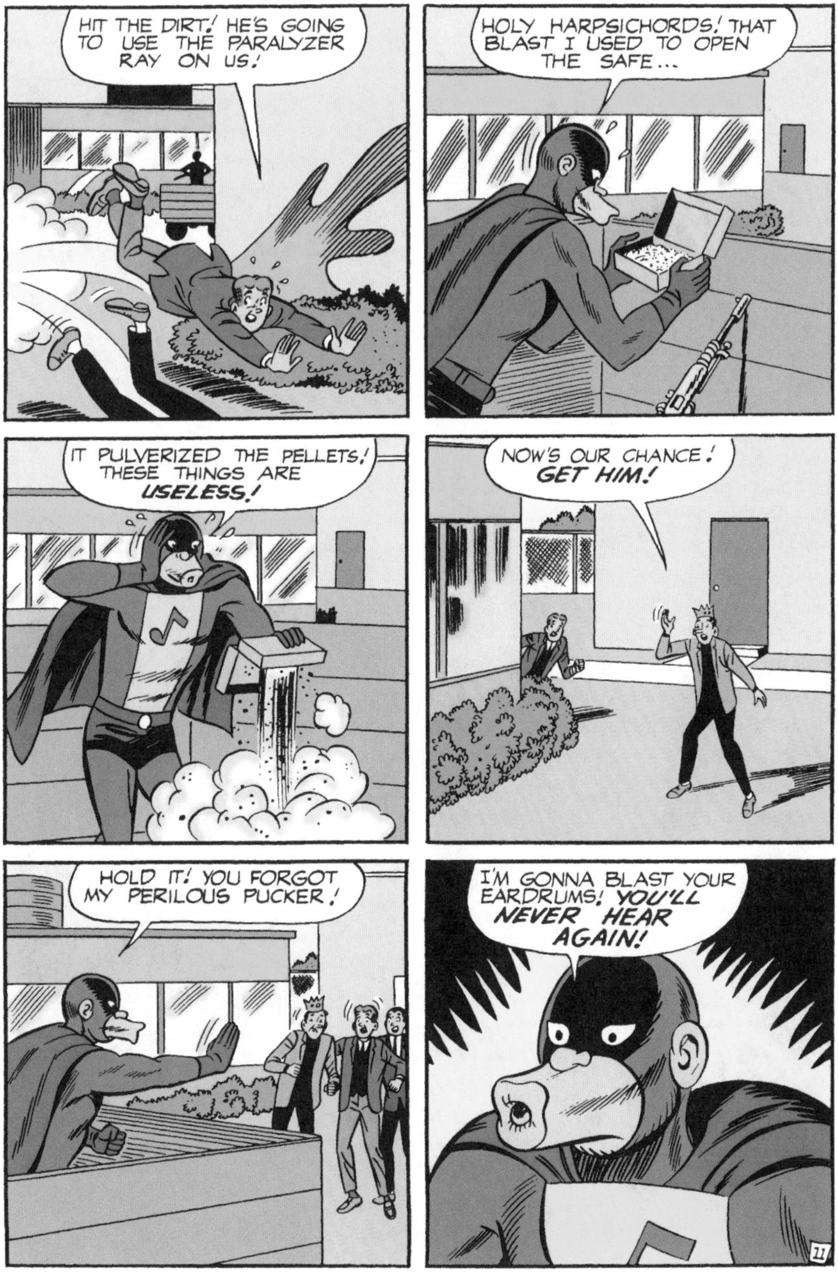
HIT THE DIRT! HE'S GOING TO USE THE PARALYZER RAY ON US!
HOLY HARPSICHORDS! THAT BLAST I USED TO OPEN THE SAFE...
IT PULVERIZED THE PELLETS! THESE THINGS ARE USELESS!
NOW'S OUR CHANCE! GET HIM!
HOLD IT! YOU FORGOT MY PERILOUS PUCKER!
I'M GONNA BLAST YOUR EARDRUMS! YOU'LL NEVER HEAR AGAIN!
11

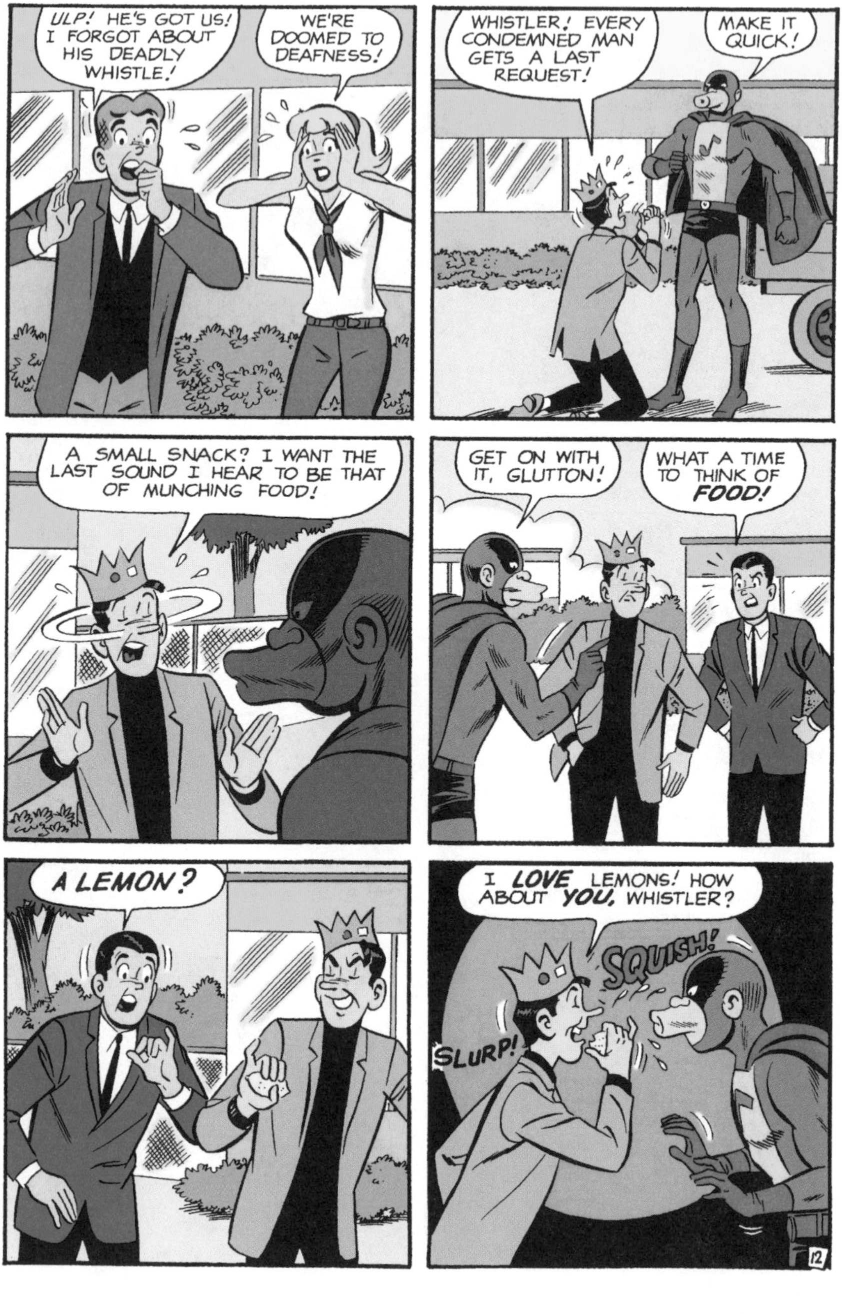
ULP! HE'S GOT US! I FORGOT ABOUT HIS DEADLY WHISTLE!
WE'RE DOOMED TO DEAFNESS!
WHISTLER! EVERY CONDEMNED MAN GETS A LAST REQUEST!
MAKE IT QUICK!
A SMALL SNACK? I WANT THE LAST SOUND I HEAR TO BE THAT OF MUNCHING FOOD!
GET ON WITH IT, GLUTTON!
WHAT A TIME TO THINK OF FOOD!
A LEMON?
I LOVE LEMONS! HOW ABOUT YOU, WHISTLER?
SQUISH!
SLURP!
12

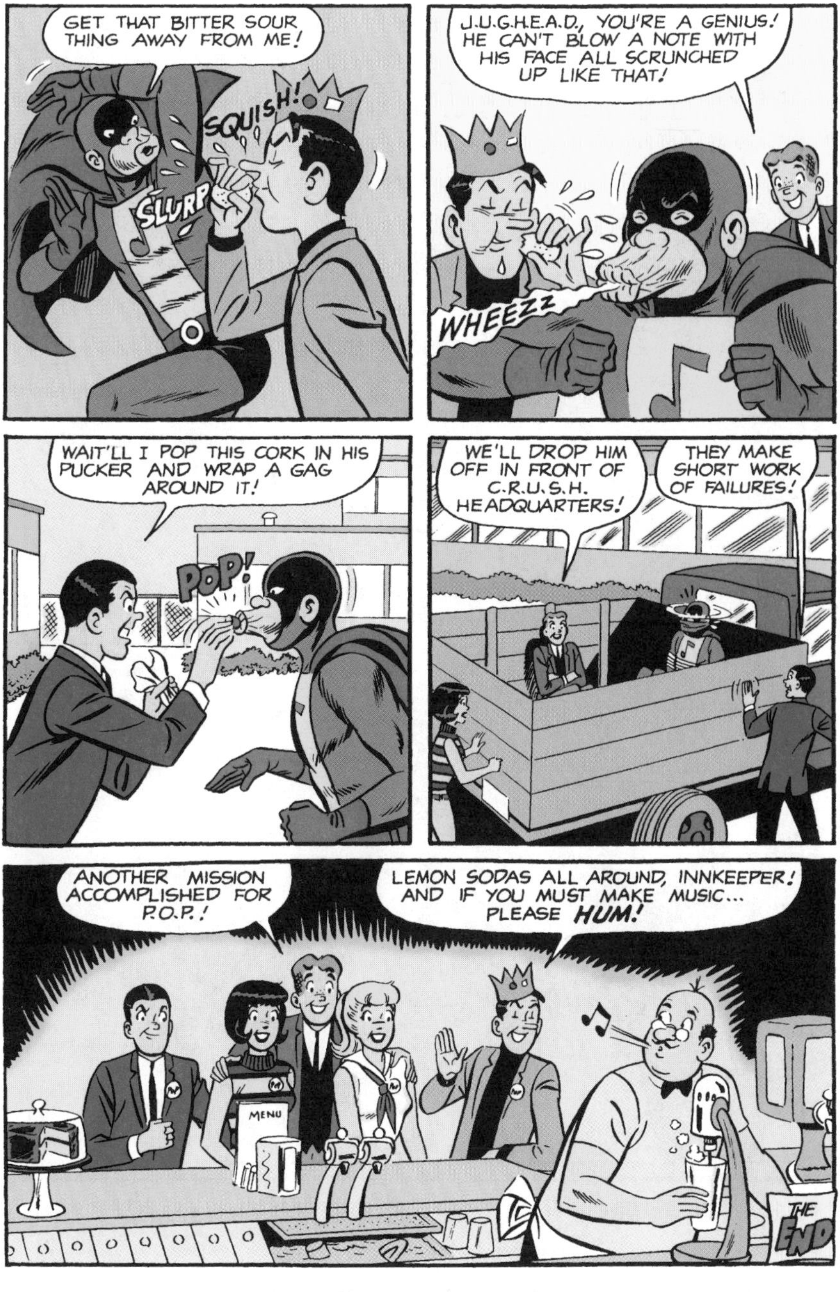
GET THAT BITTER SOUR THING AWAY FROM ME!
SQUISH!
SLURP
J.U.G.H.E.A.D., YOU'RE A GENIUS! HE CAN'T BLOW A NOTE WITH HIS FACE ALL SCRUNCHED UP LIKE THAT!
WHEEZZ
WAIT'LL I POP THIS CORK IN HIS PUCKER AND WRAP A GAG AROUND IT!
POP!
WE'LL DROP HIM OFF IN FRONT OF C.R.U.S.H. HEADQUARTERS!
THEY MAKE SHORT WORK OF FAILURES!
ANOTHER MISSION ACCOMPLISHED FOR P.O.P.!
LEMON SODAS ALL AROUND, INNKEEPER! AND IF YOU MUST MAKE MUSIC... PLEASE HUM!
MENU
THE END

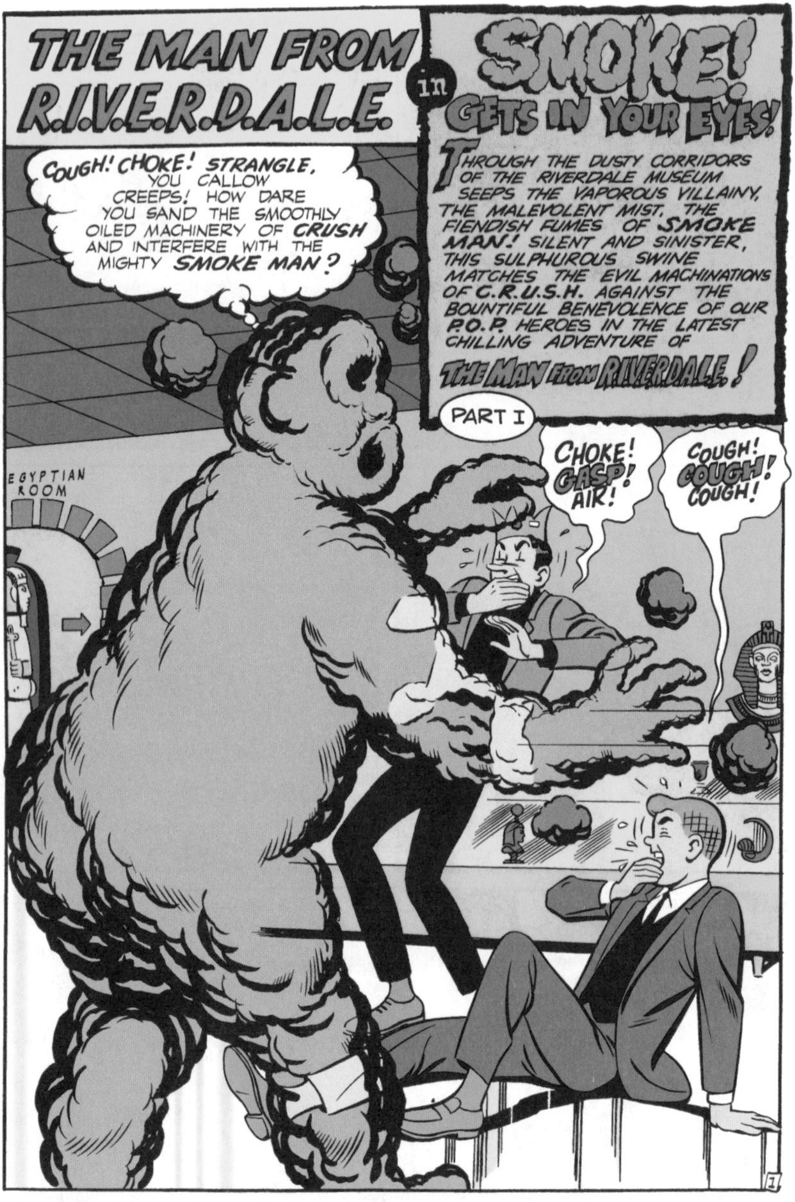
THE MAN FROM R.I.V.E.R.D.A.L.E.
in
SMOKE! GETS IN YOUR EYES!
THROUGH THE DUSTY CORRIDORS OF THE RIVERDALE MUSEUM SEEPS THE VAPOROUS VILLAINY, THE MALEVOLENT MIST, THE FIENDISH FUMES OF SMOKE MAN! SILENT AND SINISTER, THIS SULPHUROUS SWINE MATCHES THE EVIL MACHINATIONS OF C.R.U.S.H. AGAINST THE BOUNTIFUL BENEVOLENCE OF OUR P.O.P. HEROES IN THE LATEST CHILLING ADVENTURE OF THE MAN FROM R.I.V.E.R.D.A.L.E.!
PART I
COUGH! CHOKE! STRANGLE, YOU CALLOW CREEPS! HOW DARE YOU SAND THE SMOOTHLY OILED MACHINERY OF CRUSH AND INTERFERE WITH THE MIGHTY SMOKE MAN?
CHOKE! GASP! AIR!
COUGH! COUGH! COUGH!
EGYPTIAN ROOM
1

Story: Frank Doyle Pencils: Bill Vigoda
Inks & Letters: Marty Epp

Originally printed in LIFE WITH ARCHIE #52, AUGUST 1966

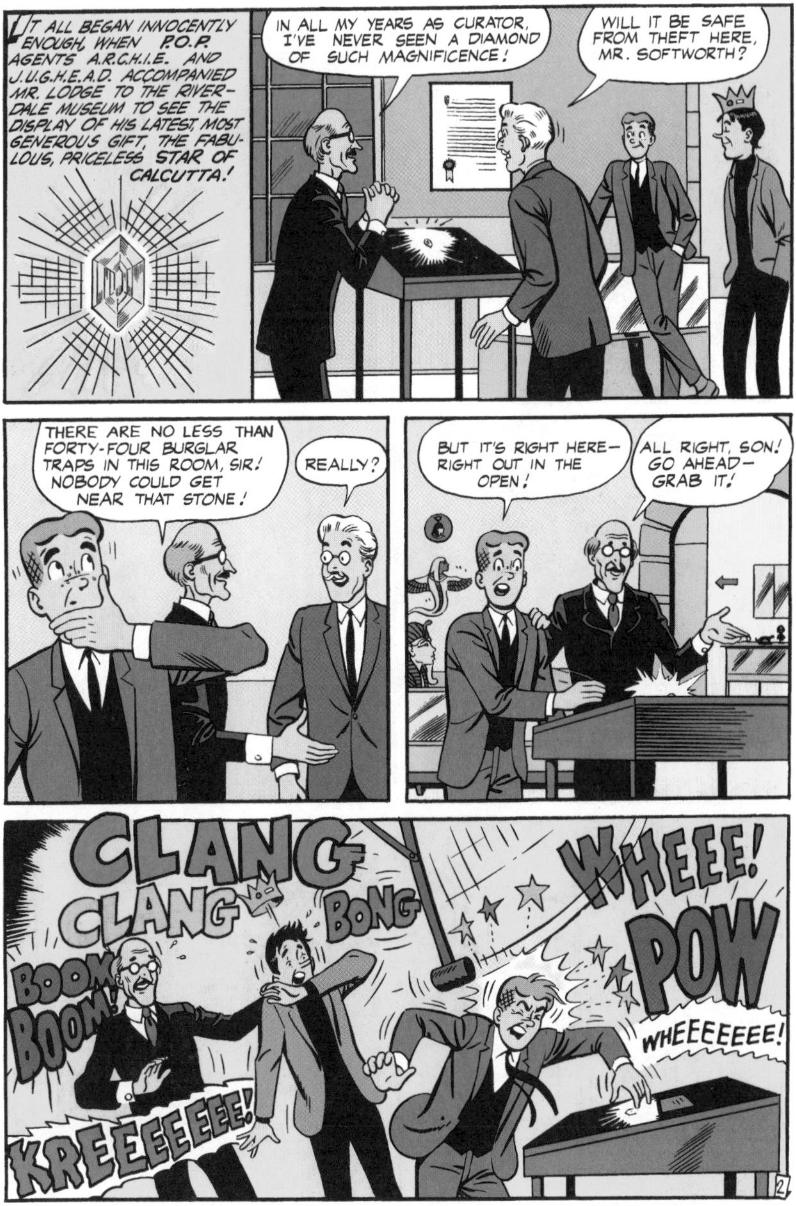
IT ALL BEGAN INNOCENTLY ENOUGH, WHEN P.O.P. AGENTS A.R.C.H.I.E. AND J.U.G.H.E.A.D. ACCOMPANIED MR. LODGE TO THE RIVERDALE MUSEUM TO SEE THE DISPLAY OF HIS LATEST, MOST GENEROUS GIFT, THE FABULOUS, PRICELESS STAR OF CALCUTTA!
IN ALL MY YEARS AS CURATOR, I'VE NEVER SEEN A DIAMOND OF SUCH MAGNIFICENCE!
WILL IT BE SAFE FROM THEFT HERE, MR. SOFTWORTH?
THERE ARE NO LESS THAN FORTY-FOUR BURGLAR TRAPS IN THIS ROOM, SIR! NOBODY COULD GET NEAR THAT STONE!
REALLY?
BUT IT'S RIGHT HERE-RIGHT OUT IN THE OPEN!
ALL RIGHT, SON! GO AHEAD-GRAB IT!
CLANG
CLANG
BONG
WHEEE!
POW
BOOM
BOOM!
BOOM
WHEEEEEEE!
KREEEEEEEE!
2

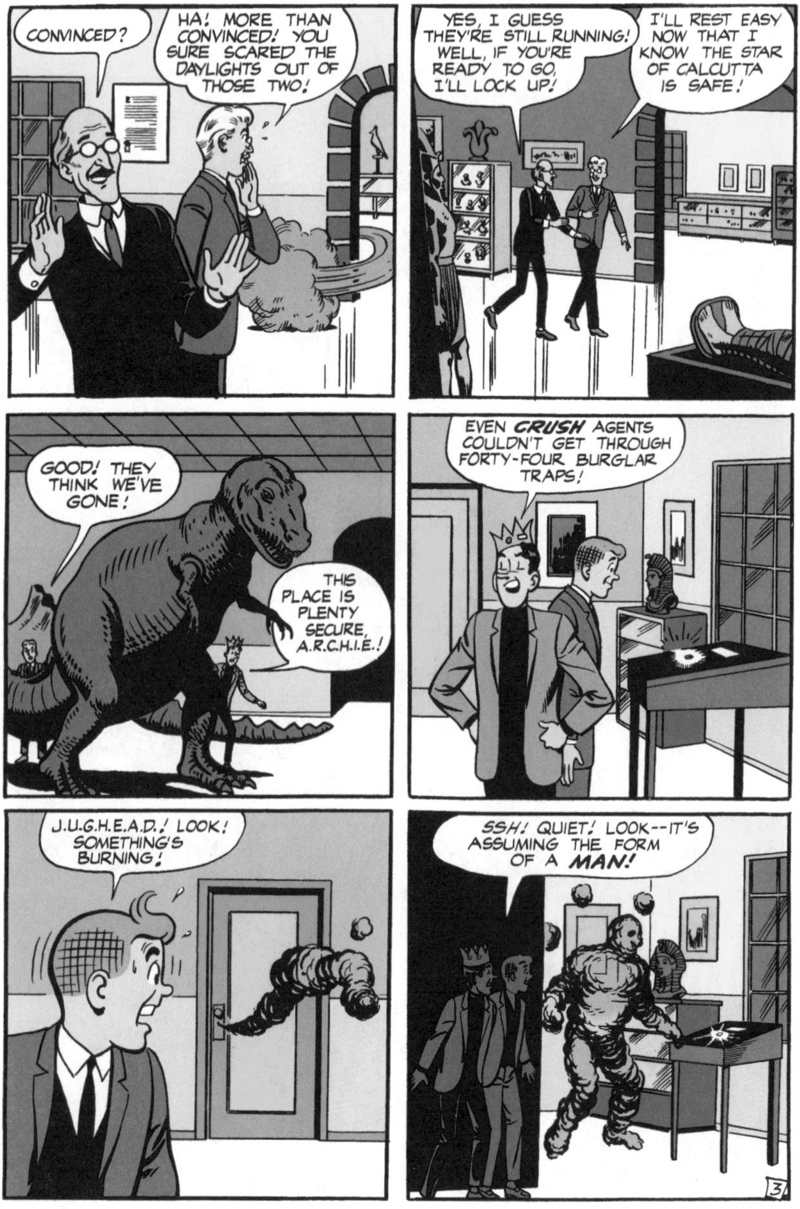
CONVINCED?
HA! MORE THAN CONVINCED! YOU SURE SCARED THE DAYLIGHTS OUT OF THOSE TWO!
YES, I GUESS THEY'RE STILL RUNNING! WELL, IF YOU'RE READY TO GO, I'LL LOCK UP!
I'LL REST EASY NOW THAT I KNOW THE STAR OF CALCUTTA IS SAFE!
GOOD! THEY THINK WE'VE GONE!
THIS PLACE IS PLENTY SECURE, A.R.C.H.I.E.!
EVEN CRUSH AGENTS COULDN'T GET THROUGH FORTY-FOUR BURGLAR TRAPS!
J.U.G.H.E.A.D.! LOOK! SOMETHING'S BURNING!
SSH! QUIET! LOOK--IT'S ASSUMING THE FORM OF A MAN!
3

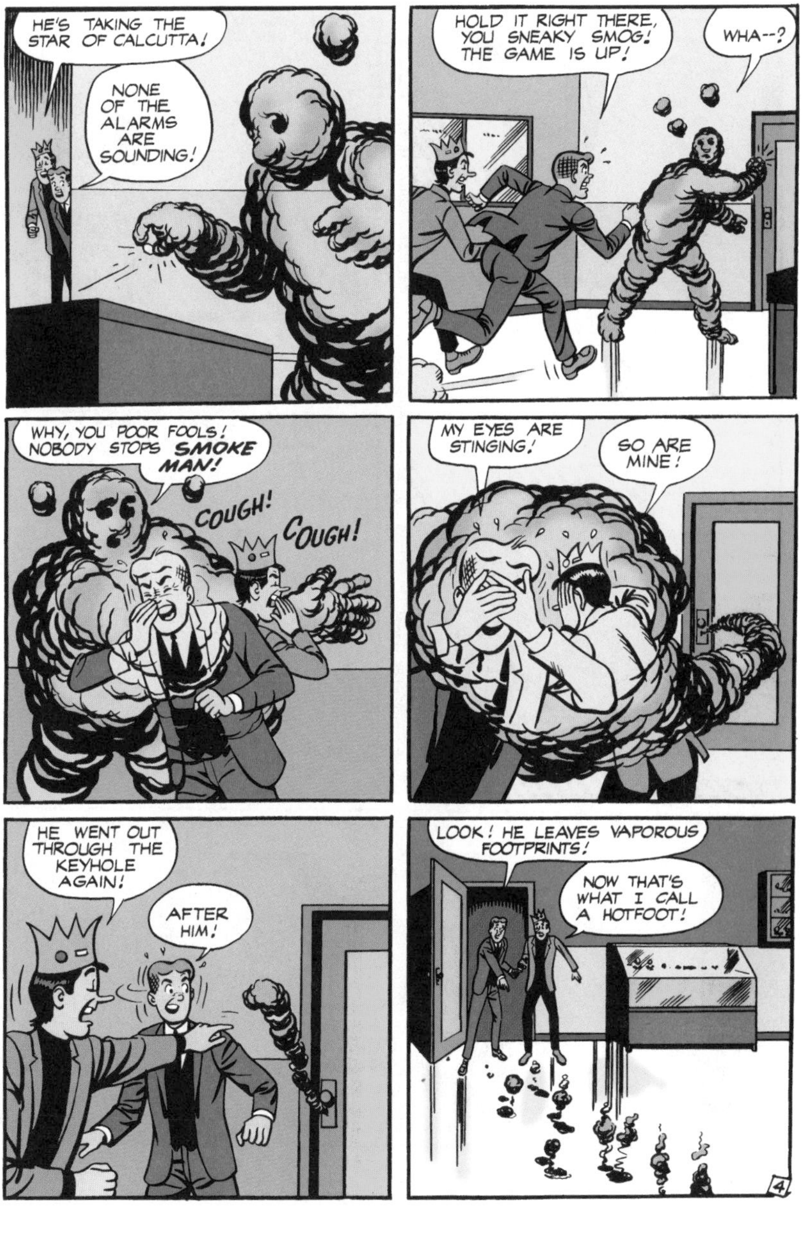
HE'S TAKING THE STAR OF CALCUTTA!
NONE OF THE ALARMS ARE SOUNDING!
HOLD IT RIGHT THERE, YOU SNEAKY SMOG! THE GAME IS UP!
WHA--?
WHY, YOU POOR FOOLS! NOBODY STOPS SMOKE MAN!
COUGH!
COUGH!
MY EYES ARE STINGING!
SO ARE MINE!
HE WENT OUT THROUGH THE KEYHOLE AGAIN!
AFTER HIM!
LOOK! HE LEAVES VAPOROUS FOOTPRINTS!
NOW THAT'S WHAT I CALL A HOTFOOT!
4

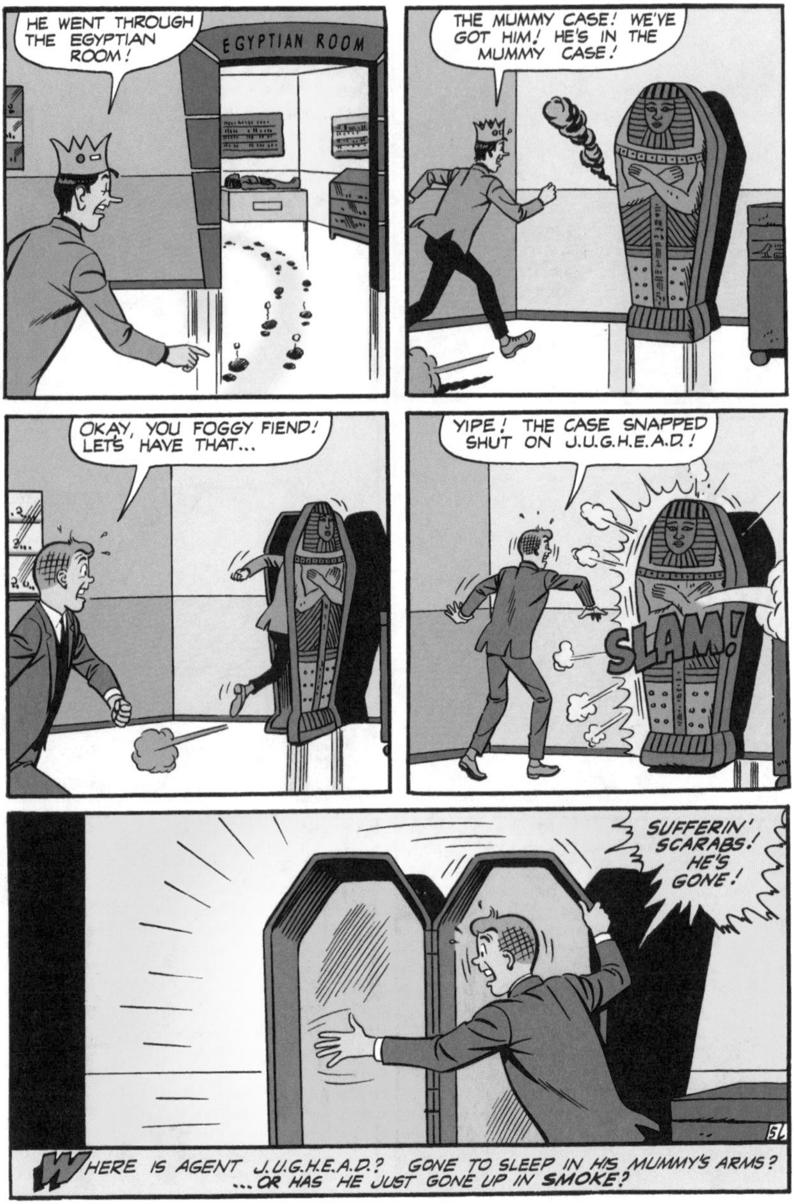
HE WENT THROUGH THE EGYPTIAN ROOM!
EGYPTIAN ROOM
THE MUMMY CASE! WE'VE GOT HIM! HE'S IN THE MUMMY CASE!
OKAY, YOU FOGGY FIEND! LET'S HAVE THAT...
YIPE! THE CASE SNAPPED SHUT ON J.U.G.H.E.A.D.!
SLAM!
SUFFERIN' SCARABS! HE'S GONE!
5
WHERE IS AGENT J.U.G.H.E.A.D.? GONE TO SLEEP IN HIS MUMMY'S ARMS? ...OR HAS HE JUST GONE UP IN SMOKE?

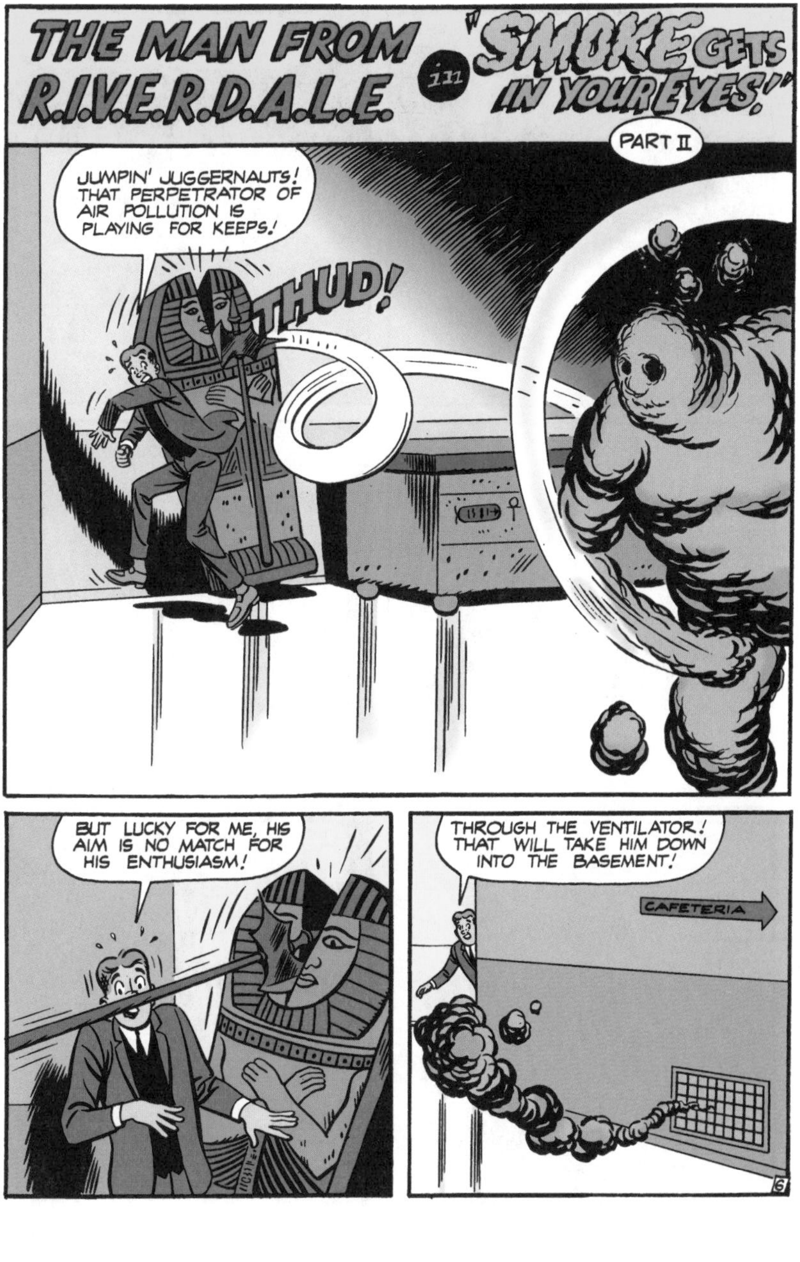
THE MAN FROM R.I.V.E.R.D.A.L.E.
"SMOKE GETS IN YOUR EYES!"
PART II
JUMPIN' JUGGERNAUTS! THAT PERPETRATOR OF AIR POLLUTION IS PLAYING FOR KEEPS!
THUD!
BUT LUCKY FOR ME, HIS AIM IS NO MATCH FOR HIS ENTHUSIASM!
THROUGH THE VENTILATOR! THAT WILL TAKE HIM DOWN INTO THE BASEMENT!
CAFETERIA
6

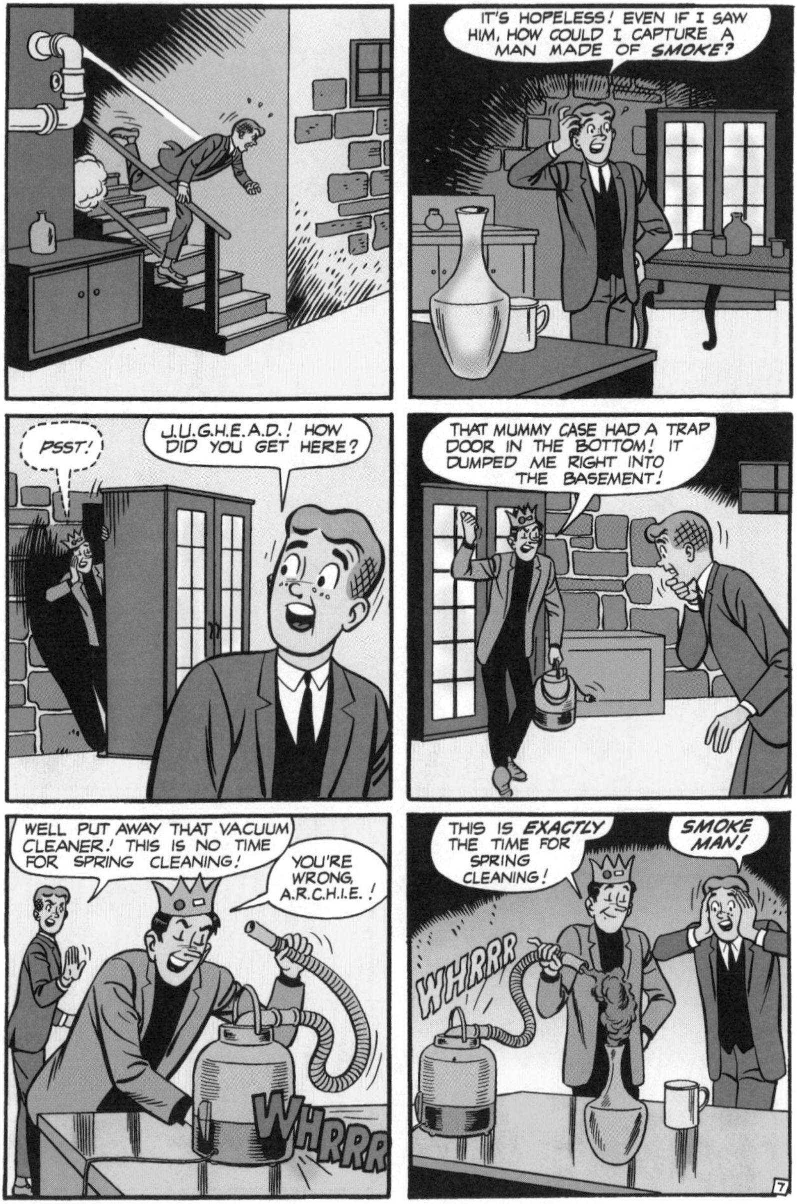
IT'S HOPELESS! EVEN IF I SAW HIM, HOW COULD I CAPTURE A MAN MADE OF SMOKE?
PSST!
J.U.G.H.E.A.D.! HOW DID YOU GET HERE?
THAT MUMMY CASE HAD A TRAP DOOR IN THE BOTTOM! IT DUMPED ME RIGHT INTO THE BASEMENT!
WELL PUT AWAY THAT VACUUM CLEANER! THIS IS NO TIME FOR SPRING CLEANING!
YOU'RE WRONG, A.R.C.H.I.E.!
WHRRR
THIS IS EXACTLY THE TIME FOR SPRING CLEANING!
SMOKE MAN!
WHRRR
7

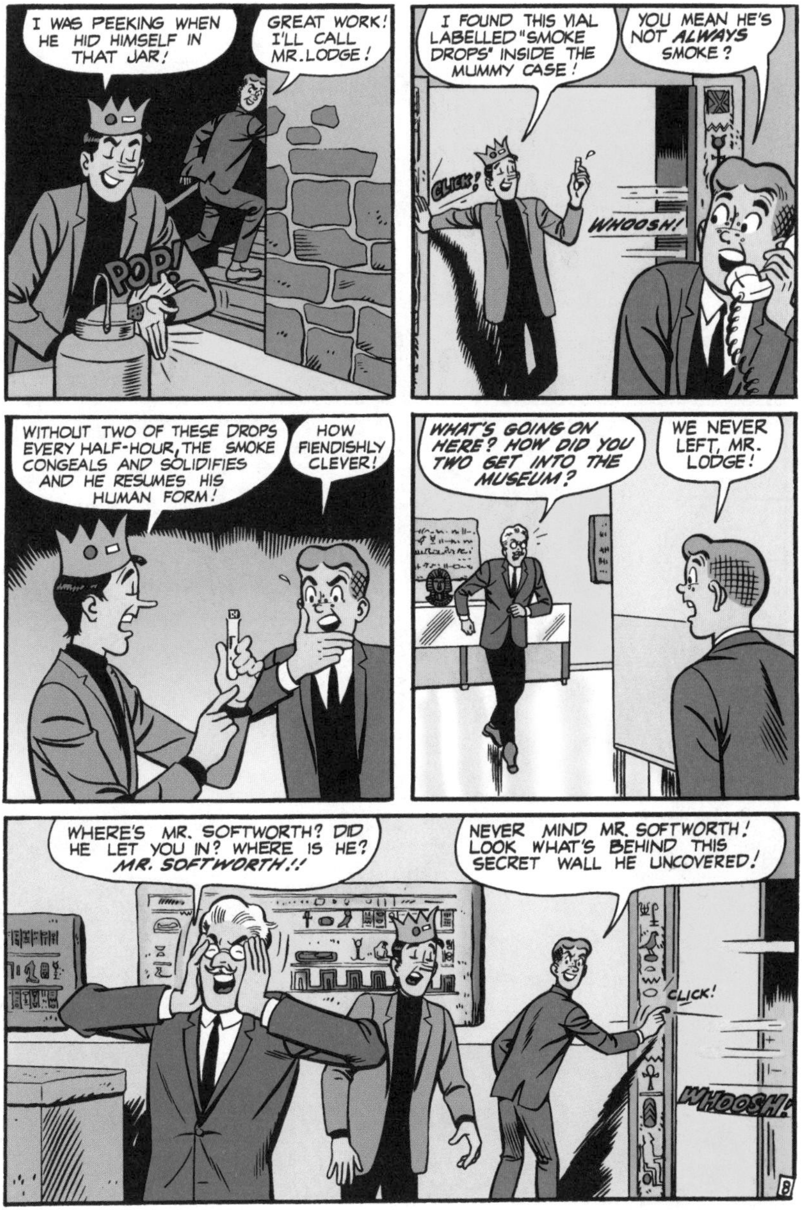
I WAS PEEKING WHEN HE HID HIMSELF IN THAT JAR!
GREAT WORK! I'LL CALL MR. LODGE!
POP!
I FOUND THIS VIAL LABELLED "SMOKE DROPS" INSIDE THE MUMMY CASE!
YOU MEAN HE'S NOT ALWAYS SMOKE?
CLICK!
WHOOSH!
WITHOUT TWO OF THESE DROPS EVERY HALF-HOUR, THE SMOKE CONGEALS AND SOLIDIFIES AND HE RESUMES HIS HUMAN FORM!
HOW FIENDISHLY CLEVER!
WHAT'S GOING ON HERE? HOW DID YOU TWO GET INTO THE MUSEUM?
WE NEVER LEFT, MR. LODGE!
WHERE'S MR. SOFTWORTH? DID HE LET YOU IN? WHERE IS HE? MR. SOFTWORTH!!
NEVER MIND MR. SOFTWORTH! LOOK WHAT'S BEHIND THIS SECRET WALL HE UNCOVERED!
CLICK!
WHOOSH!
8

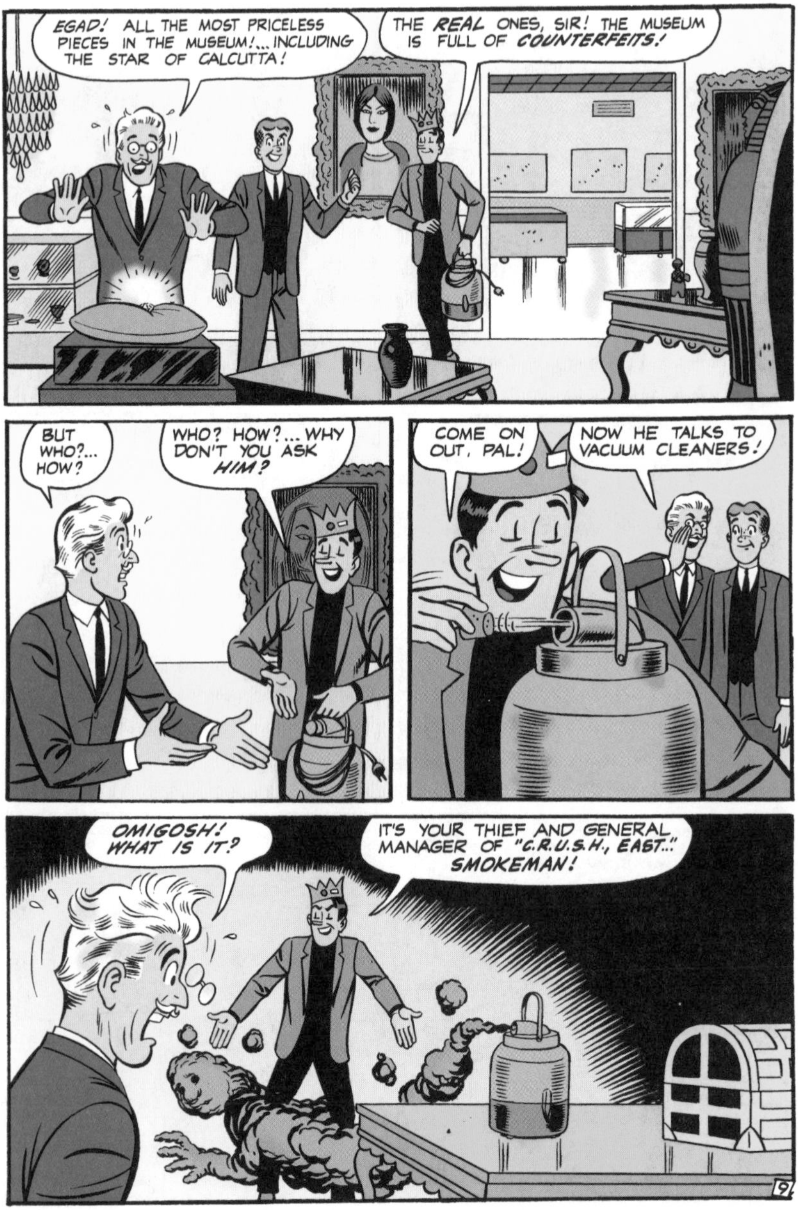
EGAD! ALL THE MOST PRICELESS PIECES IN THE MUSEUM!... INCLUDING THE STAR OF CALCUTTA!
THE REAL ONES, SIR! THE MUSEUM IS FULL OF COUNTERFEITS!
BUT WHO?... HOW?
WHO? HOW?... WHY DON'T YOU ASK HIM?
COME ON OUT, PAL!
NOW HE TALKS TO VACUUM CLEANERS!
OMIGOSH! WHAT IS IT?
IT'S YOUR THIEF AND GENERAL MANAGER OF "C.R.U.S.H., EAST..." SMOKEMAN!
9

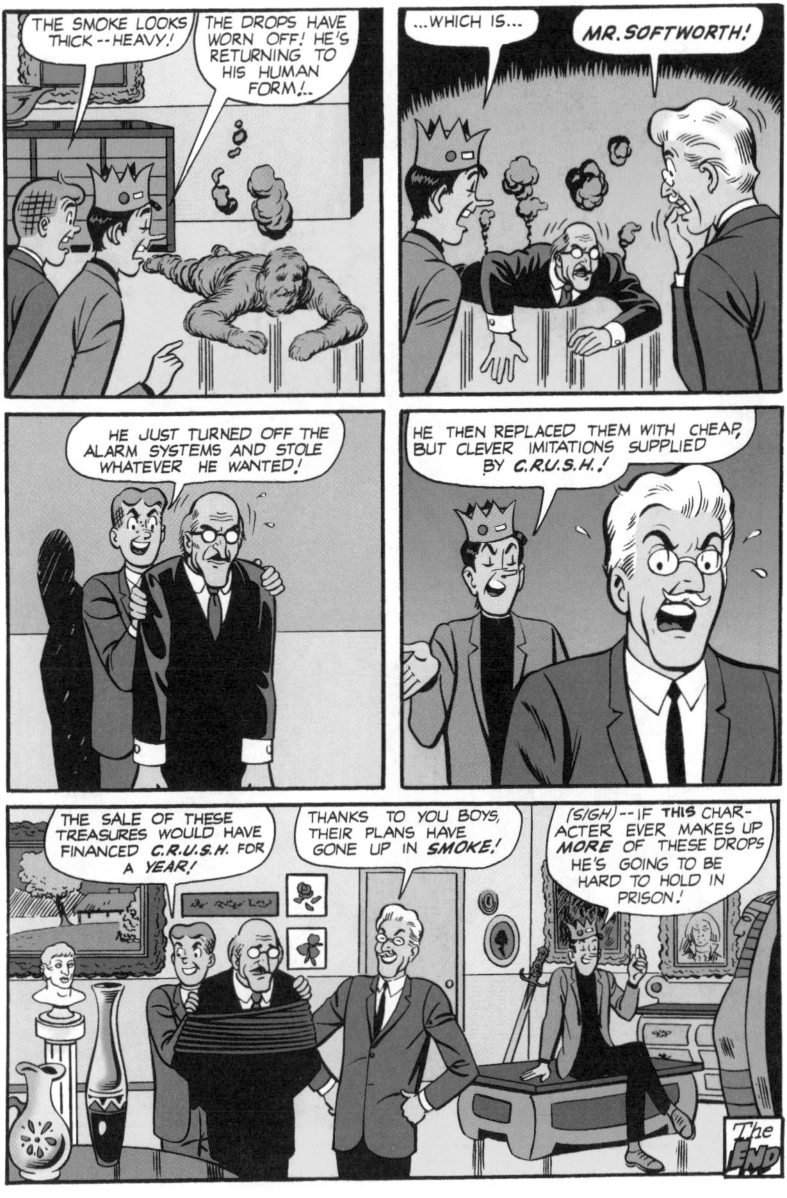
THE SMOKE LOOKS THICK -- HEAVY!
THE DROPS HAVE WORN OFF! HE'S RETURNING TO HIS HUMAN FORM!..
...WHICH IS...
MR. SOFTWORTH!
HE JUST TURNED OFF THE ALARM SYSTEMS AND STOLE WHATEVER HE WANTED!
HE THEN REPLACED THEM WITH CHEAP, BUT CLEVER IMITATIONS SUPPLIED BY C.R.U.S.H.!
THE SALE OF THESE TREASURES WOULD HAVE FINANCED C.R.U.S.H. FOR A YEAR!
THANKS TO YOU BOYS, THEIR PLANS HAVE GONE UP IN SMOKE!
(SIGH) -- IF THIS CHARACTER EVER MAKES UP MORE OF THESE DROPS HE'S GOING TO BE HARD TO HOLD IN PRISON!
The END

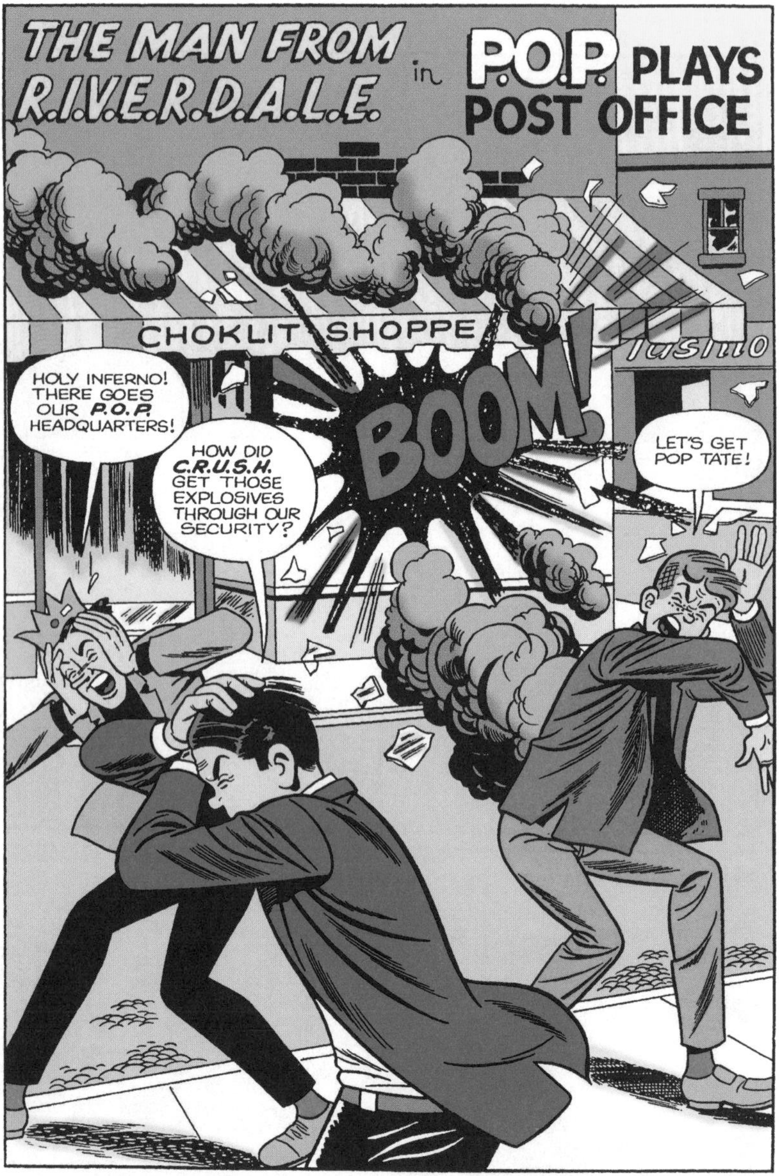
THE MAN FROM R.I.V.E.R.D.A.L.E.
in
P.O.P. PLAYS POST OFFICE
CHOKLIT SHOPPE
HOLY INFERNO! THERE GOES OUR P.O.P. HEADQUARTERS!
HOW DID C.R.U.S.H. GET THOSE EXPLOSIVES THROUGH OUR SECURITY?
BOOM!
LET'S GET POP TATE!

Story: Frank Doyle Pencils: Bob White
Inks & Letters: Mario Acquaviva

Originally printed in LIFE WITH ARCHIE #53, SEPTEMBER 1966

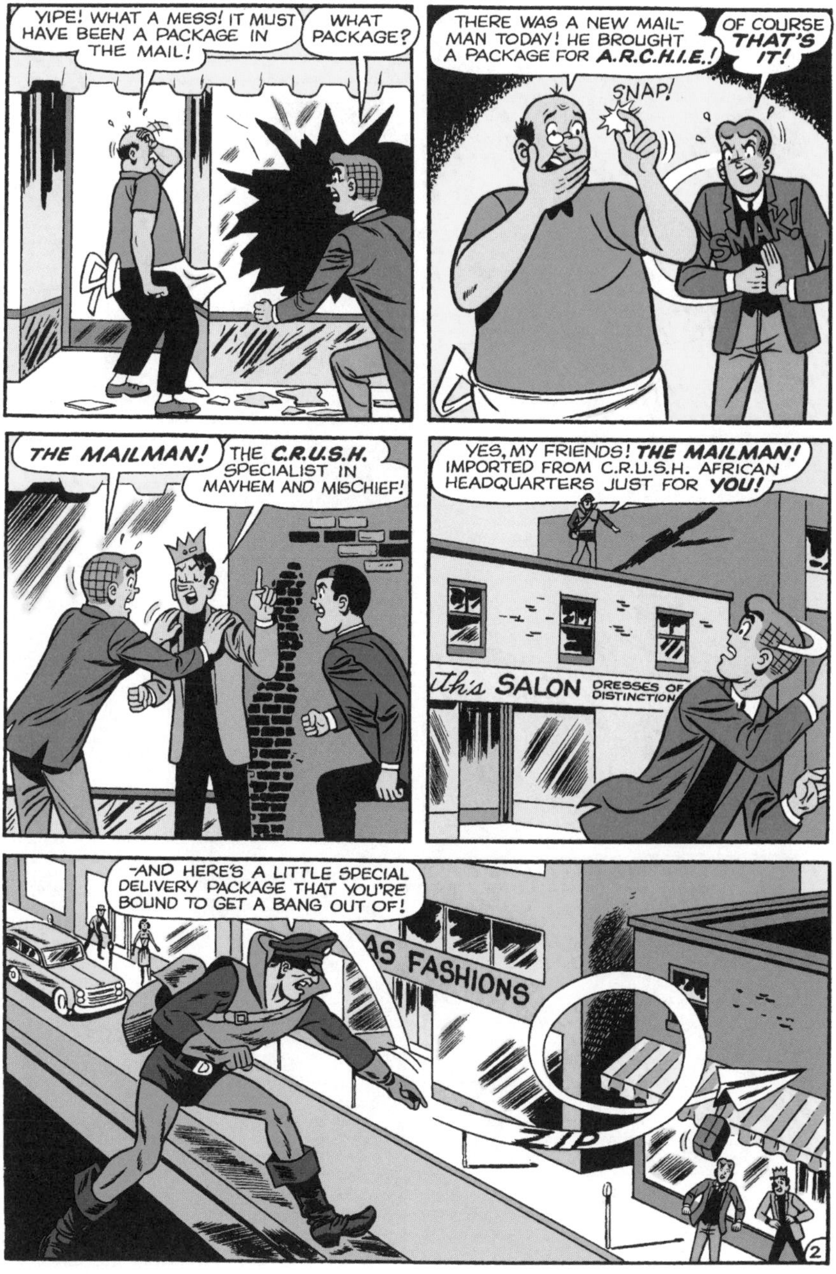
YIPE! WHAT A MESS! IT MUST HAVE BEEN A PACKAGE IN THE MAIL!
WHAT PACKAGE?
THERE WAS A NEW MAIL-MAN TODAY! HE BROUGHT A PACKAGE FOR A.R.C.H.I.E.!
SNAP!
OF COURSE THAT'S IT!
SMAK!
THE MAILMAN!
THE C.R.U.S.H. SPECIALIST IN MAYHEM AND MISCHIEF!
YES, MY FRIENDS! THE MAILMAN! IMPORTED FROM C.R.U.S.H. AFRICAN HEADQUARTERS JUST FOR YOU!
SALON DRESSES OF DISTINCTION
-AND HERE'S A LITTLE SPECIAL DELIVERY PACKAGE THAT YOU'RE BOUND TO GET A BANG OUT OF!
AS FASHIONS
ZIP
2

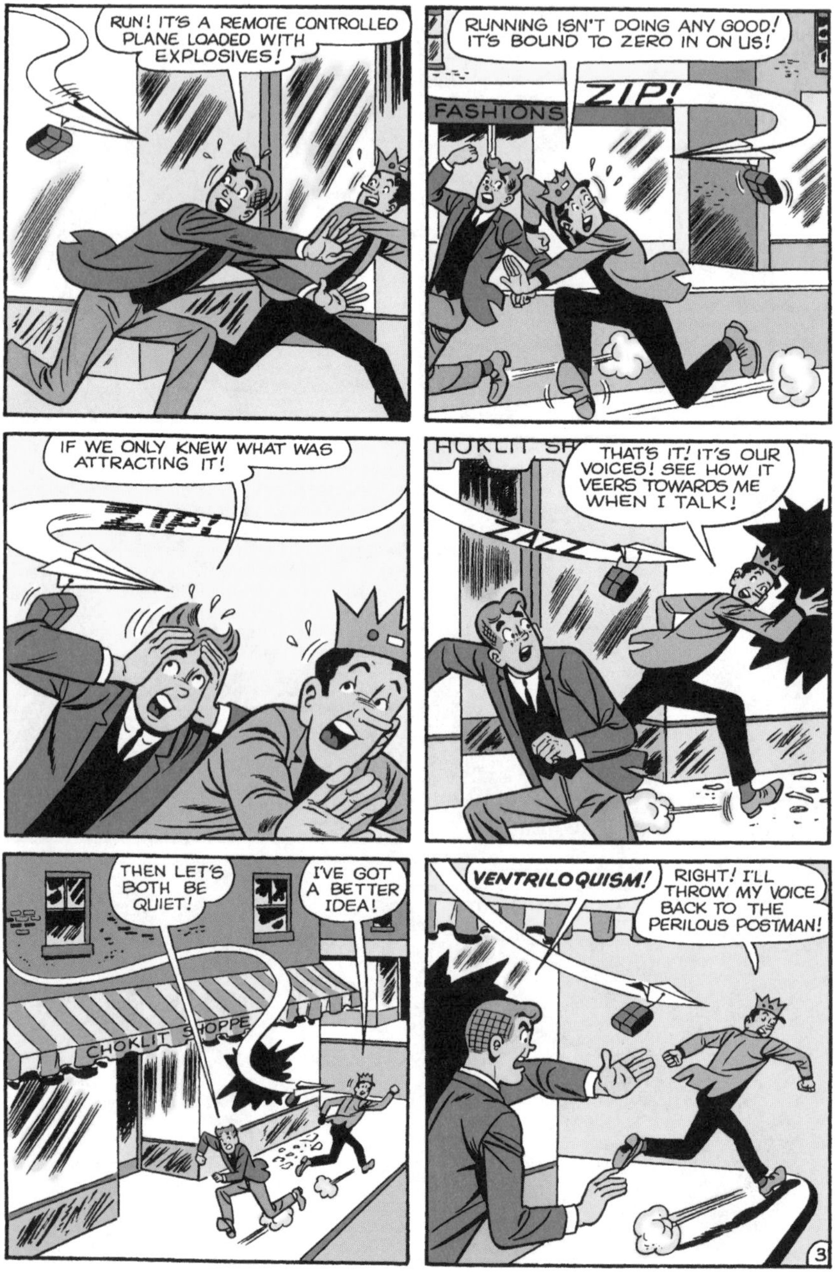
RUN! IT'S A REMOTE CONTROLLED PLANE LOADED WITH EXPLOSIVES!
RUNNING ISN'T DOING ANY GOOD! IT'S BOUND TO ZERO IN ON US!
FASHIONS
ZIP!
IF WE ONLY KNEW WHAT WAS ATTRACTING IT!
ZIP!
THAT'S IT! IT'S OUR VOICES! SEE HOW IT VEERS TOWARDS ME WHEN I TALK!
ZAZZ
THEN LET'S BOTH BE QUIET!
I'VE GOT A BETTER IDEA!
CHOKLIT SHOPPE
VENTRILOQUISM!
RIGHT! I'LL THROW MY VOICE BACK TO THE PERILOUS POSTMAN!
3

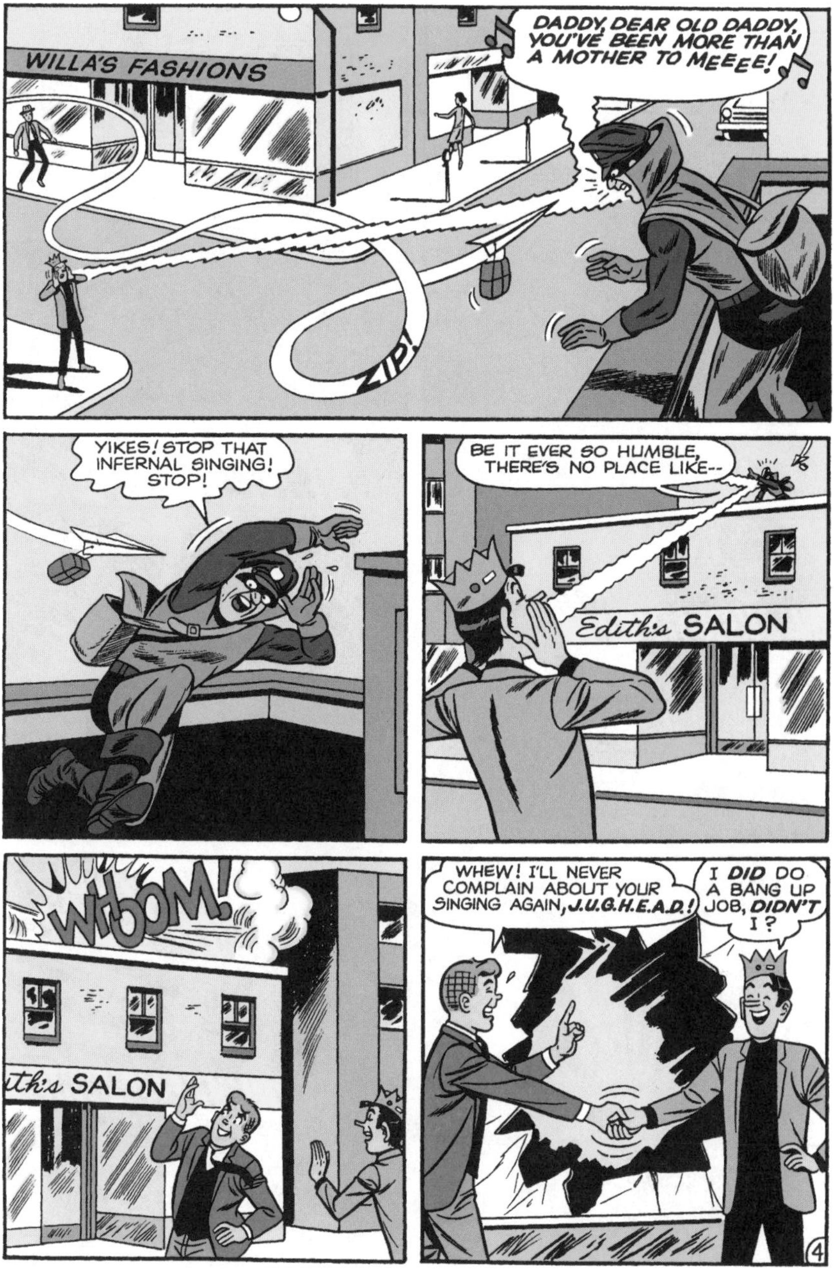
DADDY, DEAR OLD DADDY, YOU'VE BEEN MORE THAN A MOTHER TO MEEEE!
WILLA'S FASHIONS
ZIP!
YIKES! STOP THAT INFERNAL SINGING! STOP!
BE IT EVER SO HUMBLE, THERE'S NO PLACE LIKE--
Edith's SALON
WHOOM!
SALON
WHEW! I'LL NEVER COMPLAIN ABOUT YOUR SINGING AGAIN, J.U.G.H.E.A.D.!
I DID DO A BANG UP JOB, DIDN'T I?
4

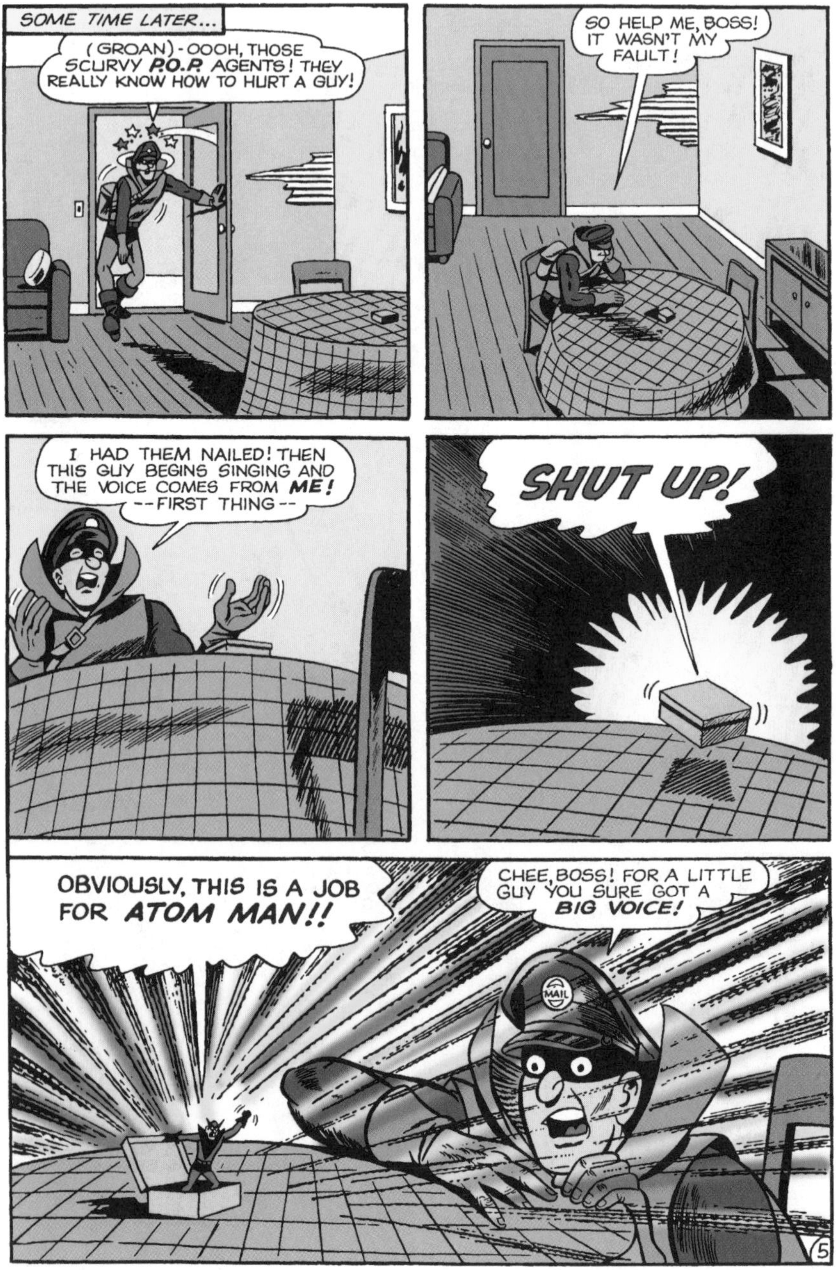
SOME TIME LATER...
(GROAN) - OOOH, THOSE SCURVY P.O.P. AGENTS! THEY REALLY KNOW HOW TO HURT A GUY!
SO HELP ME, BOSS! IT WASN'T MY FAULT!
I HAD THEM NAILED! THEN THIS GUY BEGINS SINGING AND THE VOICE COMES FROM ME! --FIRST THING--
SHUT UP!
OBVIOUSLY, THIS IS A JOB FOR ATOM MAN!!
CHEE, BOSS! FOR A LITTLE GUY YOU SURE GOT A BIG VOICE!
MAIL
5

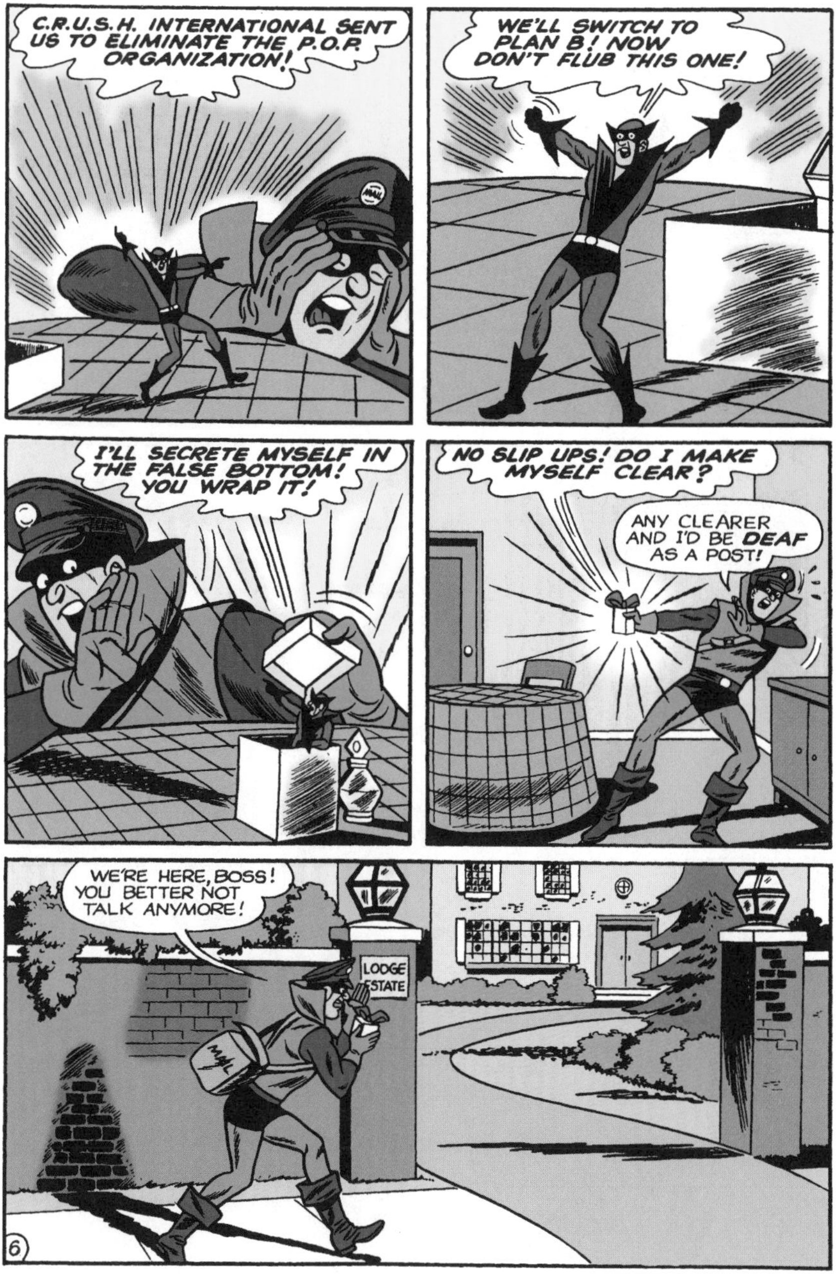
C.R.U.S.H. INTERNATIONAL SENT US TO ELIMINATE THE P.O.P. ORGANIZATION!
WE'LL SWITCH TO PLAN B! NOW DON'T FLUB THIS ONE!
I'LL SECRETE MYSELF IN THE FALSE BOTTOM! YOU WRAP IT!
NO SLIP UPS! DO I MAKE MYSELF CLEAR?
ANY CLEARER AND I'D BE DEAF AS A POST!
WE'RE HERE, BOSS! YOU BETTER NOT TALK ANYMORE!
LODGE ESTATE
6

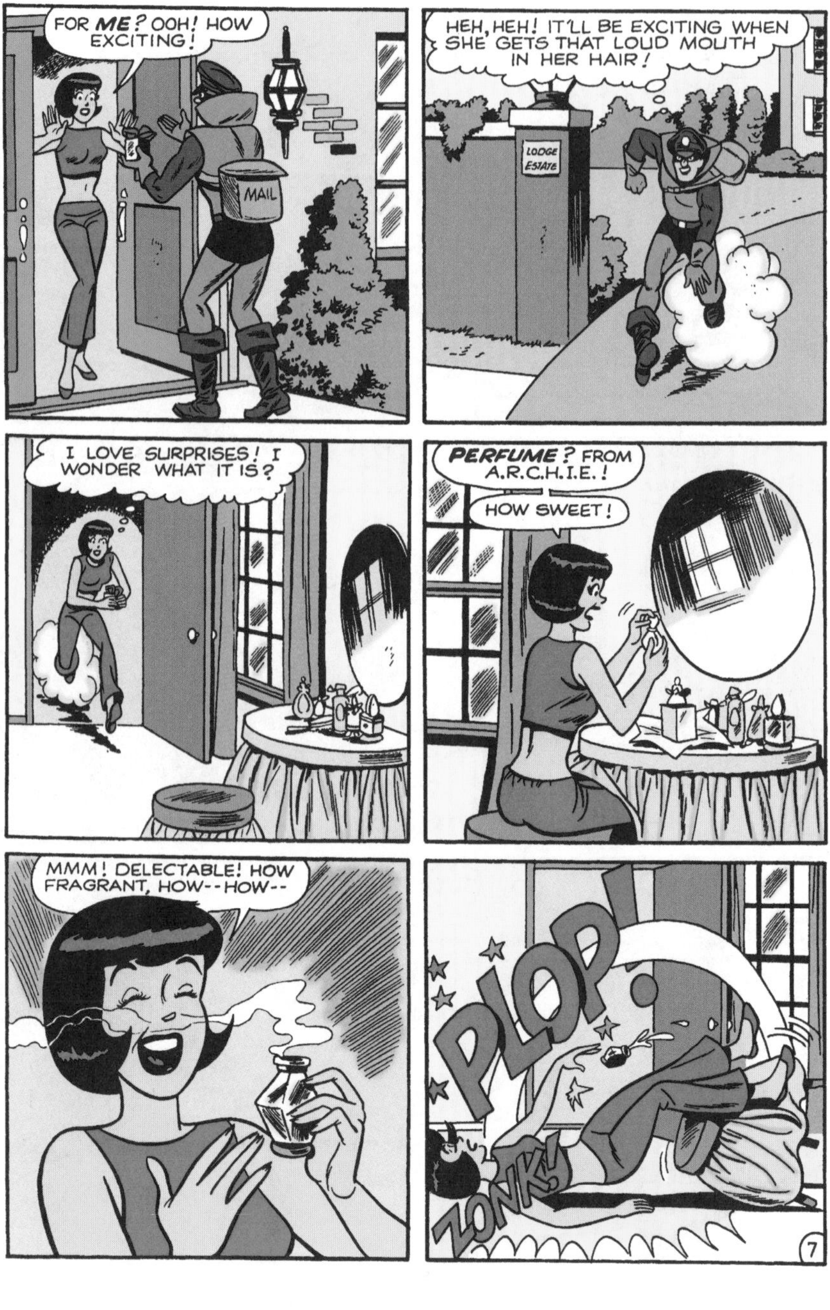
FOR ME? OOH! HOW EXCITING!
MAIL
HEH, HEH! IT'LL BE EXCITING WHEN SHE GETS THAT LOUD MOUTH IN HER HAIR!
LODGE ESTATE
I LOVE SURPRISES! I WONDER WHAT IT IS?
PERFUME? FROM A.R.C.H.I.E.!
HOW SWEET!
MMM! DELECTABLE! HOW FRAGRANT, HOW--HOW--
PLOP!
ZONK!
7

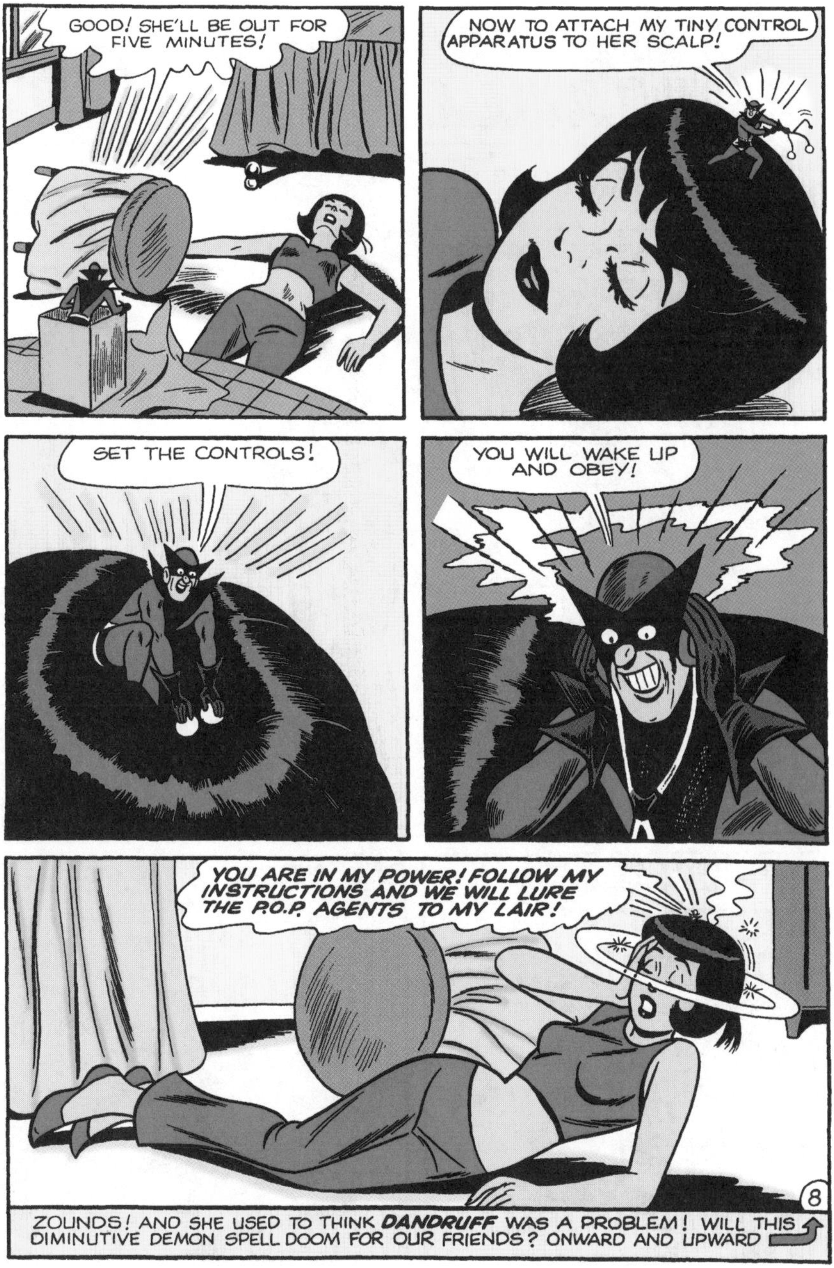
GOOD! SHE'LL BE OUT FOR FIVE MINUTES!
NOW TO ATTACH MY TINY CONTROL APPARATUS TO HER SCALP!
SET THE CONTROLS!
YOU WILL WAKE UP AND OBEY!
YOU ARE IN MY POWER! FOLLOW MY INSTRUCTIONS AND WE WILL LURE THE P.O.P. AGENTS TO MY LAIR!
8
ZOUNDS! AND SHE USED TO THINK DANDRUFF WAS A PROBLEM! WILL THIS DIMINUTIVE DEMON SPELL DOOM FOR OUR FRIENDS? ONWARD AND UPWARD

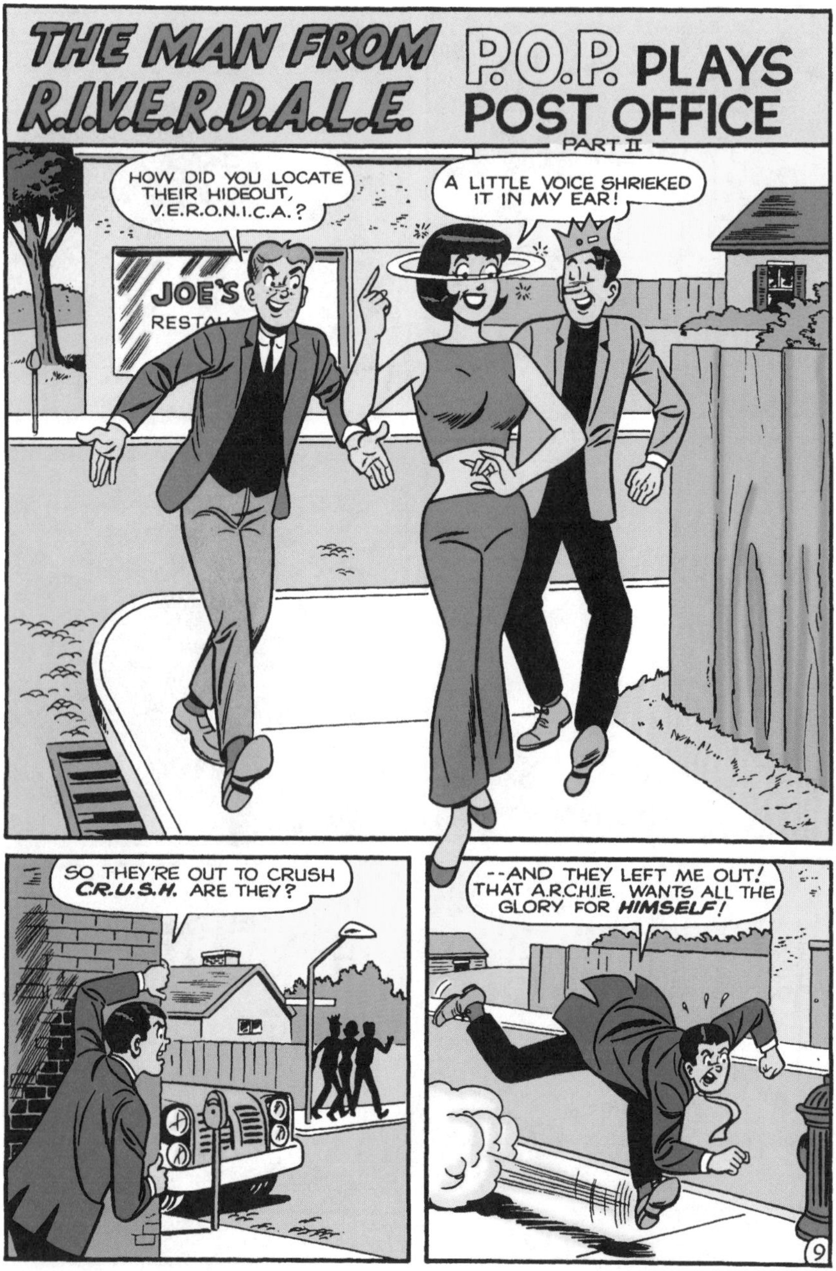
THE MAN FROM R.I.V.E.R.D.A.L.E.
P.O.P. PLAYS POST OFFICE
PART II
HOW DID YOU LOCATE THEIR HIDEOUT, V.E.R.O.N.I.C.A.?
A LITTLE VOICE SHRIEKED IT IN MY EAR!
JOE'S RESTAU
SO THEY'RE OUT TO CRUSH C.R.U.S.H. ARE THEY?
--AND THEY LEFT ME OUT! THAT A.R.C.H.I.E. WANTS ALL THE GLORY FOR HIMSELF!
9

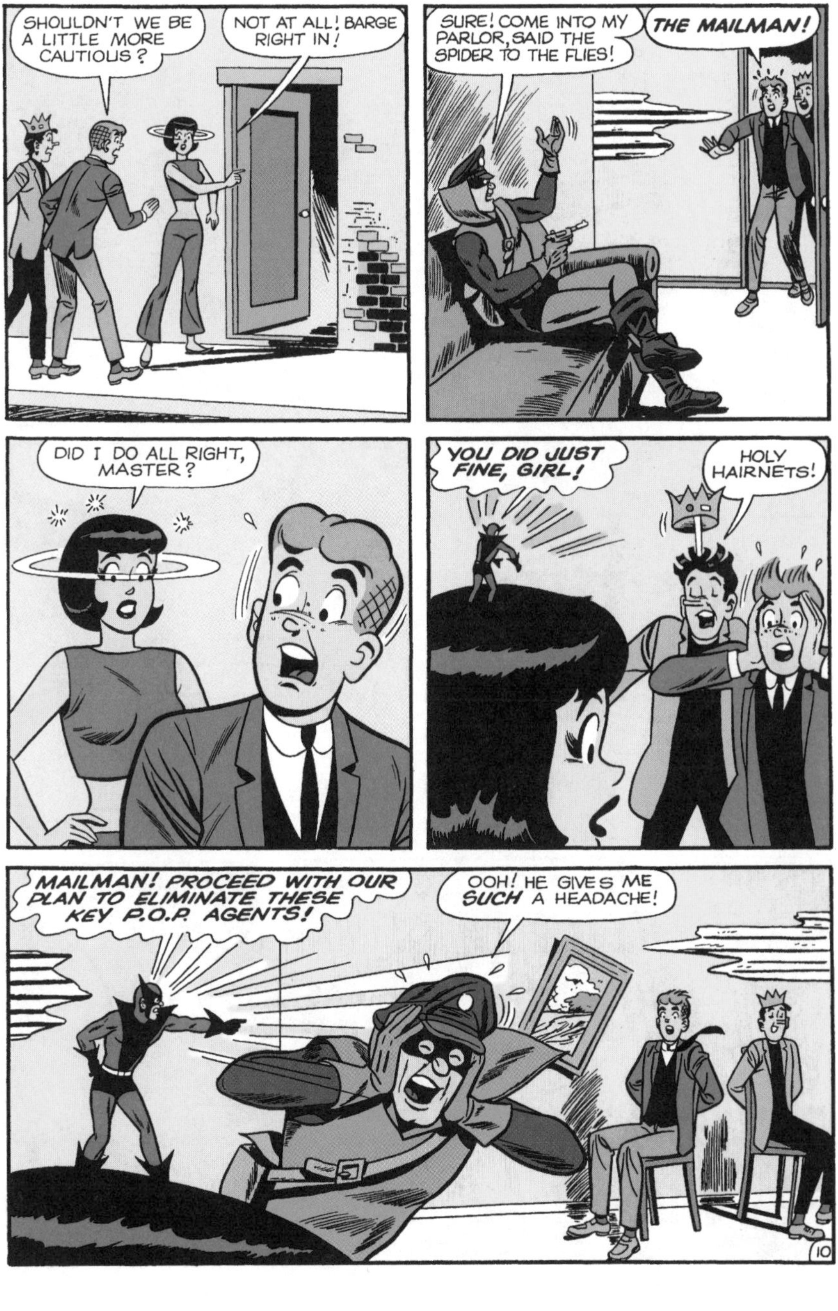
SHOULDN'T WE BE A LITTLE MORE CAUTIOUS?
NOT AT ALL! BARGE RIGHT IN!
SURE! COME INTO MY PARLOR, SAID THE SPIDER TO THE FLIES!
THE MAILMAN!
DID I DO ALL RIGHT, MASTER?
YOU DID JUST FINE, GIRL!
HOLY HAIRNETS!
MAILMAN! PROCEED WITH OUR PLAN TO ELIMINATE THESE KEY P.O.P. AGENTS!
OOH! HE GIVES ME SUCH A HEADACHE!
10

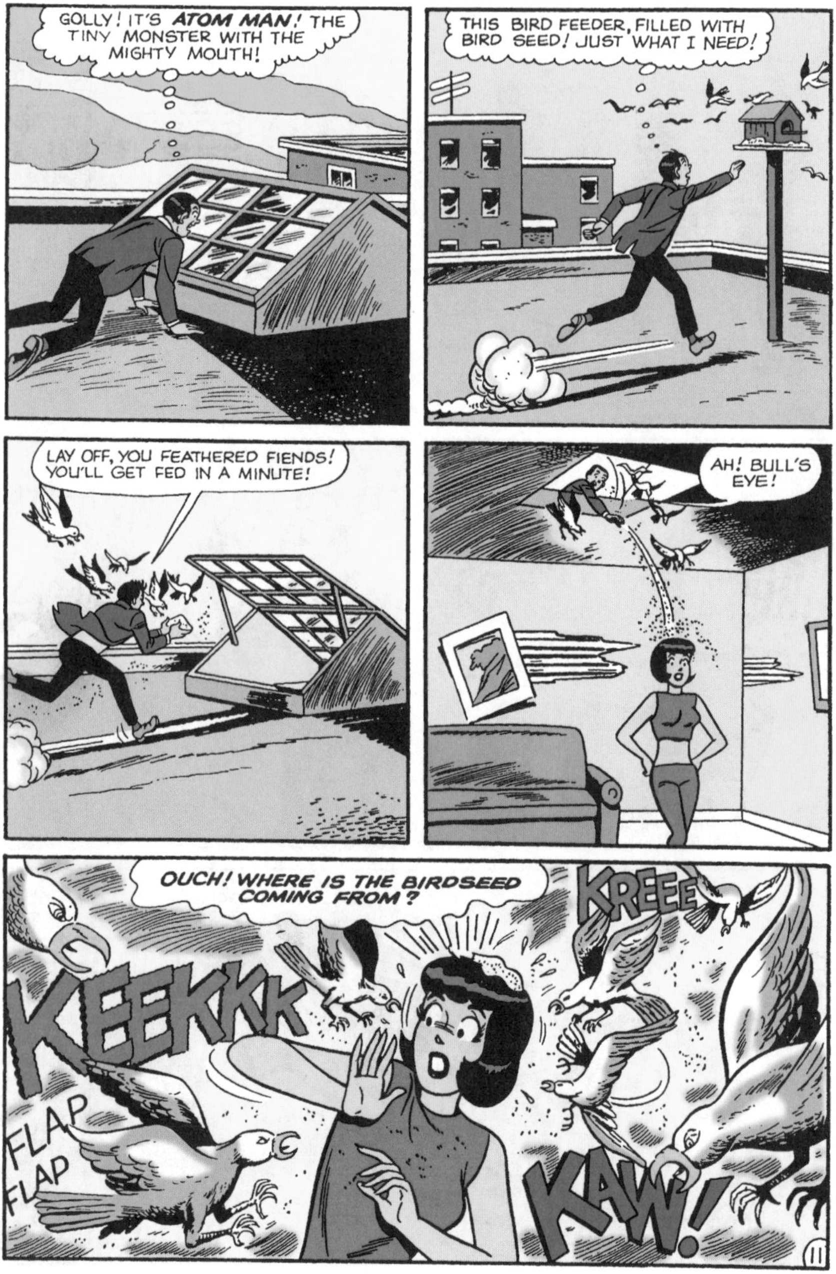
GOLLY! IT'S ATOM MAN! THE TINY MONSTER WITH THE MIGHTY MOUTH!
THIS BIRD FEEDER, FILLED WITH BIRD SEED! JUST WHAT I NEED!
LAY OFF, YOU FEATHERED FIENDS! YOU'LL GET FED IN A MINUTE!
AH! BULL'S EYE!
OUCH! WHERE IS THE BIRDSEED COMING FROM?
KREEE
KEEKKK
FLAP FLAP
KAW!

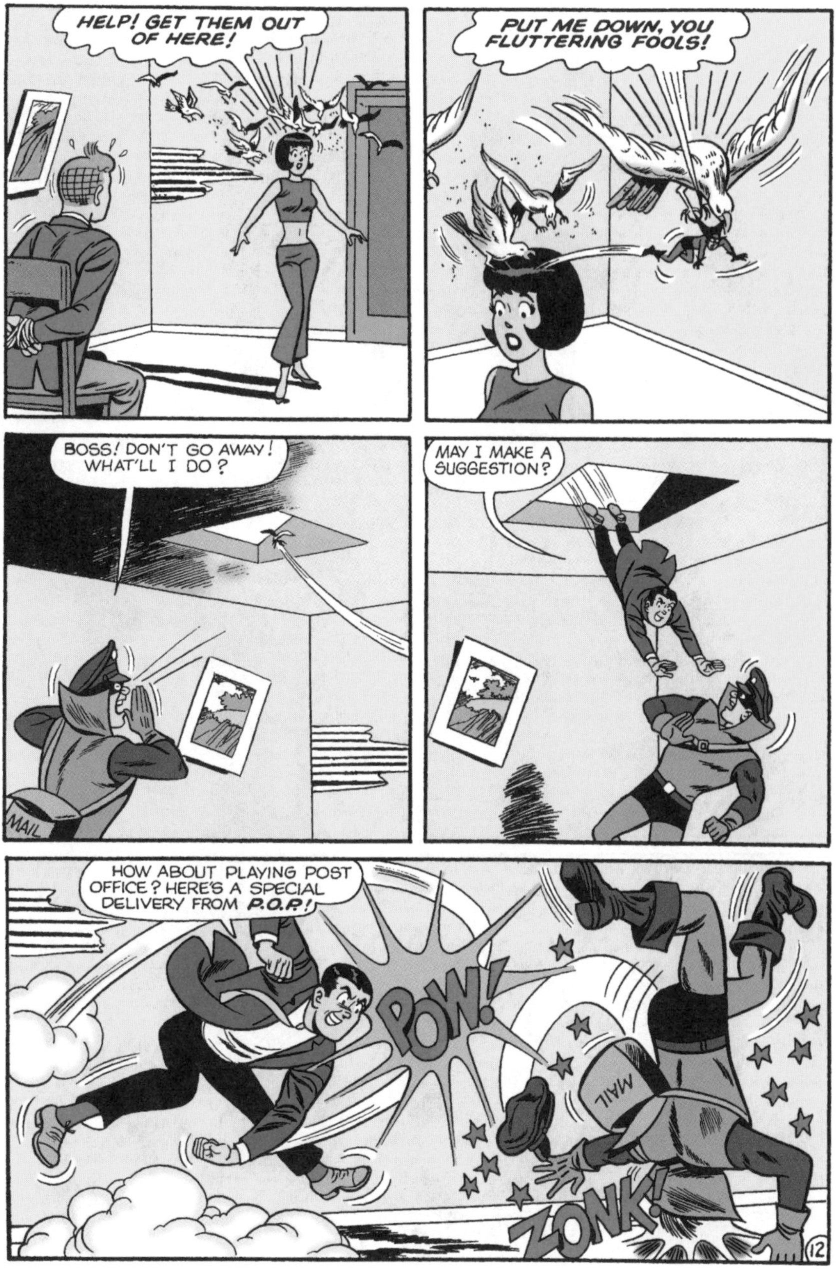
HELP! GET THEM OUT OF HERE!
PUT ME DOWN, YOU FLUTTERING FOOLS!
BOSS! DON'T GO AWAY! WHAT'LL I DO?
MAIL
MAY I MAKE A SUGGESTION?
HOW ABOUT PLAYING POST OFFICE? HERE'S A SPECIAL DELIVERY FROM P.O.P.!
POW!
MAIL
ZONK!
12

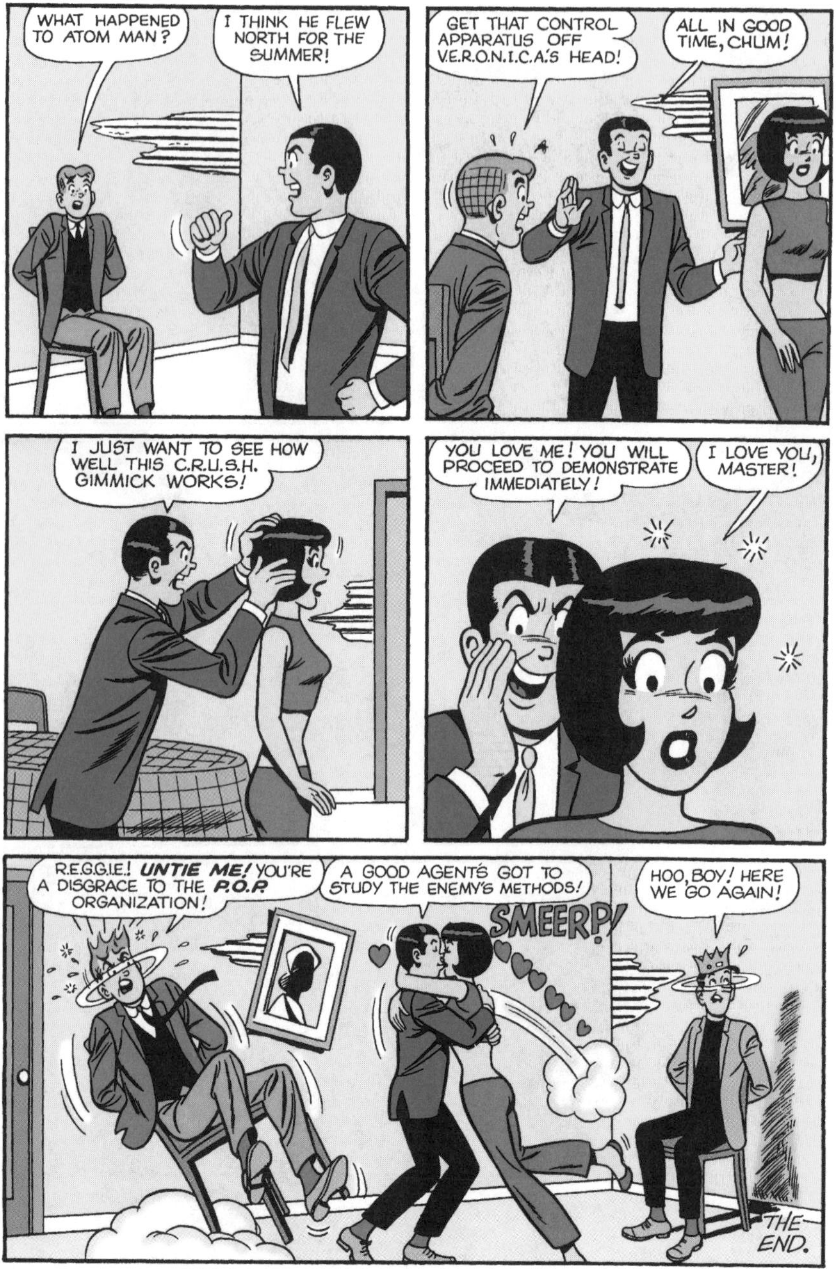
WHAT HAPPENED TO ATOM MAN?
I THINK HE FLEW NORTH FOR THE SUMMER!
GET THAT CONTROL APPARATUS OFF V.E.R.O.N.I.C.A.'S HEAD!
ALL IN GOOD TIME, CHUM!
I JUST WANT TO SEE HOW WELL THIS C.R.U.S.H. GIMMICK WORKS!
YOU LOVE ME! YOU WILL PROCEED TO DEMONSTRATE IMMEDIATELY!
I LOVE YOU, MASTER!
R.E.G.G.I.E.! UNTIE ME! YOU'RE A DISGRACE TO THE P.O.P. ORGANIZATION!
A GOOD AGENT'S GOT TO STUDY THE ENEMY'S METHODS!
SMEERP!
HOO, BOY! HERE WE GO AGAIN!
THE END.

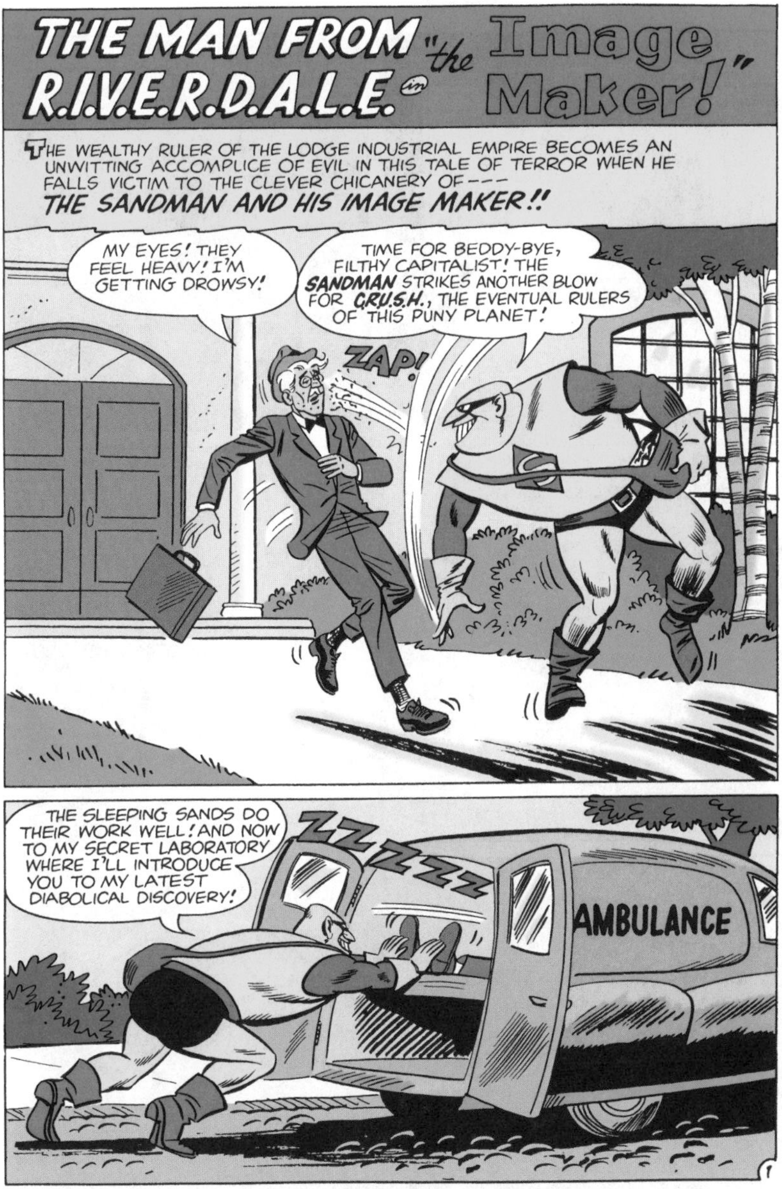
THE MAN FROM R.I.V.E.R.D.A.L.E. in "the Image Maker!"
THE WEALTHY RULER OF THE LODGE INDUSTRIAL EMPIRE BECOMES AN UNWITTING ACCOMPLICE OF EVIL IN THIS TALE OF TERROR WHEN HE FALLS VICTIM TO THE CLEVER CHICANERY OF--- THE SANDMAN AND HIS IMAGE MAKER!!
MY EYES! THEY FEEL HEAVY! I'M GETTING DROWSY!
TIME FOR BEDDY-BYE, FILTHY CAPITALIST! THE SANDMAN STRIKES ANOTHER BLOW FOR C.R.U.S.H., THE EVENTUAL RULERS OF THIS PUNY PLANET!
ZAP!
THE SLEEPING SANDS DO THEIR WORK WELL! AND NOW TO MY SECRET LABORATORY WHERE I'LL INTRODUCE YOU TO MY LATEST DIABOLICAL DISCOVERY!
ZZZZZZ
AMBULANCE
1

Story: Frank Doyle Pencils: Bill Vigoda
Inks & Letters: Marty Epp

Originally printed in LIFE WITH ARCHIE #53, SEPTEMBER 1966

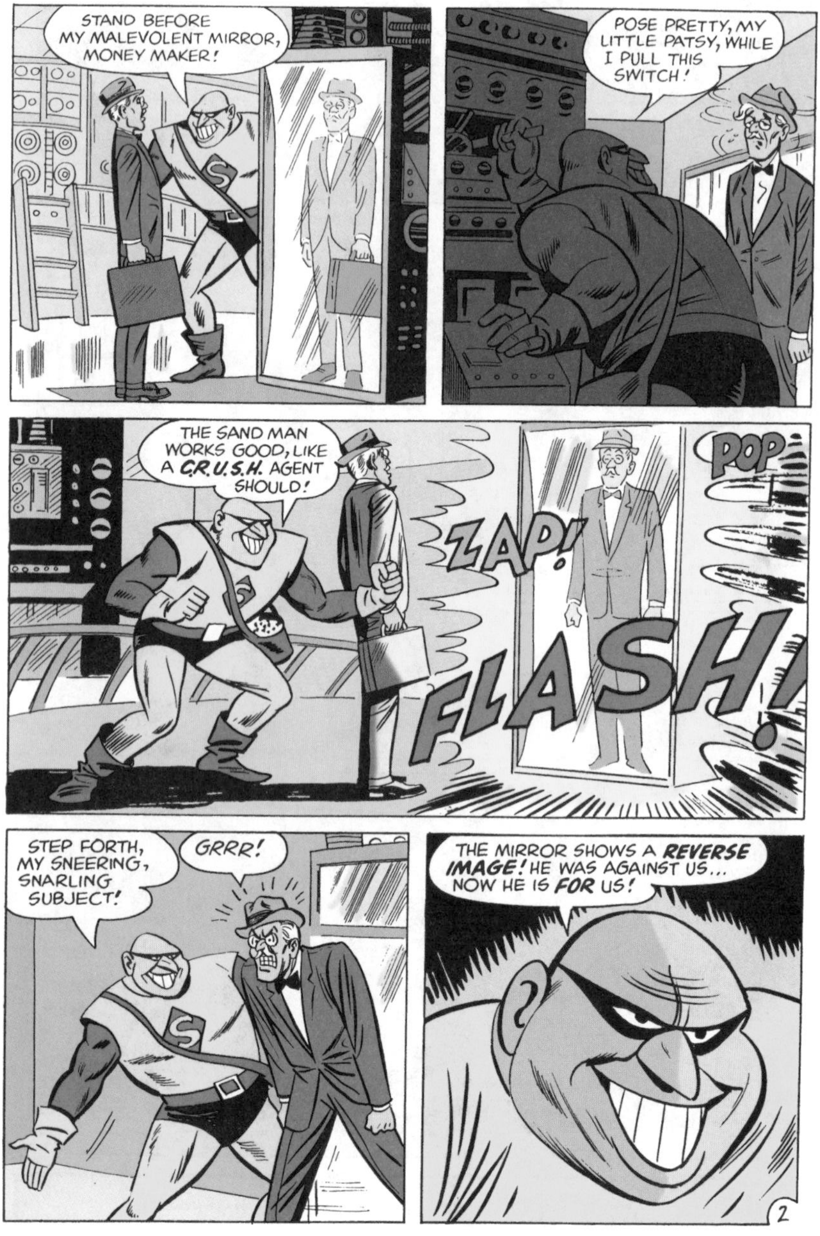
STAND BEFORE MY MALEVOLENT MIRROR, MONEY MAKER!
POSE PRETTY, MY LITTLE PATSY, WHILE I PULL THIS SWITCH!
THE SAND MAN WORKS GOOD, LIKE A C.R.U.S.H. AGENT SHOULD!
ZAP!
POP
FLASH!
STEP FORTH, MY SNEERING, SNARLING SUBJECT!
GRRR!
THE MIRROR SHOWS A REVERSE IMAGE! HE WAS AGAINST US... NOW HE IS FOR US!
2

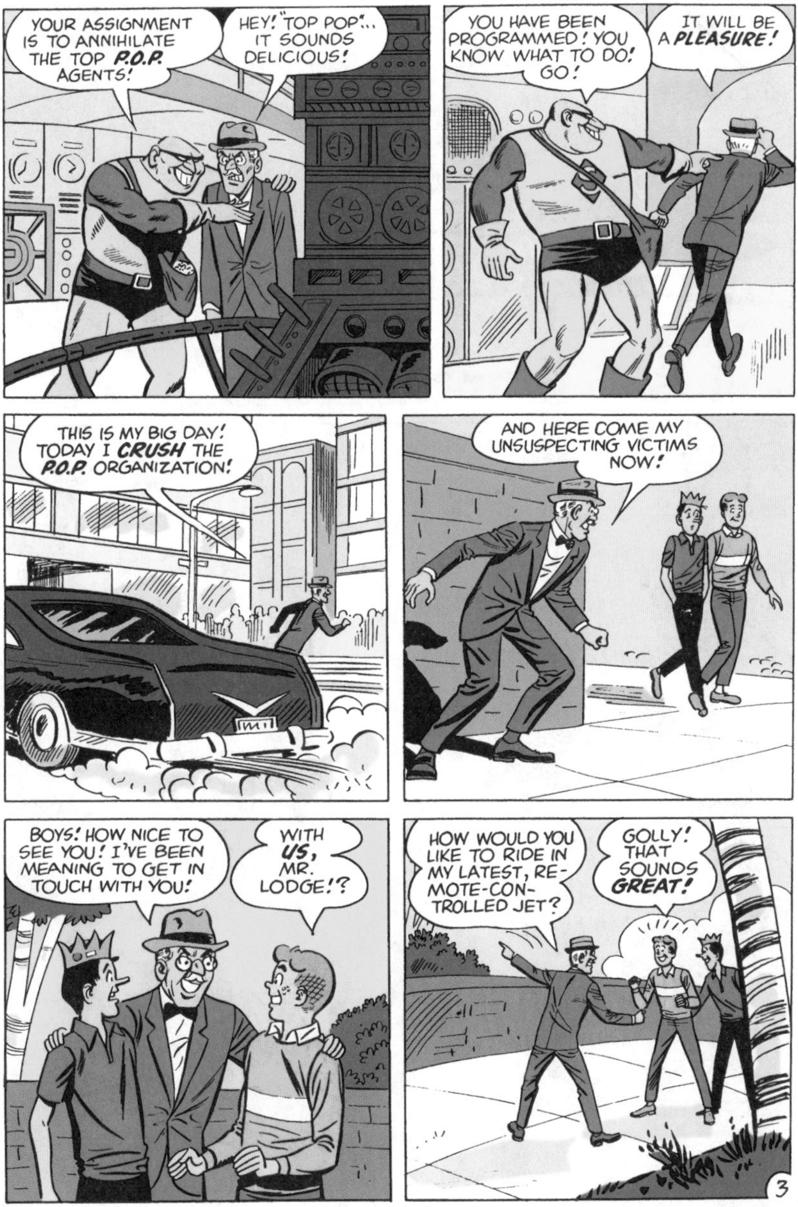
YOUR ASSIGNMENT IS TO ANNIHILATE THE TOP P.O.P. AGENTS!
HEY! "TOP POP"... IT SOUNDS DELICIOUS!
YOU HAVE BEEN PROGRAMMED! YOU KNOW WHAT TO DO! GO!
IT WILL BE A PLEASURE!
THIS IS MY BIG DAY! TODAY I CRUSH THE P.O.P. ORGANIZATION!
AND HERE COME MY UNSUSPECTING VICTIMS NOW!
BOYS! HOW NICE TO SEE YOU! I'VE BEEN MEANING TO GET IN TOUCH WITH YOU!
WITH US, MR. LODGE!?
HOW WOULD YOU LIKE TO RIDE IN MY LATEST, RE-MOTE-CON-TROLLED JET?
GOLLY! THAT SOUNDS GREAT!
3

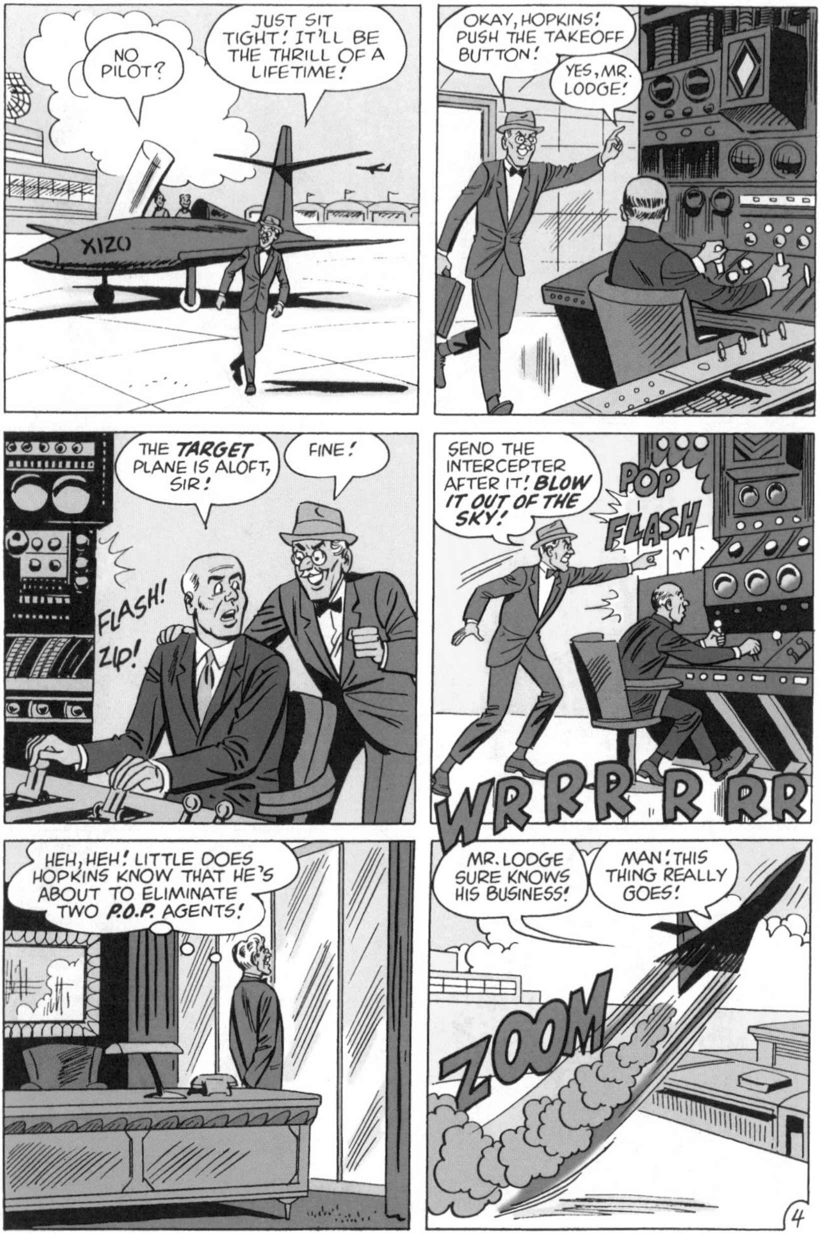
NO PILOT?
JUST SIT TIGHT! IT'LL BE THE THRILL OF A LIFETIME!
XIZO
OKAY, HOPKINS! PUSH THE TAKEOFF BUTTON!
YES, MR. LODGE!
THE TARGET PLANE IS ALOFT, SIR!
FINE!
FLASH!
ZIP!
SEND THE INTERCEPTER AFTER IT! BLOW IT OUT OF THE SKY!
POP
FLASH
WRRR R RR
HEH, HEH! LITTLE DOES HOPKINS KNOW THAT HE'S ABOUT TO ELIMINATE TWO P.O.P. AGENTS!
MR. LODGE SURE KNOWS HIS BUSINESS!
MAN! THIS THING REALLY GOES!
ZOOM
4

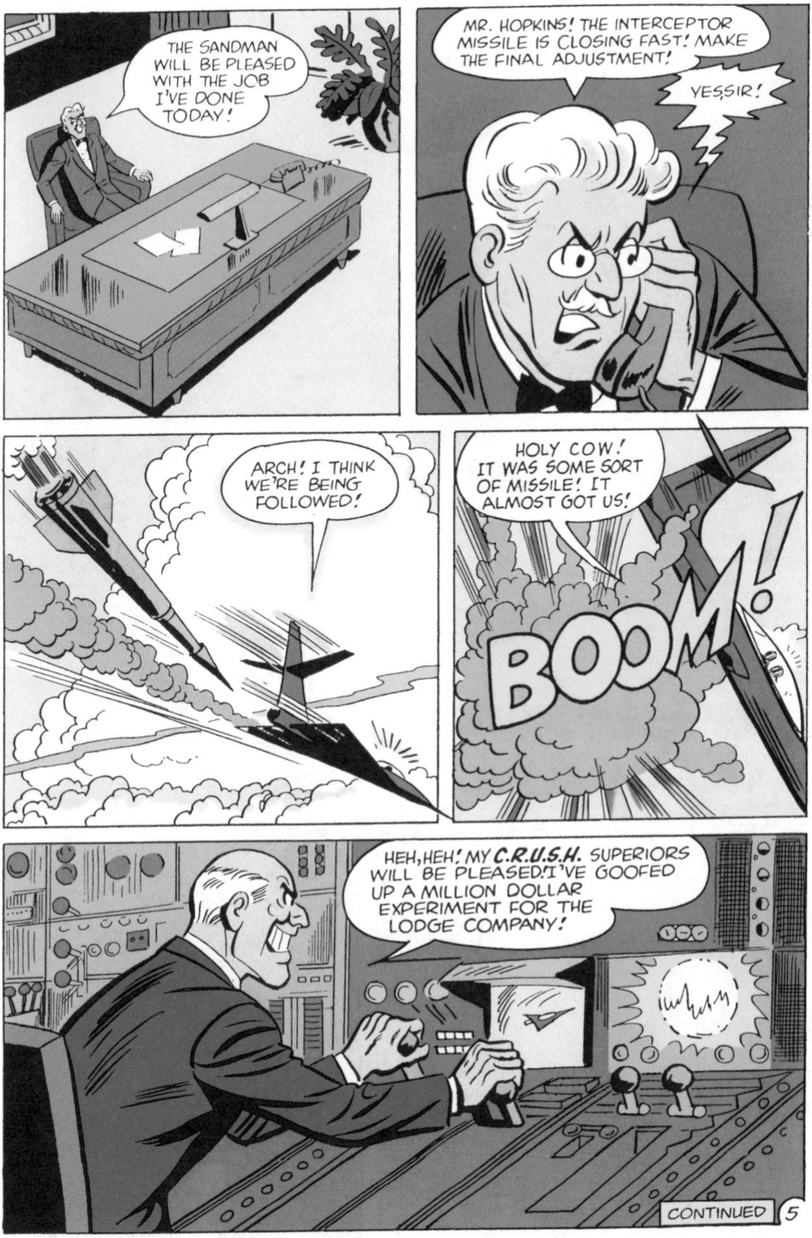
THE SANDMAN WILL BE PLEASED WITH THE JOB I'VE DONE TODAY!
MR. HOPKINS! THE INTERCEPTOR MISSILE IS CLOSING FAST! MAKE THE FINAL ADJUSTMENT!
YES,SIR!
ARCH! I THINK WE'RE BEING FOLLOWED!
HOLY COW! IT WAS SOME SORT OF MISSILE! IT ALMOST GOT US!
BOOM!
HEH,HEH! MY C.R.U.S.H. SUPERIORS WILL BE PLEASED! I'VE GOOFED UP A MILLION DOLLAR EXPERIMENT FOR THE LODGE COMPANY!
CONTINUED
5

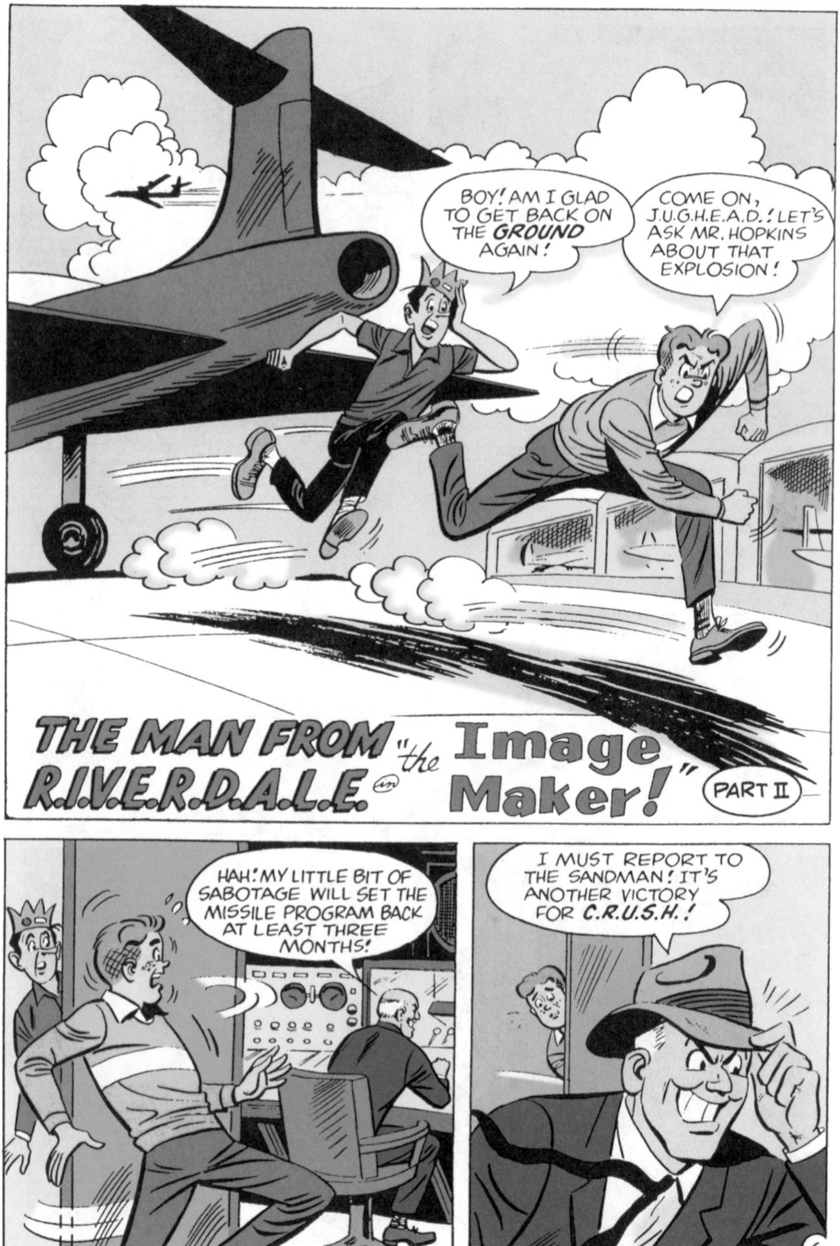
BOY! AM I GLAD TO GET BACK ON THE **GROUND** AGAIN!
COME ON, J.U.G.H.E.A.D.! LET'S ASK MR. HOPKINS ABOUT THAT EXPLOSION!
THE MAN FROM R.I.V.E.R.D.A.L.E. in "the Image Maker!" PART II
HAH! MY LITTLE BIT OF SABOTAGE WILL SET THE MISSILE PROGRAM BACK AT LEAST THREE MONTHS!
I MUST REPORT TO THE SANDMAN! IT'S ANOTHER VICTORY FOR **C.R.U.S.H.**!
6

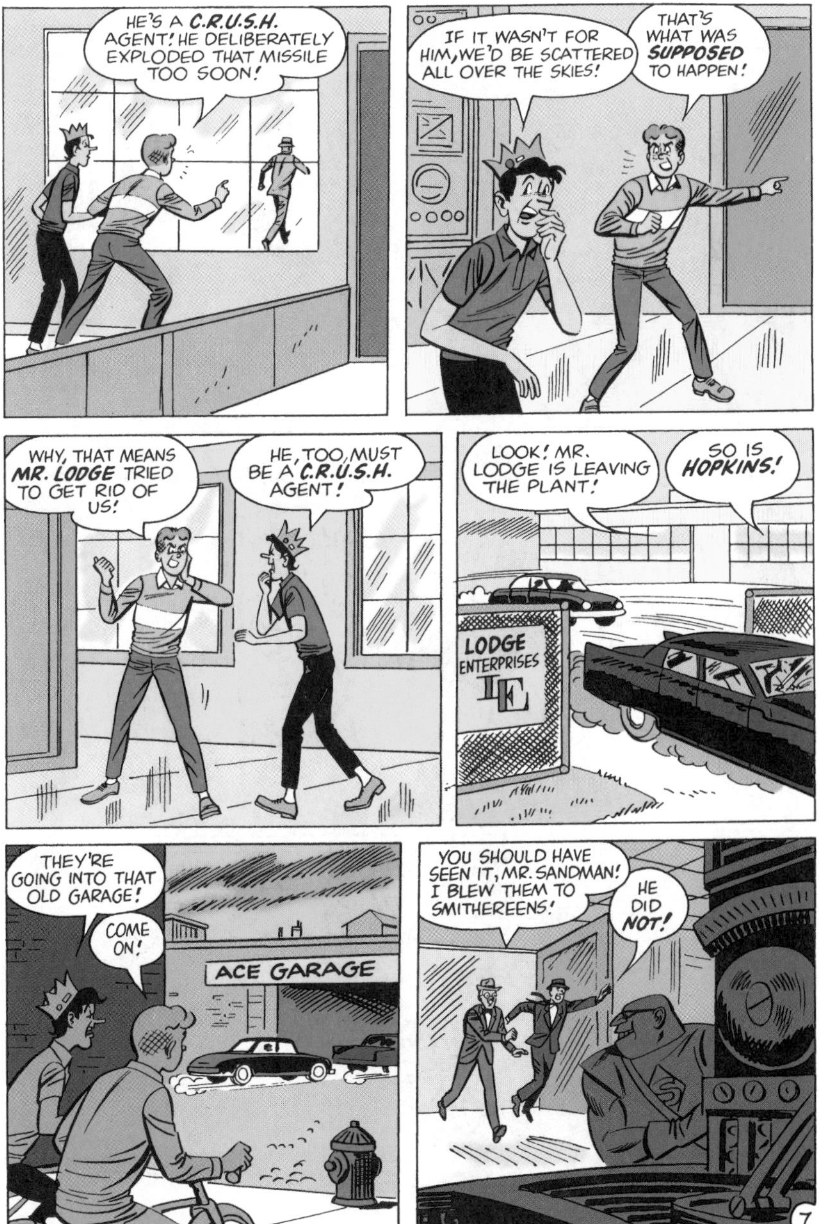
HE'S A C.R.U.S.H. AGENT! HE DELIBERATELY EXPLODED THAT MISSILE TOO SOON!
IF IT WASN'T FOR HIM, WE'D BE SCATTERED ALL OVER THE SKIES!
THAT'S WHAT WAS SUPPOSED TO HAPPEN!
WHY, THAT MEANS MR. LODGE TRIED TO GET RID OF US!
HE, TOO, MUST BE A C.R.U.S.H. AGENT!
LOOK! MR. LODGE IS LEAVING THE PLANT!
SO IS HOPKINS!
LODGE ENTERPRISES
LE
THEY'RE GOING INTO THAT OLD GARAGE!
COME ON!
ACE GARAGE
YOU SHOULD HAVE SEEN IT, MR. SANDMAN! I BLEW THEM TO SMITHEREENS!
HE DID NOT!
7

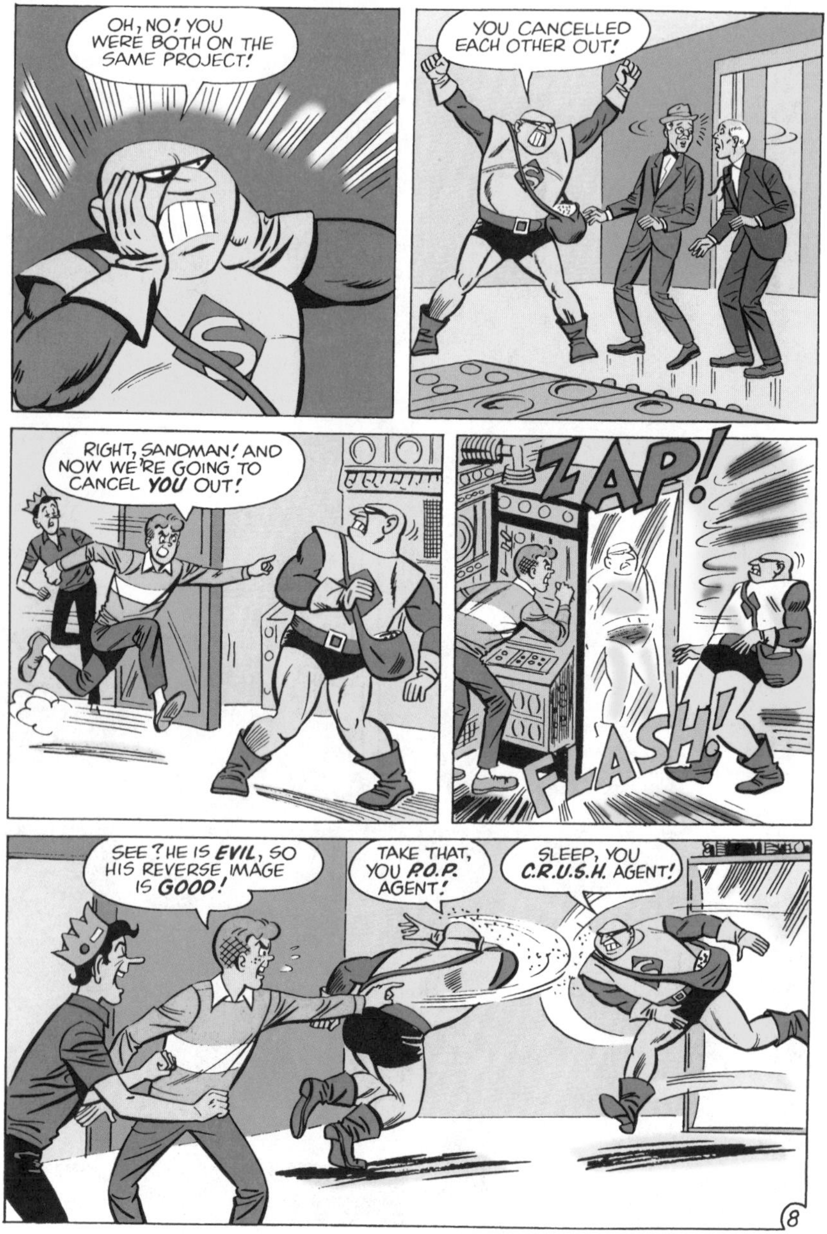
OH, NO! YOU WERE BOTH ON THE SAME PROJECT!
YOU CANCELLED EACH OTHER OUT!
RIGHT, SANDMAN! AND NOW WE'RE GOING TO CANCEL YOU OUT!
ZAP!
FLASH!
SEE? HE IS EVIL, SO HIS REVERSE IMAGE IS GOOD!
TAKE THAT, YOU P.O.P. AGENT!
SLEEP, YOU C.R.U.S.H. AGENT!
8

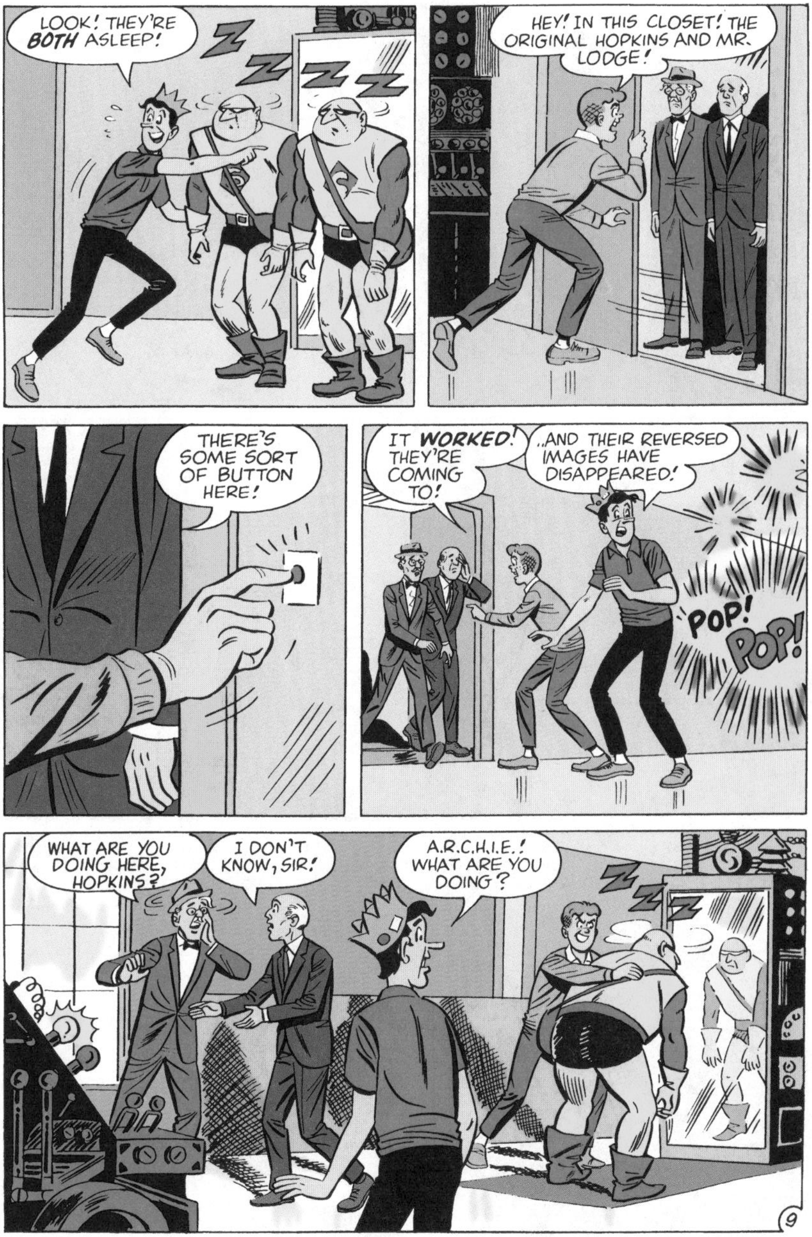
LOOK! THEY'RE BOTH ASLEEP!
Z Z Z Z
HEY! IN THIS CLOSET! THE ORIGINAL HOPKINS AND MR. LODGE!
THERE'S SOME SORT OF BUTTON HERE!
IT WORKED! THEY'RE COMING TO!
..AND THEIR REVERSED IMAGES HAVE DISAPPEARED!
POP! POP!
WHAT ARE YOU DOING HERE, HOPKINS?
I DON'T KNOW, SIR!
A.R.C.H.I.E.! WHAT ARE YOU DOING?
Z Z Z
9

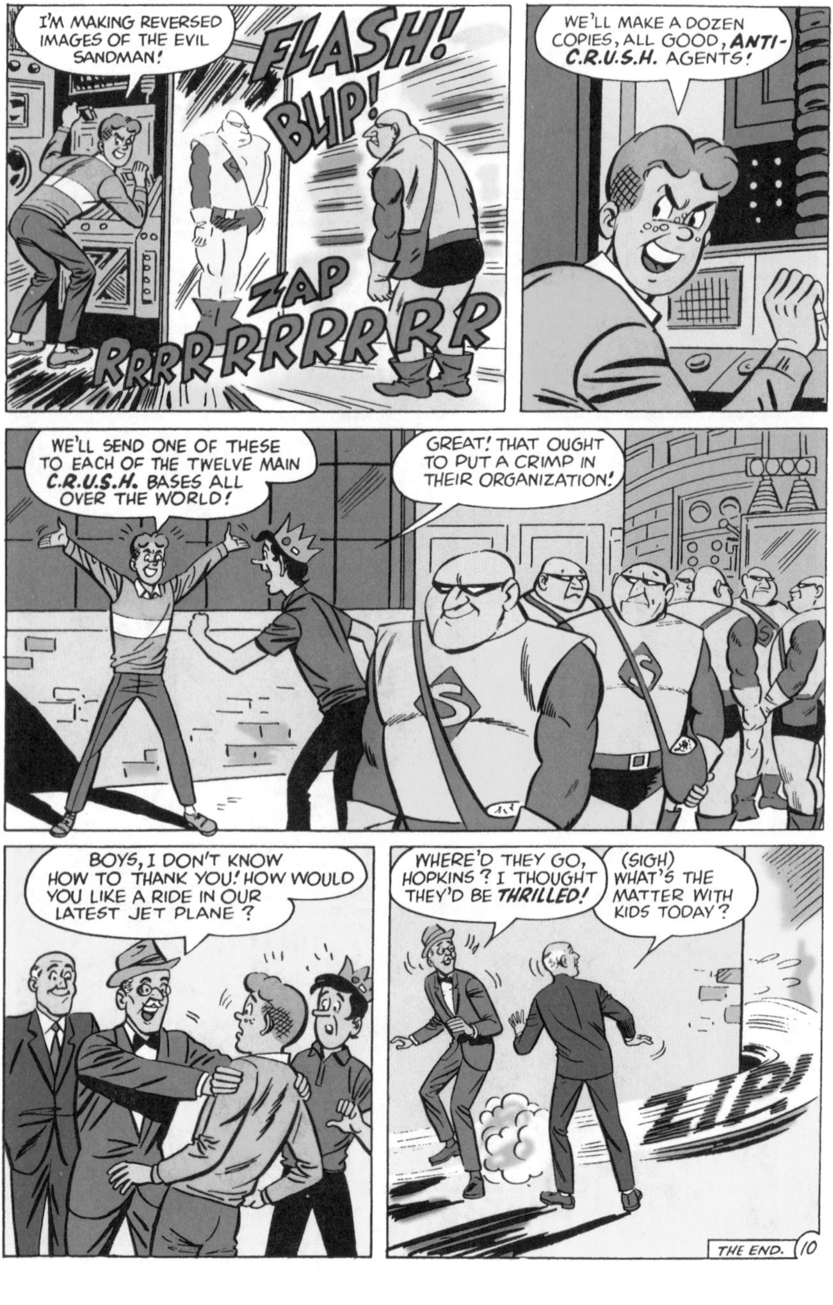
I'M MAKING REVERSED IMAGES OF THE EVIL SANDMAN!
FLASH!
BLIP!
ZAP
RRRRRRRRRR
WE'LL MAKE A DOZEN COPIES, ALL GOOD, ANTI-C.R.U.S.H. AGENTS!
WE'LL SEND ONE OF THESE TO EACH OF THE TWELVE MAIN C.R.U.S.H. BASES ALL OVER THE WORLD!
GREAT! THAT OUGHT TO PUT A CRIMP IN THEIR ORGANIZATION!
BOYS, I DON'T KNOW HOW TO THANK YOU! HOW WOULD YOU LIKE A RIDE IN OUR LATEST JET PLANE?
WHERE'D THEY GO, HOPKINS? I THOUGHT THEY'D BE THRILLED!
(SIGH) WHAT'S THE MATTER WITH KIDS TODAY?
ZIP!
THE END. 10

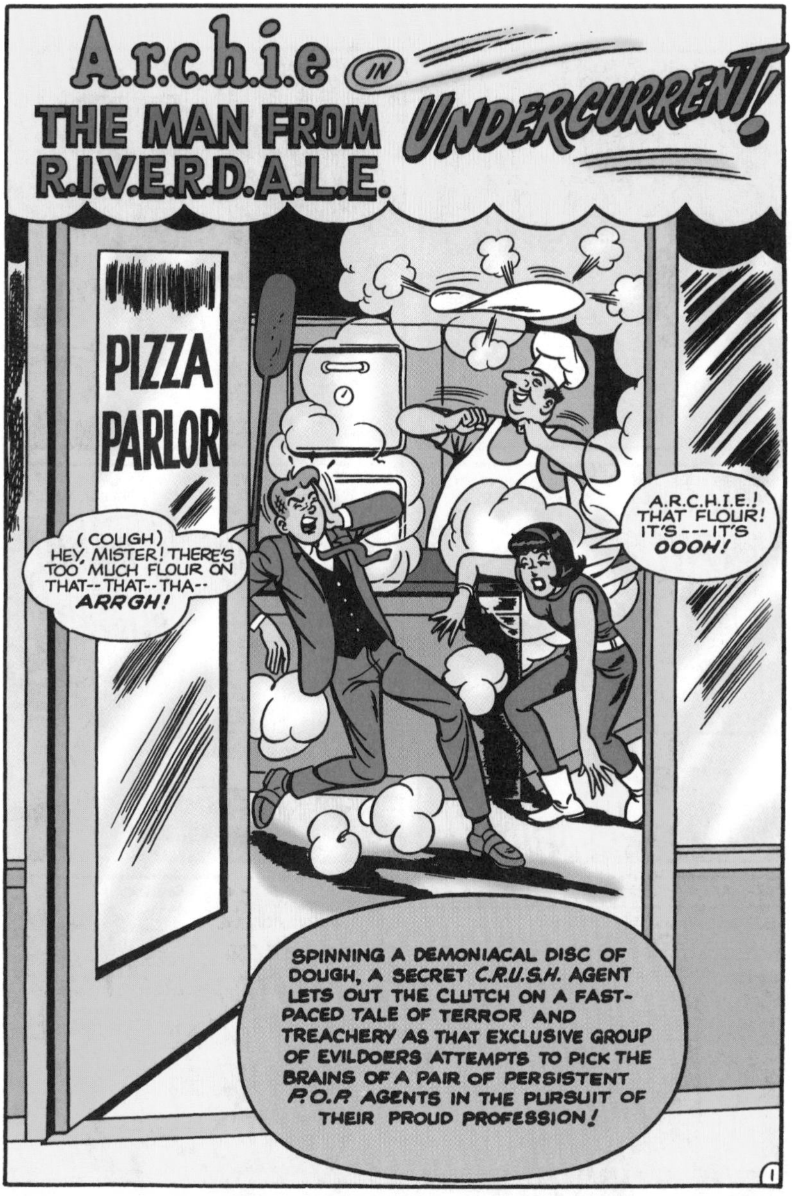
Archie IN UNDERCURRENT!
THE MAN FROM R.I.V.E.R.D.A.L.E.
PIZZA PARLOR
(COUGH) HEY, MISTER! THERE'S TOO MUCH FLOUR ON THAT--THAT--THA-- ARRGH!
A.R.C.H.I.E.! THAT FLOUR! IT'S---IT'S OOOH!
SPINNING A DEMONIACAL DISC OF DOUGH, A SECRET C.R.U.S.H. AGENT LETS OUT THE CLUTCH ON A FAST-PACED TALE OF TERROR AND TREACHERY AS THAT EXCLUSIVE GROUP OF EVILDOERS ATTEMPTS TO PICK THE BRAINS OF A PAIR OF PERSISTENT P.O.P. AGENTS IN THE PURSUIT OF THEIR PROUD PROFESSION!
1

Story: Frank Doyle Pencils: Bob White
Inks & Letters: Mario Acquaviva

Originally printed in LIFE WITH ARCHIE #54, OCTOBER 1966

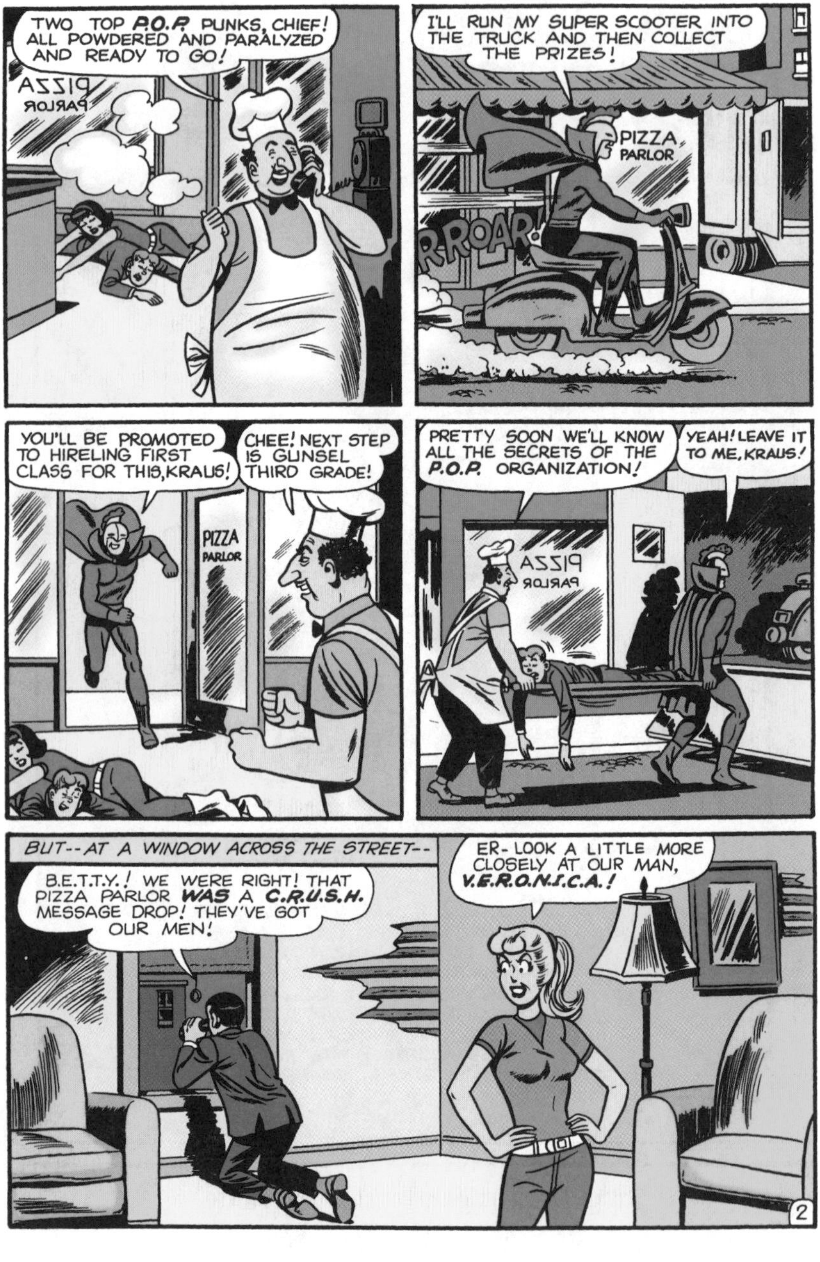
TWO TOP P.O.P. PUNKS, CHIEF! ALL POWDERED AND PARALYZED AND READY TO GO!
PIZZA PARLOR
I'LL RUN MY SUPER SCOOTER INTO THE TRUCK AND THEN COLLECT THE PRIZES!
PIZZA PARLOR
R-ROAR!
YOU'LL BE PROMOTED TO HIRELING FIRST CLASS FOR THIS, KRAUS!
CHEE! NEXT STEP IS GUNSEL THIRD GRADE!
PIZZA PARLOR
PRETTY SOON WE'LL KNOW ALL THE SECRETS OF THE P.O.P. ORGANIZATION!
YEAH! LEAVE IT TO ME, KRAUS!
PIZZA PARLOR
BUT--AT A WINDOW ACROSS THE STREET--
B.E.T.T.Y.! WE WERE RIGHT! THAT PIZZA PARLOR WAS A C.R.U.S.H. MESSAGE DROP! THEY'VE GOT OUR MEN!
ER- LOOK A LITTLE MORE CLOSELY AT OUR MAN, V.E.R.O.N.I.C.A.!
2

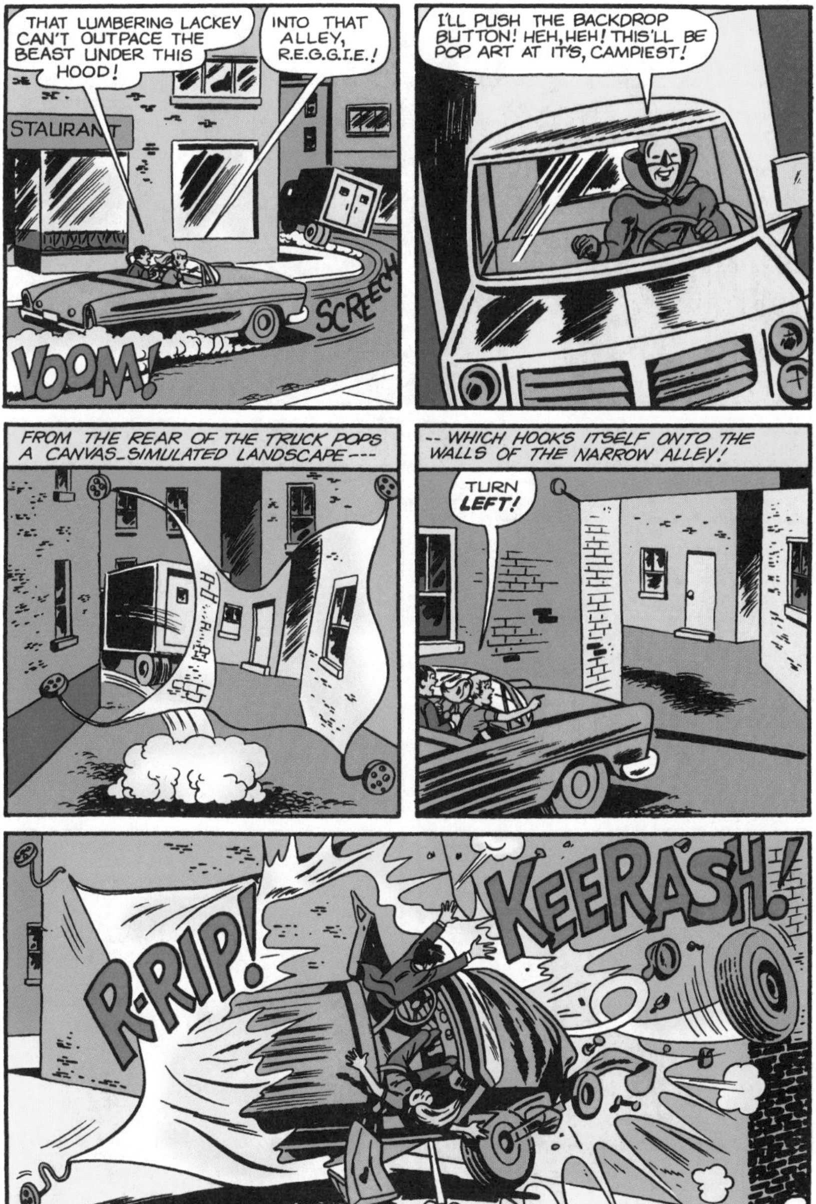
THAT LUMBERING LACKEY CAN'T OUTPACE THE BEAST UNDER THIS HOOD!
INTO THAT ALLEY, R.E.G.G.I.E.!
STAURANT
SCREECH
VOOM!
I'LL PUSH THE BACKDROP BUTTON! HEH, HEH! THIS'LL BE POP ART AT IT'S, CAMPIEST!
FROM THE REAR OF THE TRUCK POPS A CANVAS-SIMULATED LANDSCAPE---
-- WHICH HOOKS ITSELF ONTO THE WALLS OF THE NARROW ALLEY!
TURN LEFT!
R-RIP!
KEERASH!
3

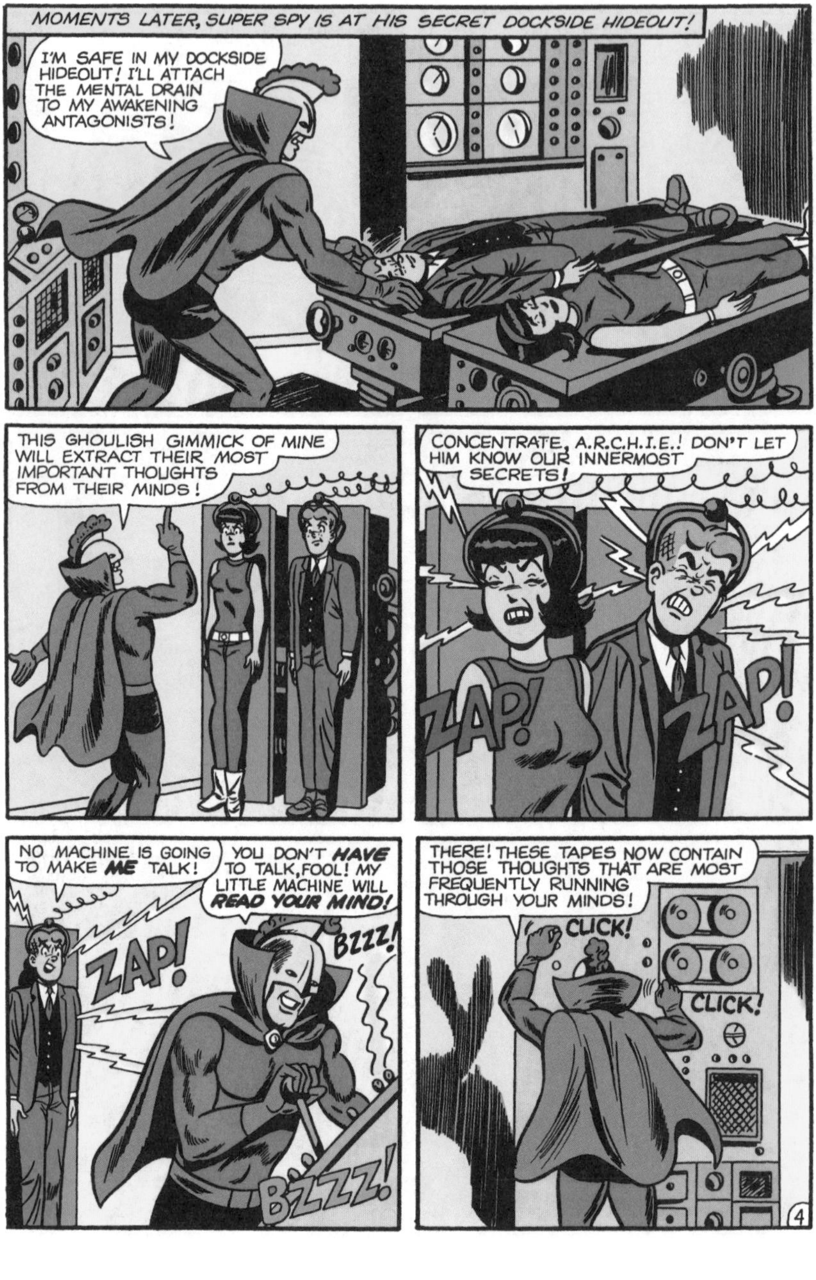
MOMENTS LATER, SUPER SPY IS AT HIS SECRET DOCKSIDE HIDEOUT!
I'M SAFE IN MY DOCKSIDE HIDEOUT! I'LL ATTACH THE MENTAL DRAIN TO MY AWAKENING ANTAGONISTS!
THIS GHOULISH GIMMICK OF MINE WILL EXTRACT THEIR MOST IMPORTANT THOUGHTS FROM THEIR MINDS!
CONCENTRATE, A.R.C.H.I.E.! DON'T LET HIM KNOW OUR INNERMOST SECRETS!
ZAP!
ZAP!
NO MACHINE IS GOING TO MAKE **ME** TALK!
YOU DON'T **HAVE** TO TALK, FOOL! MY LITTLE MACHINE WILL **READ YOUR MIND!**
ZAP!
BZZZ!
BZZZ!
THERE! THESE TAPES NOW CONTAIN THOSE THOUGHTS THAT ARE MOST FREQUENTLY RUNNING THROUGH YOUR MINDS!
CLICK!
CLICK!
4

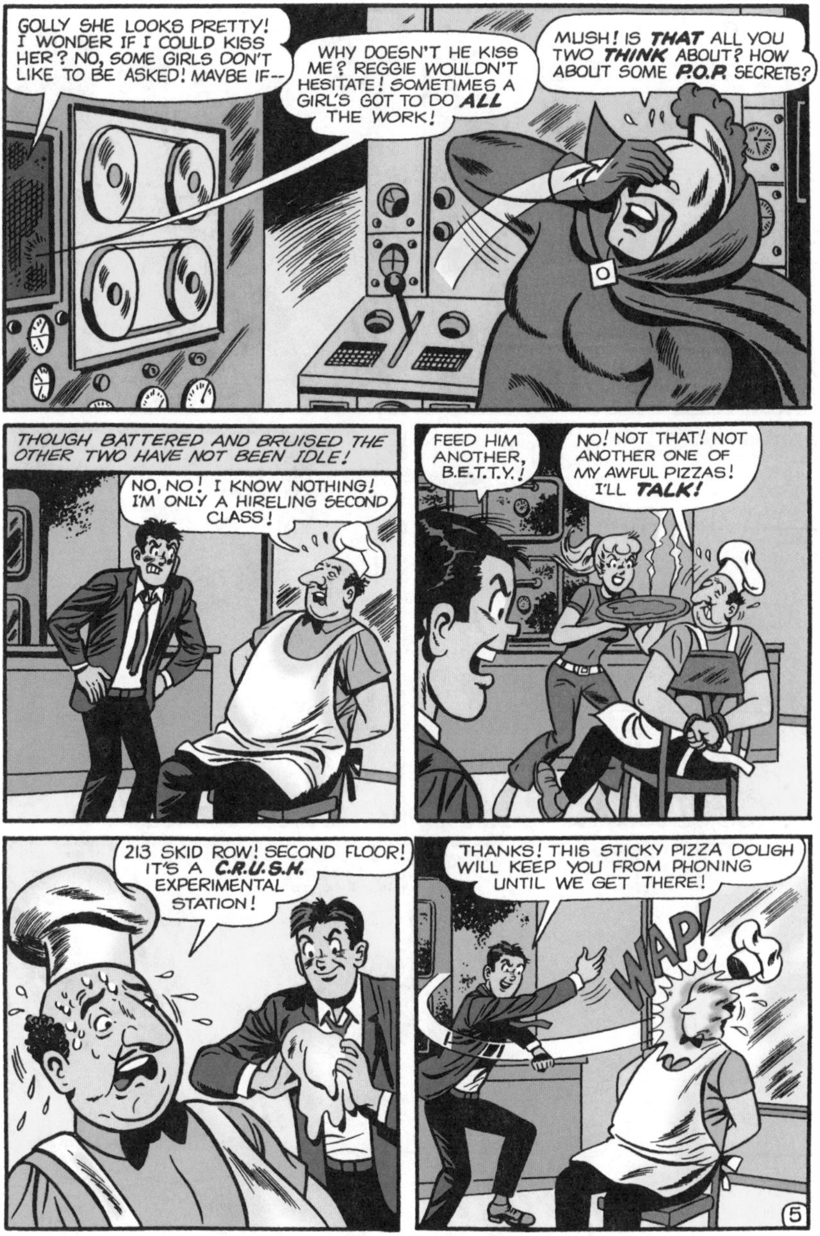
GOLLY SHE LOOKS PRETTY! I WONDER IF I COULD KISS HER? NO, SOME GIRLS DON'T LIKE TO BE ASKED! MAYBE IF--
WHY DOESN'T HE KISS ME? REGGIE WOULDN'T HESITATE! SOMETIMES A GIRL'S GOT TO DO **ALL** THE WORK!
MUSH! IS **THAT** ALL YOU TWO **THINK** ABOUT? HOW ABOUT SOME **P.O.P.** SECRETS?
THOUGH BATTERED AND BRUISED THE OTHER TWO HAVE NOT BEEN IDLE!
NO, NO! I KNOW NOTHING! I'M ONLY A HIRELING SECOND CLASS!
FEED HIM ANOTHER, B.E.T.T.Y.!
NO! NOT THAT! NOT ANOTHER ONE OF MY AWFUL PIZZAS! I'LL **TALK!**
213 SKID ROW! SECOND FLOOR! IT'S A **C.R.U.S.H.** EXPERIMENTAL STATION!
THANKS! THIS STICKY PIZZA DOUGH WILL KEEP YOU FROM PHONING UNTIL WE GET THERE!
WAP!
5

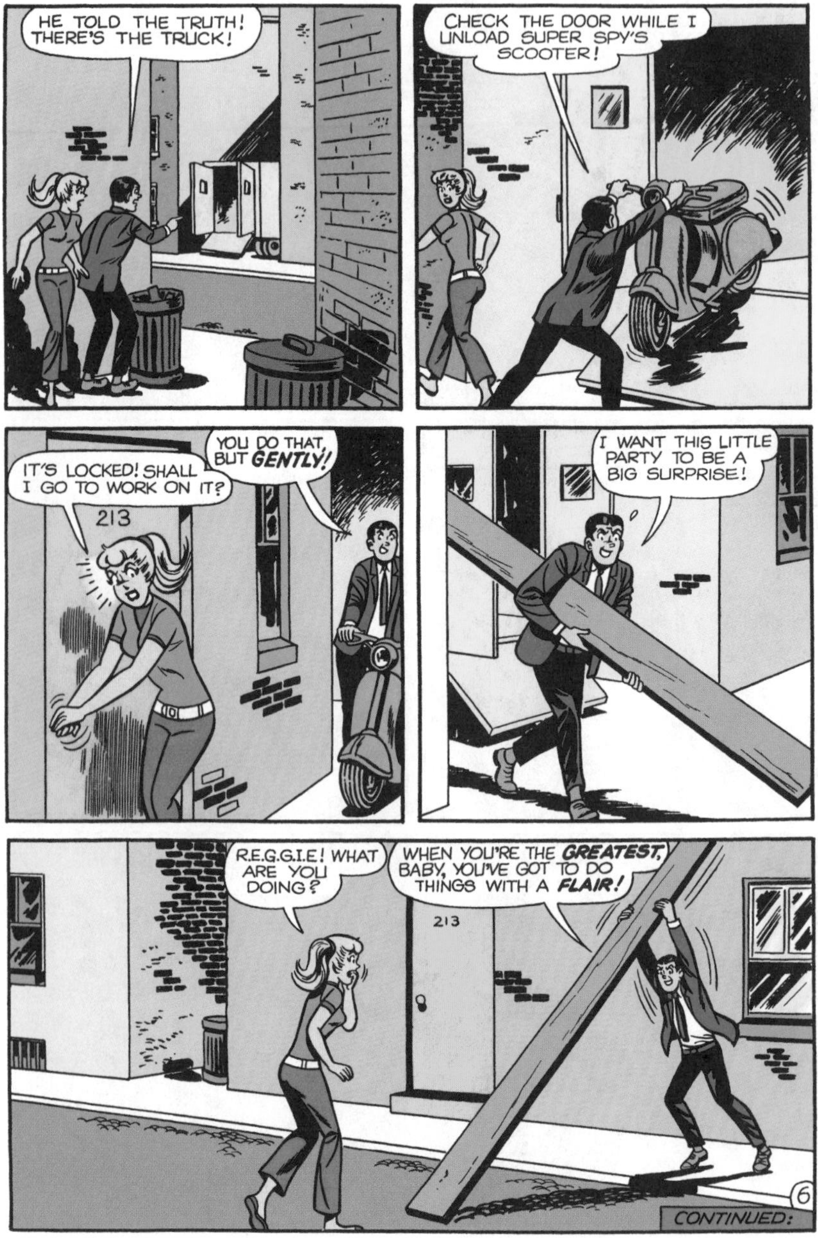
HE TOLD THE TRUTH! THERE'S THE TRUCK!
CHECK THE DOOR WHILE I UNLOAD SUPER SPY'S SCOOTER!
IT'S LOCKED! SHALL I GO TO WORK ON IT?
213
YOU DO THAT, BUT **GENTLY**!
I WANT THIS LITTLE PARTY TO BE A BIG SURPRISE!
R.E.G.G.I.E! WHAT ARE YOU DOING?
213
WHEN YOU'RE THE **GREATEST**, BABY, YOU'VE GOT TO DO THINGS WITH A **FLAIR**!
6
CONTINUED:

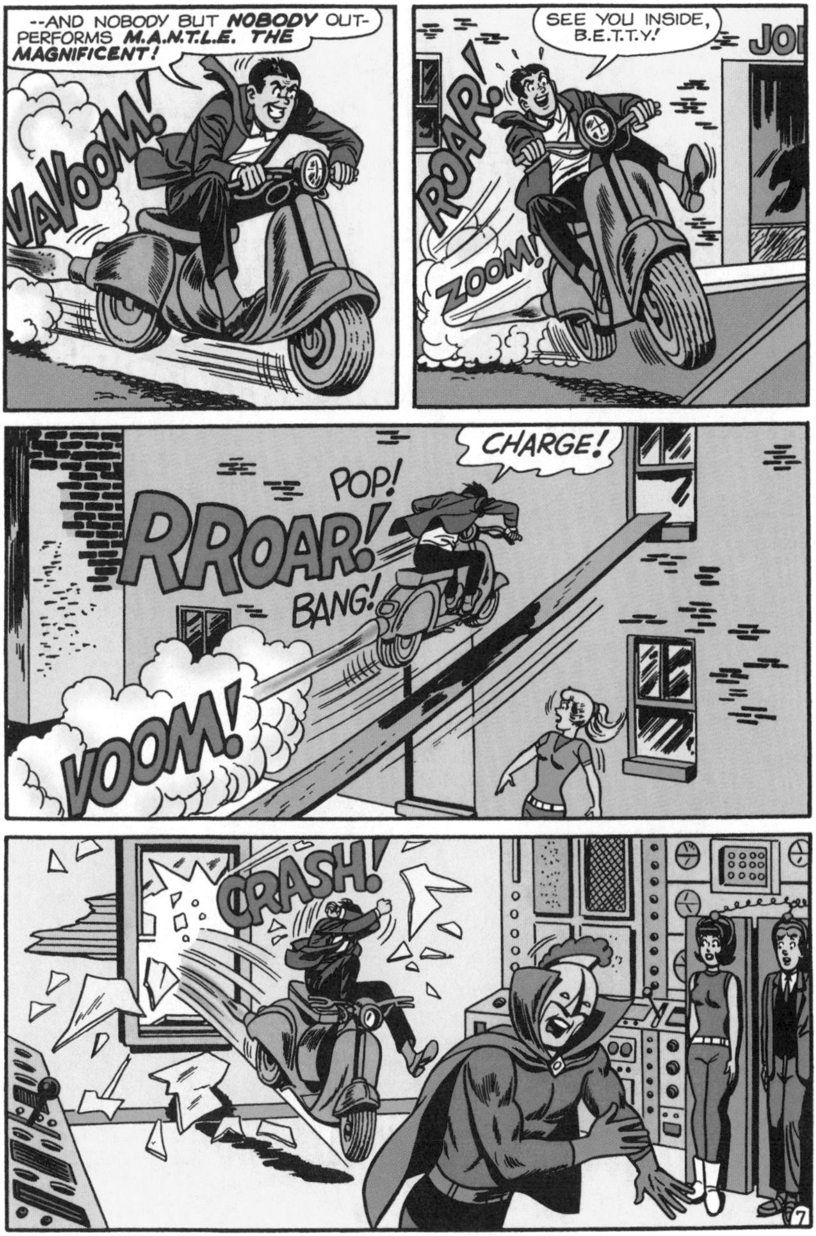
--AND NOBODY BUT NOBODY OUT-PERFORMS M.A.N.T.L.E. THE MAGNIFICENT!
VAVOOM!
SEE YOU INSIDE, B.E.T.T.Y.!
ROAR!
ZOOM!
CHARGE!
POP!
RROAR!
BANG!
VOOM!
CRASH!

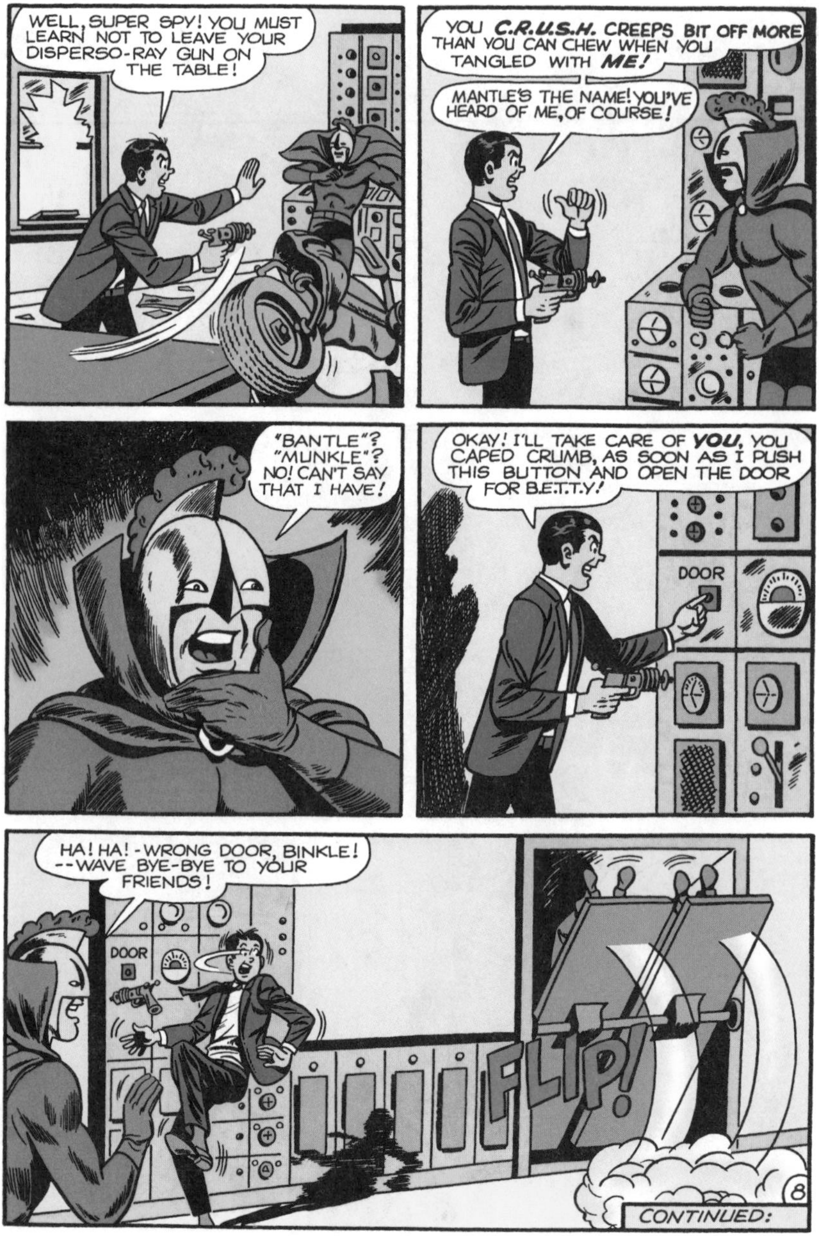
WELL, SUPER SPY! YOU MUST LEARN NOT TO LEAVE YOUR DISPERSO-RAY GUN ON THE TABLE!
YOU C.R.U.S.H. CREEPS BIT OFF MORE THAN YOU CAN CHEW WHEN YOU TANGLED WITH ME!
MANTLE'S THE NAME! YOU'VE HEARD OF ME, OF COURSE!
"BANTLE"? "MUNKLE"? NO! CAN'T SAY THAT I HAVE!
OKAY! I'LL TAKE CARE OF YOU, YOU CAPED CRUMB, AS SOON AS I PUSH THIS BUTTON AND OPEN THE DOOR FOR B.E.T.T.Y.!
DOOR
HA! HA! -WRONG DOOR, BINKLE! --WAVE BYE-BYE TO YOUR FRIENDS!
DOOR
FLIP!
8
CONTINUED:

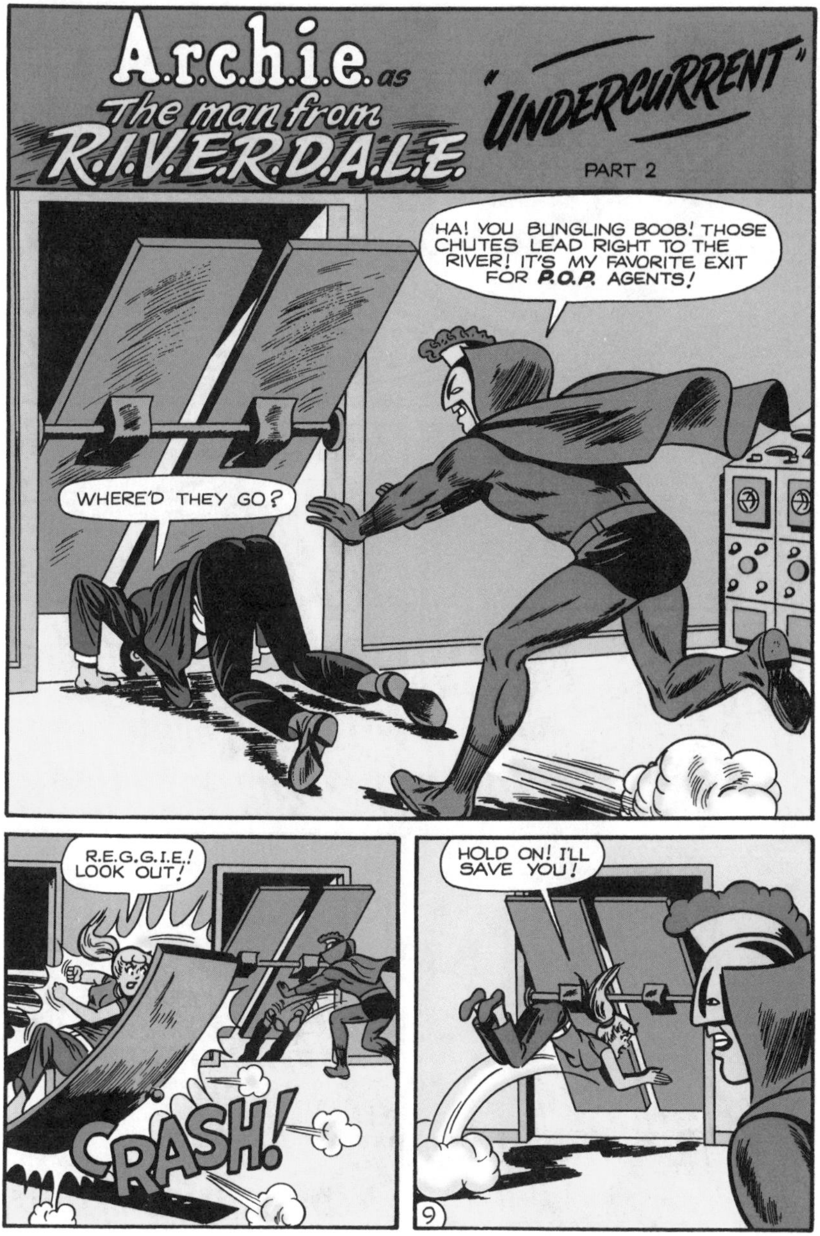
Archie as
The man from
R.I.V.E.R.D.A.L.E.
"UNDERCURRENT"
PART 2
HA! YOU BUNGLING BOOB! THOSE CHUTES LEAD RIGHT TO THE RIVER! IT'S MY FAVORITE EXIT FOR P.O.P. AGENTS!
WHERE'D THEY GO?
R.E.G.G.I.E.! LOOK OUT!
CRASH!
HOLD ON! I'LL SAVE YOU!
9

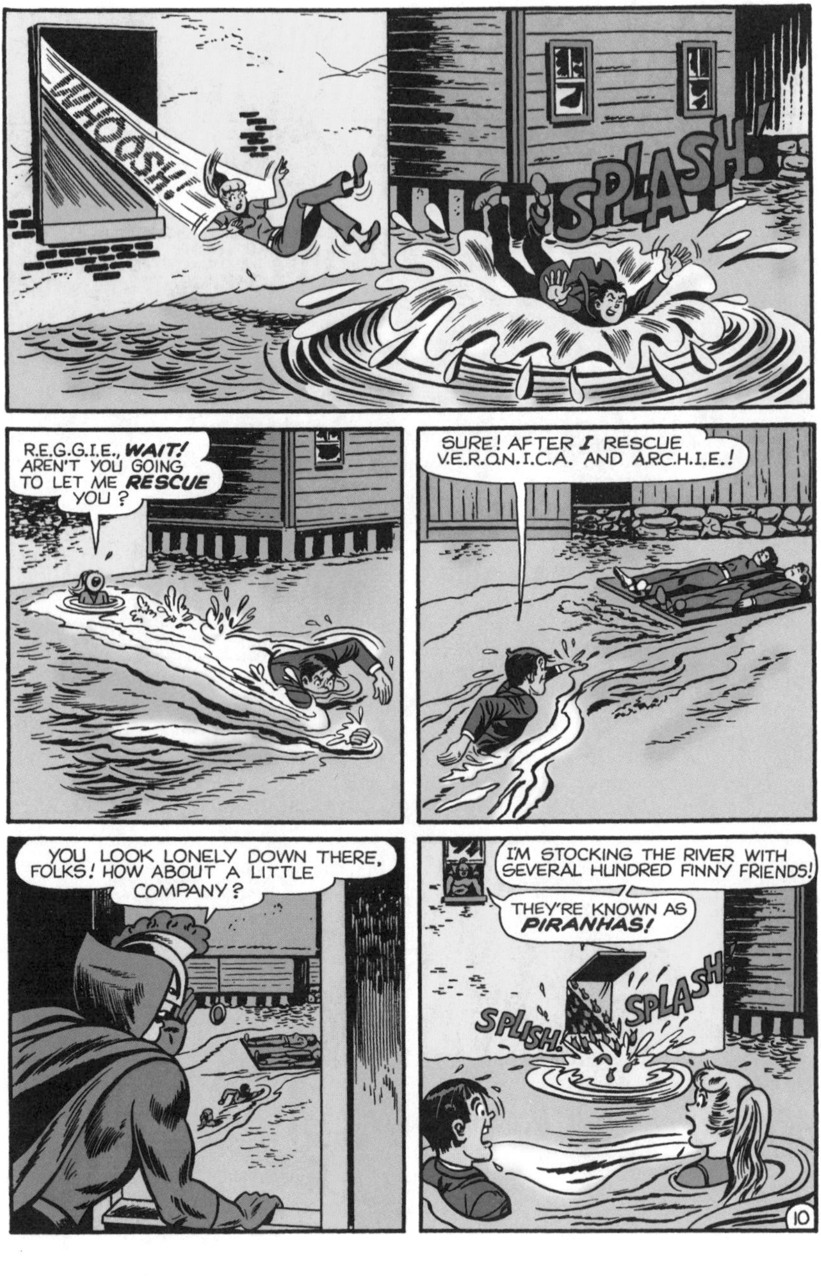
WHOOSH!!
SPLASH!
R.E.G.G.I.E., WAIT! AREN'T YOU GOING TO LET ME RESCUE YOU?
SURE! AFTER I RESCUE V.E.R.O.N.I.C.A. AND A.R.C.H.I.E.!
YOU LOOK LONELY DOWN THERE, FOLKS! HOW ABOUT A LITTLE COMPANY?
I'M STOCKING THE RIVER WITH SEVERAL HUNDRED FINNY FRIENDS!
THEY'RE KNOWN AS PIRANHAS!
SPLISH!
SPLASH
10

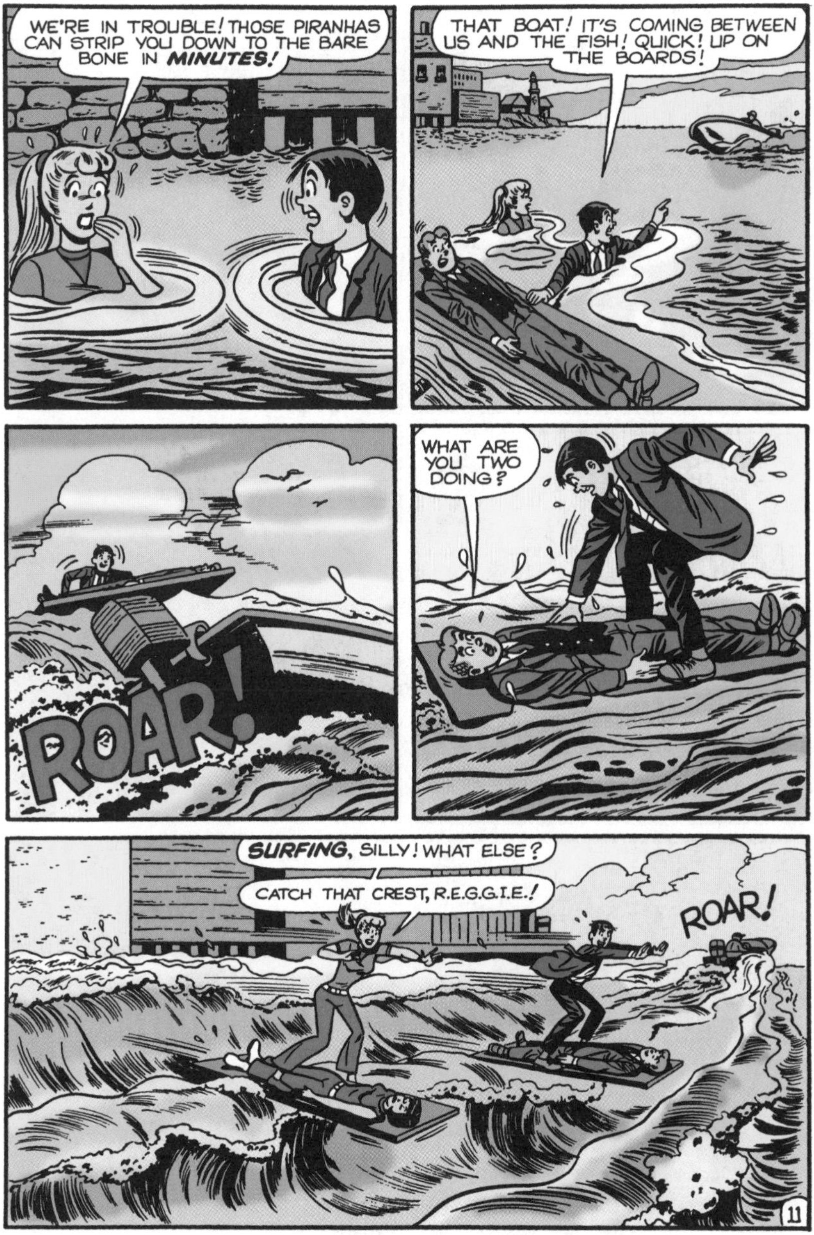
WE'RE IN TROUBLE! THOSE PIRANHAS CAN STRIP YOU DOWN TO THE BARE BONE IN MINUTES!
THAT BOAT! IT'S COMING BETWEEN US AND THE FISH! QUICK! UP ON THE BOARDS!
ROAR!
WHAT ARE YOU TWO DOING?
SURFING, SILLY! WHAT ELSE?
CATCH THAT CREST, R.E.G.G.I.E.!
ROAR!
11

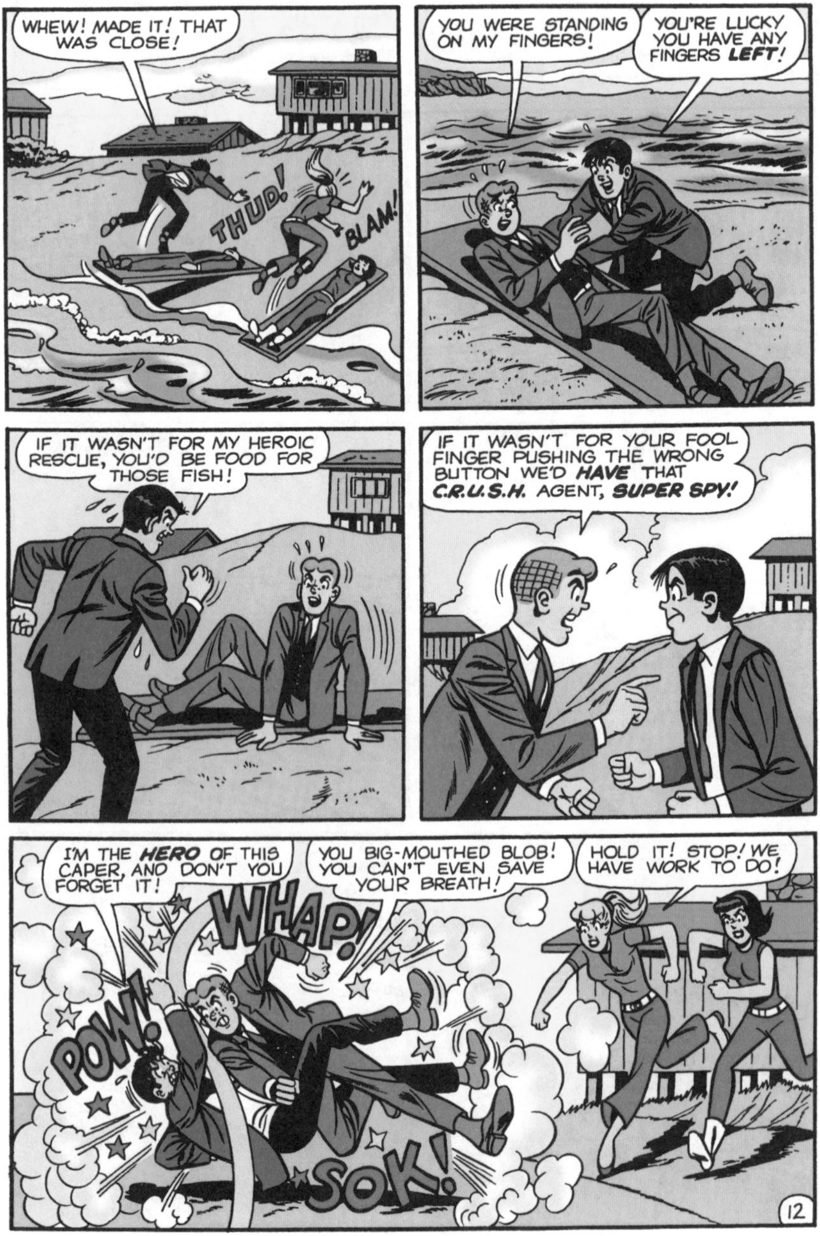
WHEW! MADE IT! THAT WAS CLOSE!
THUD!
BLAM!
YOU WERE STANDING ON MY FINGERS!
YOU'RE LUCKY YOU HAVE ANY FINGERS LEFT!
IF IT WASN'T FOR MY HEROIC RESCUE, YOU'D BE FOOD FOR THOSE FISH!
IF IT WASN'T FOR YOUR FOOL FINGER PUSHING THE WRONG BUTTON WE'D HAVE THAT C.R.U.S.H. AGENT, SUPER SPY!
I'M THE HERO OF THIS CAPER, AND DON'T YOU FORGET IT!
YOU BIG-MOUTHED BLOB! YOU CAN'T EVEN SAVE YOUR BREATH!
HOLD IT! STOP! WE HAVE WORK TO DO!
WHAP!
POW!
SOK!
12

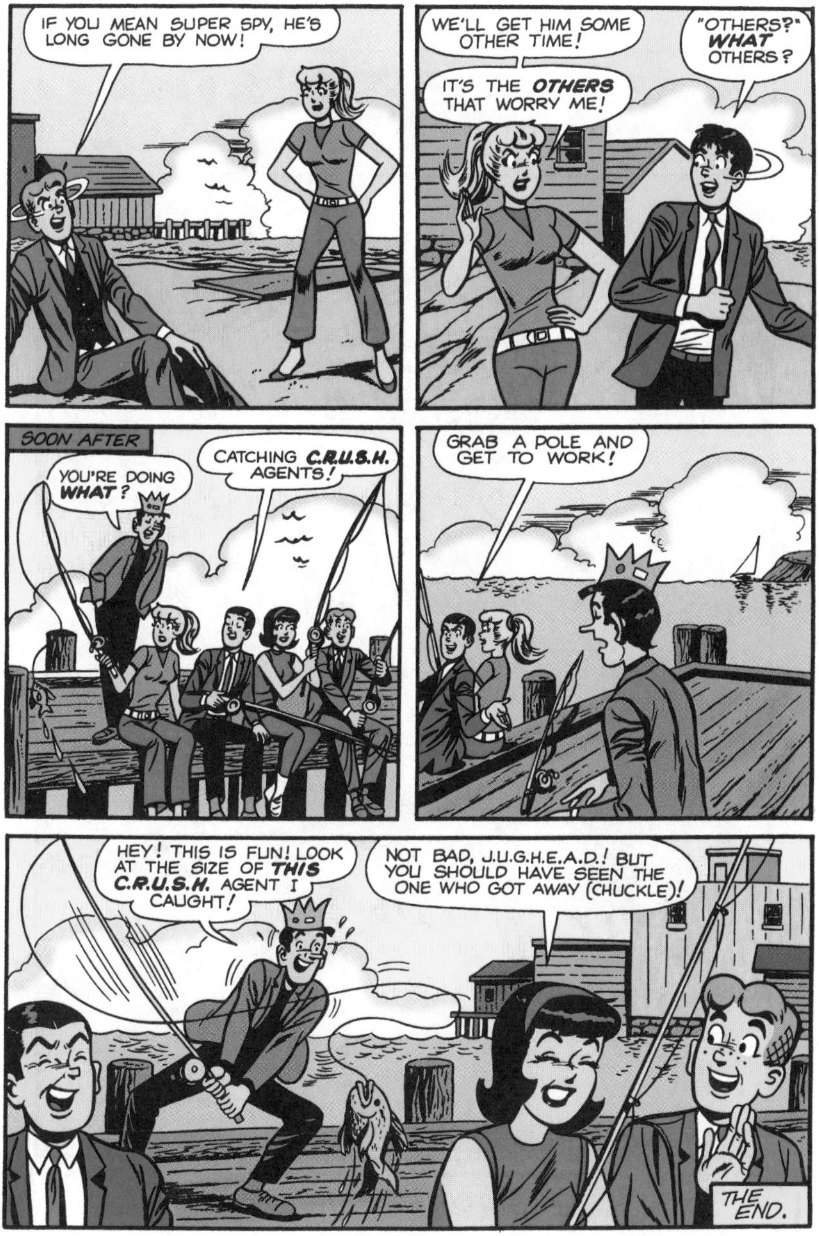

IF YOU MEAN SUPER SPY, HE'S LONG GONE BY NOW!
WE'LL GET HIM SOME OTHER TIME!
IT'S THE **OTHERS** THAT WORRY ME!
"OTHERS?" **WHAT** OTHERS?
SOON AFTER
YOU'RE DOING **WHAT**?
CATCHING **C.R.U.S.H.** AGENTS!
GRAB A POLE AND GET TO WORK!
HEY! THIS IS FUN! LOOK AT THE SIZE OF **THIS C.R.U.S.H.** AGENT I CAUGHT!
NOT BAD, J.U.G.H.E.A.D.! BUT YOU SHOULD HAVE SEEN THE ONE WHO GOT AWAY (CHUCKLE)!
THE END.

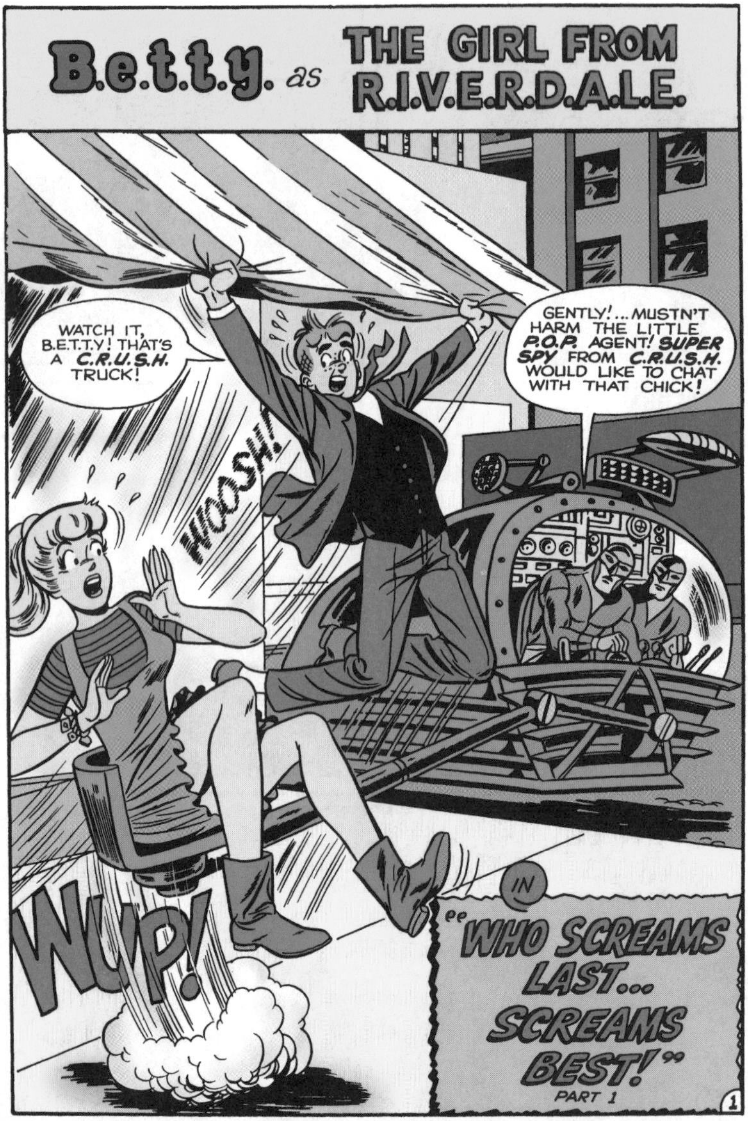
B.e.t.t.y. as THE GIRL FROM R.I.V.E.R.D.A.L.E.
WATCH IT, B.E.T.T.Y! THAT'S A C.R.U.S.H. TRUCK!
GENTLY!...MUSTN'T HARM THE LITTLE P.O.P. AGENT! SUPER SPY FROM C.R.U.S.H. WOULD LIKE TO CHAT WITH THAT CHICK!
WOOSH!!
WUP!
IN "WHO SCREAMS LAST... SCREAMS BEST!" PART 1
1

Story: Frank Doyle Pencils: Bob White
Inks & Letters: Mario Acquaviva

Originally printed in LIFE WITH ARCHIE #54, OCTOBER 1966

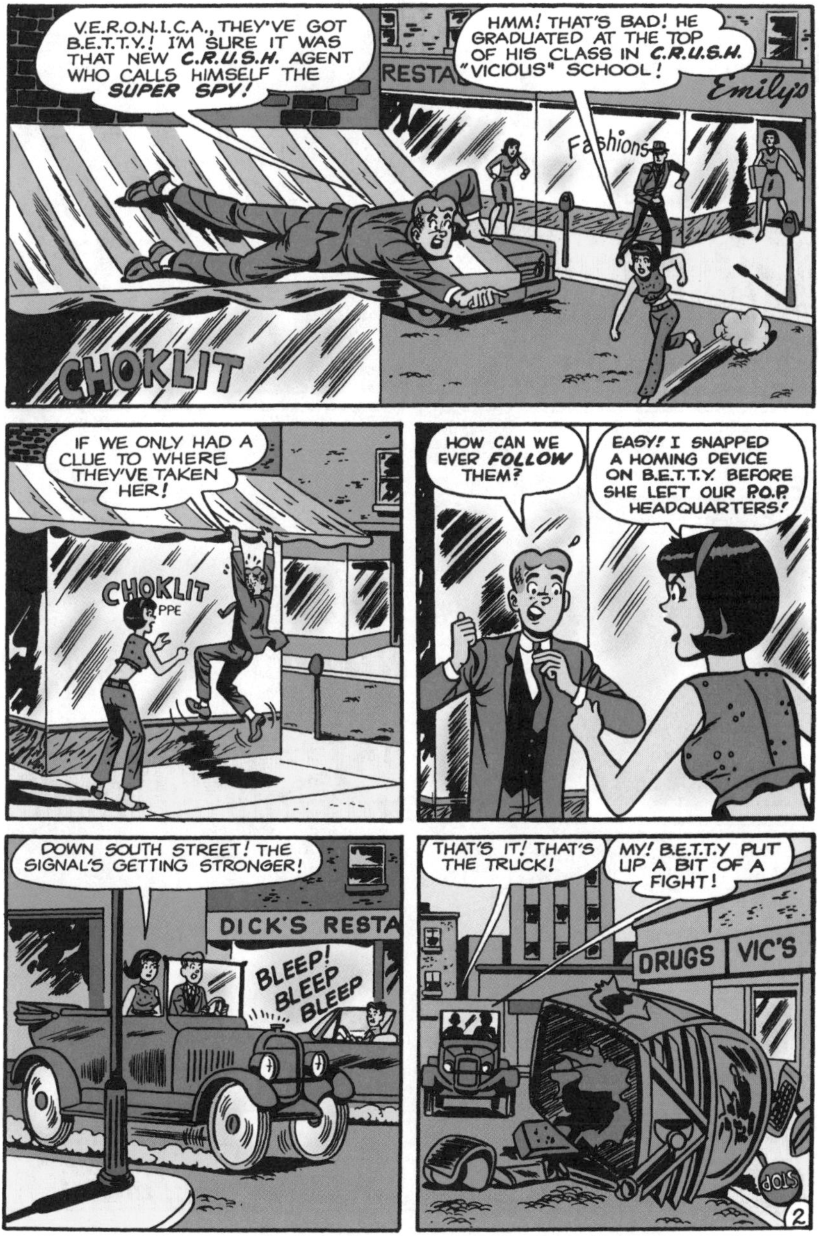
V.E.R.O.N.I.C.A., THEY'VE GOT B.E.T.T.Y.! I'M SURE IT WAS THAT NEW C.R.U.S.H. AGENT WHO CALLS HIMSELF THE SUPER SPY!
HMM! THAT'S BAD! HE GRADUATED AT THE TOP OF HIS CLASS IN C.R.U.S.H. "VICIOUS" SCHOOL!
RESTA
Emily's
Fashions
CHOKLIT
IF WE ONLY HAD A CLUE TO WHERE THEY'VE TAKEN HER!
CHOKLIT
PPE
HOW CAN WE EVER FOLLOW THEM?
EASY! I SNAPPED A HOMING DEVICE ON B.E.T.T.Y. BEFORE SHE LEFT OUR P.O.P. HEADQUARTERS!
DOWN SOUTH STREET! THE SIGNAL'S GETTING STRONGER!
DICK'S RESTA
BLEEP! BLEEP BLEEP
THAT'S IT! THAT'S THE TRUCK!
MY! B.E.T.T.Y PUT UP A BIT OF A FIGHT!
DRUGS
VIC'S
STOP
2

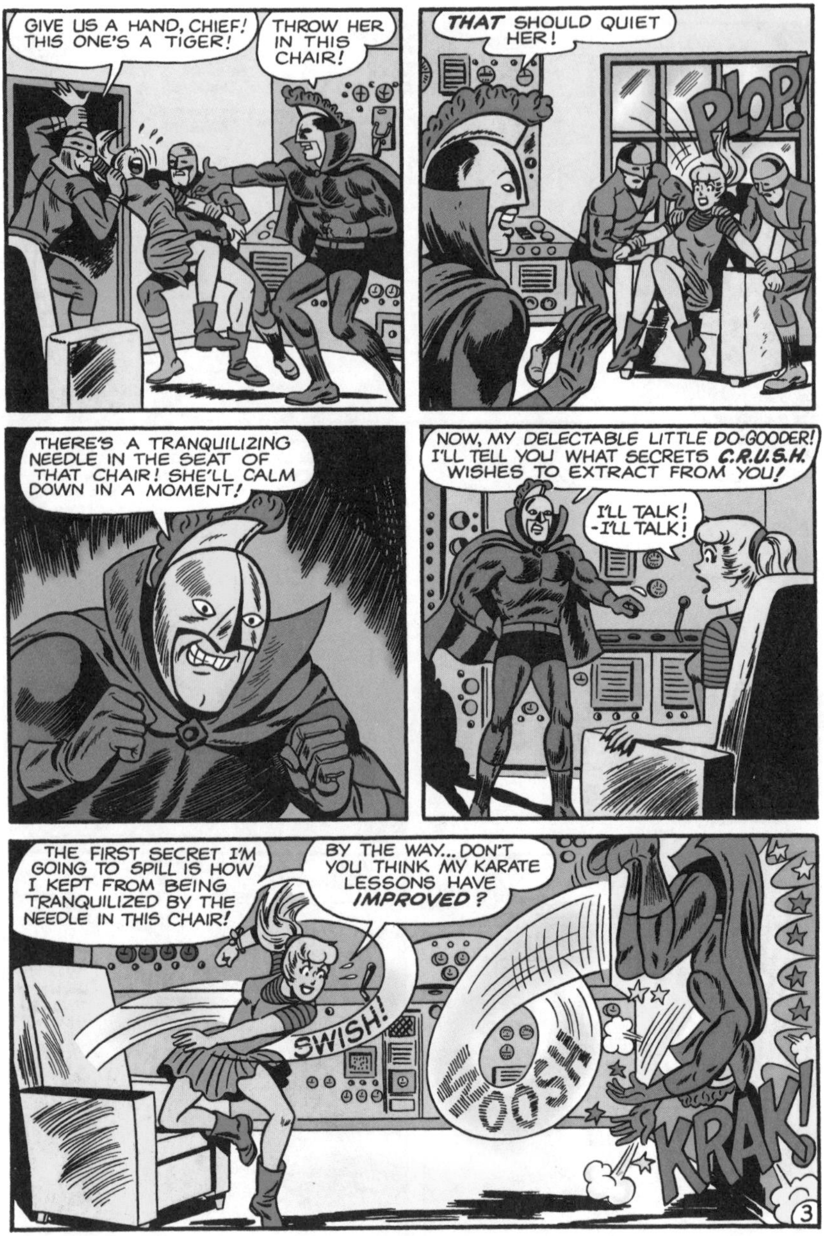
GIVE US A HAND, CHIEF! THIS ONE'S A TIGER!
THROW HER IN THIS CHAIR!
THAT SHOULD QUIET HER!
PLOP!
THERE'S A TRANQUILIZING NEEDLE IN THE SEAT OF THAT CHAIR! SHE'LL CALM DOWN IN A MOMENT!
NOW, MY DELECTABLE LITTLE DO-GOODER! I'LL TELL YOU WHAT SECRETS C.R.U.S.H. WISHES TO EXTRACT FROM YOU!
I'LL TALK! -I'LL TALK!
THE FIRST SECRET I'M GOING TO SPILL IS HOW I KEPT FROM BEING TRANQUILIZED BY THE NEEDLE IN THIS CHAIR!
BY THE WAY... DON'T YOU THINK MY KARATE LESSONS HAVE IMPROVED?
SWISH!
WOOSH
KRAK!
3

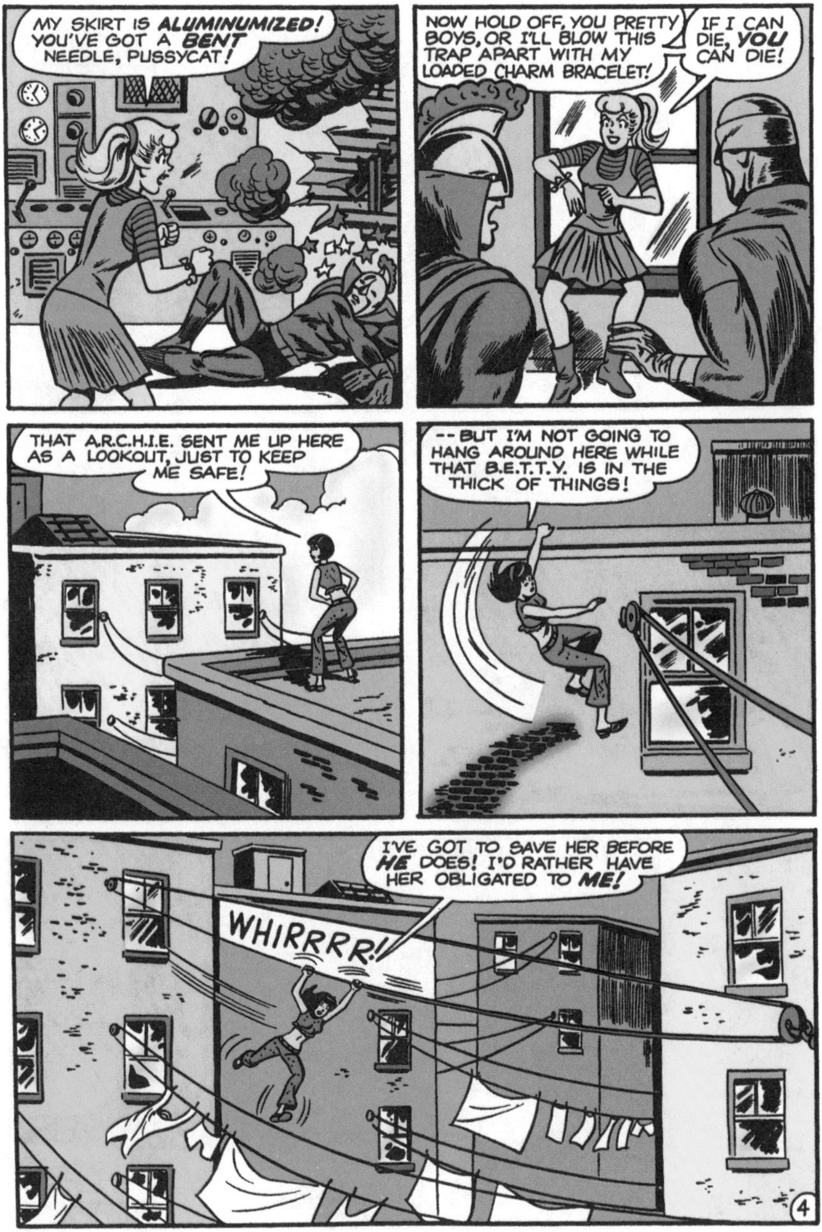
MY SKIRT IS ALUMINUMIZED! YOU'VE GOT A BENT NEEDLE, PUSSYCAT!
NOW HOLD OFF, YOU PRETTY BOYS, OR I'LL BLOW THIS TRAP APART WITH MY LOADED CHARM BRACELET!
IF I CAN DIE, YOU CAN DIE!
THAT A.R.C.H.I.E. SENT ME UP HERE AS A LOOKOUT, JUST TO KEEP ME SAFE!
--BUT I'M NOT GOING TO HANG AROUND HERE WHILE THAT B.E.T.T.Y. IS IN THE THICK OF THINGS!
I'VE GOT TO SAVE HER BEFORE HE DOES! I'D RATHER HAVE HER OBLIGATED TO ME!
WHIRRRR!
4

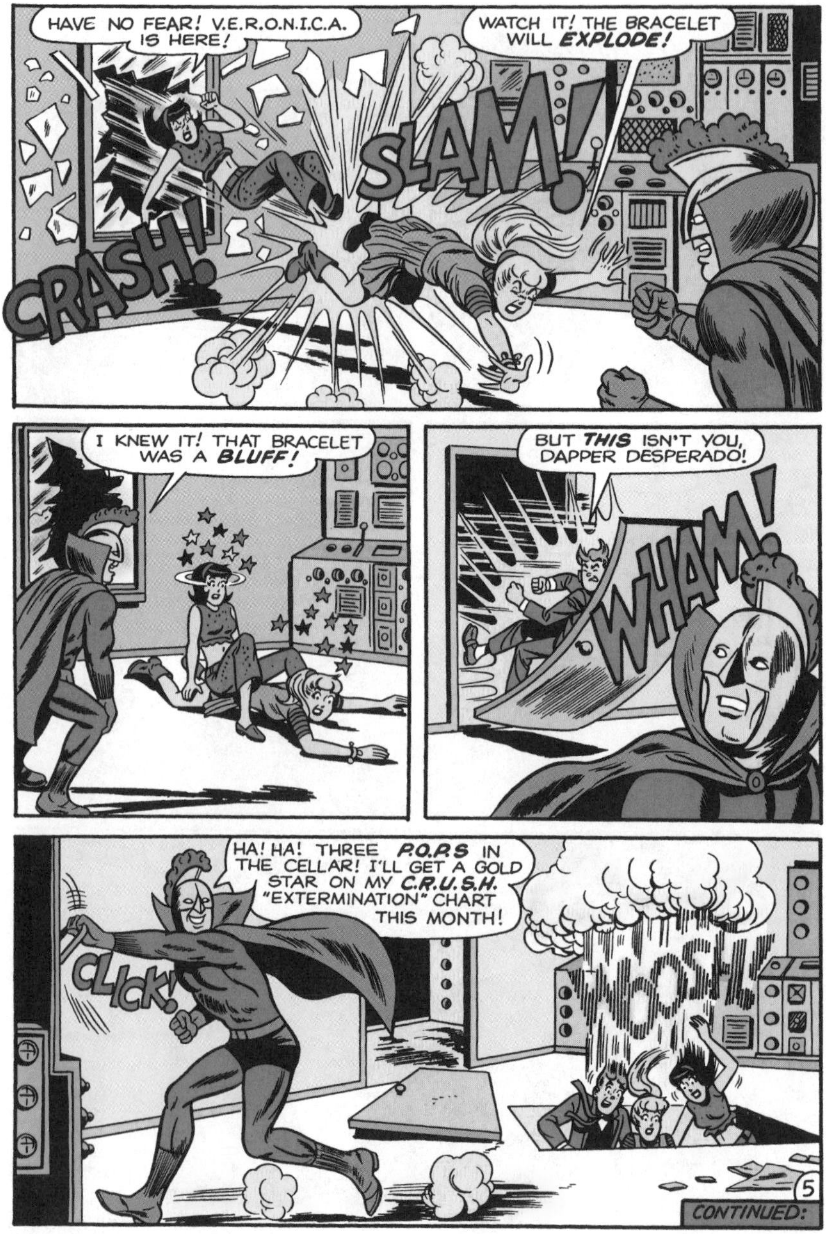
HAVE NO FEAR! V.E.R.O.N.I.C.A. IS HERE!
WATCH IT! THE BRACELET WILL EXPLODE!
SLAM!
CRASH!
I KNEW IT! THAT BRACELET WAS A BLUFF!
BUT THIS ISN'T YOU, DAPPER DESPERADO!
WHAM!
HA! HA! THREE P.O.P.S IN THE CELLAR! I'LL GET A GOLD STAR ON MY C.R.U.S.H. "EXTERMINATION" CHART THIS MONTH!
CLICK!
WOOSH!
5
CONTINUED:

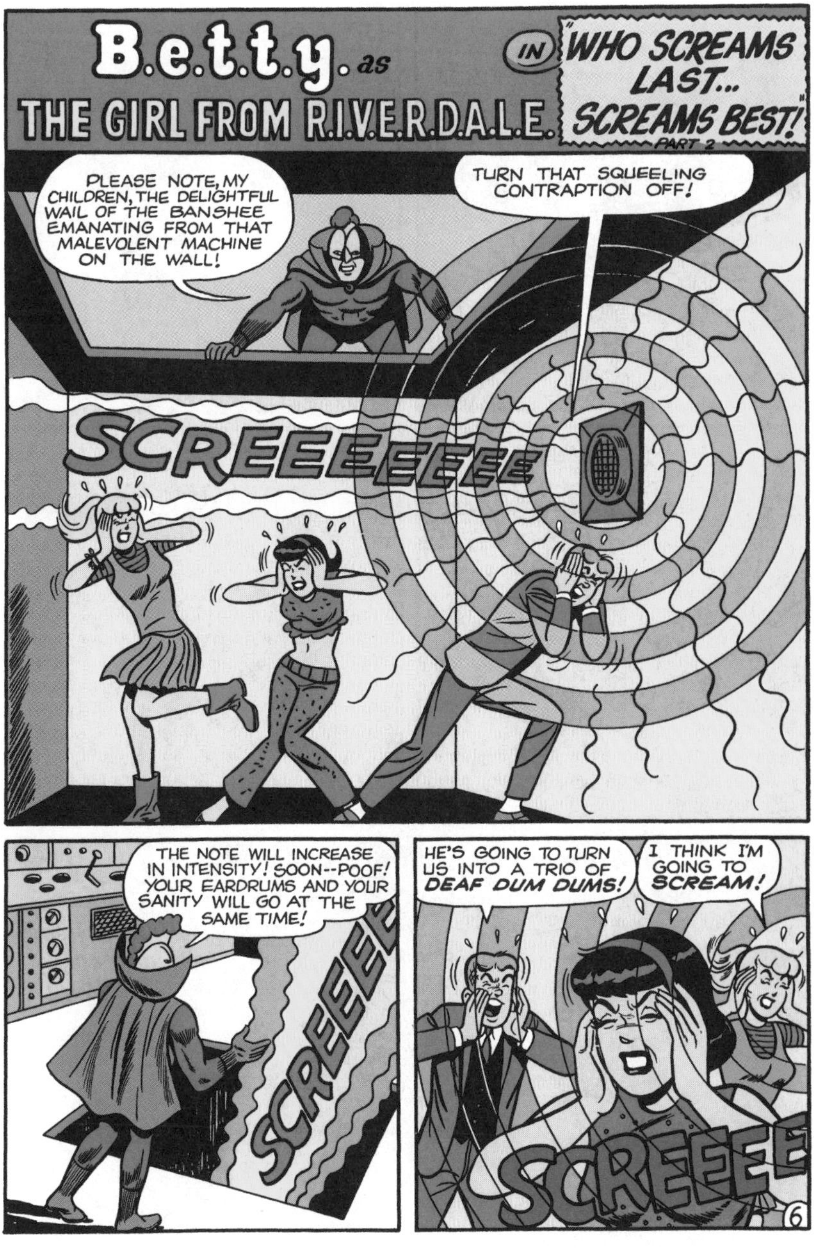
B.e.t.t.y. as
THE GIRL FROM R.I.V.E.R.D.A.L.E.
IN
"WHO SCREAMS LAST... SCREAMS BEST!"
PART 2
PLEASE NOTE, MY CHILDREN, THE DELIGHTFUL WAIL OF THE BANSHEE EMANATING FROM THAT MALEVOLENT MACHINE ON THE WALL!
TURN THAT SQUEELING CONTRAPTION OFF!
SCREEEEEEE
THE NOTE WILL INCREASE IN INTENSITY! SOON--POOF! YOUR EARDRUMS AND YOUR SANITY WILL GO AT THE SAME TIME!
SCREEEE
HE'S GOING TO TURN US INTO A TRIO OF DEAF DUM DUMS!
I THINK I'M GOING TO SCREAM!
SCREEEE
6

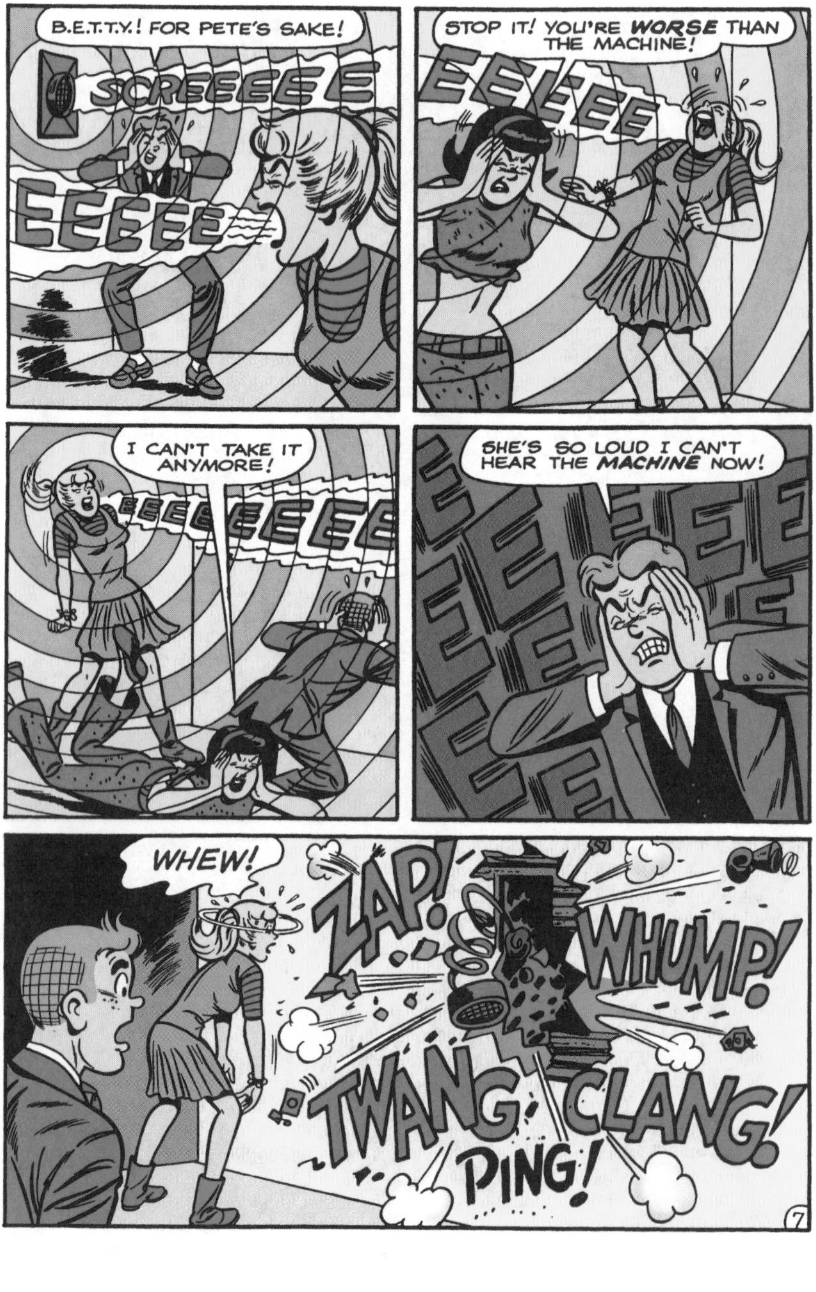
B.E.T.T.Y.! FOR PETE'S SAKE!
SCREEEEEE
EEEEE
STOP IT! YOU'RE WORSE THAN THE MACHINE!
EEEEE
I CAN'T TAKE IT ANYMORE!
EEEEEEEEE
SHE'S SO LOUD I CAN'T HEAR THE MACHINE NOW!
WHEW!
ZAP!
WHUMP!
TWANG!
CLANG!
PING!
7

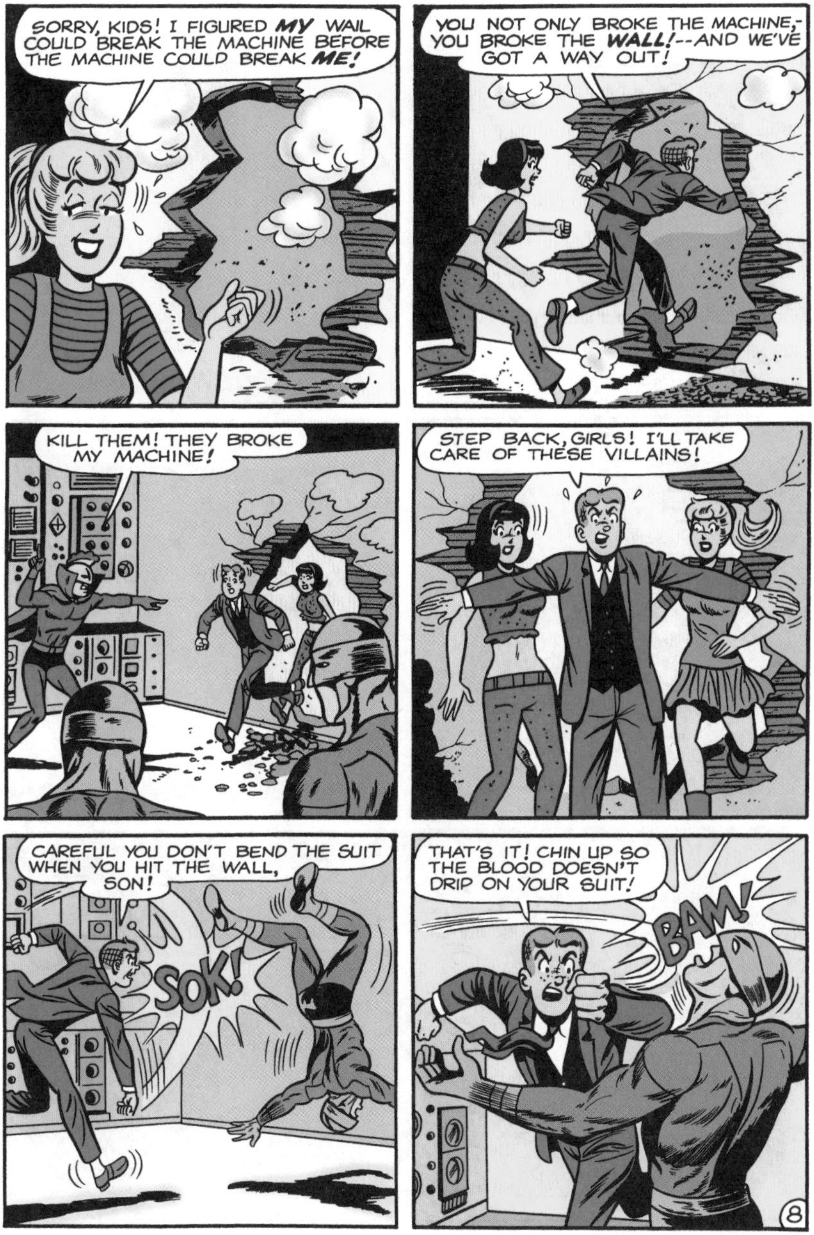
SORRY, KIDS! I FIGURED MY WAIL COULD BREAK THE MACHINE BEFORE THE MACHINE COULD BREAK ME!
YOU NOT ONLY BROKE THE MACHINE,- YOU BROKE THE WALL!--AND WE'VE GOT A WAY OUT!
KILL THEM! THEY BROKE MY MACHINE!
STEP BACK, GIRLS! I'LL TAKE CARE OF THESE VILLAINS!
CAREFUL YOU DON'T BEND THE SUIT WHEN YOU HIT THE WALL, SON!
SOK!
THAT'S IT! CHIN UP SO THE BLOOD DOESN'T DRIP ON YOUR SUIT!
BAM!
8

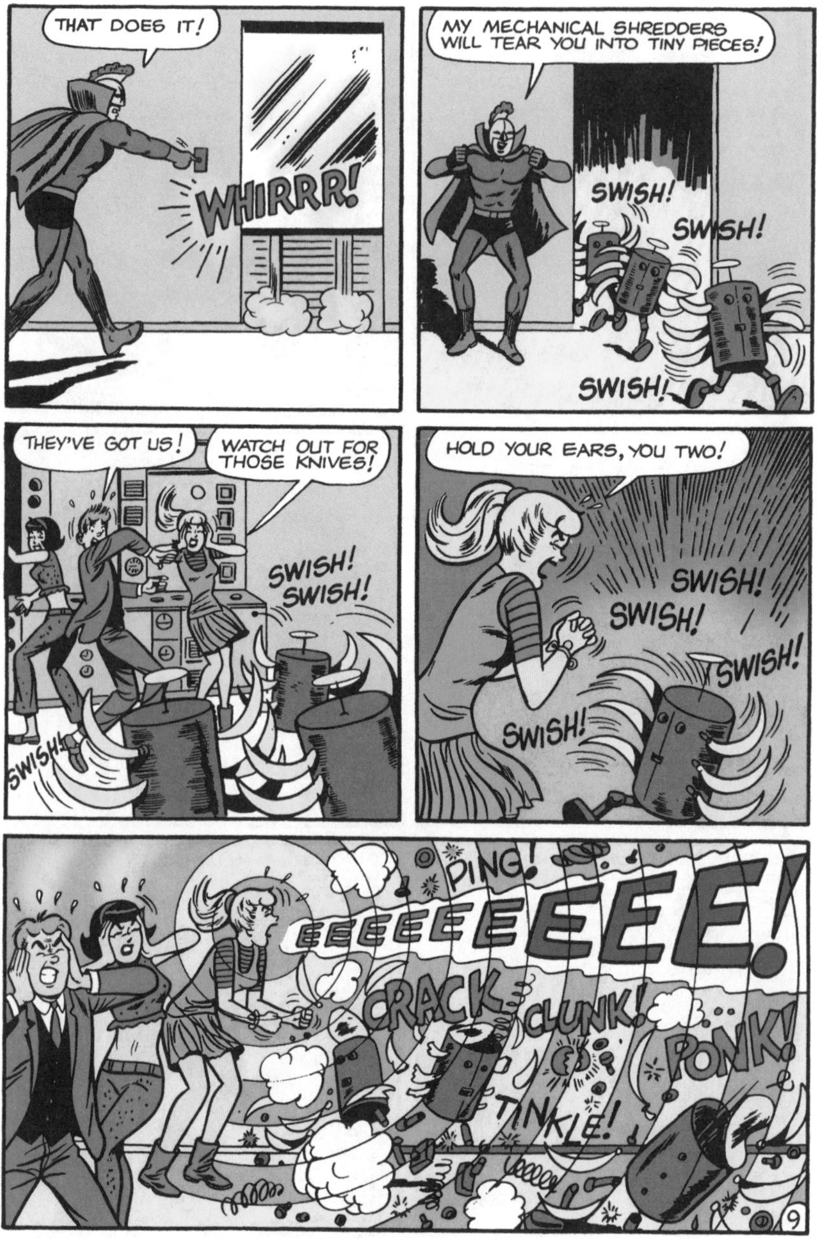
THAT DOES IT!
WHIRRR!
MY MECHANICAL SHREDDERS WILL TEAR YOU INTO TINY PIECES!
SWISH!
SWISH!
SWISH!
THEY'VE GOT US!
WATCH OUT FOR THOSE KNIVES!
SWISH! SWISH!
SWISH!
HOLD YOUR EARS, YOU TWO!
SWISH!
SWISH!
SWISH!
SWISH!
PING!
EEEEEEEEE!
CRACK
CLUNK!
PONK!
TINKLE!
9

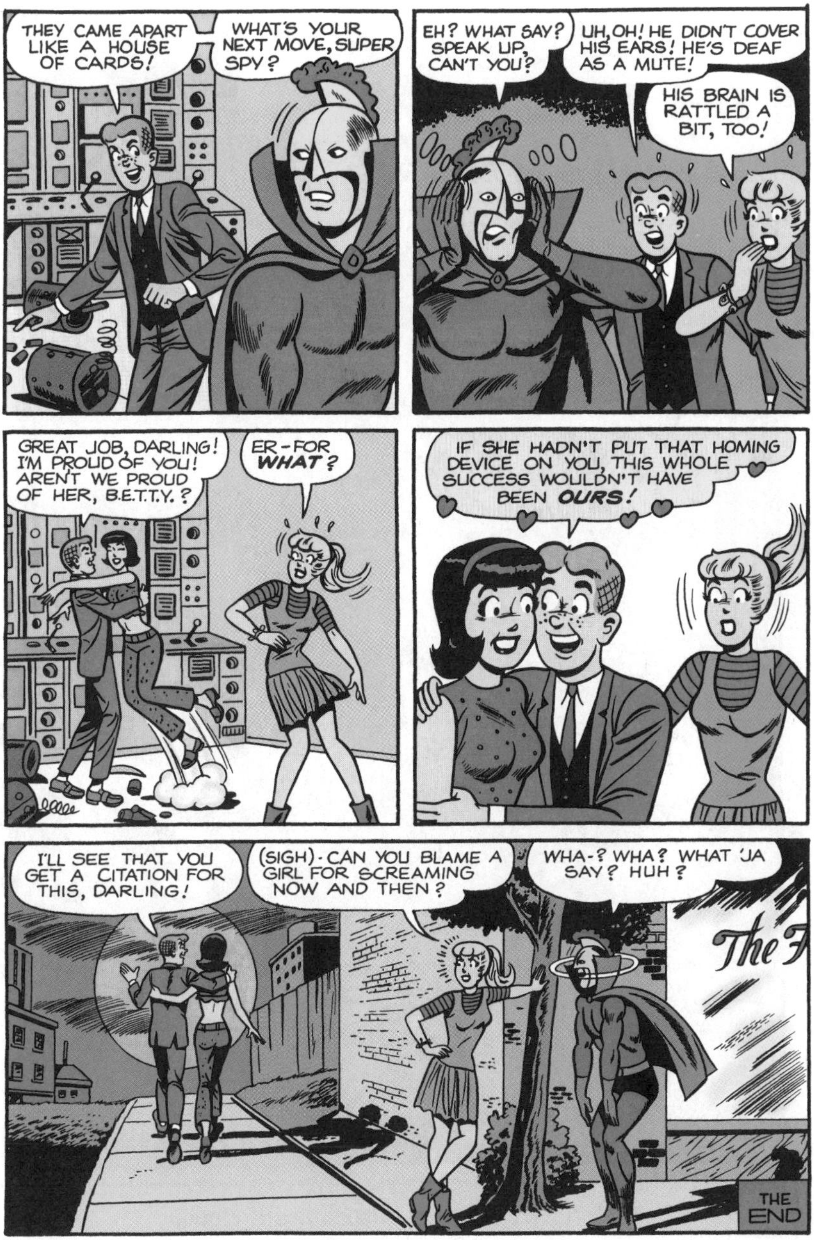
THEY CAME APART LIKE A HOUSE OF CARDS!
WHAT'S YOUR NEXT MOVE, SUPER SPY?
EH? WHAT SAY? SPEAK UP, CAN'T YOU?
UH, OH! HE DIDN'T COVER HIS EARS! HE'S DEAF AS A MUTE!
HIS BRAIN IS RATTLED A BIT, TOO!
GREAT JOB, DARLING! I'M PROUD OF YOU! AREN'T WE PROUD OF HER, B.E.T.T.Y.?
ER-FOR WHAT?
IF SHE HADN'T PUT THAT HOMING DEVICE ON YOU, THIS WHOLE SUCCESS WOULDN'T HAVE BEEN OURS!
I'LL SEE THAT YOU GET A CITATION FOR THIS, DARLING!
(SIGH)-CAN YOU BLAME A GIRL FOR SCREAMING NOW AND THEN?
WHA-? WHA? WHAT 'JA SAY? HUH?
THE END

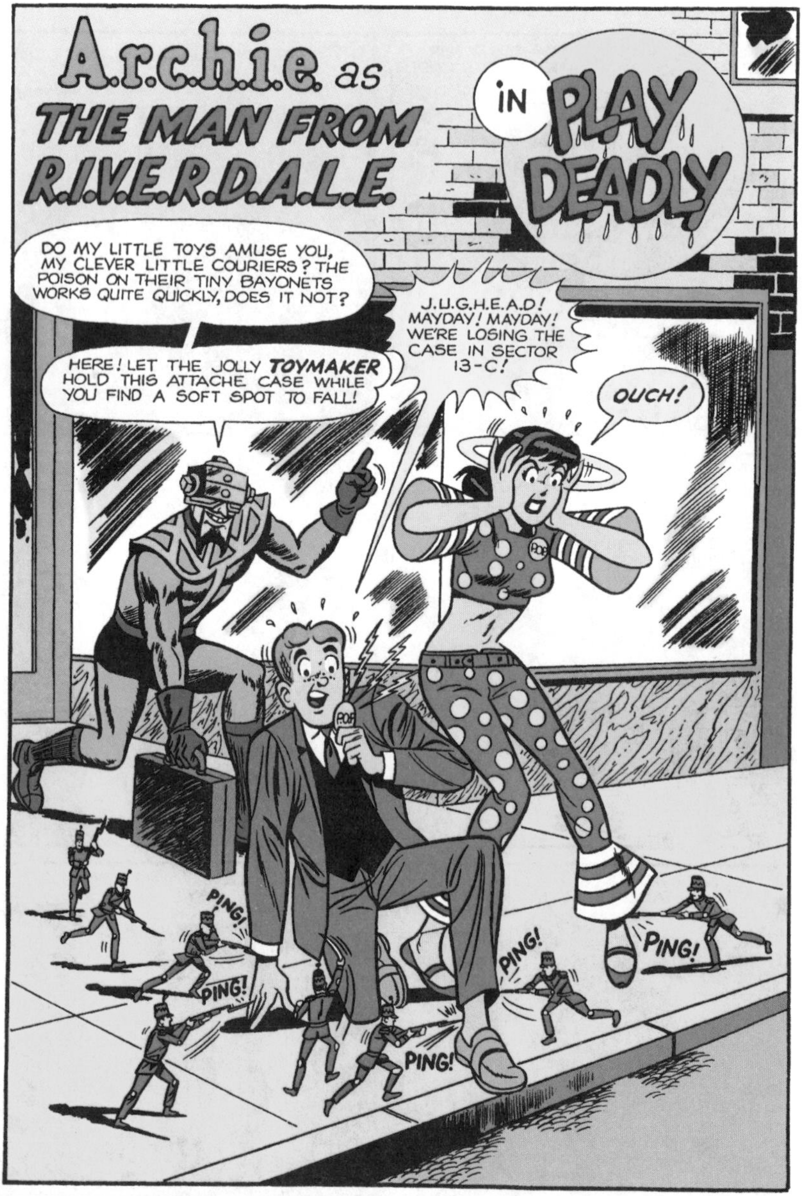
Archie as
THE MAN FROM R.I.V.E.R.D.A.L.E.
IN PLAY DEADLY
DO MY LITTLE TOYS AMUSE YOU, MY CLEVER LITTLE COURIERS? THE POISON ON THEIR TINY BAYONETS WORKS QUITE QUICKLY, DOES IT NOT?
HERE! LET THE JOLLY TOYMAKER HOLD THIS ATTACHE CASE WHILE YOU FIND A SOFT SPOT TO FALL!
J.U.G.H.E.A.D! MAYDAY! MAYDAY! WE'RE LOSING THE CASE IN SECTOR 13-C!
OUCH!
PING!
PING!
PING!
PING!
PING!
PING!

Story: Frank Doyle Pencils: Bill Vigoda
Inks & Letters: Mario Acquaviva

Originally printed in LIFE WITH ARCHIE #55, NOVEMBER 1966

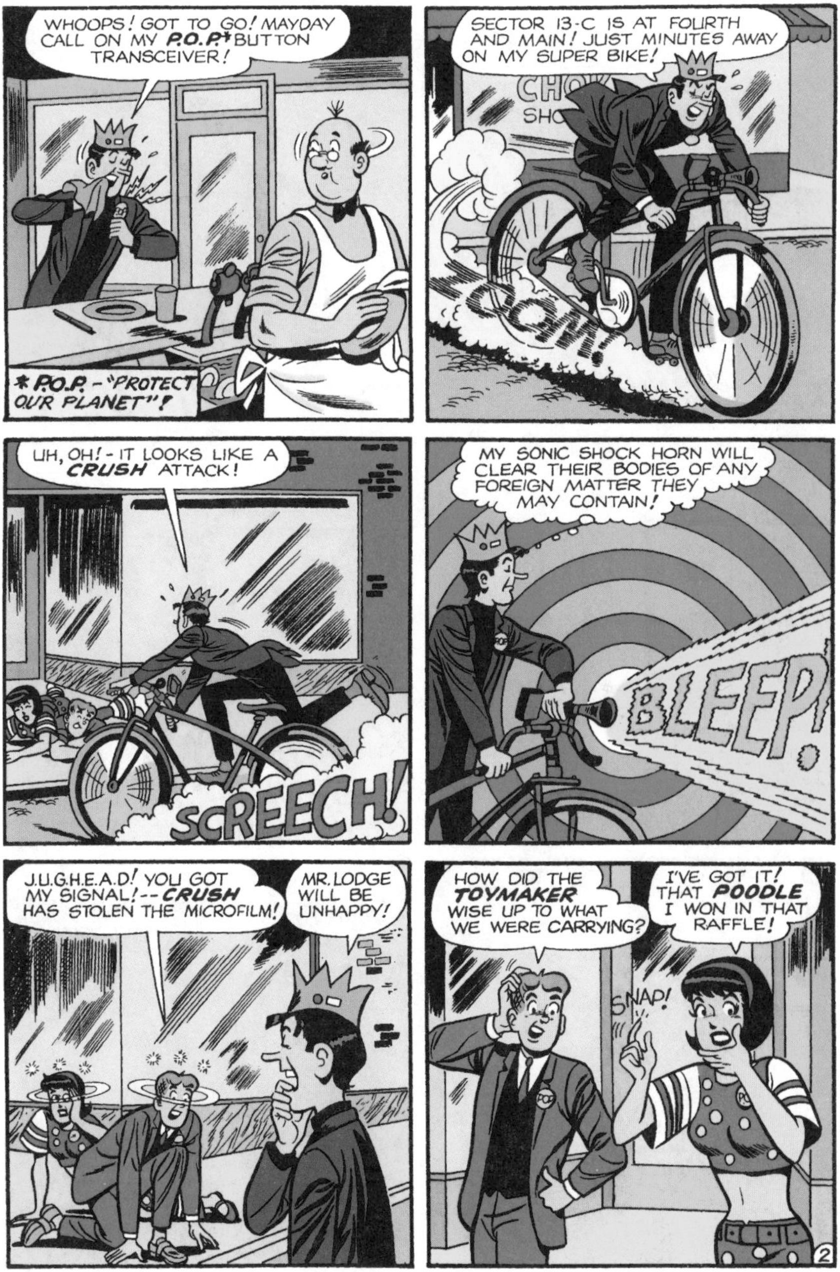
WHOOPS! GOT TO GO! MAYDAY CALL ON MY P.O.P.* BUTTON TRANSCEIVER!
* P.O.P. - "PROTECT OUR PLANET"!
SECTOR 13-C IS AT FOURTH AND MAIN! JUST MINUTES AWAY ON MY SUPER BIKE!
ZOOM!
UH, OH! - IT LOOKS LIKE A CRUSH ATTACK!
SCREECH!
MY SONIC SHOCK HORN WILL CLEAR THEIR BODIES OF ANY FOREIGN MATTER THEY MAY CONTAIN!
BLEEP!
J.U.G.H.E.A.D! YOU GOT MY SIGNAL! -- CRUSH HAS STOLEN THE MICROFILM!
MR. LODGE WILL BE UNHAPPY!
HOW DID THE TOYMAKER WISE UP TO WHAT WE WERE CARRYING?
I'VE GOT IT! THAT POODLE I WON IN THAT RAFFLE!
SNAP!
2

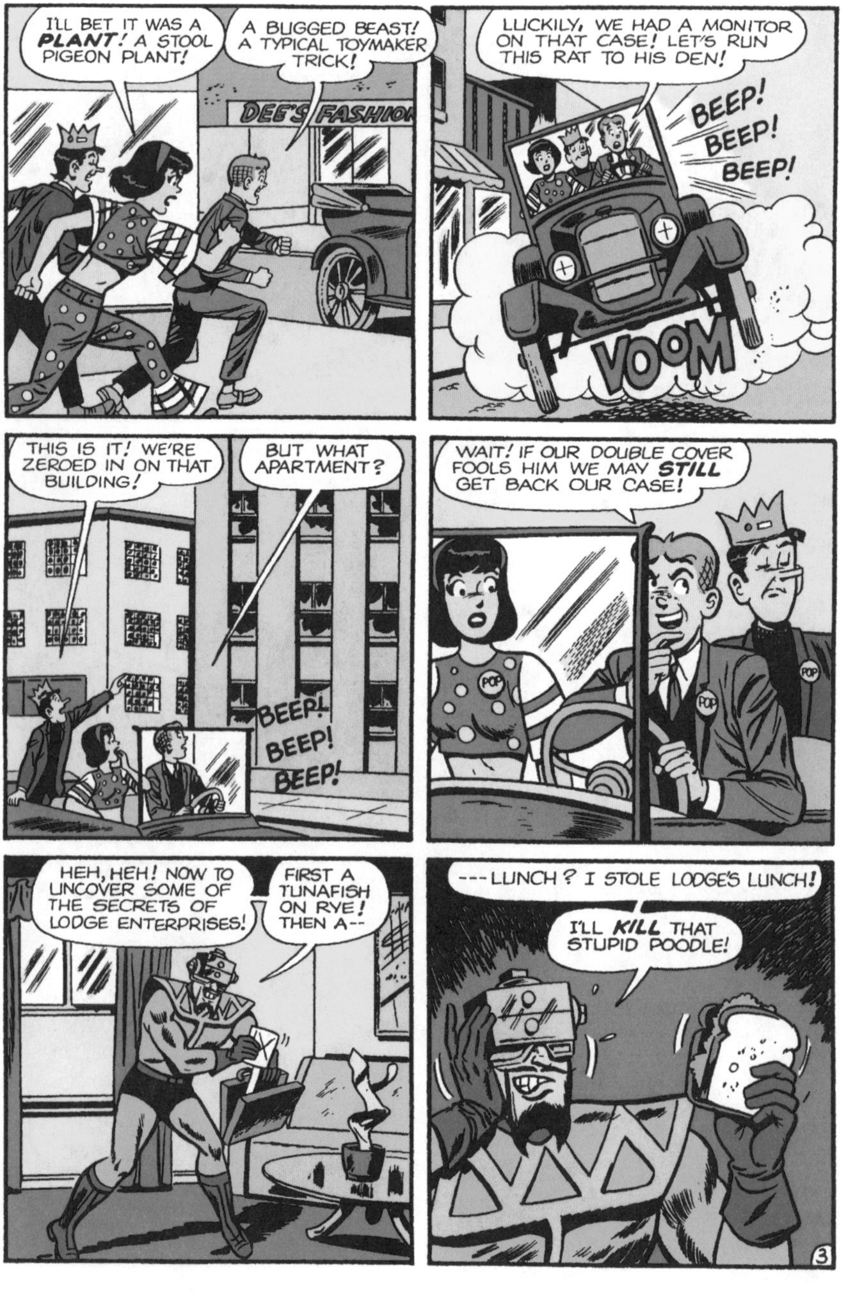
I'LL BET IT WAS A PLANT! A STOOL PIGEON PLANT!
A BUGGED BEAST! A TYPICAL TOYMAKER TRICK!
DEE'S FASHION
LUCKILY, WE HAD A MONITOR ON THAT CASE! LET'S RUN THIS RAT TO HIS DEN!
BEEP! BEEP! BEEP!
VOOM
THIS IS IT! WE'RE ZEROED IN ON THAT BUILDING!
BUT WHAT APARTMENT?
BEEP! BEEP! BEEP!
WAIT! IF OUR DOUBLE COVER FOOLS HIM WE MAY STILL GET BACK OUR CASE!
POP
HEH, HEH! NOW TO UNCOVER SOME OF THE SECRETS OF LODGE ENTERPRISES!
FIRST A TUNAFISH ON RYE! THEN A--
---LUNCH? I STOLE LODGE'S LUNCH!
I'LL KILL THAT STUPID POODLE!
3

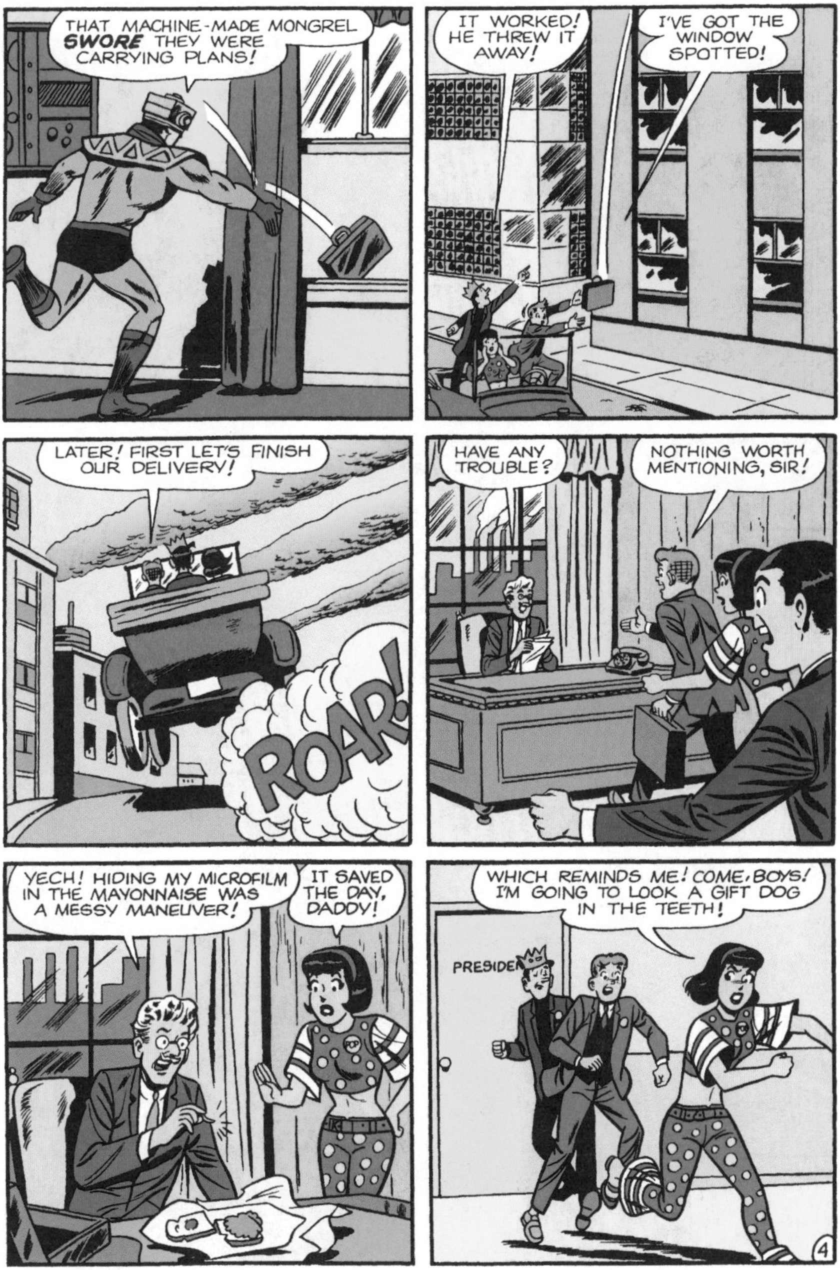
THAT MACHINE-MADE MONGREL SWORE THEY WERE CARRYING PLANS!
IT WORKED! HE THREW IT AWAY!
I'VE GOT THE WINDOW SPOTTED!
LATER! FIRST LET'S FINISH OUR DELIVERY!
ROAR!
HAVE ANY TROUBLE?
NOTHING WORTH MENTIONING, SIR!
YECH! HIDING MY MICROFILM IN THE MAYONNAISE WAS A MESSY MANEUVER!
IT SAVED THE DAY, DADDY!
WHICH REMINDS ME! COME, BOYS! I'M GOING TO LOOK A GIFT DOG IN THE TEETH!
PRESIDE
4

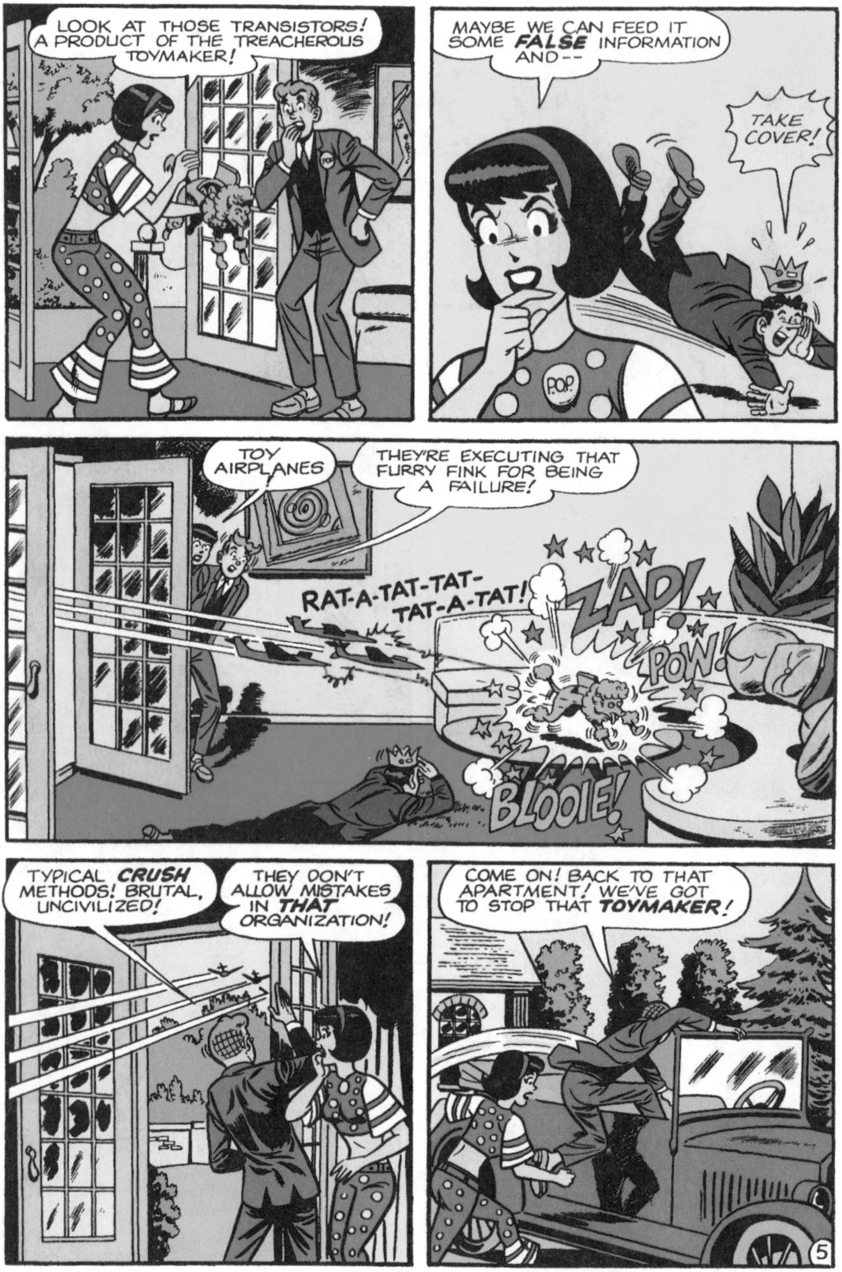
LOOK AT THOSE TRANSISTORS! A PRODUCT OF THE TREACHEROUS TOYMAKER!
MAYBE WE CAN FEED IT SOME FALSE INFORMATION AND--
TAKE COVER!
P.O.P.
TOY AIRPLANES
THEY'RE EXECUTING THAT FURRY FINK FOR BEING A FAILURE!
RAT-A-TAT-TAT-TAT-A-TAT!
ZAP!
POW!
BLOOIE!
TYPICAL CRUSH METHODS! BRUTAL, UNCIVILIZED!
THEY DON'T ALLOW MISTAKES IN THAT ORGANIZATION!
COME ON! BACK TO THAT APARTMENT! WE'VE GOT TO STOP THAT TOYMAKER!
5

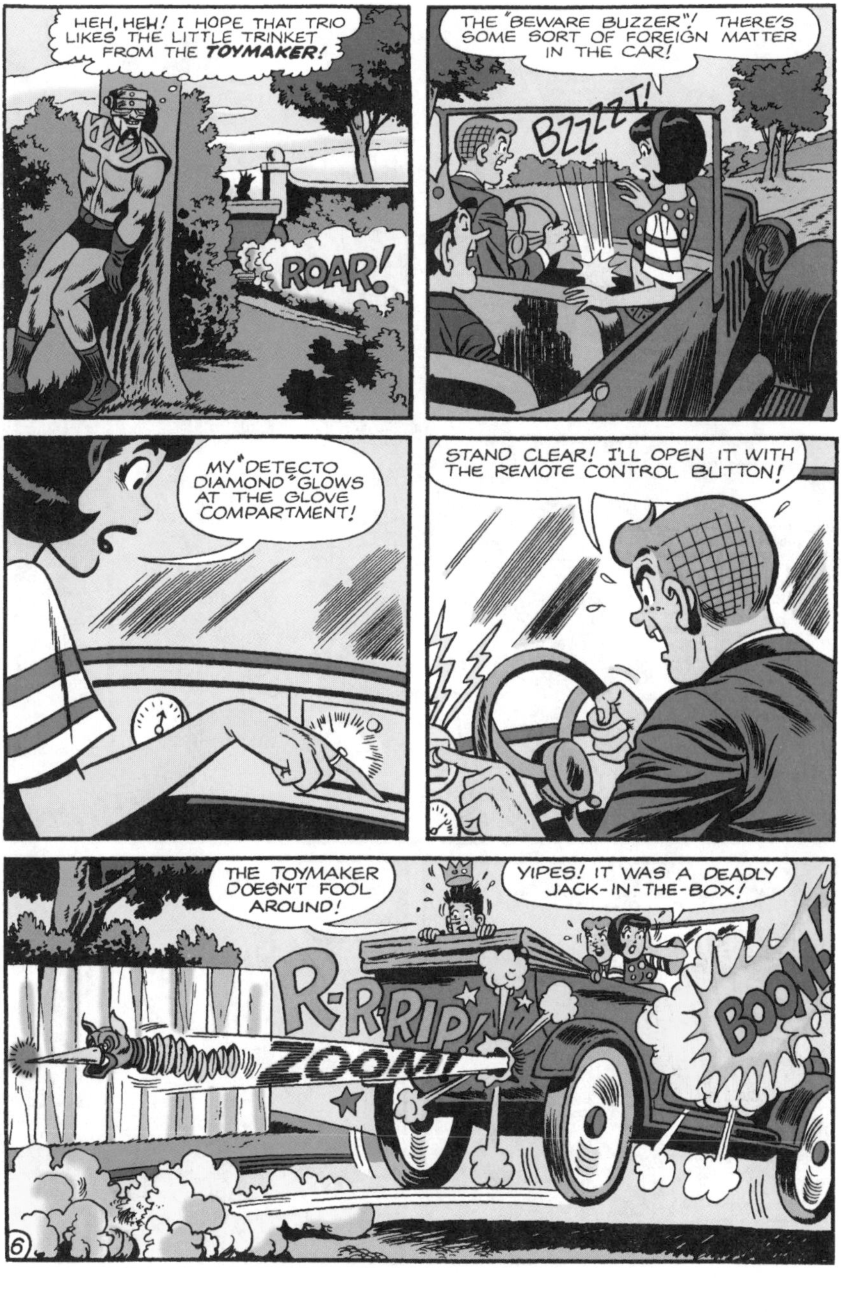
HEH, HEH! I HOPE THAT TRIO LIKES THE LITTLE TRINKET FROM THE TOYMAKER!
ROAR!
THE "BEWARE BUZZER"! THERE'S SOME SORT OF FOREIGN MATTER IN THE CAR!
BZZZZT!
MY "DETECTO DIAMOND" GLOWS AT THE GLOVE COMPARTMENT!
STAND CLEAR! I'LL OPEN IT WITH THE REMOTE CONTROL BUTTON!
THE TOYMAKER DOESN'T FOOL AROUND!
YIPES! IT WAS A DEADLY JACK-IN-THE-BOX!
R-R-RIP!
ZOOM!
BOOM!
6

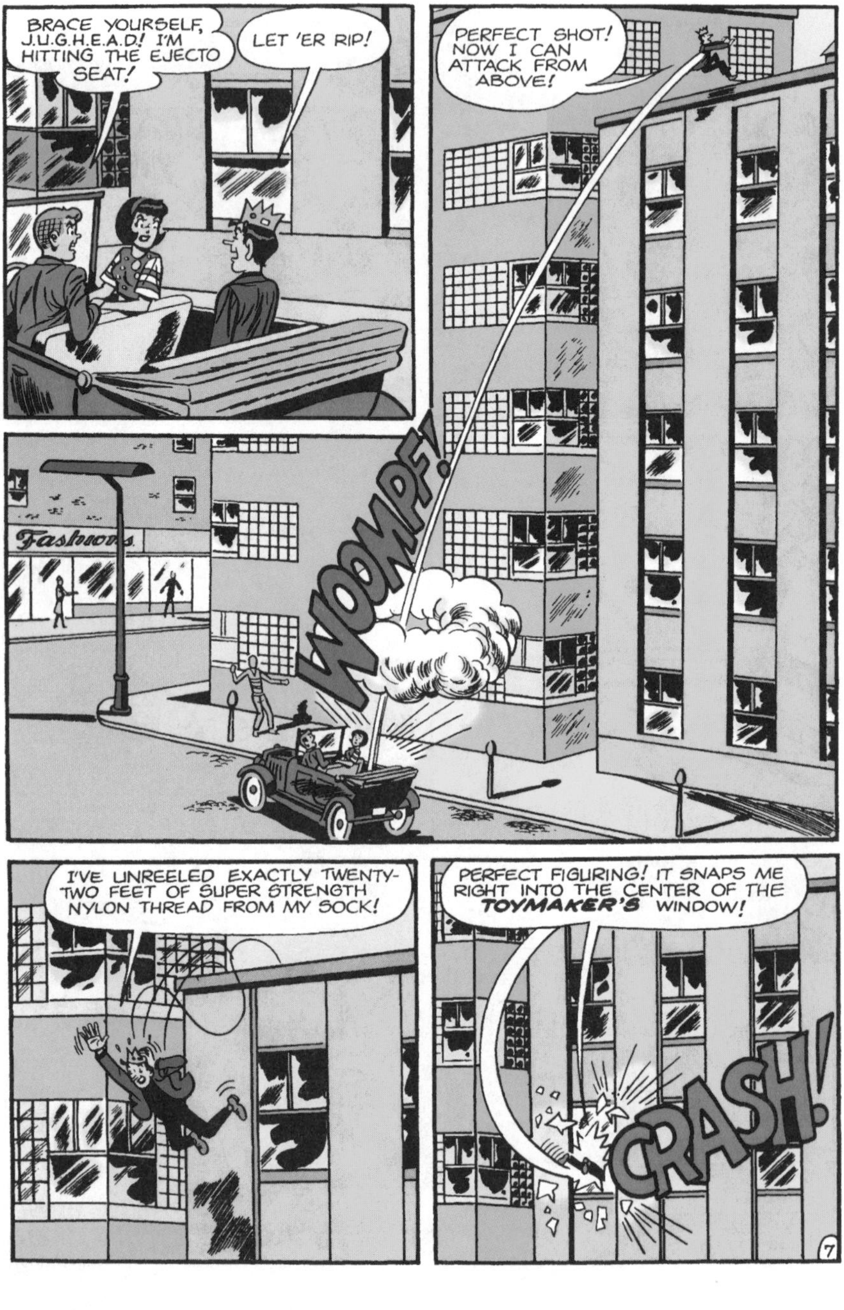
BRACE YOURSELF, J.U.G.H.E.A.D! I'M HITTING THE EJECTO SEAT!
LET 'ER RIP!
PERFECT SHOT! NOW I CAN ATTACK FROM ABOVE!
Fashions
WOOMPF!
I'VE UNREELED EXACTLY TWENTY-TWO FEET OF SUPER STRENGTH NYLON THREAD FROM MY SOCK!
PERFECT FIGURING! IT SNAPS ME RIGHT INTO THE CENTER OF THE TOYMAKER'S WINDOW!
CRASH!
7

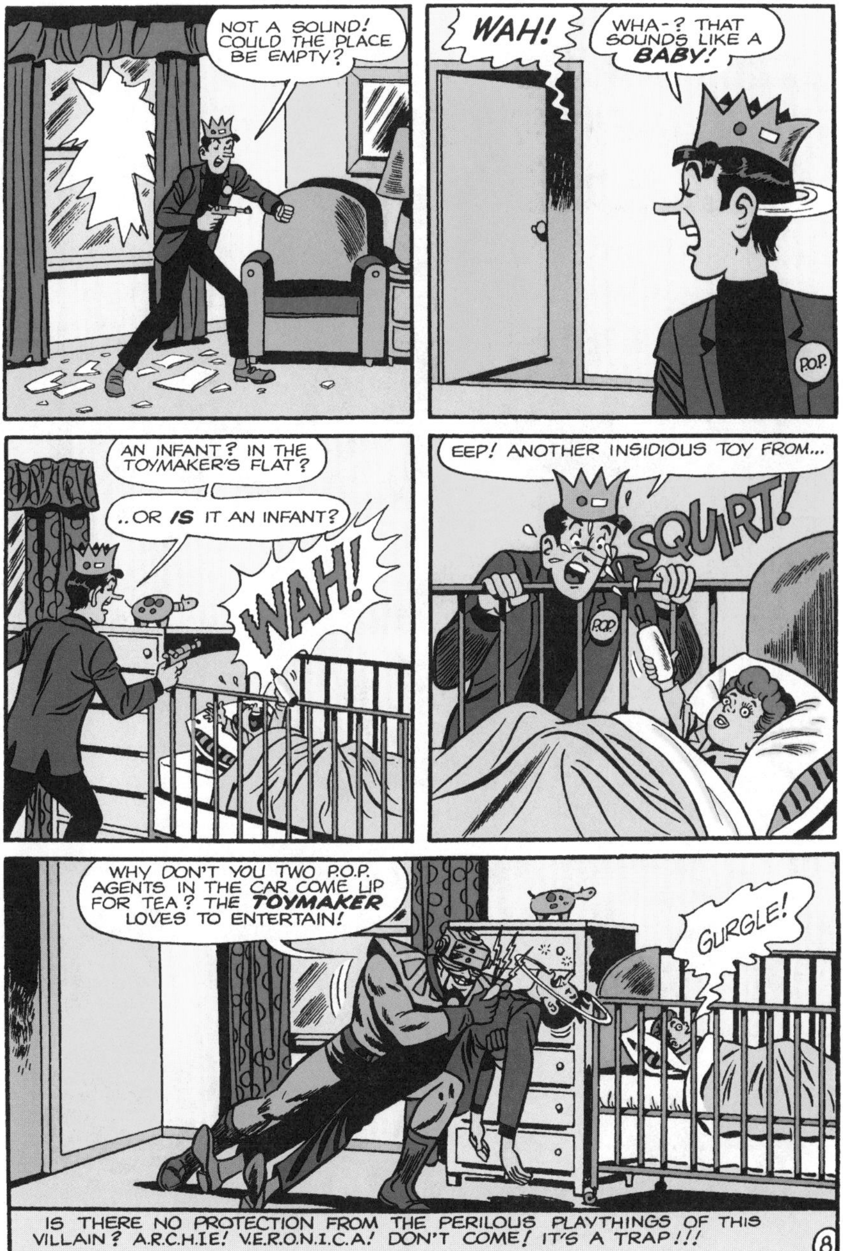
NOT A SOUND! COULD THE PLACE BE EMPTY?
WAH!
WHA-? THAT SOUNDS LIKE A BABY!
P.O.P.
AN INFANT? IN THE TOYMAKER'S FLAT?
..OR IS IT AN INFANT?
WAH!
EEP! ANOTHER INSIDIOUS TOY FROM...
SQUIRT!
P.O.P.
WHY DON'T YOU TWO P.O.P. AGENTS IN THE CAR COME UP FOR TEA? THE TOYMAKER LOVES TO ENTERTAIN!
GURGLE!
IS THERE NO PROTECTION FROM THE PERILOUS PLAYTHINGS OF THIS VILLAIN? A.R.C.H.I.E! V.E.R.O.N.I.C.A! DON'T COME! IT'S A TRAP!!!
8

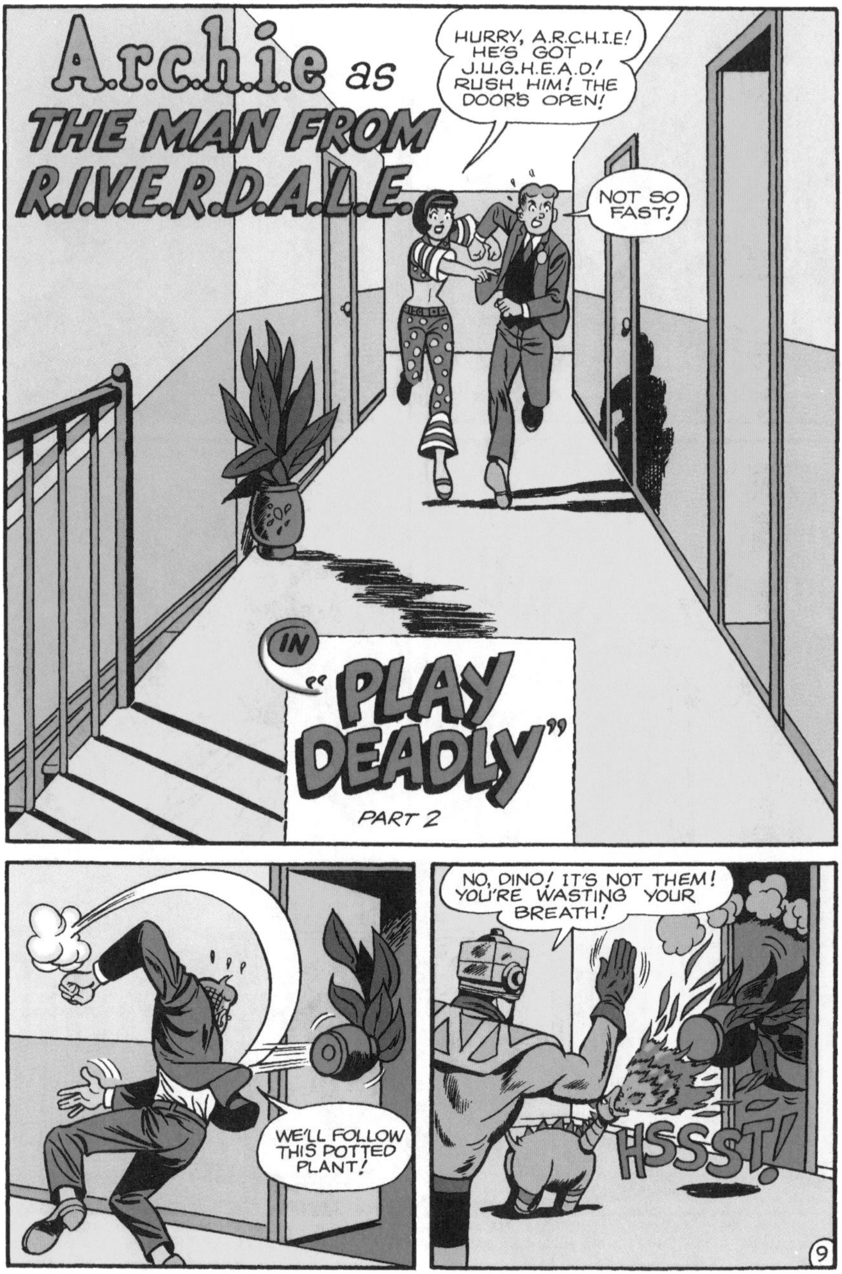
A.r.c.h.i.e as
THE MAN FROM R.I.V.E.R.D.A.L.E.
HURRY, A.R.C.H.I.E! HE'S GOT J.U.G.H.E.A.D! RUSH HIM! THE DOOR'S OPEN!
NOT SO FAST!
IN "PLAY DEADLY"
PART 2
WE'LL FOLLOW THIS POTTED PLANT!
NO, DINO! IT'S NOT THEM! YOU'RE WASTING YOUR BREATH!
HSSST!
9

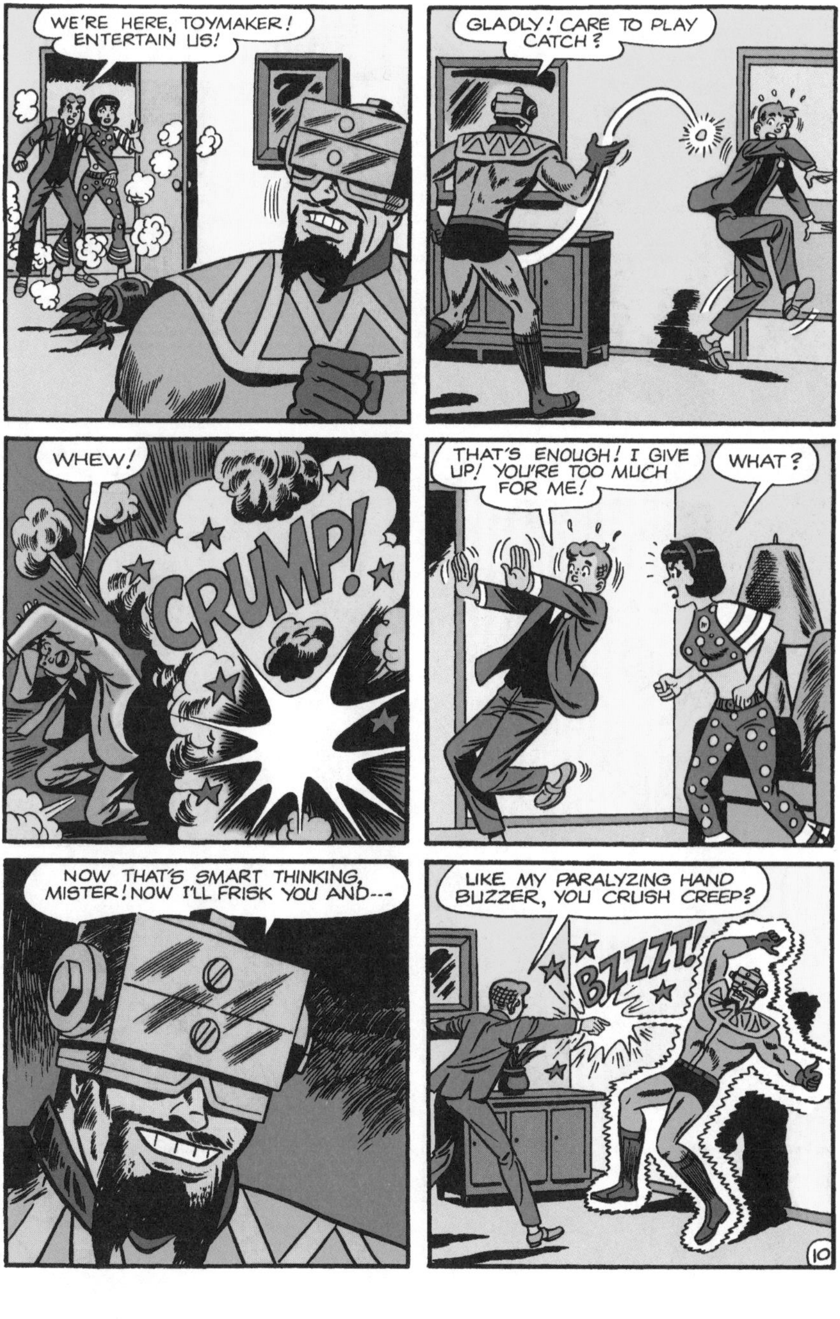
WE'RE HERE, TOYMAKER! ENTERTAIN US!
GLADLY! CARE TO PLAY CATCH?
WHEW!
CRUMP!
THAT'S ENOUGH! I GIVE UP! YOU'RE TOO MUCH FOR ME!
WHAT?
NOW THAT'S SMART THINKING, MISTER! NOW I'LL FRISK YOU AND---
LIKE MY PARALYZING HAND BUZZER, YOU CRUSH CREEP?
BZZZT!
10

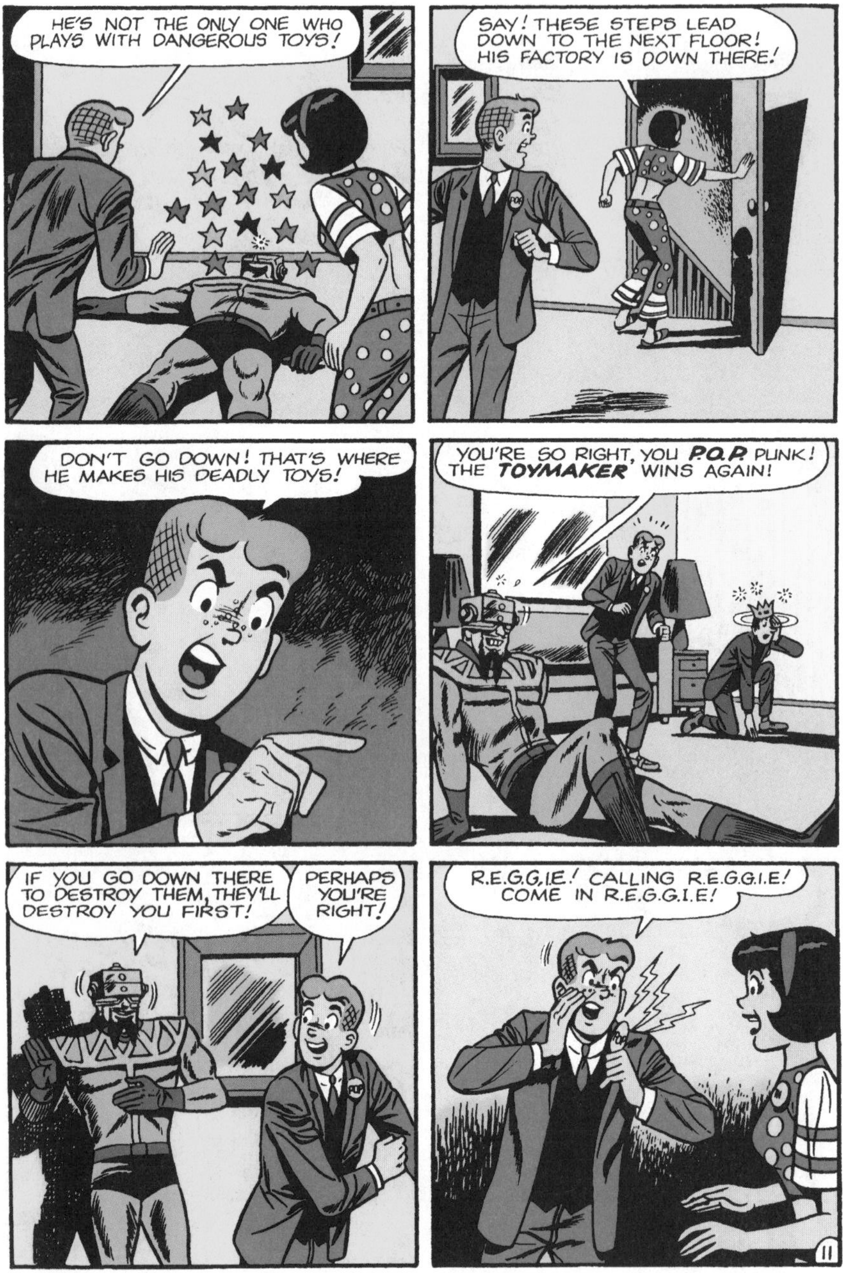
HE'S NOT THE ONLY ONE WHO PLAYS WITH DANGEROUS TOYS!
SAY! THESE STEPS LEAD DOWN TO THE NEXT FLOOR! HIS FACTORY IS DOWN THERE!
DON'T GO DOWN! THAT'S WHERE HE MAKES HIS DEADLY TOYS!
YOU'RE SO RIGHT, YOU P.O.P. PUNK! THE TOYMAKER WINS AGAIN!
IF YOU GO DOWN THERE TO DESTROY THEM, THEY'LL DESTROY YOU FIRST!
PERHAPS YOU'RE RIGHT!
R.E.G.G.I.E.! CALLING R.E.G.G.I.E.! COME IN R.E.G.G.I.E.!
11

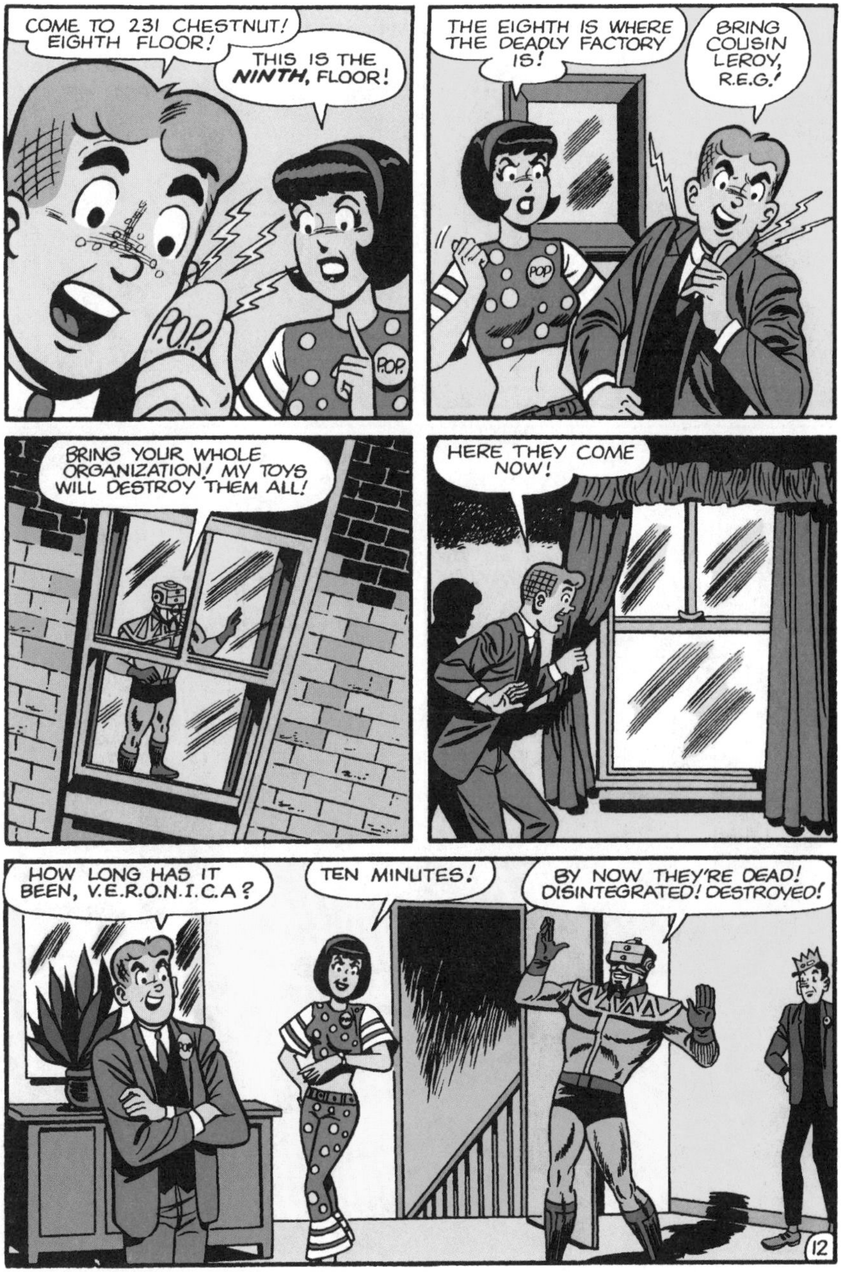
COME TO 231 CHESTNUT! EIGHTH FLOOR!
THIS IS THE *NINTH*, FLOOR!
THE EIGHTH IS WHERE THE DEADLY FACTORY IS!
BRING COUSIN LEROY, R.E.G.!
BRING YOUR WHOLE ORGANIZATION! MY TOYS WILL DESTROY THEM ALL!
HERE THEY COME NOW!
HOW LONG HAS IT BEEN, V.E.R.O.N.I.C.A?
TEN MINUTES!
BY NOW THEY'RE DEAD! DISINTEGRATED! DESTROYED!
12

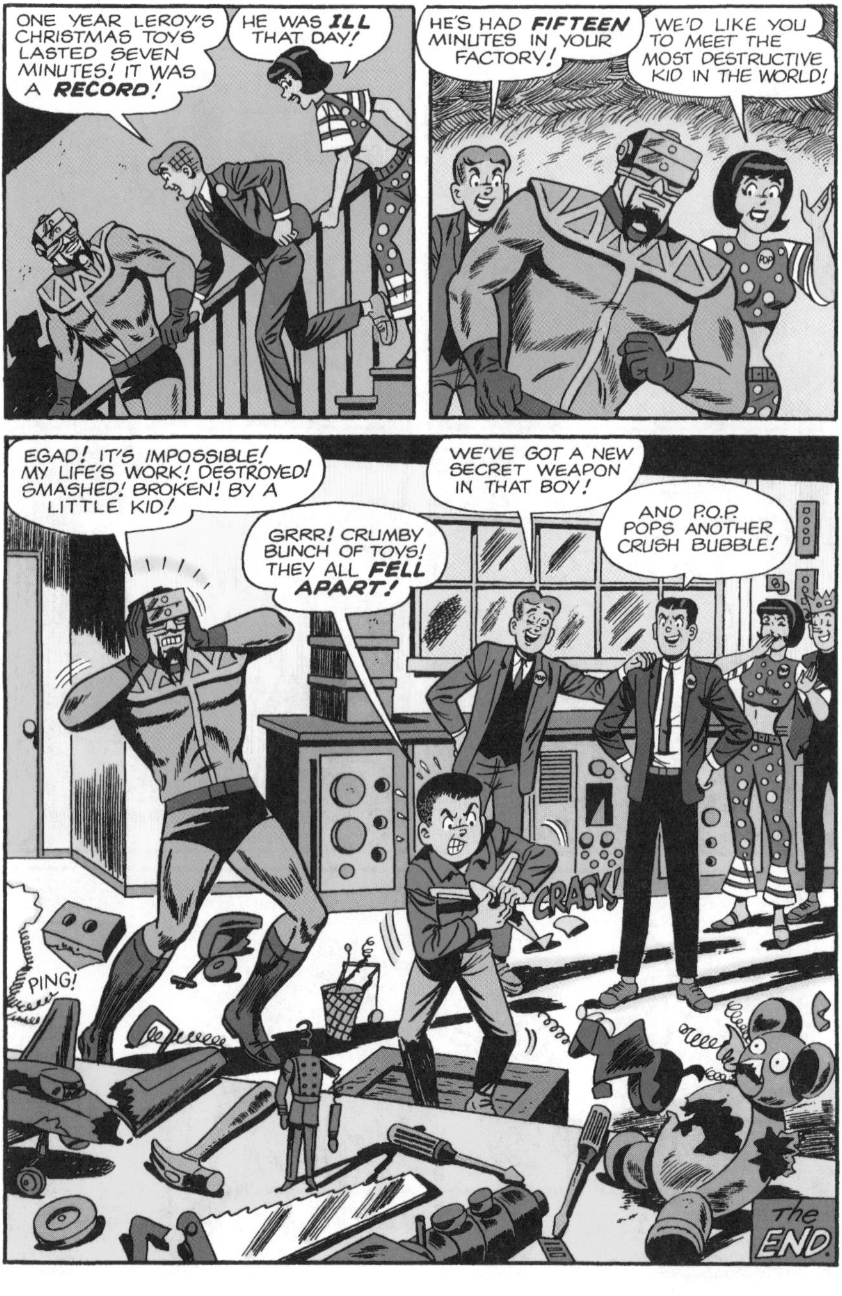
ONE YEAR LEROY'S CHRISTMAS TOYS LASTED SEVEN MINUTES! IT WAS A **RECORD**!
HE WAS **ILL** THAT DAY!
HE'S HAD **FIFTEEN** MINUTES IN YOUR FACTORY!
WE'D LIKE YOU TO MEET THE MOST DESTRUCTIVE KID IN THE WORLD!
EGAD! IT'S IMPOSSIBLE! MY LIFE'S WORK! DESTROYED! SMASHED! BROKEN! BY A LITTLE KID!
GRRR! CRUMBY BUNCH OF TOYS! THEY ALL **FELL APART**!
WE'VE GOT A NEW SECRET WEAPON IN THAT BOY!
AND P.O.P. POPS ANOTHER CRUSH BUBBLE!
CRACK!
PING!
The END.

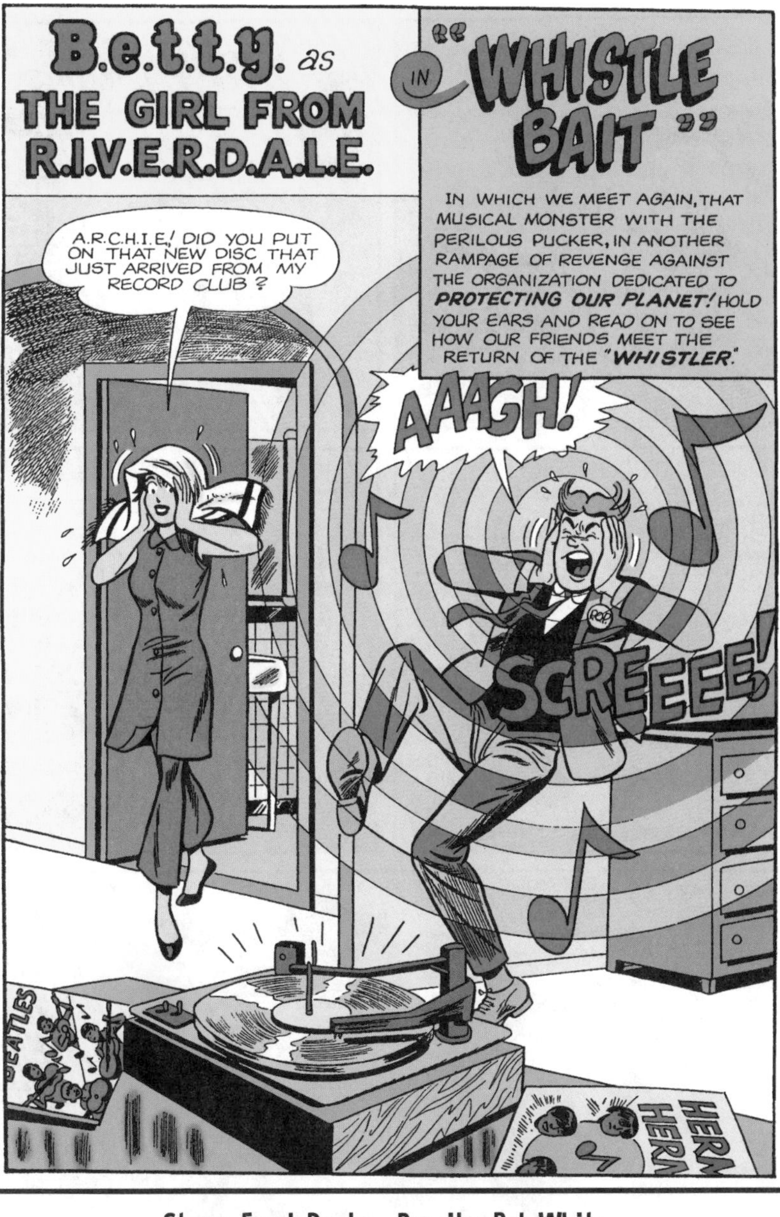
B.e.t.t.y. as
THE GIRL FROM R.I.V.E.R.D.A.L.E.
IN "WHISTLE BAIT"
IN WHICH WE MEET AGAIN, THAT MUSICAL MONSTER WITH THE PERILOUS PUCKER, IN ANOTHER RAMPAGE OF REVENGE AGAINST THE ORGANIZATION DEDICATED TO PROTECTING OUR PLANET! HOLD YOUR EARS AND READ ON TO SEE HOW OUR FRIENDS MEET THE RETURN OF THE "WHISTLER."
A.R.C.H.I.E.! DID YOU PUT ON THAT NEW DISC THAT JUST ARRIVED FROM MY RECORD CLUB?
AAAGH!
SCREEEE!

Story: Frank Doyle Pencils: Bob White
Inks & Letters: Mario Acquaviva

Originally printed in LIFE WITH ARCHIE #55, NOVEMBER 1966

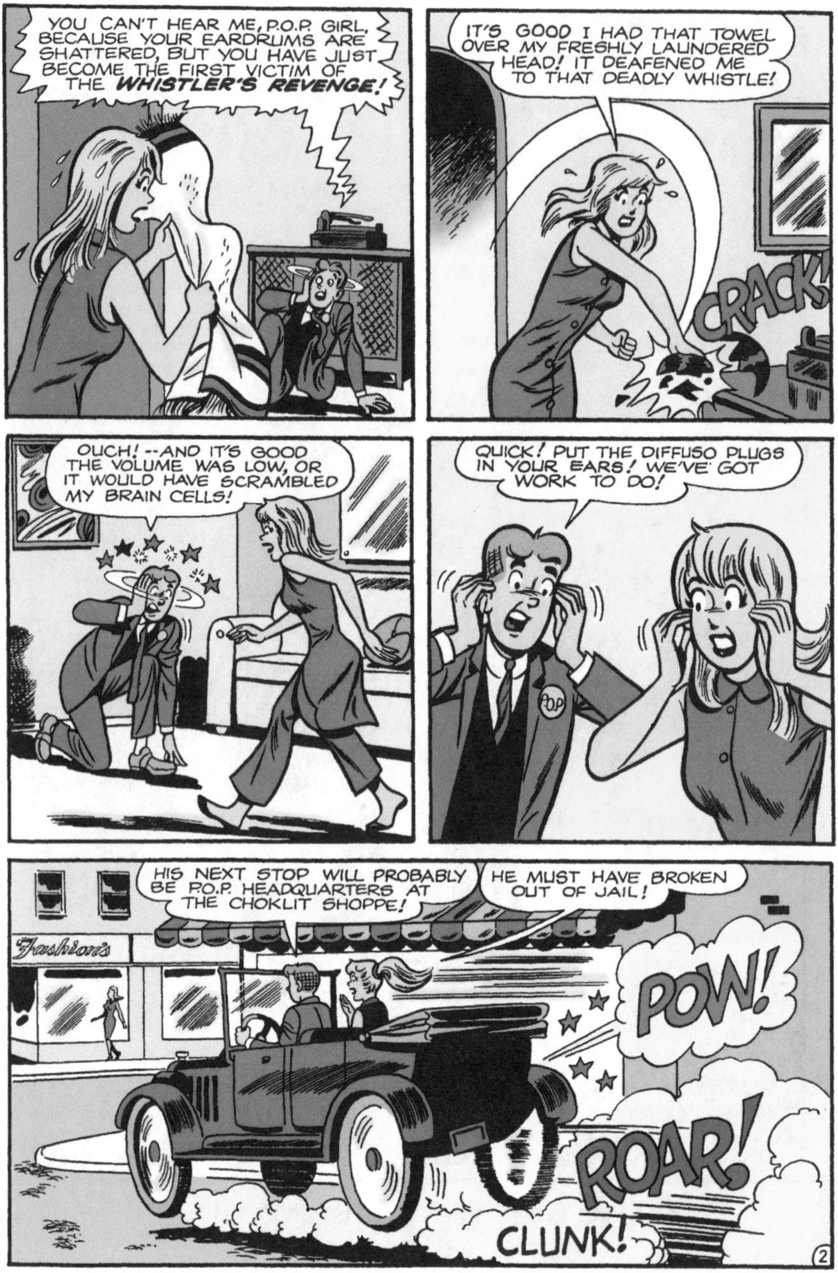
YOU CAN'T HEAR ME, P.O.P. GIRL, BECAUSE YOUR EARDRUMS ARE SHATTERED, BUT YOU HAVE JUST BECOME THE FIRST VICTIM OF THE WHISTLER'S REVENGE!
IT'S GOOD I HAD THAT TOWEL OVER MY FRESHLY LAUNDERED HEAD! IT DEAFENED ME TO THAT DEADLY WHISTLE!
CRACK!
OUCH! --AND IT'S GOOD THE VOLUME WAS LOW, OR IT WOULD HAVE SCRAMBLED MY BRAIN CELLS!
QUICK! PUT THE DIFFUSO PLUGS IN YOUR EARS! WE'VE GOT WORK TO DO!
P.O.P.
HIS NEXT STOP WILL PROBABLY BE P.O.P. HEADQUARTERS AT THE CHOKLIT SHOPPE!
HE MUST HAVE BROKEN OUT OF JAIL!
Fashions
POW!
ROAR!
CLUNK!
2

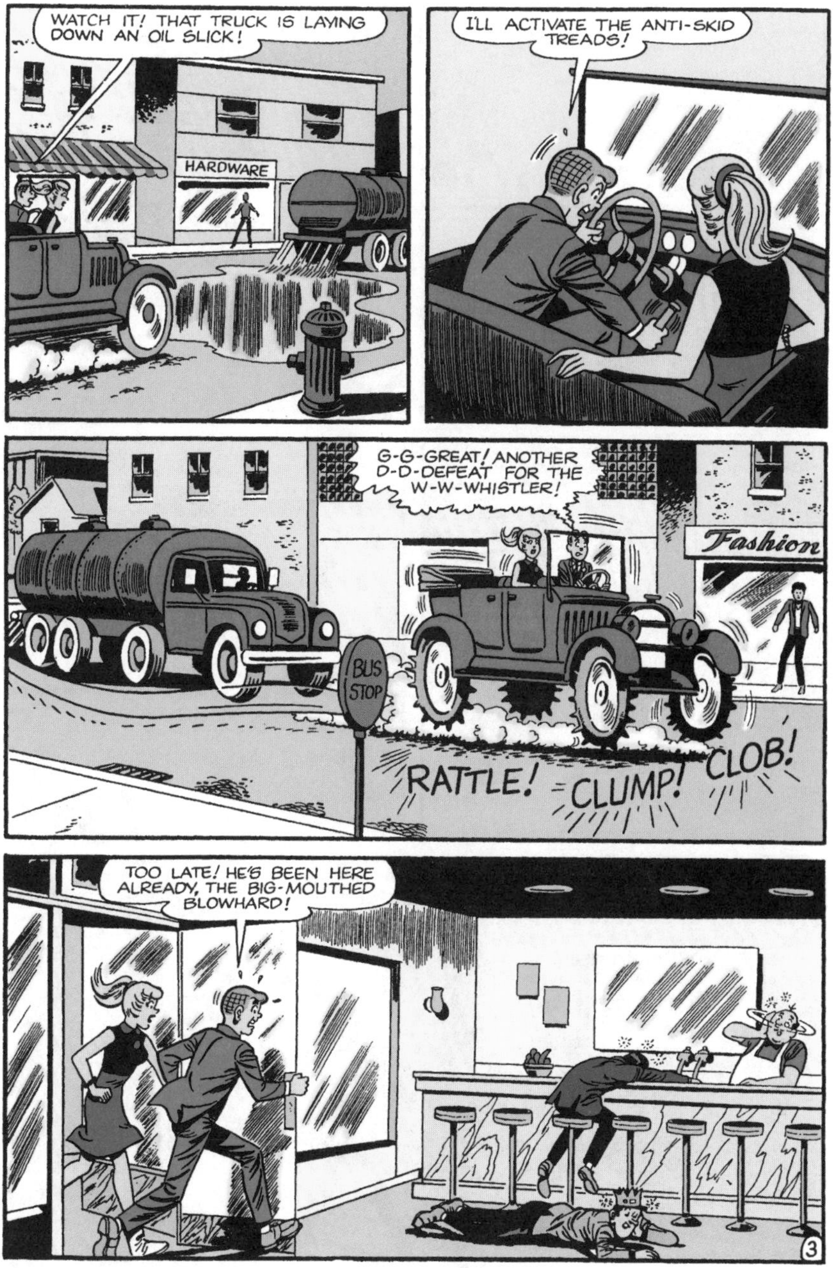
WATCH IT! THAT TRUCK IS LAYING DOWN AN OIL SLICK!
HARDWARE
I'LL ACTIVATE THE ANTI-SKID TREADS!
G-G-GREAT! ANOTHER D-D-DEFEAT FOR THE W-W-WHISTLER!
Fashion
BUS STOP
RATTLE! CLUMP! CLOB!
TOO LATE! HE'S BEEN HERE ALREADY, THE BIG-MOUTHED BLOWHARD!
3

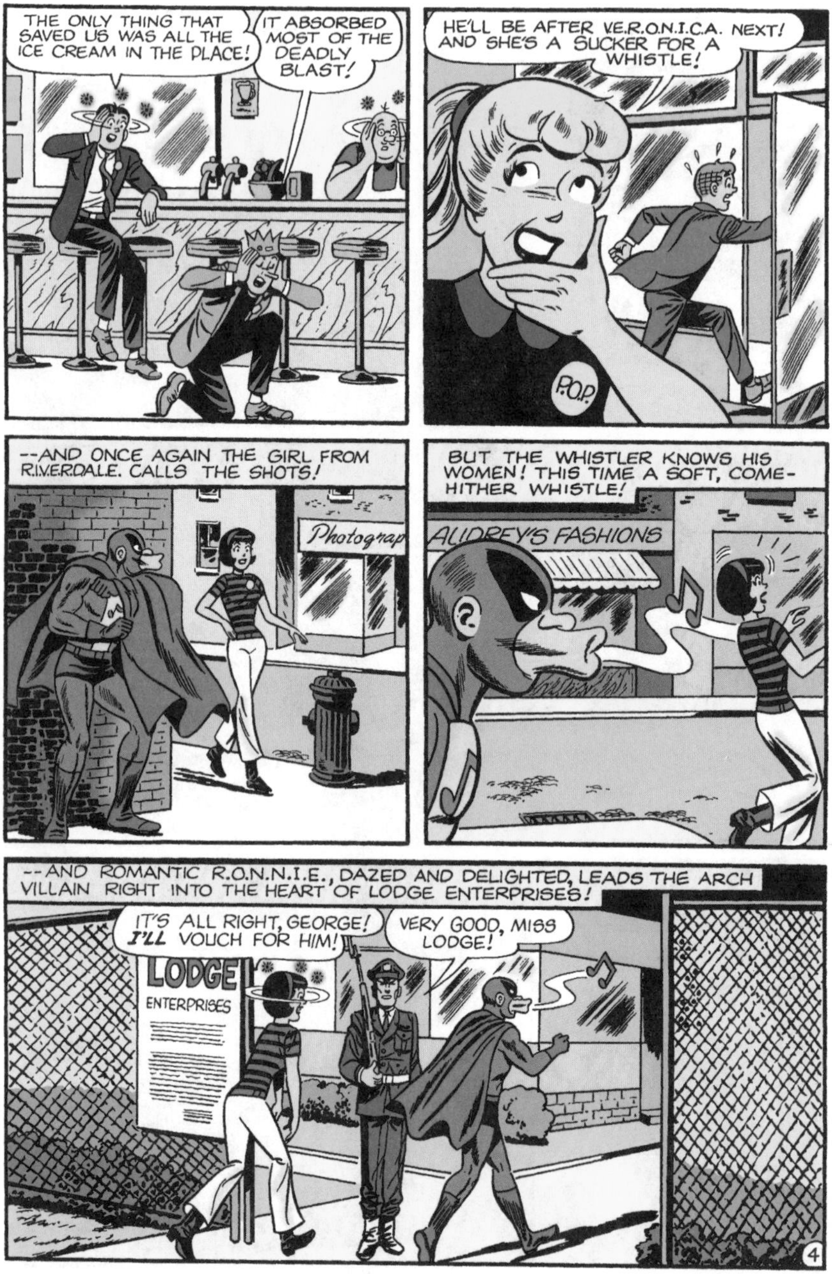
THE ONLY THING THAT SAVED US WAS ALL THE ICE CREAM IN THE PLACE!
IT ABSORBED MOST OF THE DEADLY BLAST!
HE'LL BE AFTER V.E.R.O.N.I.C.A. NEXT! AND SHE'S A SUCKER FOR A WHISTLE!
P.O.P.
--AND ONCE AGAIN THE GIRL FROM R.I.V.E.R.D.A.L.E. CALLS THE SHOTS!
Photograp
BUT THE WHISTLER KNOWS HIS WOMEN! THIS TIME A SOFT, COME-HITHER WHISTLE!
AUDREY'S FASHIONS
--AND ROMANTIC R.O.N.N.I.E., DAZED AND DELIGHTED, LEADS THE ARCH VILLAIN RIGHT INTO THE HEART OF LODGE ENTERPRISES!
IT'S ALL RIGHT, GEORGE! I'LL VOUCH FOR HIM!
VERY GOOD, MISS LODGE!
LODGE
ENTERPRISES
4

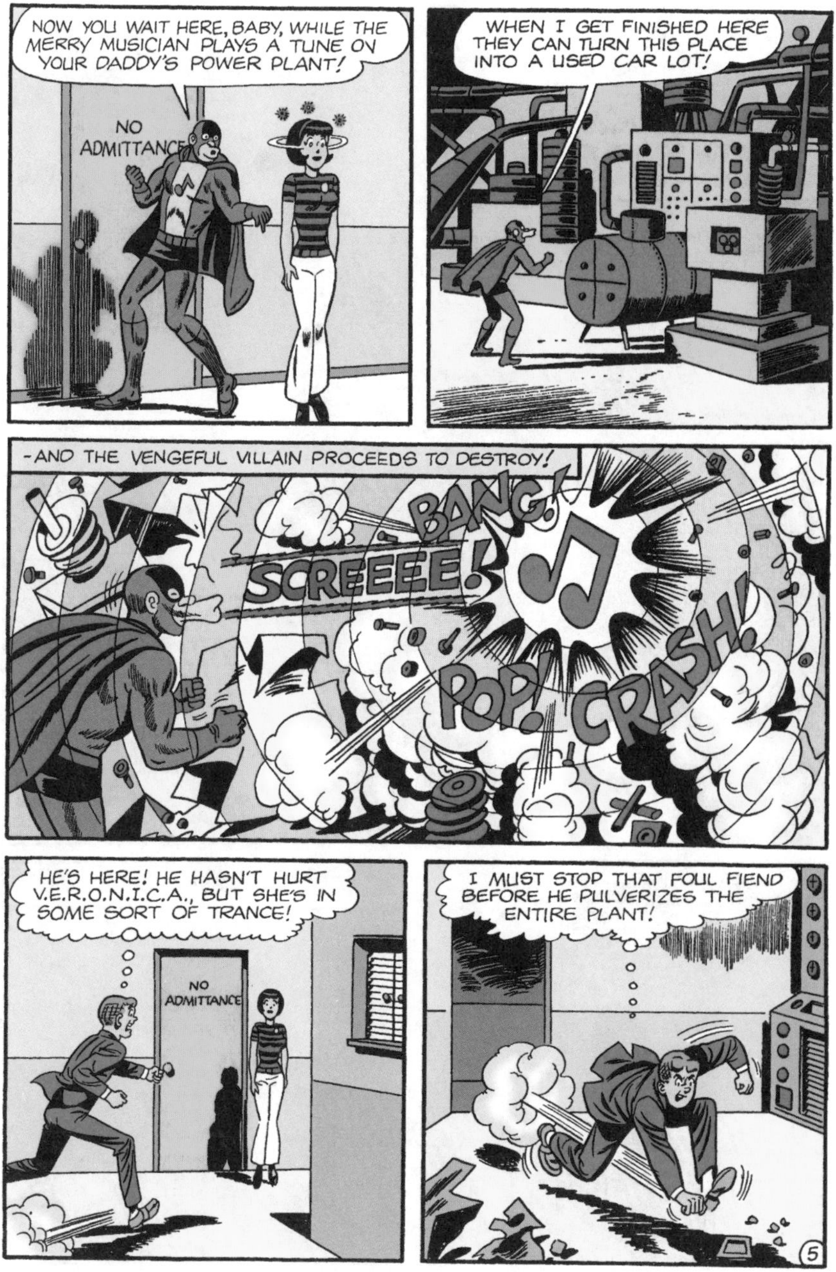
NOW YOU WAIT HERE, BABY, WHILE THE MERRY MUSICIAN PLAYS A TUNE ON YOUR DADDY'S POWER PLANT!
NO ADMITTANCE
WHEN I GET FINISHED HERE THEY CAN TURN THIS PLACE INTO A USED CAR LOT!
-AND THE VENGEFUL VILLAIN PROCEEDS TO DESTROY!
BANG!
SCREEEE!
POP!
CRASH!
HE'S HERE! HE HASN'T HURT V.E.R.O.N.I.C.A., BUT SHE'S IN SOME SORT OF TRANCE!
NO ADMITTANCE
I MUST STOP THAT FOUL FIEND BEFORE HE PULVERIZES THE ENTIRE PLANT!
5

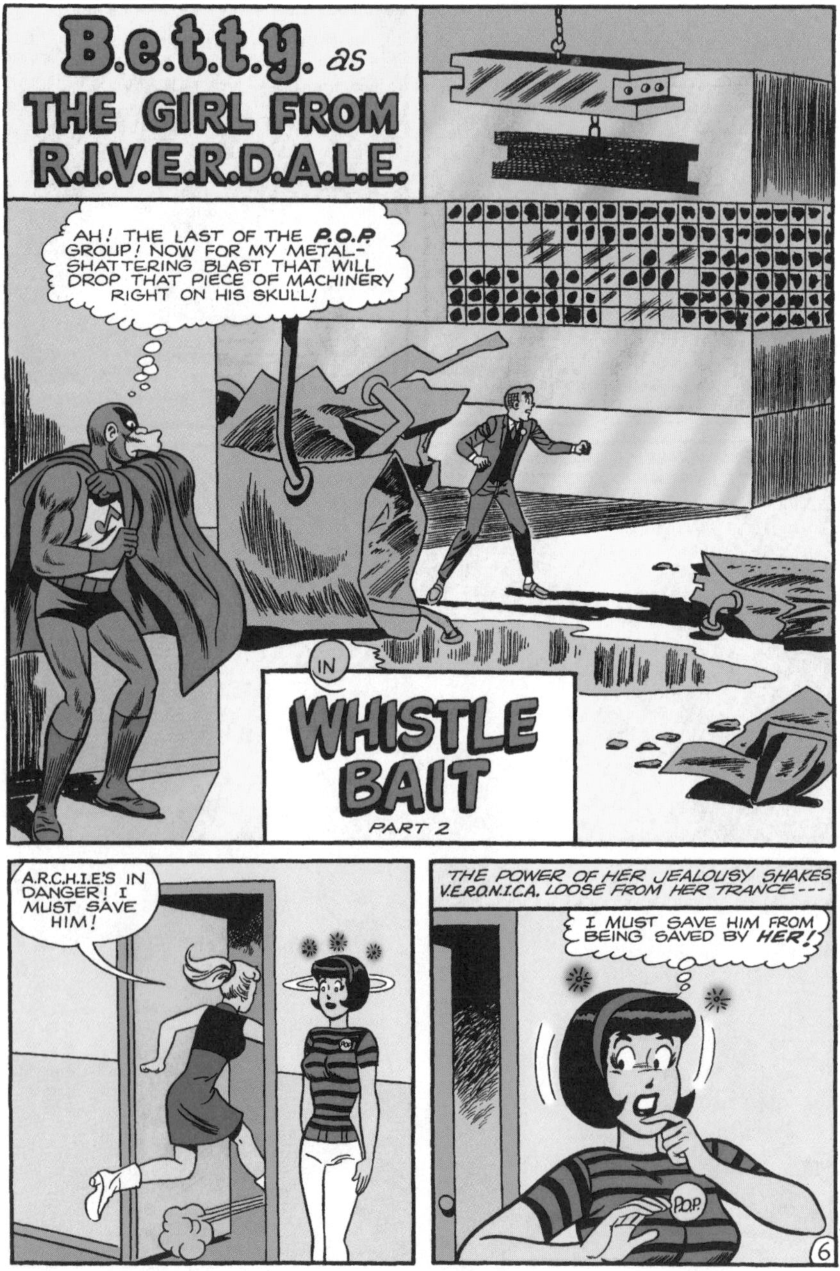
B.e.t.t.y. as
THE GIRL FROM R.I.V.E.R.D.A.L.E.
AH! THE LAST OF THE P.O.P. GROUP! NOW FOR MY METAL-SHATTERING BLAST THAT WILL DROP THAT PIECE OF MACHINERY RIGHT ON HIS SKULL!
IN
WHISTLE BAIT
PART 2
A.R.C.H.I.E.'S IN DANGER! I MUST SAVE HIM!
POP
THE POWER OF HER JEALOUSY SHAKES V.E.R.O.N.I.C.A. LOOSE FROM HER TRANCE---
I MUST SAVE HIM FROM BEING SAVED BY HER!
P.O.P.
6

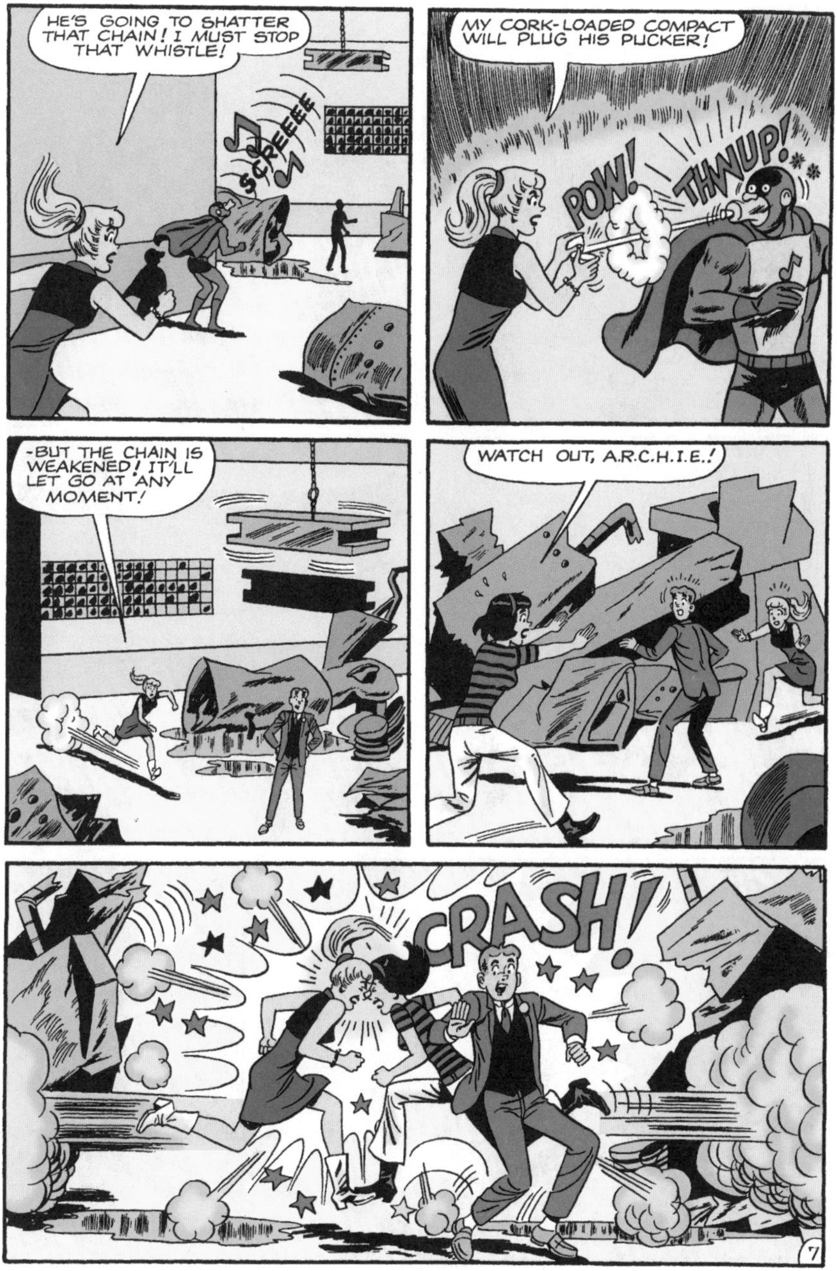
HE'S GOING TO SHATTER THAT CHAIN! I MUST STOP THAT WHISTLE!
SCREEEEE
MY CORK-LOADED COMPACT WILL PLUG HIS PUCKER!
POW!
THWUP!
-BUT THE CHAIN IS WEAKENED! IT'LL LET GO AT ANY MOMENT!
WATCH OUT, A.R.C.H.I.E.!
CRASH!
7

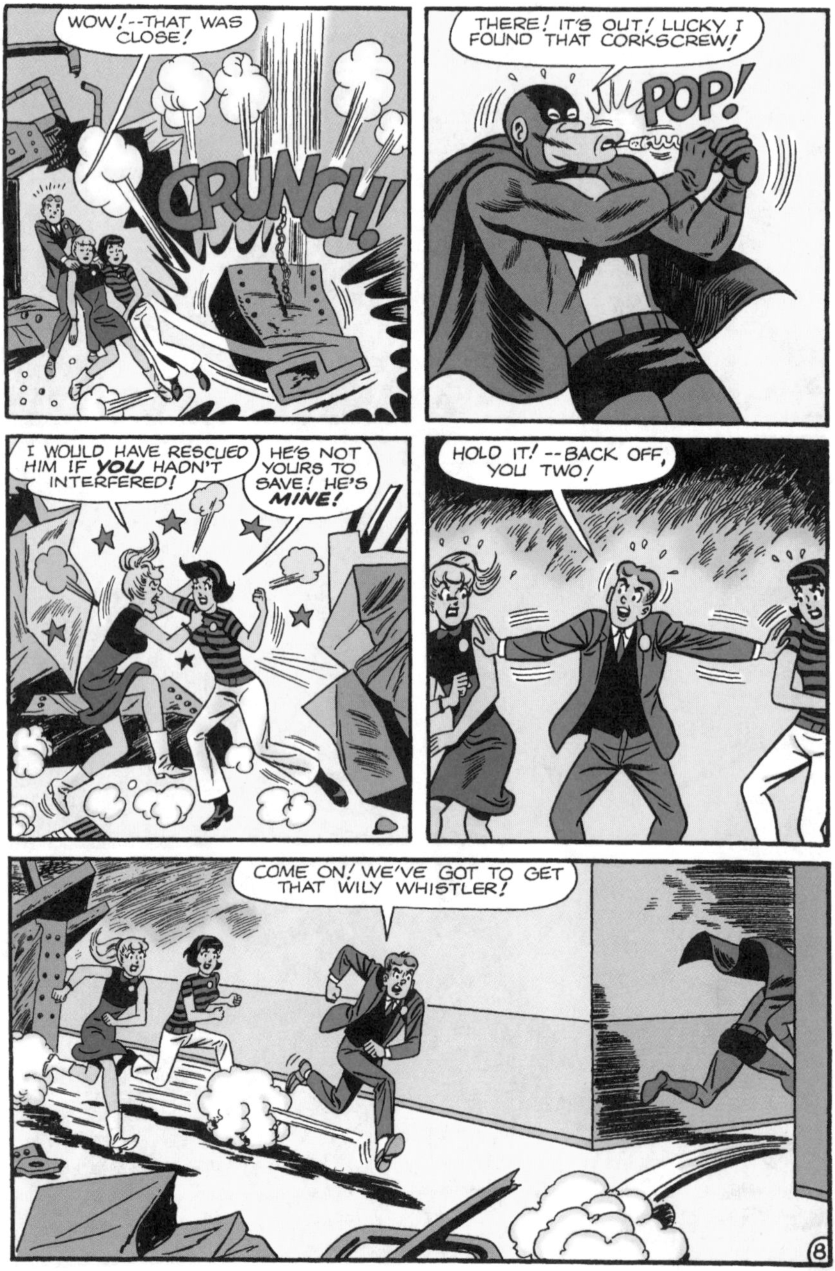
WOW!--THAT WAS CLOSE!
CRUNCH!
THERE! IT'S OUT! LUCKY I FOUND THAT CORKSCREW!
POP!
I WOULD HAVE RESCUED HIM IF YOU HADN'T INTERFERED!
HE'S NOT YOURS TO SAVE! HE'S MINE!
HOLD IT! --BACK OFF, YOU TWO!
COME ON! WE'VE GOT TO GET THAT WILY WHISTLER!
8

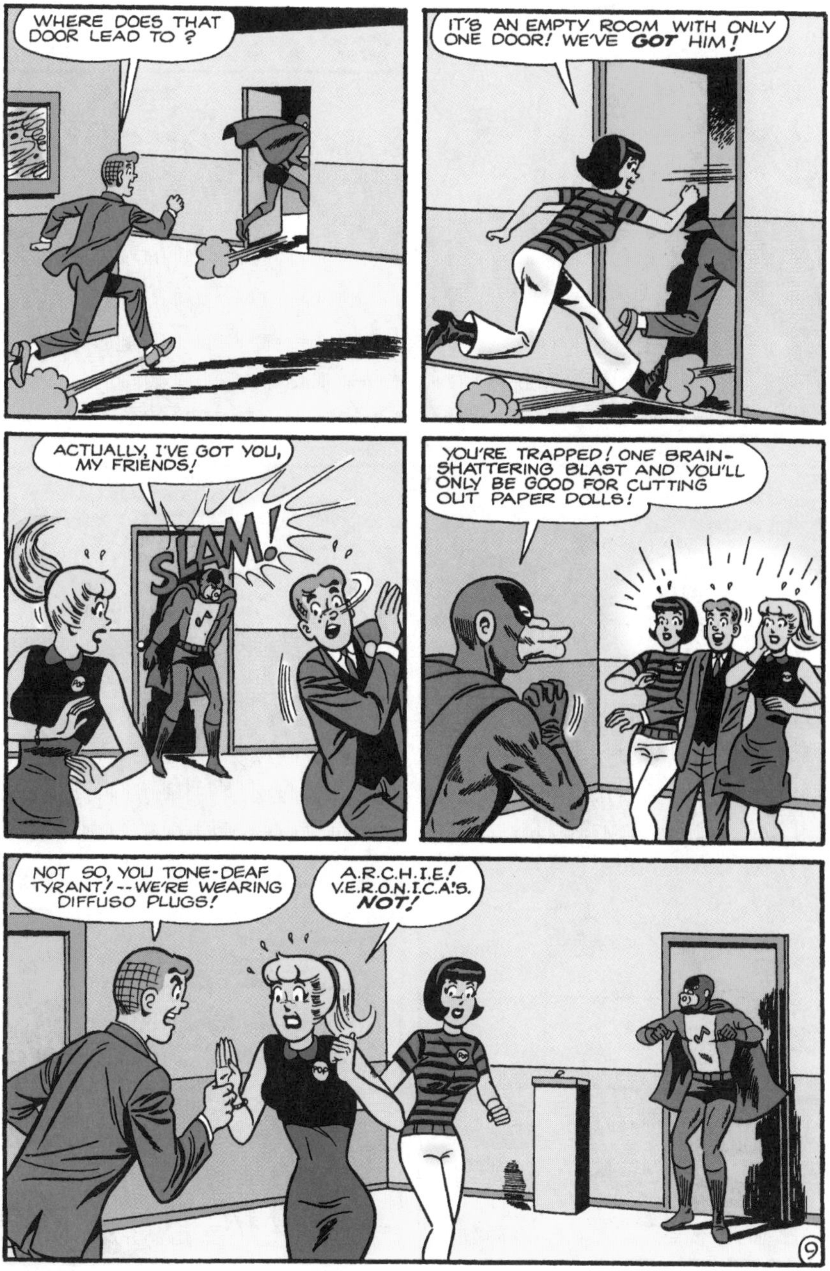
WHERE DOES THAT DOOR LEAD TO ?
IT'S AN EMPTY ROOM WITH ONLY ONE DOOR! WE'VE GOT HIM!
ACTUALLY, I'VE GOT YOU, MY FRIENDS!
SLAM!
YOU'RE TRAPPED! ONE BRAIN-SHATTERING BLAST AND YOU'LL ONLY BE GOOD FOR CUTTING OUT PAPER DOLLS!
NOT SO, YOU TONE-DEAF TYRANT! --WE'RE WEARING DIFFUSO PLUGS!
A.R.C.H.I.E! V.E.R.O.N.I.C.A!S. NOT!
9

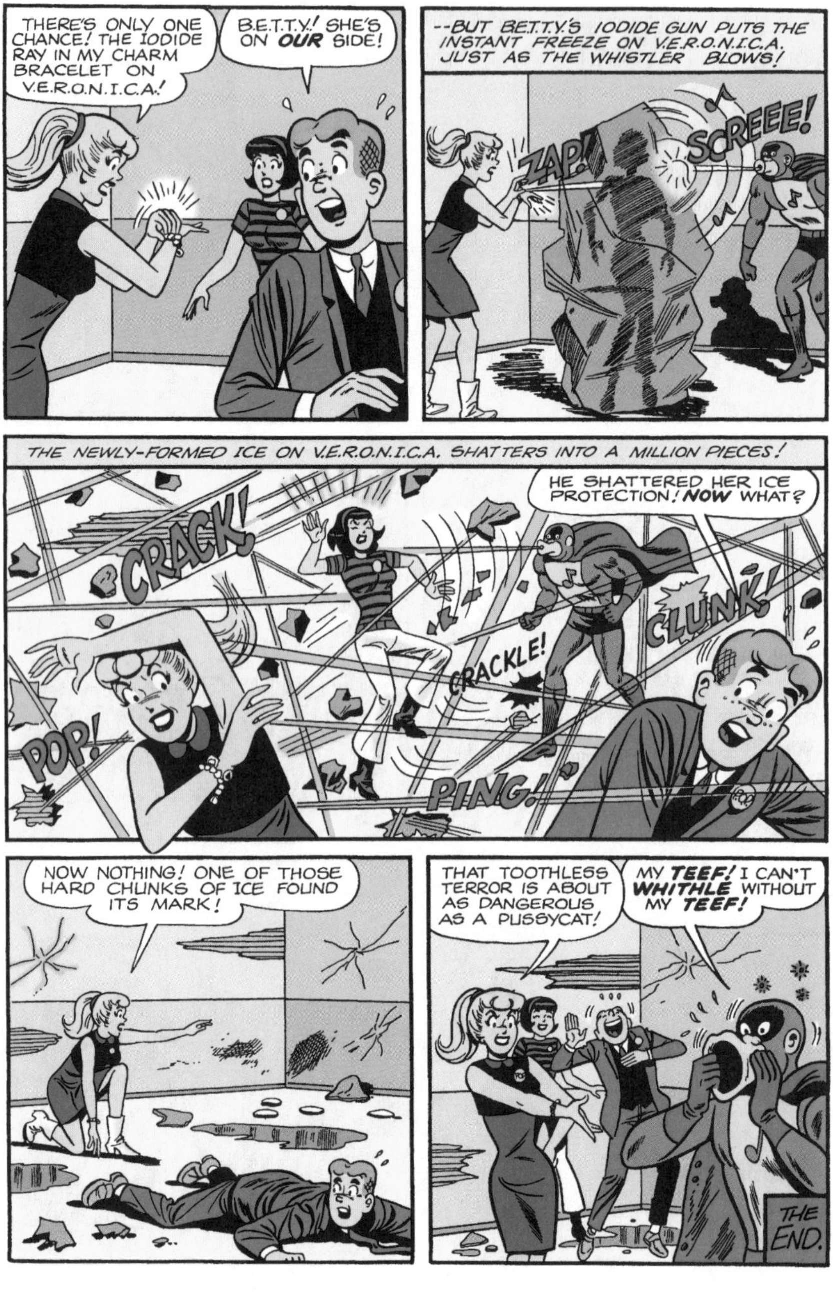
THERE'S ONLY ONE CHANCE! THE IODIDE RAY IN MY CHARM BRACELET ON V.E.R.O.N.I.C.A.!
B.E.T.T.Y.! SHE'S ON OUR SIDE!
--BUT BETTY'S IODIDE GUN PUTS THE INSTANT FREEZE ON V.E.R.O.N.I.C.A. JUST AS THE WHISTLER BLOWS!
ZAP!
SCREEEE!
THE NEWLY-FORMED ICE ON V.E.R.O.N.I.C.A. SHATTERS INTO A MILLION PIECES!
HE SHATTERED HER ICE PROTECTION! NOW WHAT?
CRACK!
CLUNK!
CRACKLE!
POP!
PING!
NOW NOTHING! ONE OF THOSE HARD CHUNKS OF ICE FOUND ITS MARK!
THAT TOOTHLESS TERROR IS ABOUT AS DANGEROUS AS A PUSSYCAT!
MY TEEF! I CAN'T WHITHLE WITHOUT MY TEEF!
THE END.

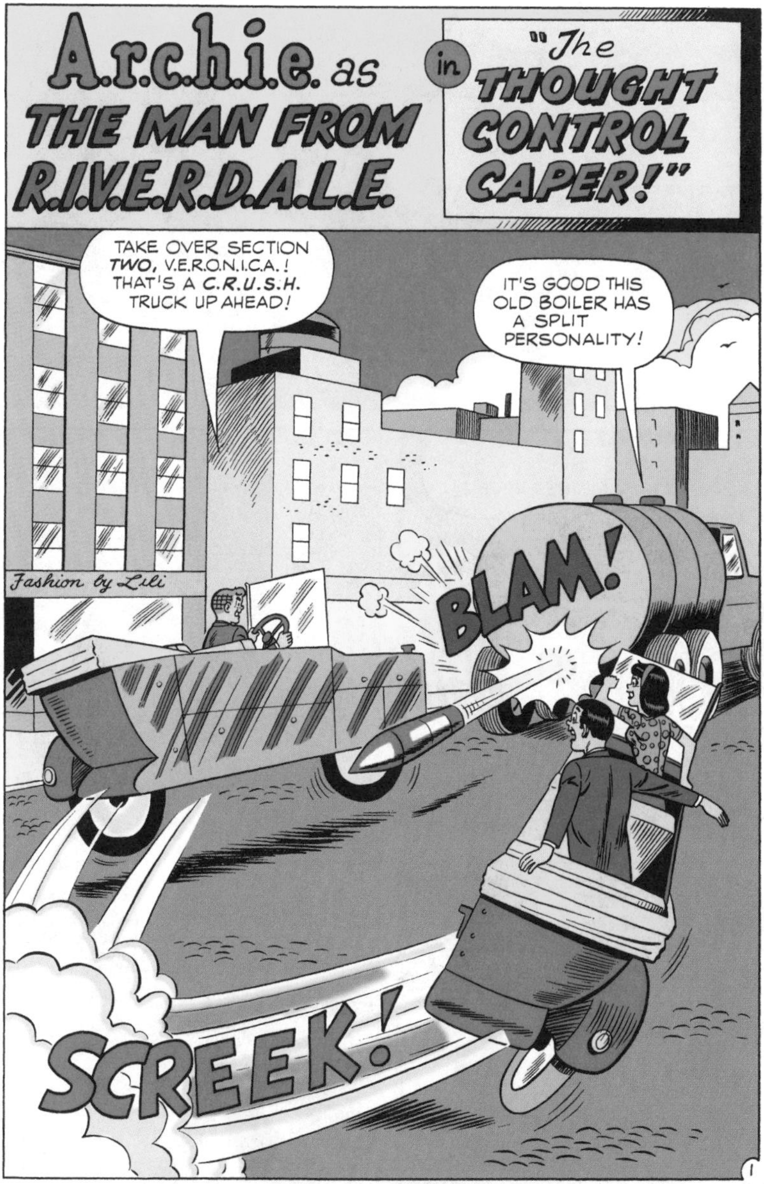
Archie as THE MAN FROM R.I.V.E.R.D.A.L.E.
in "The THOUGHT CONTROL CAPER!"
TAKE OVER SECTION TWO, V.E.R.O.N.I.C.A.! THAT'S A C.R.U.S.H. TRUCK UP AHEAD!
IT'S GOOD THIS OLD BOILER HAS A SPLIT PERSONALITY!
Fashion by Lili
BLAM!
SCREEK!
1

Story: Frank Doyle Pencils: Bob White
Inks & Letters: Jon D'Agostino

Originally printed in LIFE WITH ARCHIE #56, DECEMBER 1966

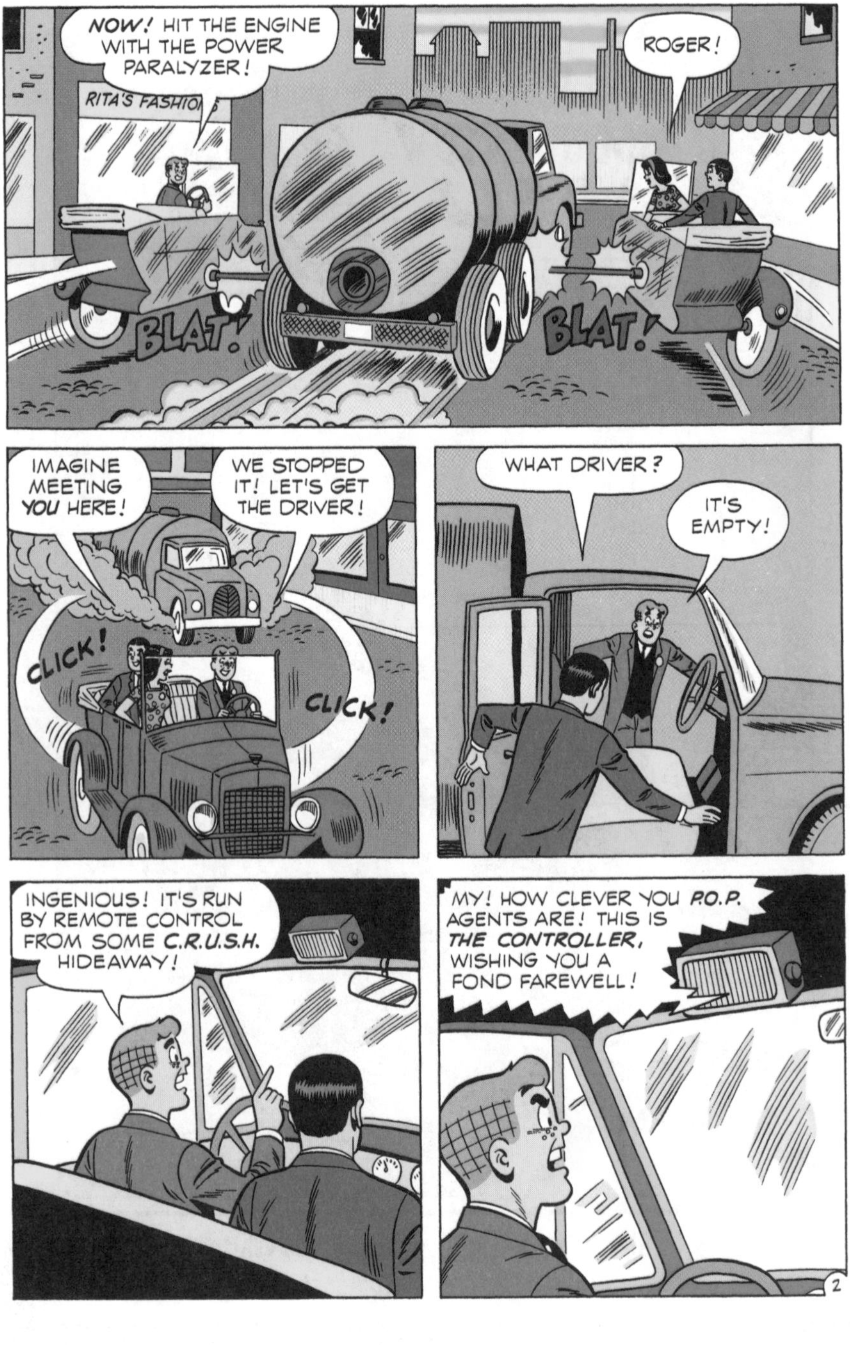
NOW! HIT THE ENGINE WITH THE POWER PARALYZER!
RITA'S FASHIONS
ROGER!
BLAT!
BLAT!
IMAGINE MEETING YOU HERE!
WE STOPPED IT! LET'S GET THE DRIVER!
CLICK!
CLICK!
WHAT DRIVER?
IT'S EMPTY!
INGENIOUS! IT'S RUN BY REMOTE CONTROL FROM SOME C.R.U.S.H. HIDEAWAY!
MY! HOW CLEVER YOU P.O.P. AGENTS ARE! THIS IS THE CONTROLLER, WISHING YOU A FOND FAREWELL!
2

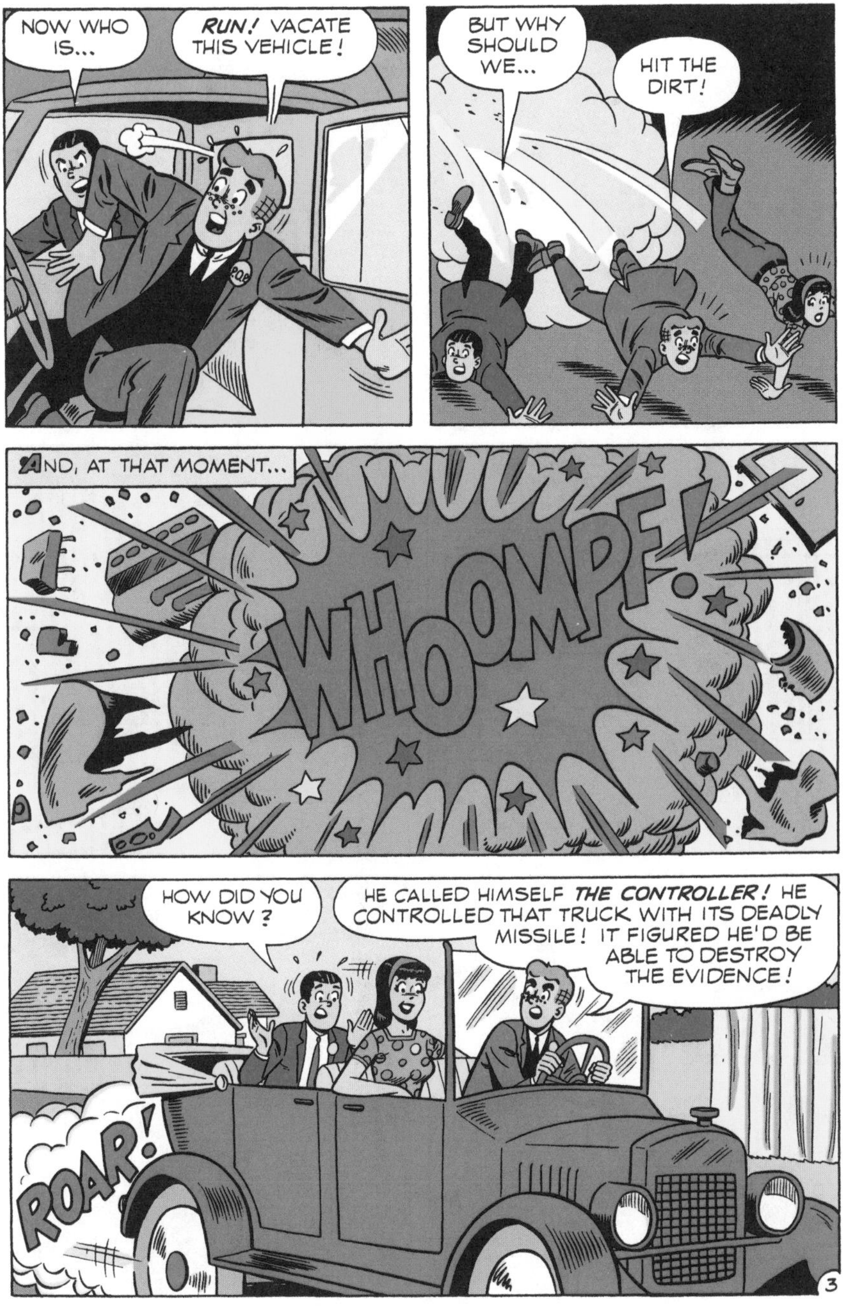
NOW WHO IS...
RUN! VACATE THIS VEHICLE!
BUT WHY SHOULD WE...
HIT THE DIRT!
AND, AT THAT MOMENT...
WHOOMPF!
HOW DID YOU KNOW?
HE CALLED HIMSELF THE CONTROLLER! HE CONTROLLED THAT TRUCK WITH ITS DEADLY MISSILE! IT FIGURED HE'D BE ABLE TO DESTROY THE EVIDENCE!
ROAR!
3

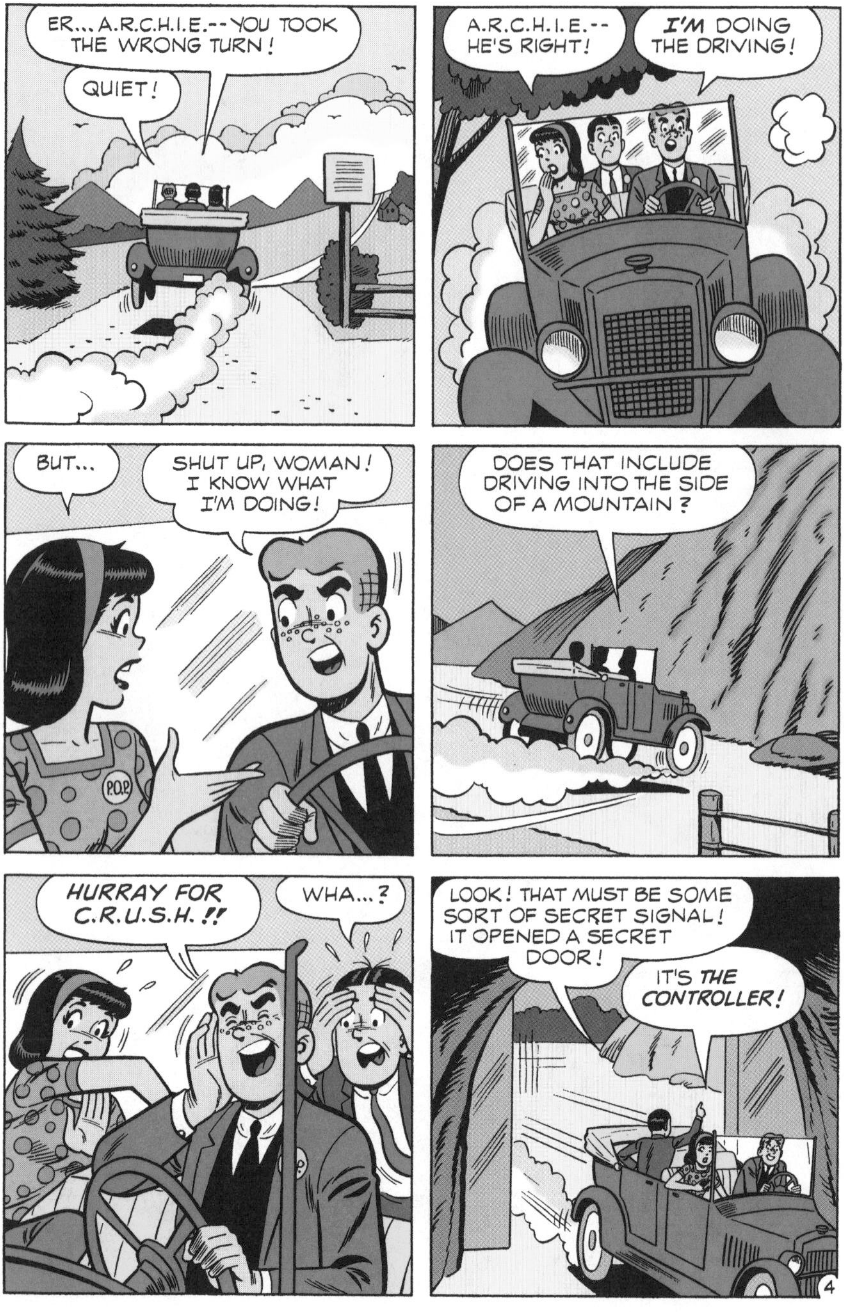
ER... A.R.C.H.I.E.-- YOU TOOK THE WRONG TURN!
QUIET!
A.R.C.H.I.E.-- HE'S RIGHT!
I'M DOING THE DRIVING!
BUT...
SHUT UP, WOMAN! I KNOW WHAT I'M DOING!
P.O.P.
DOES THAT INCLUDE DRIVING INTO THE SIDE OF A MOUNTAIN?
HURRAY FOR C.R.U.S.H.!!
WHA...?
LOOK! THAT MUST BE SOME SORT OF SECRET SIGNAL! IT OPENED A SECRET DOOR!
IT'S THE CONTROLLER!
4

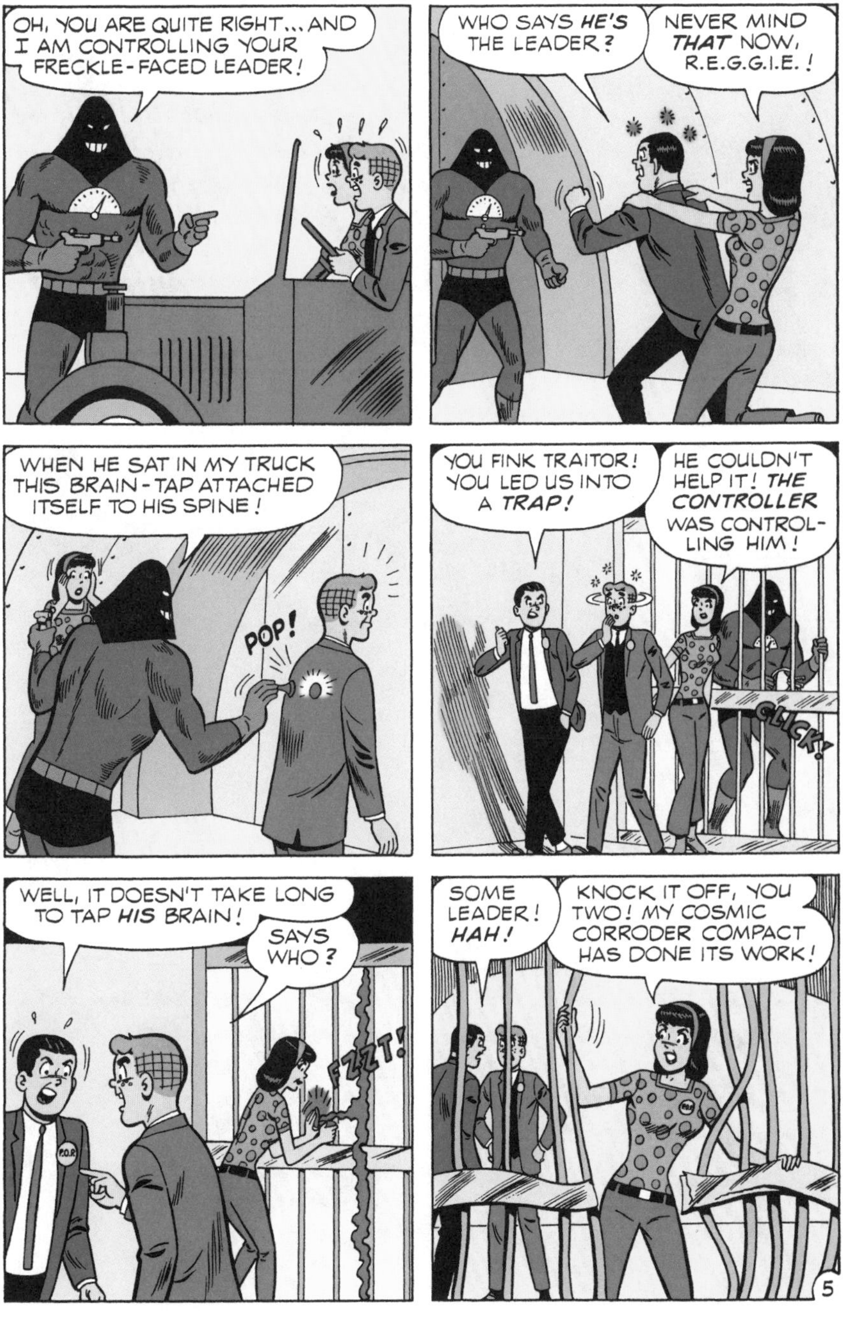
OH, YOU ARE QUITE RIGHT... AND I AM CONTROLLING YOUR FRECKLE-FACED LEADER!
WHO SAYS HE'S THE LEADER?
NEVER MIND THAT NOW, R.E.G.G.I.E.!
WHEN HE SAT IN MY TRUCK THIS BRAIN-TAP ATTACHED ITSELF TO HIS SPINE!
POP!
YOU FINK TRAITOR! YOU LED US INTO A TRAP!
HE COULDN'T HELP IT! THE CONTROLLER WAS CONTROLLING HIM!
CLICK!
WELL, IT DOESN'T TAKE LONG TO TAP HIS BRAIN!
SAYS WHO?
FZZZT!
SOME LEADER! HAH!
KNOCK IT OFF, YOU TWO! MY COSMIC CORRODER COMPACT HAS DONE ITS WORK!
5

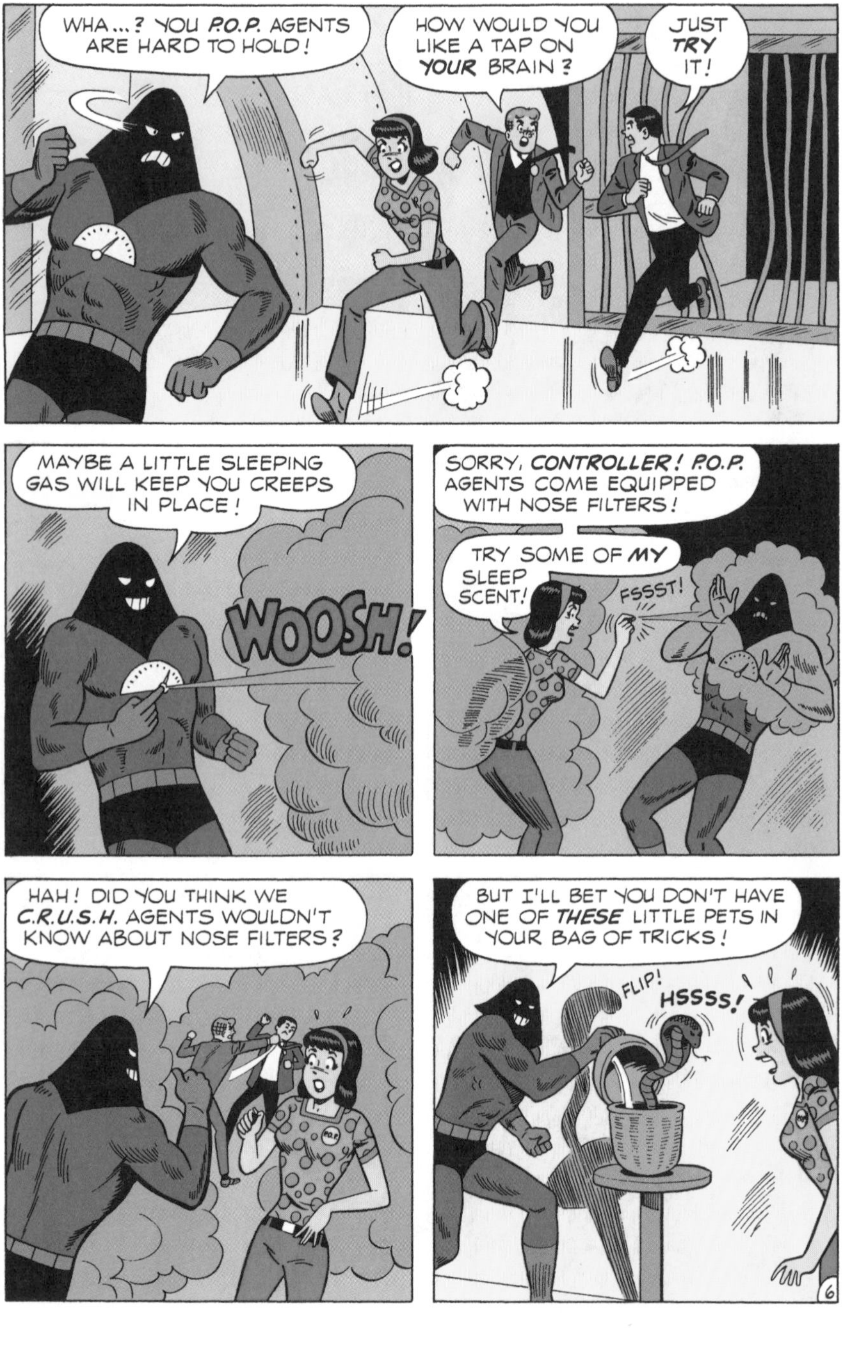
WHA...? YOU P.O.P. AGENTS ARE HARD TO HOLD!
HOW WOULD YOU LIKE A TAP ON YOUR BRAIN?
JUST TRY IT!
MAYBE A LITTLE SLEEPING GAS WILL KEEP YOU CREEPS IN PLACE!
WOOSH!
SORRY, CONTROLLER! P.O.P. AGENTS COME EQUIPPED WITH NOSE FILTERS!
TRY SOME OF MY SLEEP SCENT!
FSSST!
HAH! DID YOU THINK WE C.R.U.S.H. AGENTS WOULDN'T KNOW ABOUT NOSE FILTERS?
BUT I'LL BET YOU DON'T HAVE ONE OF THESE LITTLE PETS IN YOUR BAG OF TRICKS!
FLIP!
HSSSS!
6

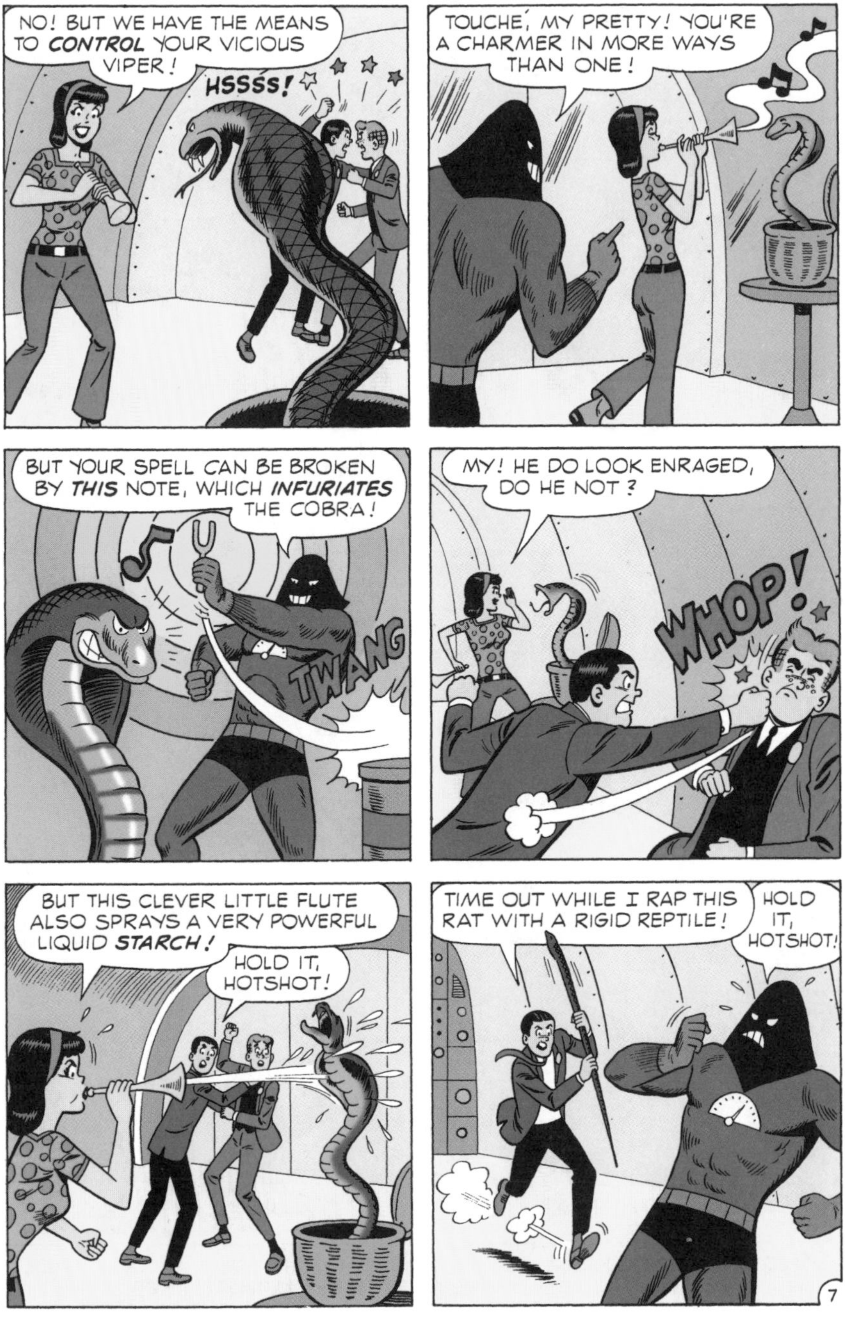
NO! BUT WE HAVE THE MEANS TO CONTROL YOUR VICIOUS VIPER!
HSSSS!
TOUCHE, MY PRETTY! YOU'RE A CHARMER IN MORE WAYS THAN ONE!
BUT YOUR SPELL CAN BE BROKEN BY THIS NOTE, WHICH INFURIATES THE COBRA!
TWANG
MY! HE DO LOOK ENRAGED, DO HE NOT?
WHOP!
BUT THIS CLEVER LITTLE FLUTE ALSO SPRAYS A VERY POWERFUL LIQUID STARCH!
HOLD IT, HOTSHOT!
TIME OUT WHILE I RAP THIS RAT WITH A RIGID REPTILE!
HOLD IT, HOTSHOT!
7

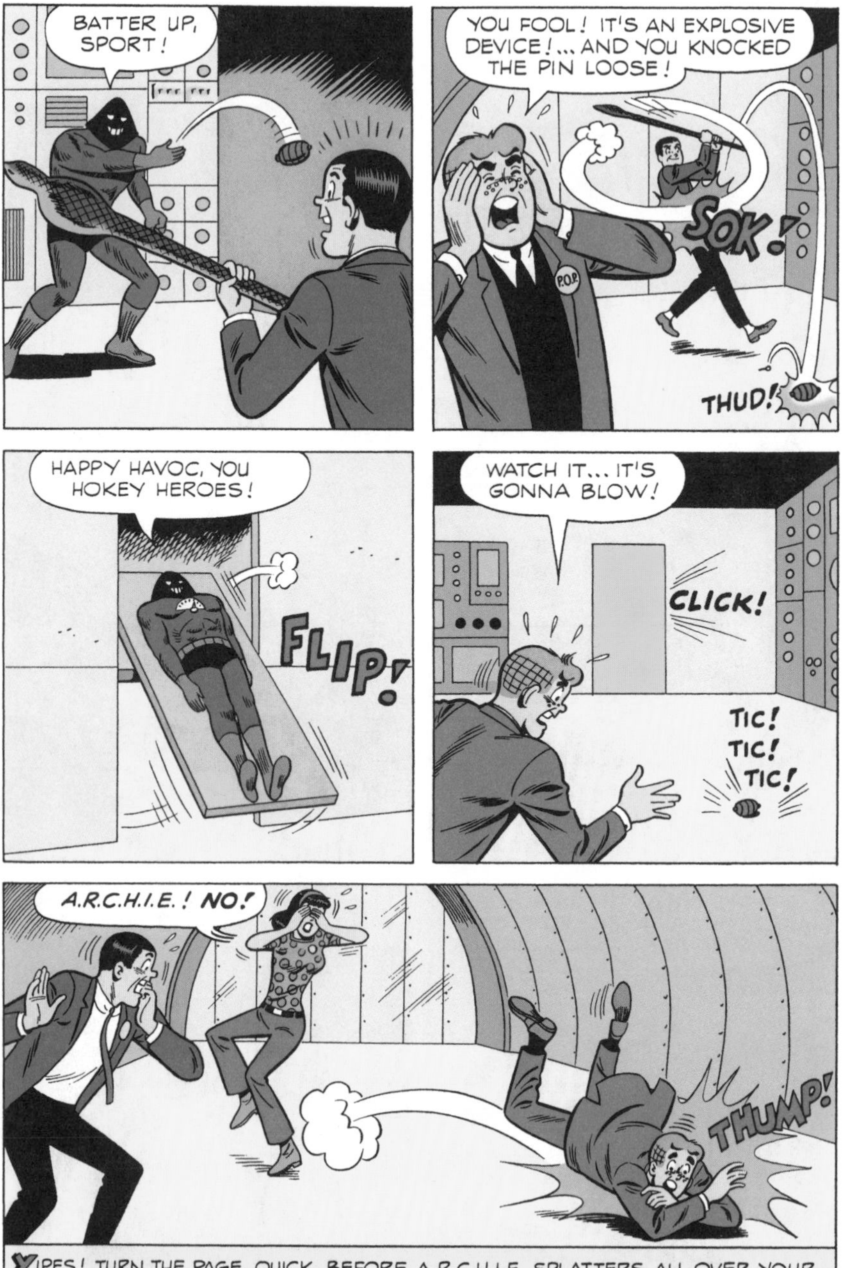
BATTER UP, SPORT!
YOU FOOL! IT'S AN EXPLOSIVE DEVICE!... AND YOU KNOCKED THE PIN LOOSE!
SOK!
P.O.P.
THUD!
HAPPY HAVOC, YOU HOKEY HEROES!
FLIP!
WATCH IT... IT'S GONNA BLOW!
CLICK!
TIC! TIC! TIC!
A.R.C.H.I.E.! NO!
THUMP!
YIPES! TURN THE PAGE, QUICK, BEFORE A.R.C.H.I.E. SPLATTERS ALL OVER YOUR NEIGHBORHOOD!--SCORE ONE FOR THE CONTROLLER!
8

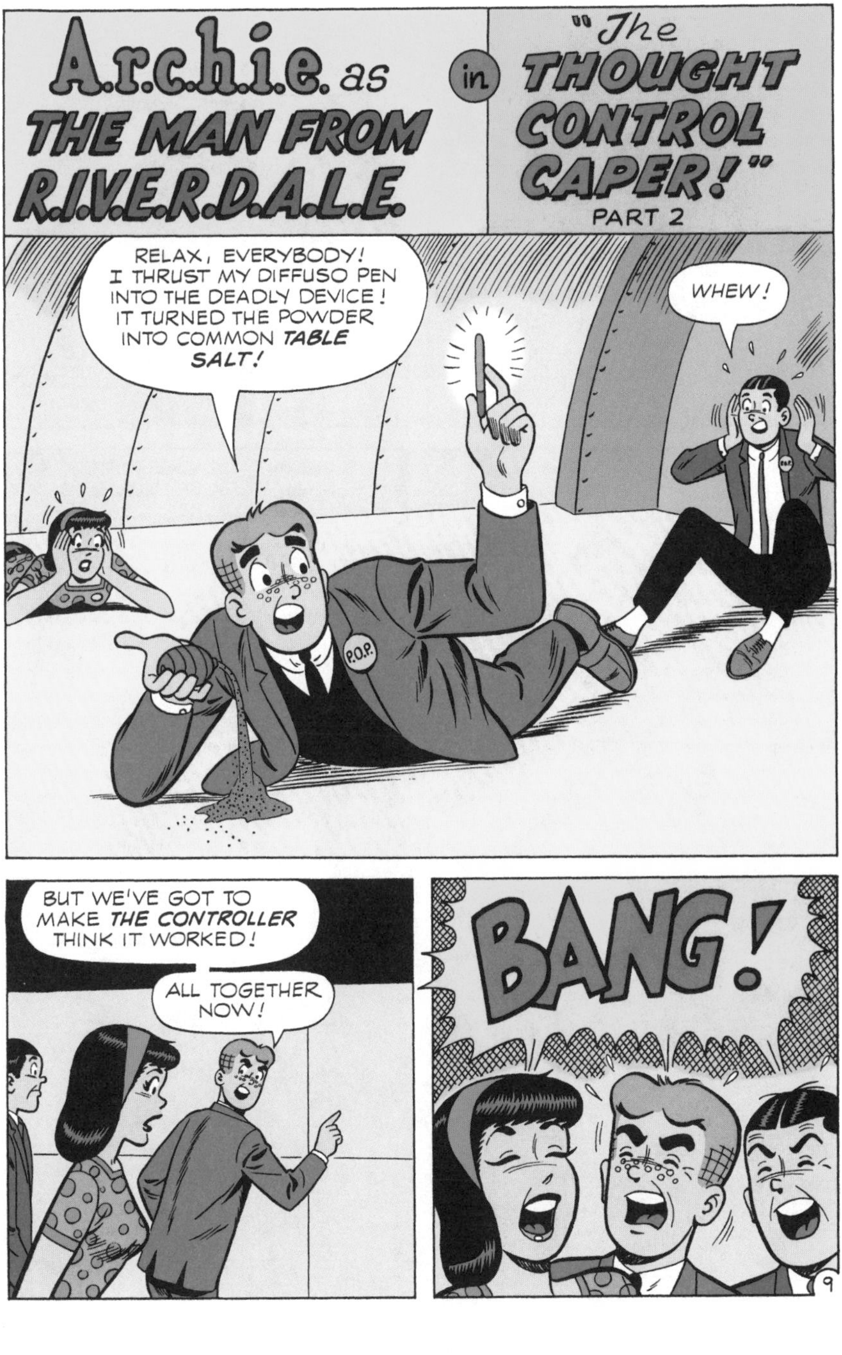

Archie as THE MAN FROM R.I.V.E.R.D.A.L.E.
in "The THOUGHT CONTROL CAPER!"
PART 2
RELAX, EVERYBODY! I THRUST MY DIFFUSO PEN INTO THE DEADLY DEVICE! IT TURNED THE POWDER INTO COMMON TABLE SALT!
WHEW!
P.O.P.
BUT WE'VE GOT TO MAKE THE CONTROLLER THINK IT WORKED!
ALL TOGETHER NOW!
BANG!
9

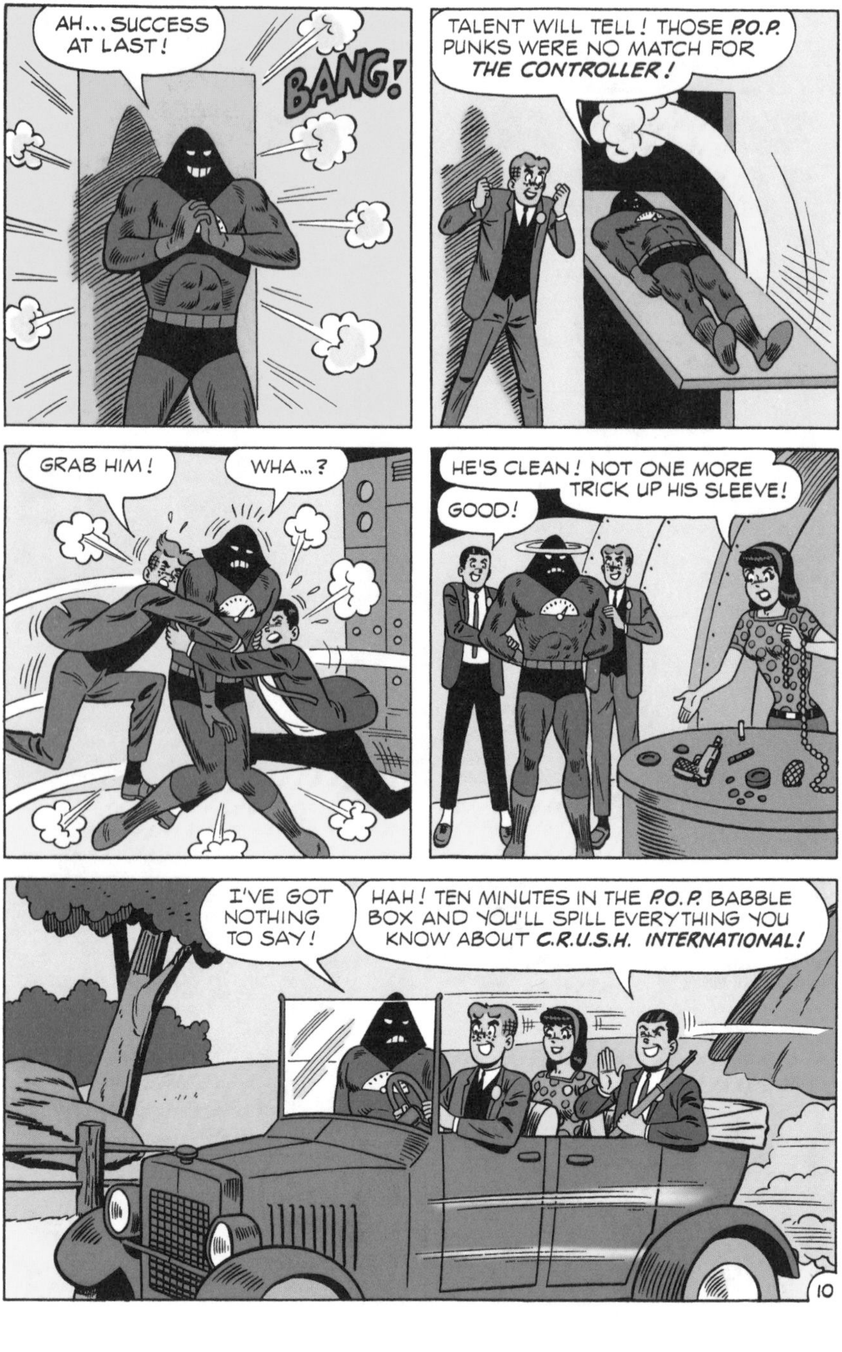
AH... SUCCESS AT LAST!
BANG!
TALENT WILL TELL! THOSE P.O.P. PUNKS WERE NO MATCH FOR THE CONTROLLER!
GRAB HIM!
WHA...?
HE'S CLEAN! NOT ONE MORE TRICK UP HIS SLEEVE!
GOOD!
I'VE GOT NOTHING TO SAY!
HAH! TEN MINUTES IN THE P.O.P. BABBLE BOX AND YOU'LL SPILL EVERYTHING YOU KNOW ABOUT C.R.U.S.H. INTERNATIONAL!
10

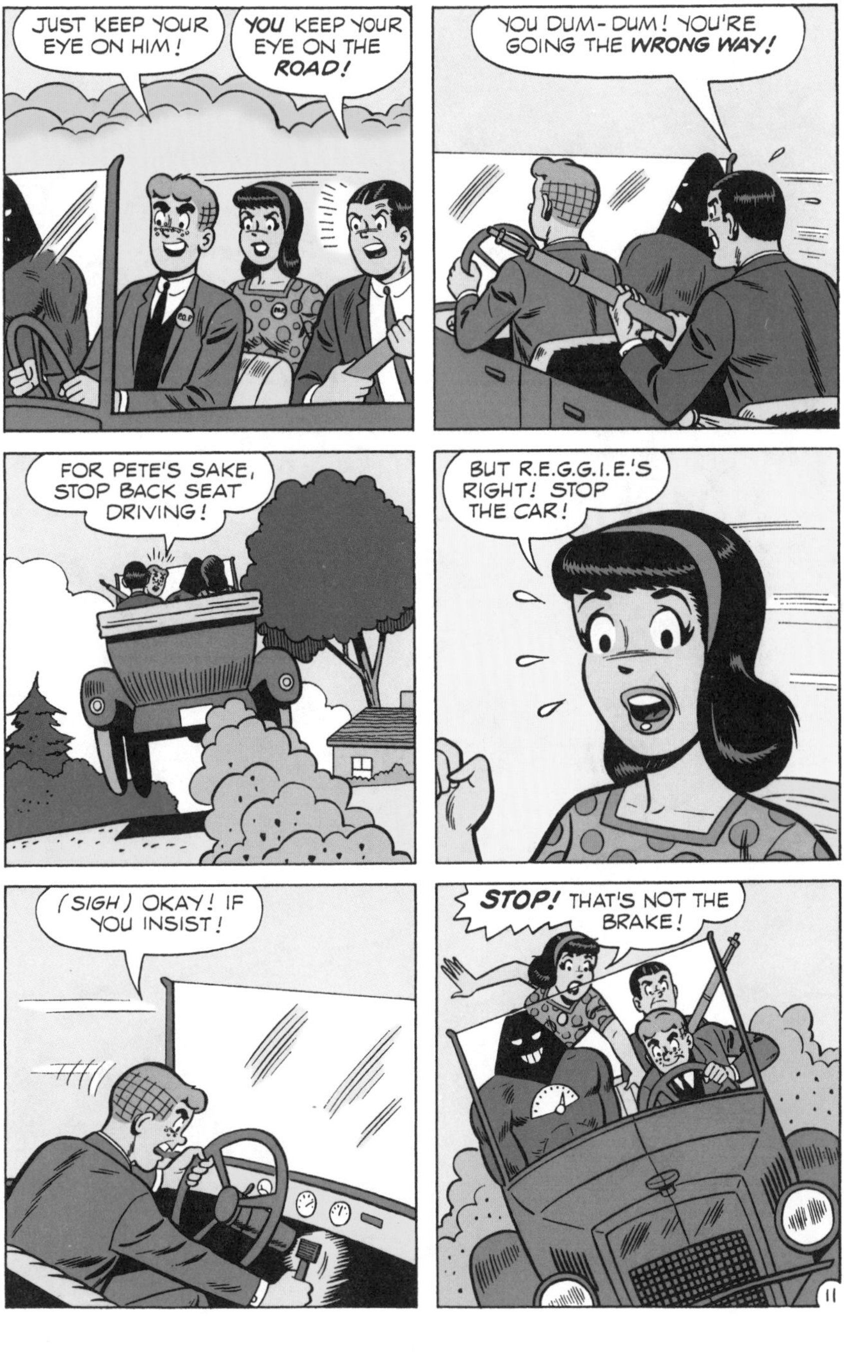
JUST KEEP YOUR EYE ON HIM!
YOU KEEP YOUR EYE ON THE ROAD!
YOU DUM-DUM! YOU'RE GOING THE WRONG WAY!
FOR PETE'S SAKE, STOP BACK SEAT DRIVING!
BUT R.E.G.G.I.E.'S RIGHT! STOP THE CAR!
(SIGH) OKAY! IF YOU INSIST!
STOP! THAT'S NOT THE BRAKE!
11

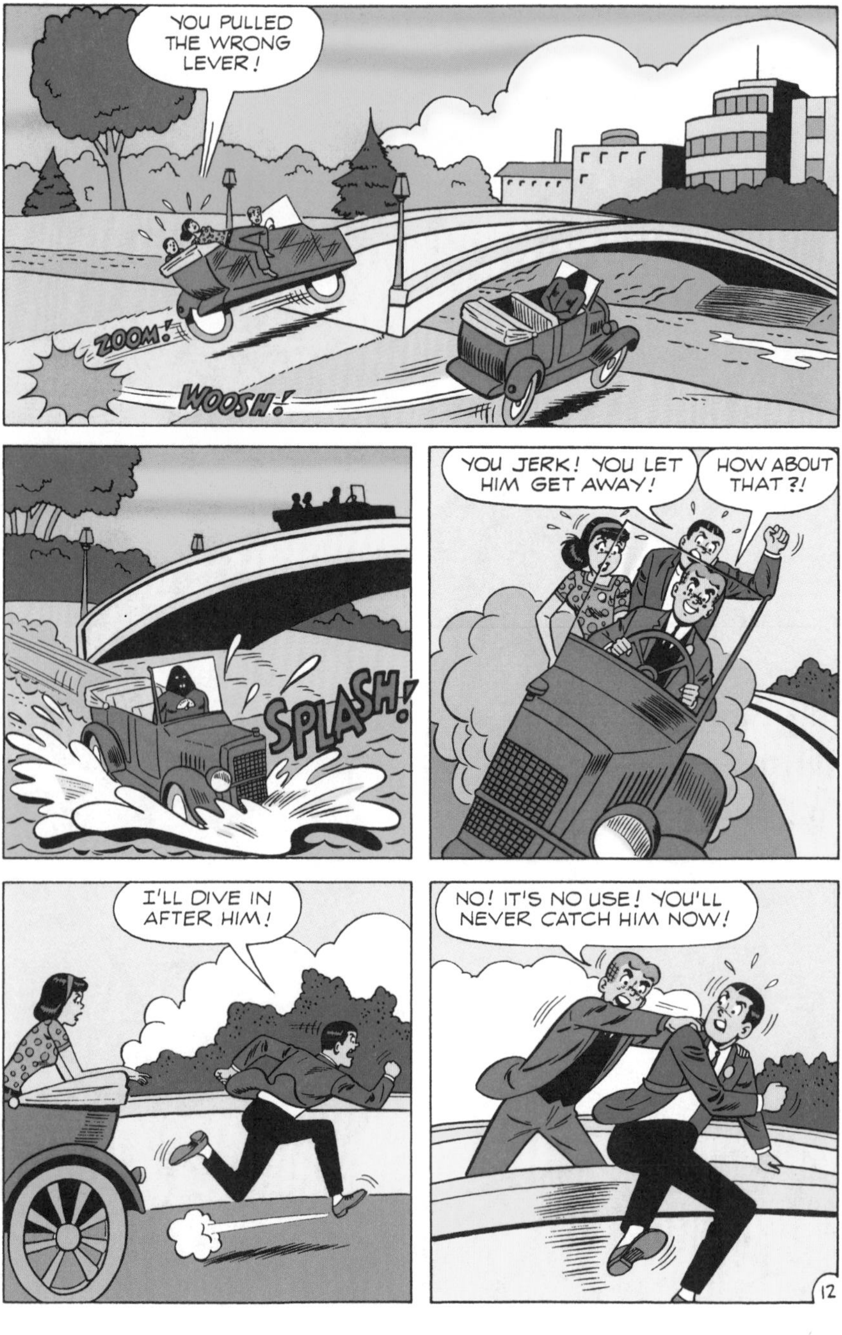
YOU PULLED THE WRONG LEVER!
ZOOM!
WOOSH!
SPLASH!
YOU JERK! YOU LET HIM GET AWAY!
HOW ABOUT THAT?!
I'LL DIVE IN AFTER HIM!
NO! IT'S NO USE! YOU'LL NEVER CATCH HIM NOW!
12

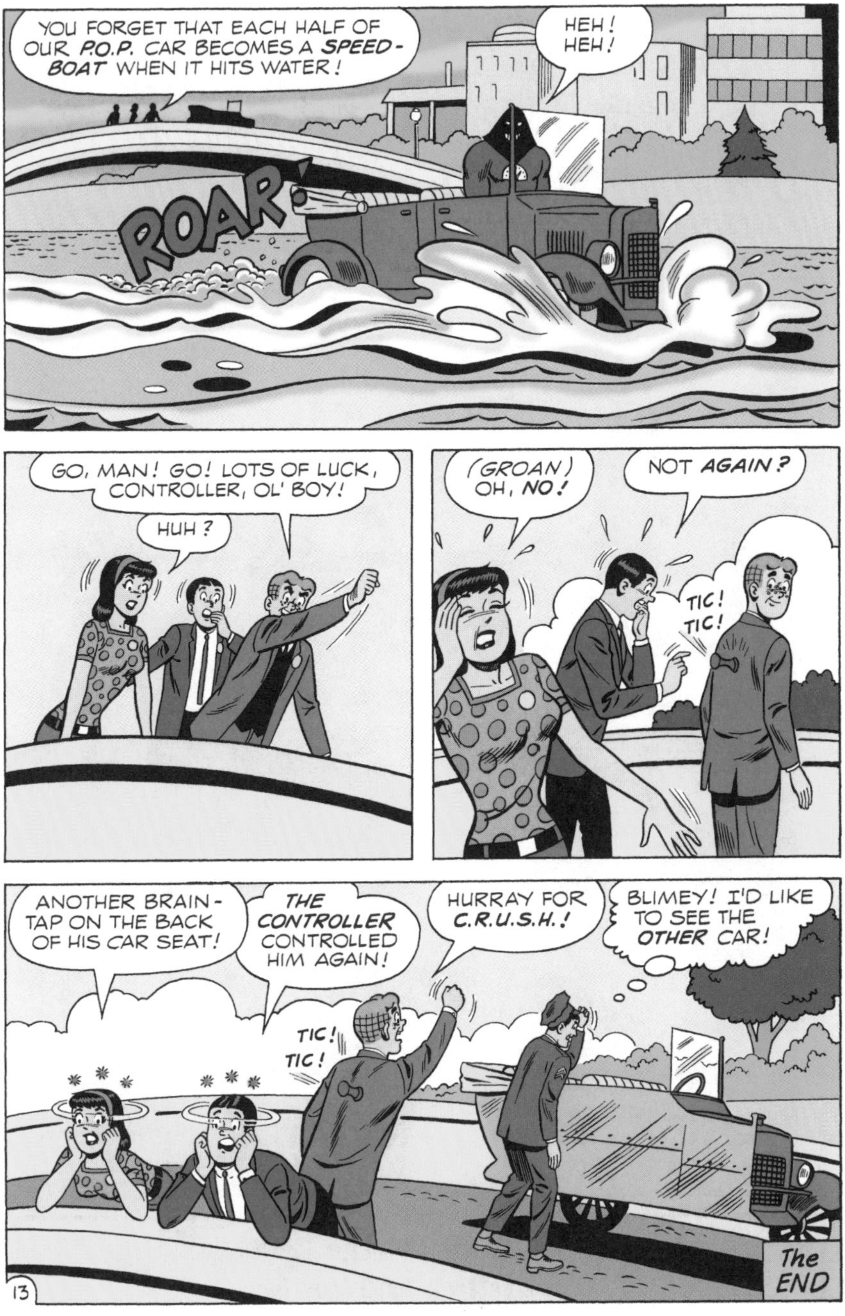
YOU FORGET THAT EACH HALF OF OUR P.O.P. CAR BECOMES A SPEED-BOAT WHEN IT HITS WATER!
HEH! HEH!
ROAR!
GO, MAN! GO! LOTS OF LUCK, CONTROLLER, OL' BOY!
HUH?
(GROAN) OH, NO!
NOT AGAIN?
TIC! TIC!
ANOTHER BRAIN-TAP ON THE BACK OF HIS CAR SEAT!
THE CONTROLLER CONTROLLED HIM AGAIN!
HURRAY FOR C.R.U.S.H.!
BLIMEY! I'D LIKE TO SEE THE OTHER CAR!
TIC! TIC!
13
The END

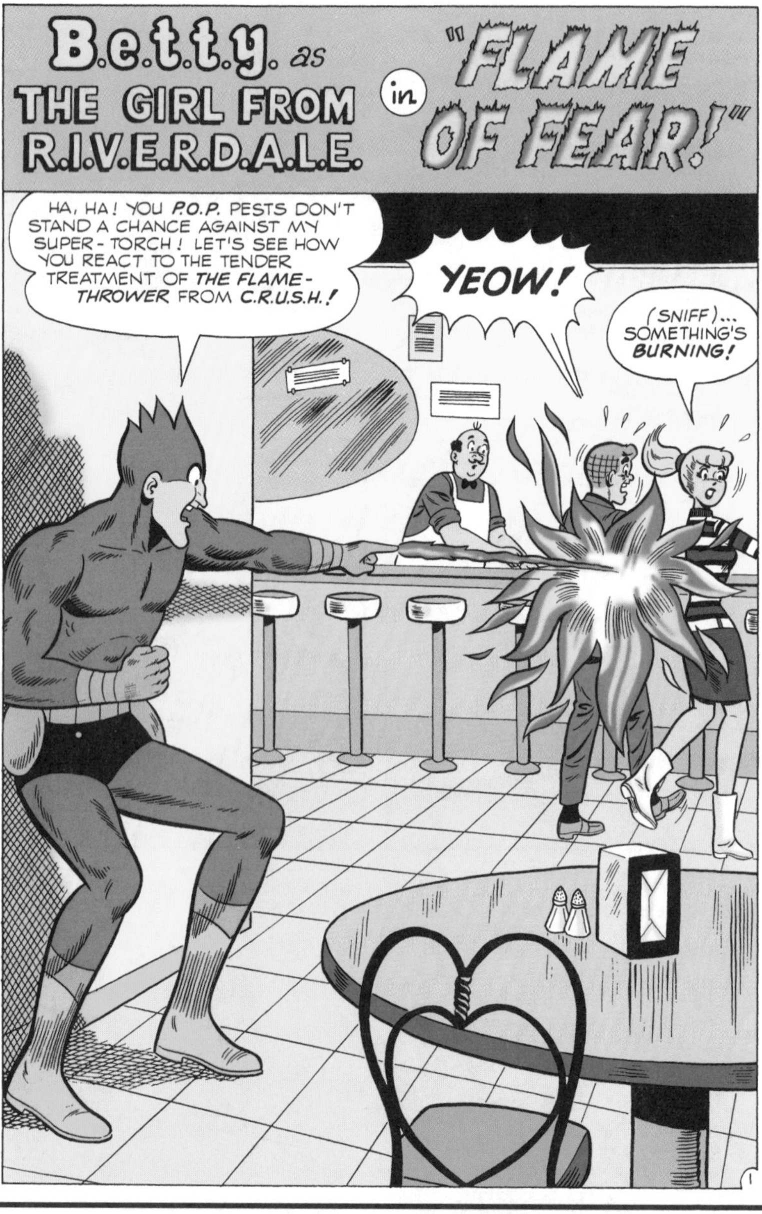
B.e.t.t.y. as THE GIRL FROM R.I.V.E.R.D.A.L.E. in "FLAME OF FEAR!"
HA, HA! YOU P.O.P. PESTS DON'T STAND A CHANCE AGAINST MY SUPER-TORCH! LET'S SEE HOW YOU REACT TO THE TENDER TREATMENT OF THE FLAME-THROWER FROM C.R.U.S.H.!
YEOW!
(SNIFF)... SOMETHING'S BURNING!

Story: Frank Doyle Pencils: Bob White
Inks & Letters: Jon D'Agostino

Originally printed in LIFE WITH ARCHIE #56, DECEMBER 1966

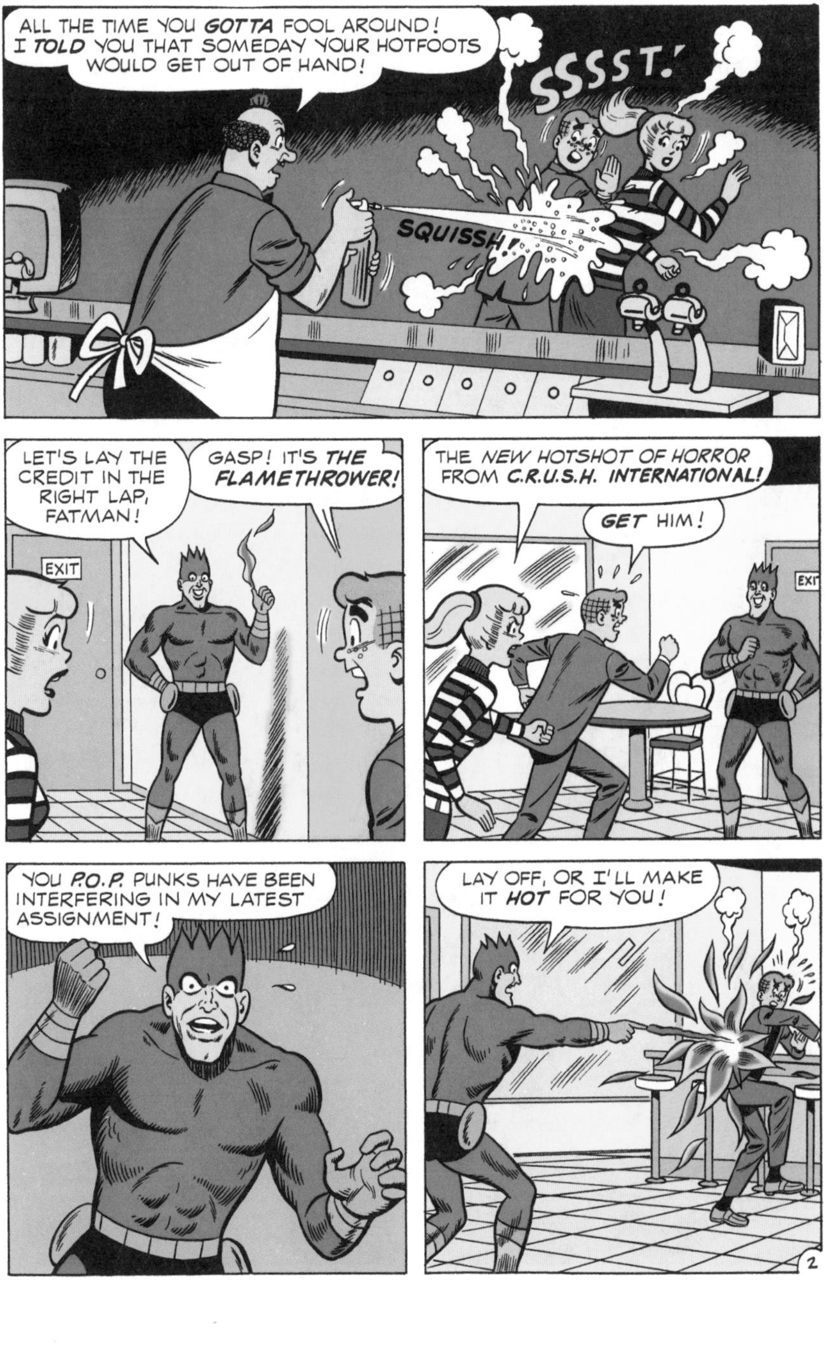
ALL THE TIME YOU GOTTA FOOL AROUND! I TOLD YOU THAT SOMEDAY YOUR HOTFOOTS WOULD GET OUT OF HAND!
SSSST!
SQUISSH!
LET'S LAY THE CREDIT IN THE RIGHT LAP, FATMAN!
GASP! IT'S THE FLAMETHROWER!
EXIT
THE NEW HOTSHOT OF HORROR FROM C.R.U.S.H. INTERNATIONAL!
GET HIM!
YOU P.O.P. PUNKS HAVE BEEN INTERFERING IN MY LATEST ASSIGNMENT!
LAY OFF, OR I'LL MAKE IT HOT FOR YOU!
2

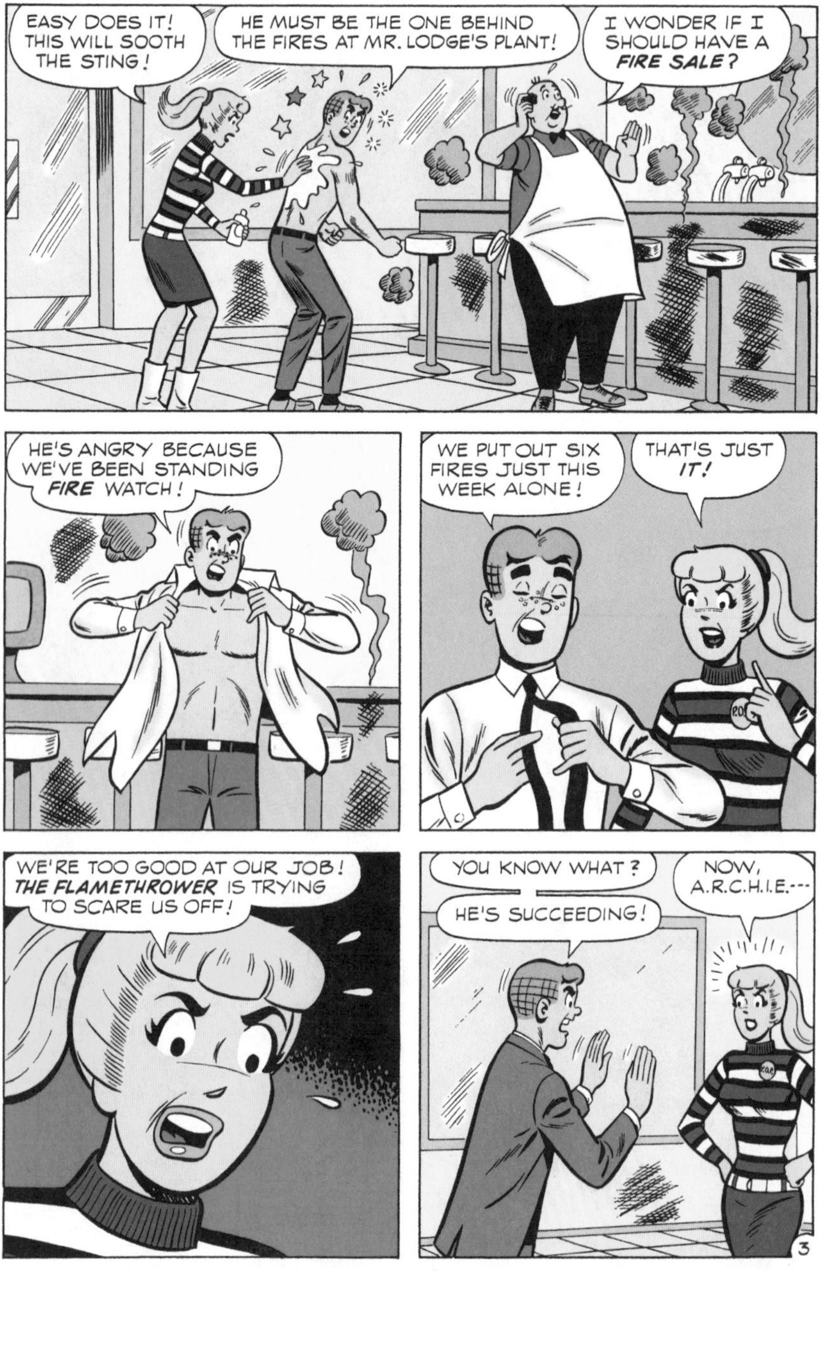
EASY DOES IT! THIS WILL SOOTH THE STING!
HE MUST BE THE ONE BEHIND THE FIRES AT MR. LODGE'S PLANT!
I WONDER IF I SHOULD HAVE A FIRE SALE?
HE'S ANGRY BECAUSE WE'VE BEEN STANDING FIRE WATCH!
WE PUT OUT SIX FIRES JUST THIS WEEK ALONE!
THAT'S JUST IT!
WE'RE TOO GOOD AT OUR JOB! THE FLAMETHROWER IS TRYING TO SCARE US OFF!
YOU KNOW WHAT?
HE'S SUCCEEDING!
NOW, A.R.C.H.I.E.---
3

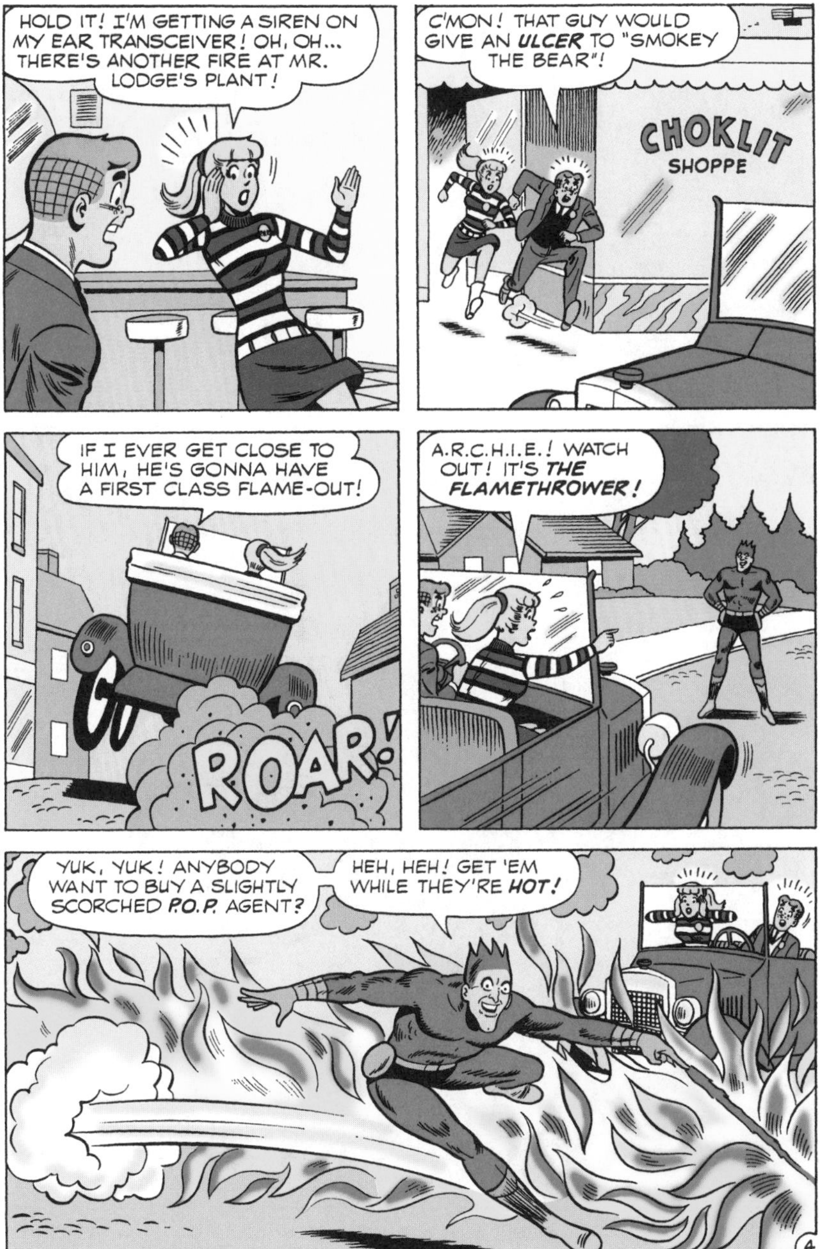
HOLD IT! I'M GETTING A SIREN ON MY EAR TRANSCEIVER! OH, OH... THERE'S ANOTHER FIRE AT MR. LODGE'S PLANT!
C'MON! THAT GUY WOULD GIVE AN ULCER TO "SMOKEY THE BEAR"!
CHOKLIT SHOPPE
IF I EVER GET CLOSE TO HIM, HE'S GONNA HAVE A FIRST CLASS FLAME-OUT!
ROAR!
A.R.C.H.I.E.! WATCH OUT! IT'S THE FLAMETHROWER!
YUK, YUK! ANYBODY WANT TO BUY A SLIGHTLY SCORCHED P.O.P. AGENT?
HEH, HEH! GET 'EM WHILE THEY'RE HOT!
4

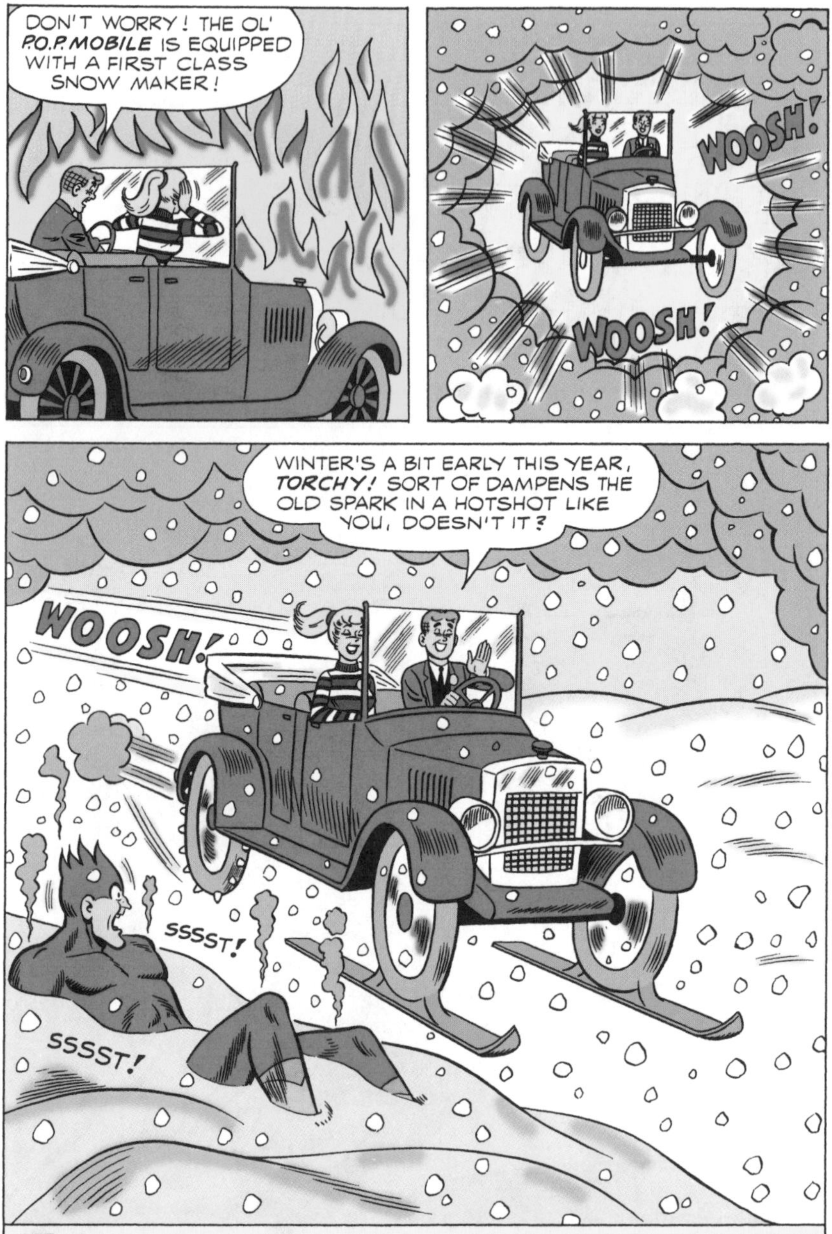
DON'T WORRY! THE OL' P.O.P. MOBILE IS EQUIPPED WITH A FIRST CLASS SNOW MAKER!
WOOSH!
WOOSH!
WINTER'S A BIT EARLY THIS YEAR, TORCHY! SORT OF DAMPENS THE OLD SPARK IN A HOTSHOT LIKE YOU, DOESN'T IT?
WOOSH!
SSSST!
SSSST!
THAT'S ONE FOR OUR SIDE! BUT HOW DO YOU HANDLE A HOT-HEADED HOOD LIKE THIS ONE? A GUY LIKE THAT BURNS YOU UP, DOESN'T HE?
5

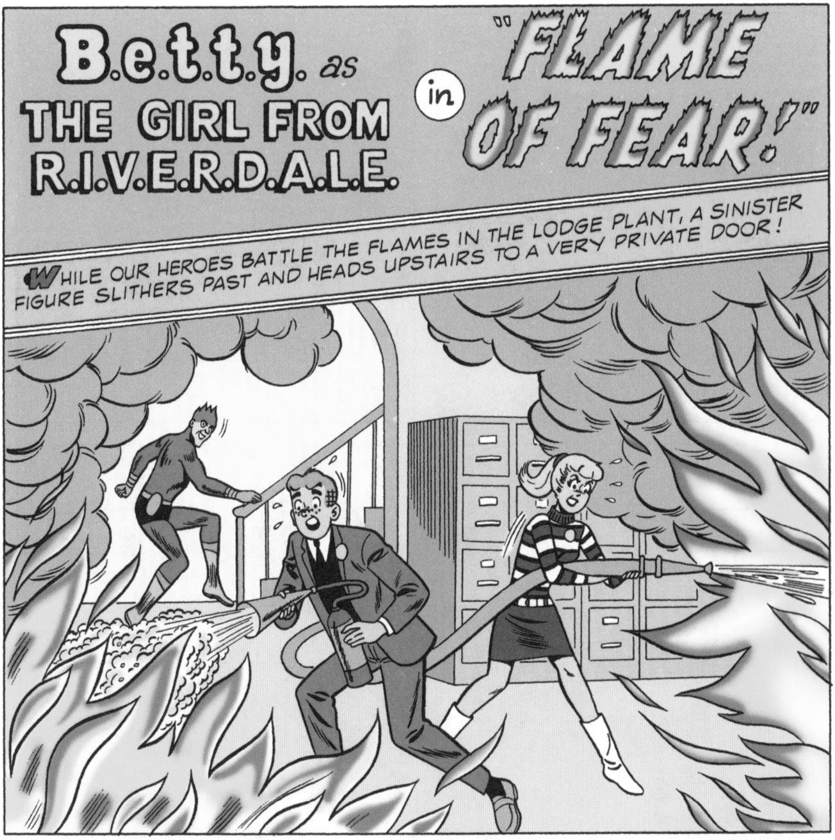

B.e.t.t.y. as THE GIRL FROM R.I.V.E.R.D.A.L.E. in "FLAME OF FEAR!"
WHILE OUR HEROES BATTLE THE FLAMES IN THE LODGE PLANT, A SINISTER FIGURE SLITHERS PAST AND HEADS UPSTAIRS TO A VERY PRIVATE DOOR!

...AND STRIKES AT THE HEART OF THE LODGE EMPIRE! -- *LODGE HIMSELF!*

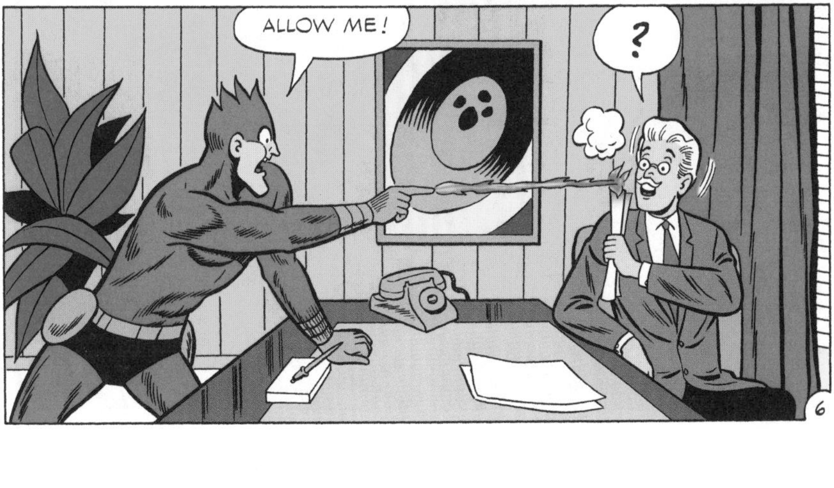

ALLOW ME!
?
6

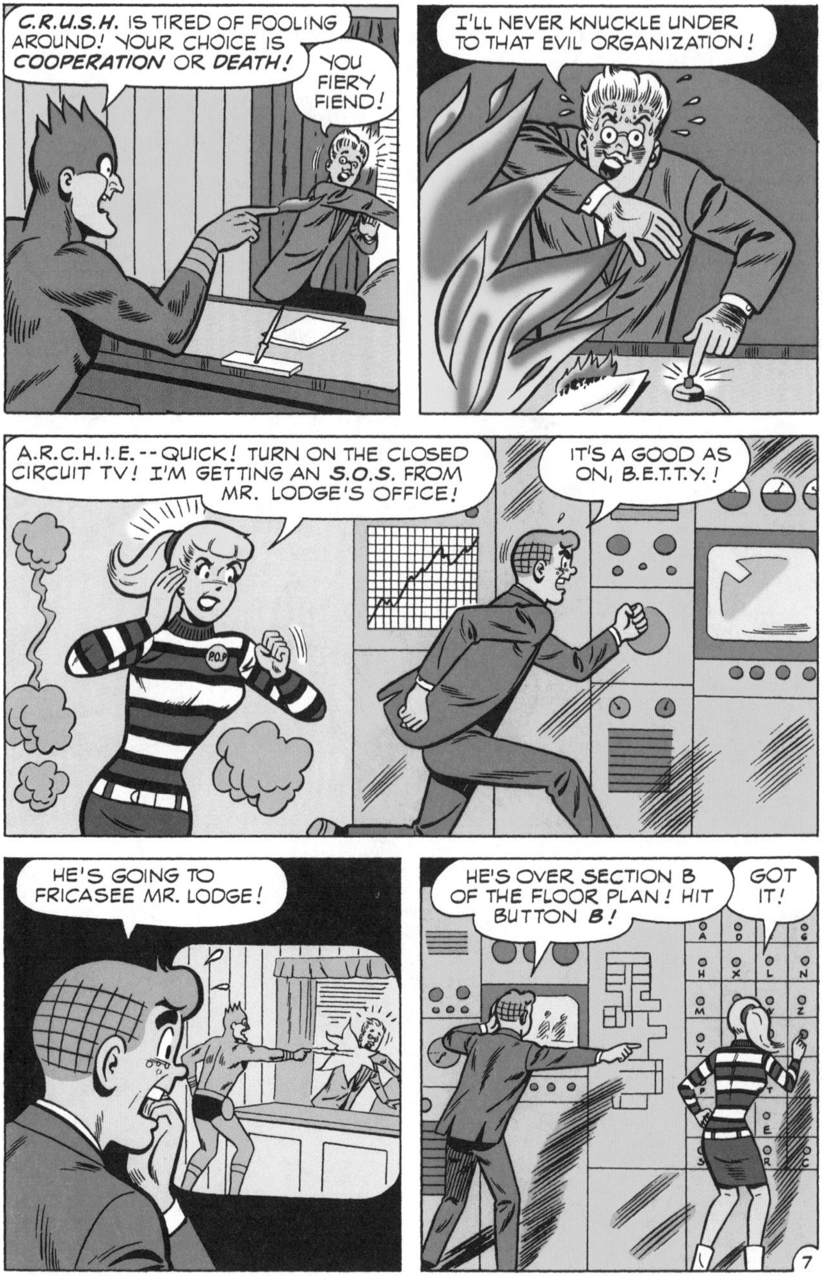
C.R.U.S.H. IS TIRED OF FOOLING AROUND! YOUR CHOICE IS COOPERATION OR DEATH!
YOU FIERY FIEND!
I'LL NEVER KNUCKLE UNDER TO THAT EVIL ORGANIZATION!
A.R.C.H.I.E.--QUICK! TURN ON THE CLOSED CIRCUIT TV! I'M GETTING AN S.O.S. FROM MR. LODGE'S OFFICE!
IT'S A GOOD AS ON, B.E.T.T.Y.!
P.O.P
HE'S GOING TO FRICASEE MR. LODGE!
HE'S OVER SECTION B OF THE FLOOR PLAN! HIT BUTTON B!
GOT IT!
7

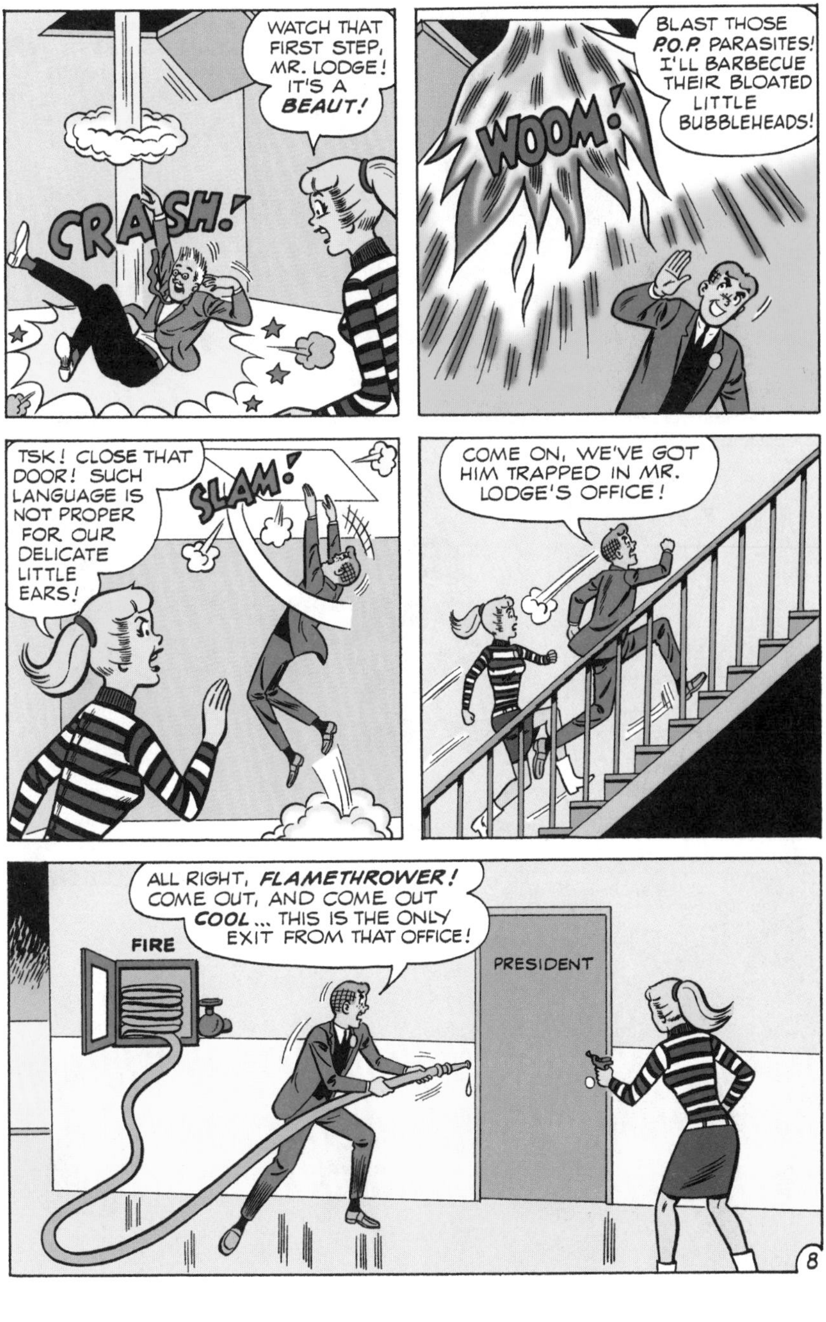
WATCH THAT FIRST STEP, MR. LODGE! IT'S A BEAUT!
CRASH!
BLAST THOSE P.O.P. PARASITES! I'LL BARBECUE THEIR BLOATED LITTLE BUBBLEHEADS!
WOOM!
TSK! CLOSE THAT DOOR! SUCH LANGUAGE IS NOT PROPER FOR OUR DELICATE LITTLE EARS!
SLAM!
COME ON, WE'VE GOT HIM TRAPPED IN MR. LODGE'S OFFICE!
ALL RIGHT, FLAMETHROWER! COME OUT, AND COME OUT COOL... THIS IS THE ONLY EXIT FROM THAT OFFICE!
FIRE
PRESIDENT
8

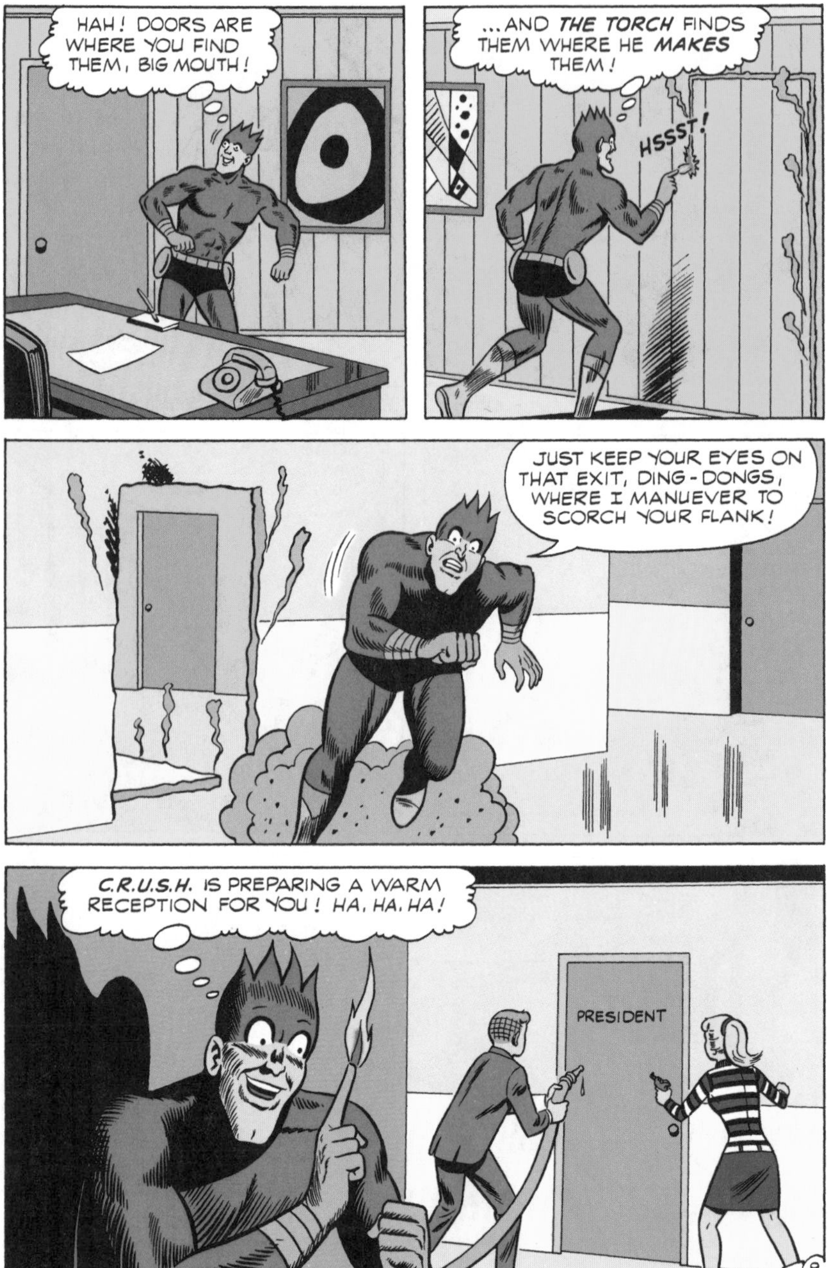
HAH! DOORS ARE WHERE YOU FIND THEM, BIG MOUTH!
...AND THE TORCH FINDS THEM WHERE HE MAKES THEM!
HSSST!
JUST KEEP YOUR EYES ON THAT EXIT, DING-DONGS, WHERE I MANUEVER TO SCORCH YOUR FLANK!
C.R.U.S.H. IS PREPARING A WARM RECEPTION FOR YOU! HA, HA, HA!
PRESIDENT
9

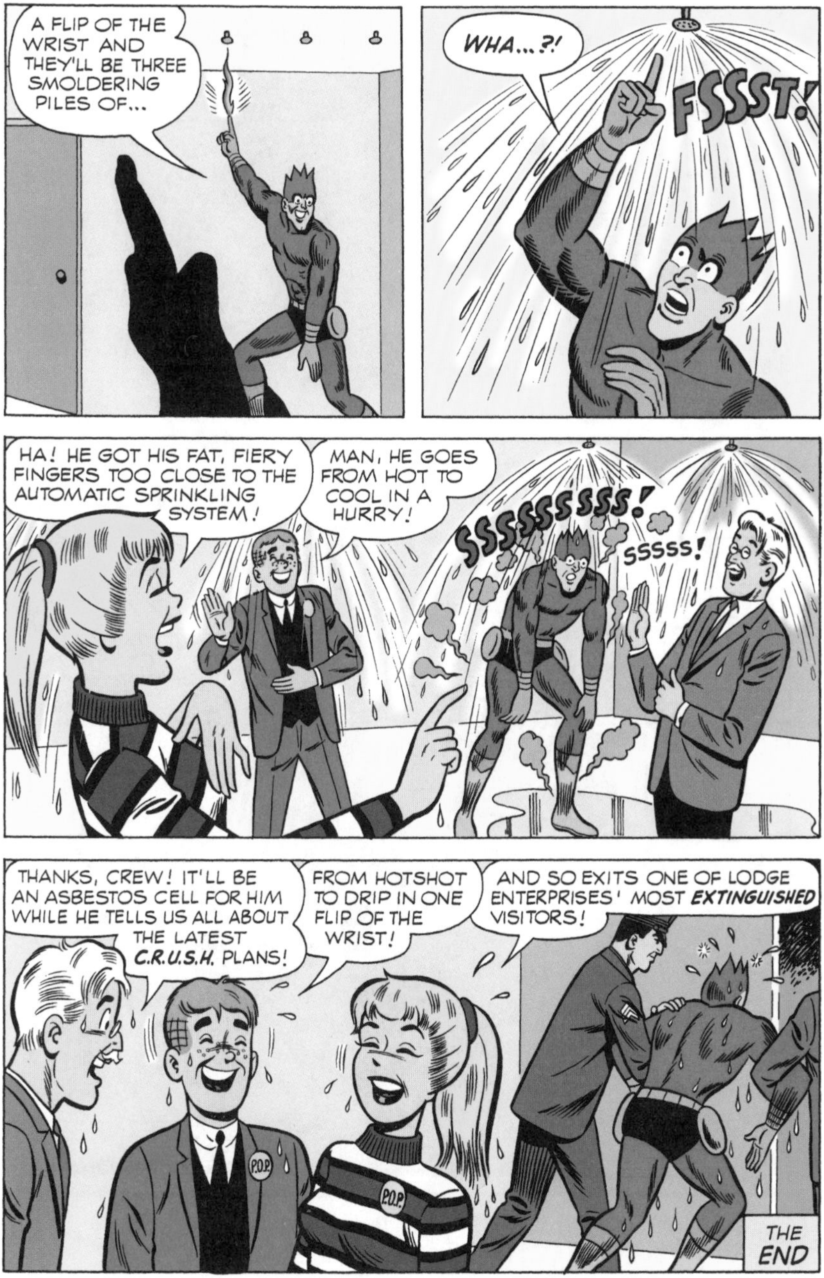

A FLIP OF THE WRIST AND THEY'LL BE THREE SMOLDERING PILES OF...
WHA...?!
FSSST!
HA! HE GOT HIS FAT, FIERY FINGERS TOO CLOSE TO THE AUTOMATIC SPRINKLING SYSTEM!
MAN, HE GOES FROM HOT TO COOL IN A HURRY!
SSSSSSSSS!
SSSSS!
THANKS, CREW! IT'LL BE AN ASBESTOS CELL FOR HIM WHILE HE TELLS US ALL ABOUT THE LATEST C.R.U.S.H. PLANS!
FROM HOTSHOT TO DRIP IN ONE FLIP OF THE WRIST!
AND SO EXITS ONE OF LODGE ENTERPRISES' MOST EXTINGUISHED VISITORS!
P.O.P.
P.O.P.
THE END

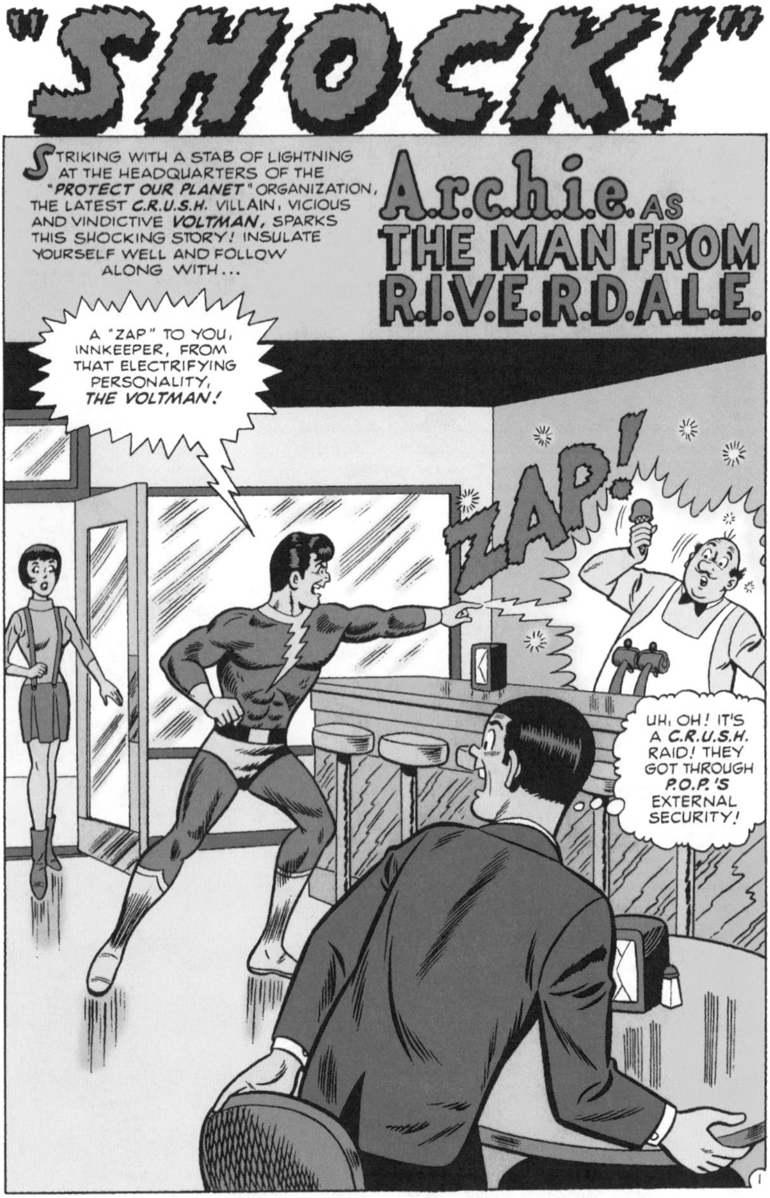
"SHOCK!"
STRIKING WITH A STAB OF LIGHTNING AT THE HEADQUARTERS OF THE "PROTECT OUR PLANET" ORGANIZATION, THE LATEST C.R.U.S.H. VILLAIN, VICIOUS AND VINDICTIVE VOLTMAN, SPARKS THIS SHOCKING STORY! INSULATE YOURSELF WELL AND FOLLOW ALONG WITH...
Archie AS THE MAN FROM R.I.V.E.R.D.A.L.E.
A "ZAP" TO YOU, INNKEEPER, FROM THAT ELECTRIFYING PERSONALITY, THE VOLTMAN!
ZAP!
UH, OH! IT'S A C.R.U.S.H. RAID! THEY GOT THROUGH P.O.P.'S EXTERNAL SECURITY!
1

Story: Frank Doyle Pencils: Bob White
Inks & Letters: Jon D'Agostino

Originally printed in LIFE WITH ARCHIE #58, FEBRUARY 1967

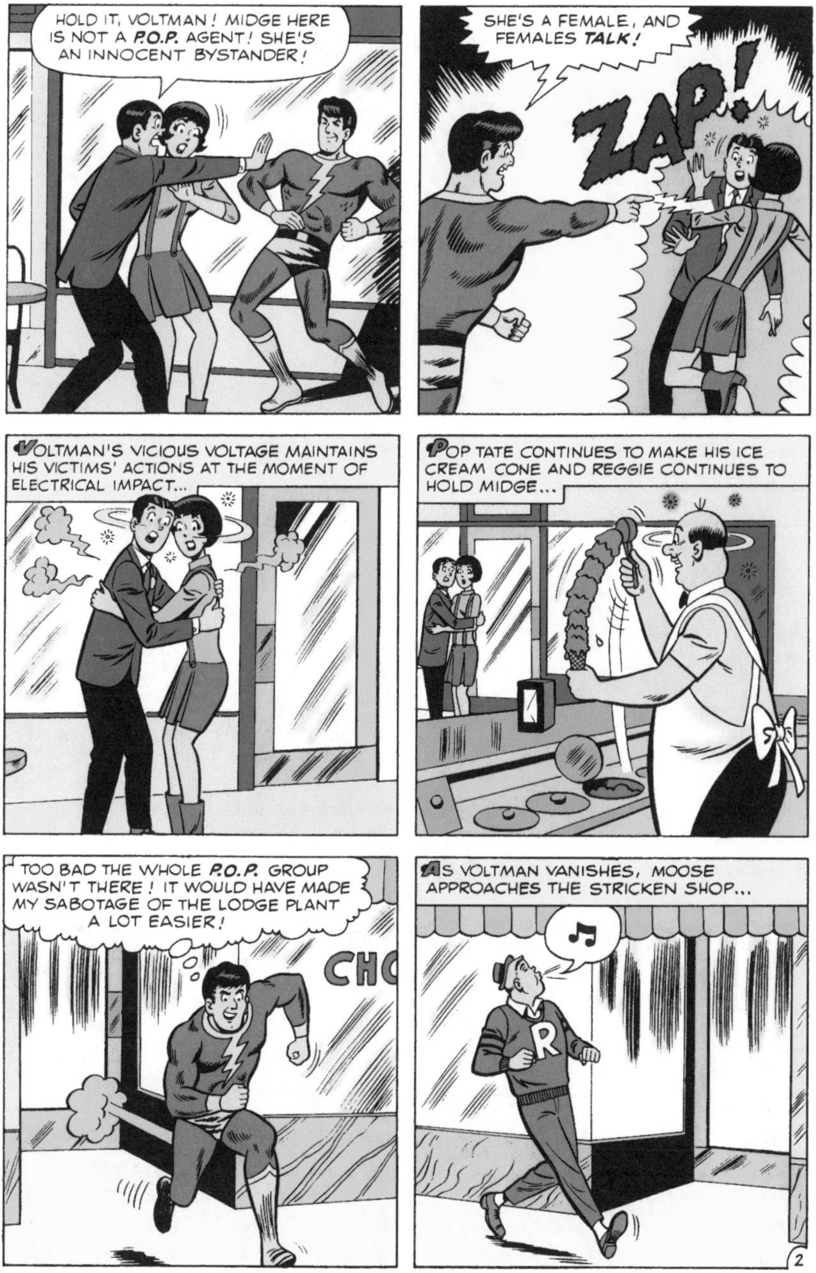
HOLD IT, VOLTMAN! MIDGE HERE IS NOT A P.O.P. AGENT! SHE'S AN INNOCENT BYSTANDER!
SHE'S A FEMALE, AND FEMALES TALK!
ZAP!
VOLTMAN'S VICIOUS VOLTAGE MAINTAINS HIS VICTIMS' ACTIONS AT THE MOMENT OF ELECTRICAL IMPACT...
POP TATE CONTINUES TO MAKE HIS ICE CREAM CONE AND REGGIE CONTINUES TO HOLD MIDGE...
TOO BAD THE WHOLE P.O.P. GROUP WASN'T THERE! IT WOULD HAVE MADE MY SABOTAGE OF THE LODGE PLANT A LOT EASIER!
CHO
AS VOLTMAN VANISHES, MOOSE APPROACHES THE STRICKEN SHOP...
R
2

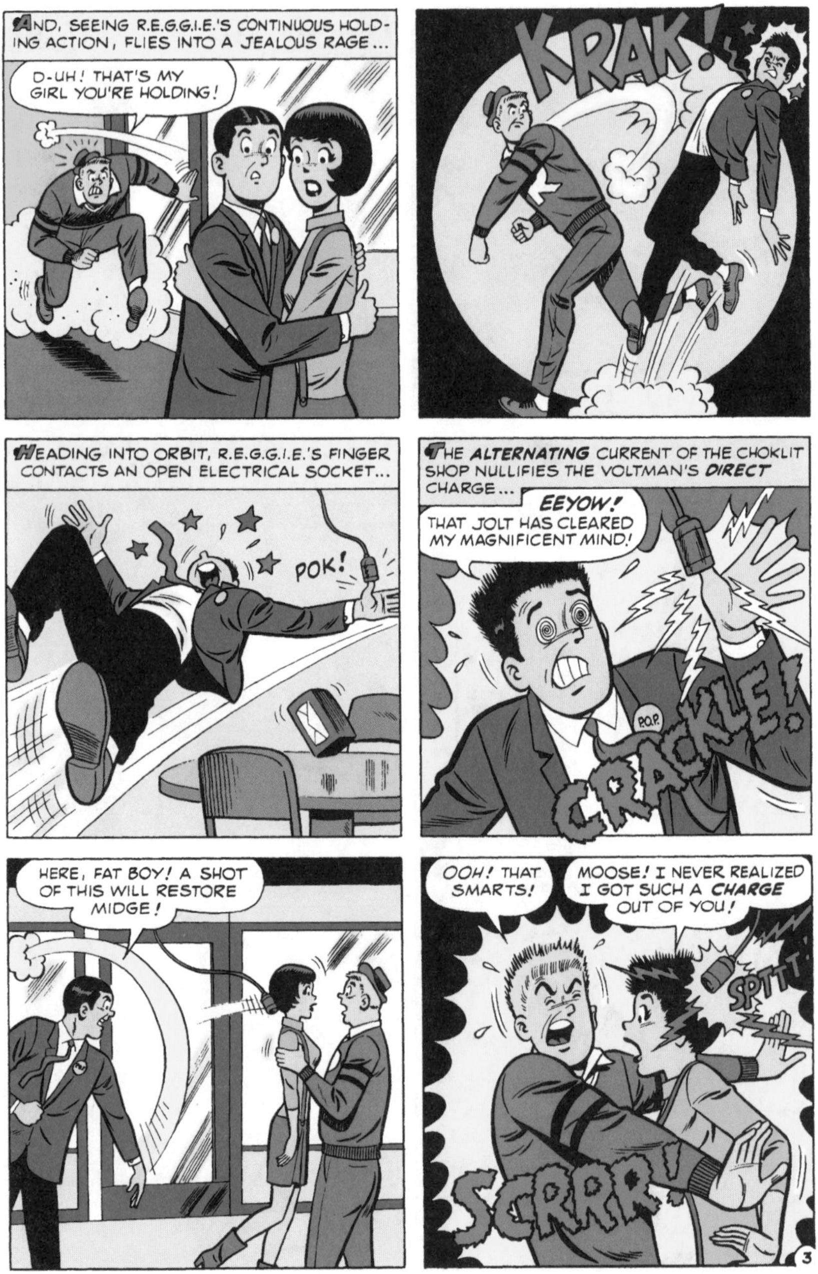
AND, SEEING R.E.G.G.I.E.'S CONTINUOUS HOLDING ACTION, FLIES INTO A JEALOUS RAGE...
D-UH! THAT'S MY GIRL YOU'RE HOLDING!
KRAK!
HEADING INTO ORBIT, R.E.G.G.I.E.'S FINGER CONTACTS AN OPEN ELECTRICAL SOCKET...
POK!
THE ALTERNATING CURRENT OF THE CHOKLIT SHOP NULLIFIES THE VOLTMAN'S DIRECT CHARGE...
EEYOW! THAT JOLT HAS CLEARED MY MAGNIFICENT MIND!
P.O.P.
CRACKLE!
HERE, FAT BOY! A SHOT OF THIS WILL RESTORE MIDGE!
OOH! THAT SMARTS!
MOOSE! I NEVER REALIZED I GOT SUCH A CHARGE OUT OF YOU!
SPTTT
SCRRR!
3

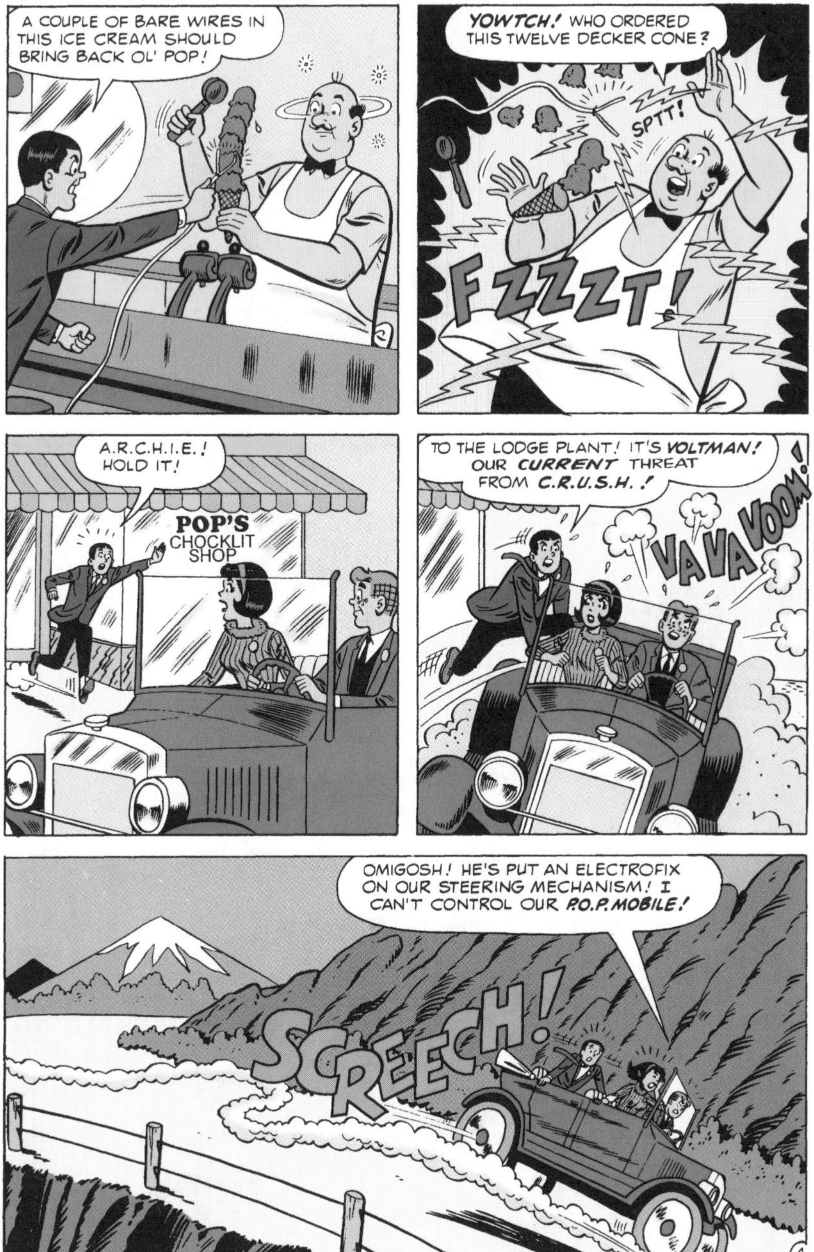
A COUPLE OF BARE WIRES IN THIS ICE CREAM SHOULD BRING BACK OL' POP!
YOWTCH! WHO ORDERED THIS TWELVE DECKER CONE?
SPTT!
FZZZZT!
A.R.C.H.I.E.! HOLD IT!
POP'S CHOCKLIT SHOP
TO THE LODGE PLANT! IT'S VOLTMAN! OUR CURRENT THREAT FROM C.R.U.S.H.!
VAVAVOOM!
OMIGOSH! HE'S PUT AN ELECTROFIX ON OUR STEERING MECHANISM! I CAN'T CONTROL OUR P.O.P. MOBILE!
SCREECH!

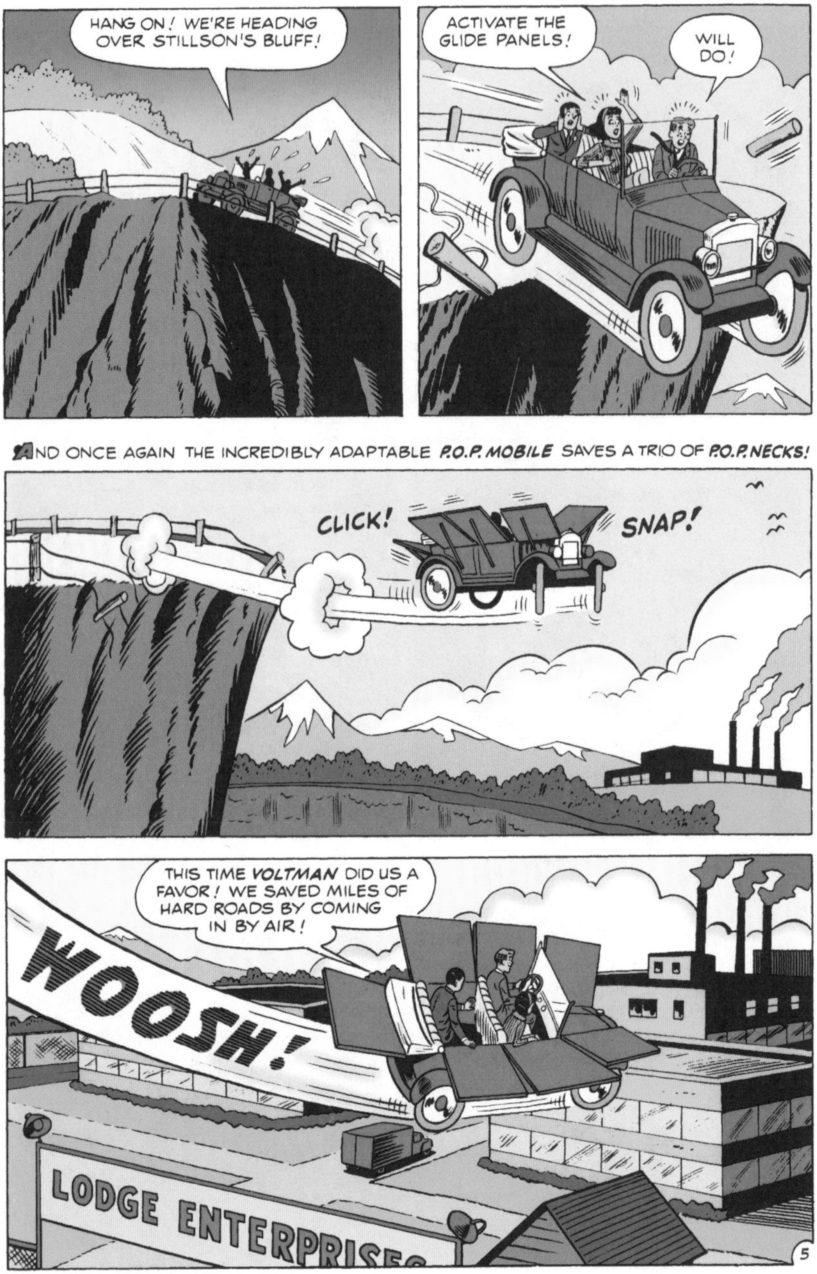
HANG ON! WE'RE HEADING OVER STILLSON'S BLUFF!
ACTIVATE THE GLIDE PANELS!
WILL DO!
AND ONCE AGAIN THE INCREDIBLY ADAPTABLE P.O.P. MOBILE SAVES A TRIO OF P.O.P. NECKS!
CLICK!
SNAP!
THIS TIME VOLTMAN DID US A FAVOR! WE SAVED MILES OF HARD ROADS BY COMING IN BY AIR!
WOOSH!
LODGE ENTERPRISES
5

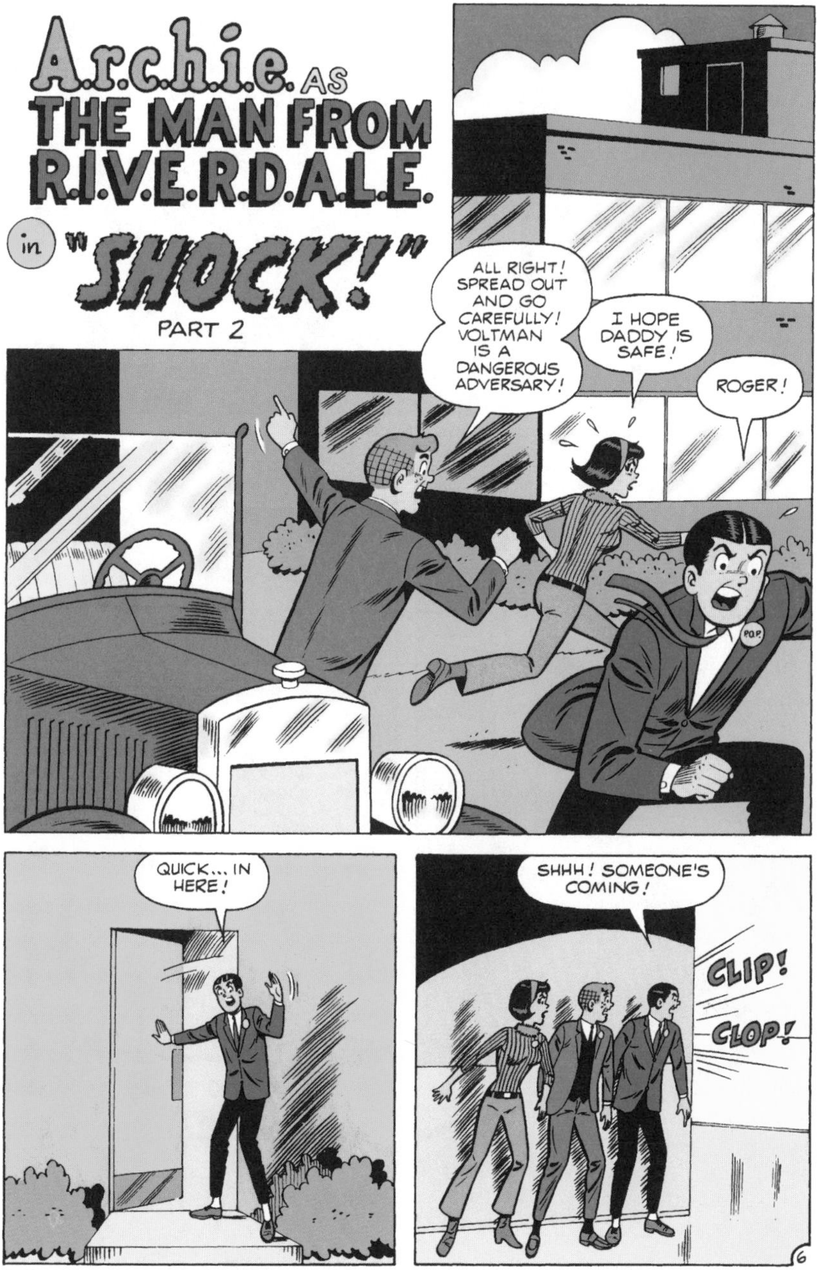
Archie AS
THE MAN FROM R.I.V.E.R.D.A.L.E.
in "SHOCK!"
PART 2
ALL RIGHT! SPREAD OUT AND GO CAREFULLY! VOLTMAN IS A DANGEROUS ADVERSARY!
I HOPE DADDY IS SAFE!
ROGER!
P.O.P.
QUICK... IN HERE!
SHHH! SOMEONE'S COMING!
CLIP!
CLOP!
6

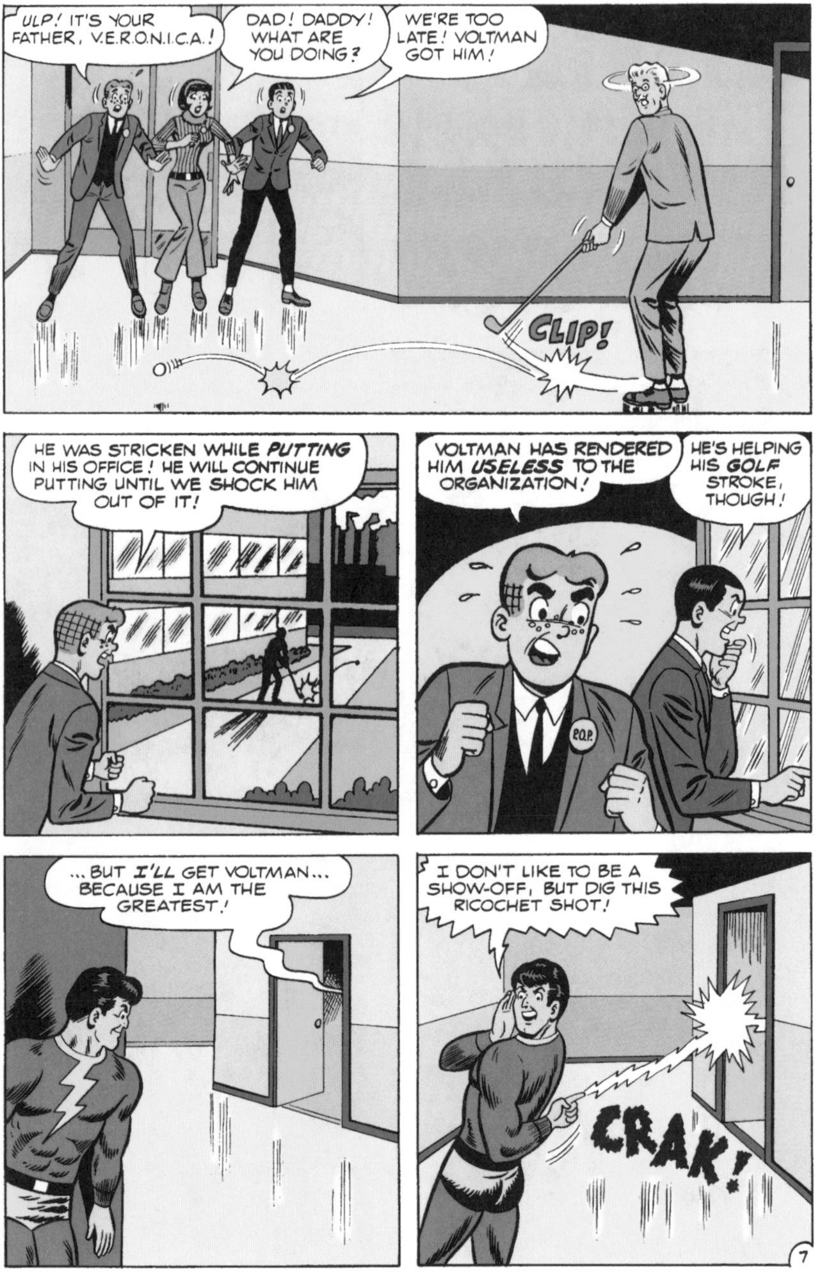
ULP! IT'S YOUR FATHER, V.E.R.O.N.I.C.A.!
DAD! DADDY! WHAT ARE YOU DOING?
WE'RE TOO LATE! VOLTMAN GOT HIM!
CLIP!
HE WAS STRICKEN WHILE PUTTING IN HIS OFFICE! HE WILL CONTINUE PUTTING UNTIL WE SHOCK HIM OUT OF IT!
VOLTMAN HAS RENDERED HIM USELESS TO THE ORGANIZATION!
HE'S HELPING HIS GOLF STROKE, THOUGH!
R.O.P.
...BUT I'LL GET VOLTMAN... BECAUSE I AM THE GREATEST!
I DON'T LIKE TO BE A SHOW-OFF, BUT DIG THIS RICOCHET SHOT!
CRAK!
7

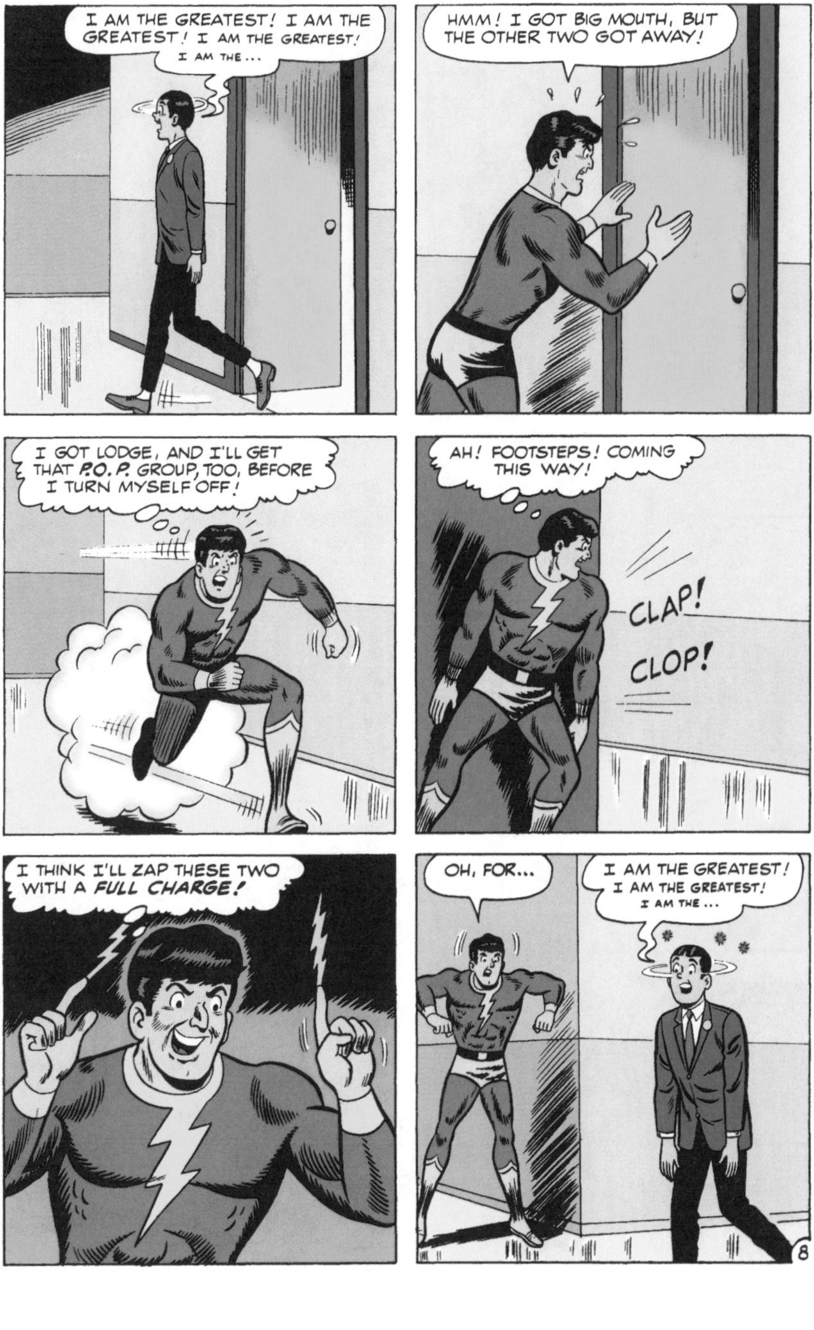
I AM THE GREATEST! I AM THE GREATEST! I AM THE GREATEST! I AM THE...
HMM! I GOT BIG MOUTH, BUT THE OTHER TWO GOT AWAY!
I GOT LODGE, AND I'LL GET THAT P.O.P. GROUP, TOO, BEFORE I TURN MYSELF OFF!
AH! FOOTSTEPS! COMING THIS WAY!
CLAP!
CLOP!
I THINK I'LL ZAP THESE TWO WITH A FULL CHARGE!
OH, FOR...
I AM THE GREATEST! I AM THE GREATEST! I AM THE...
8

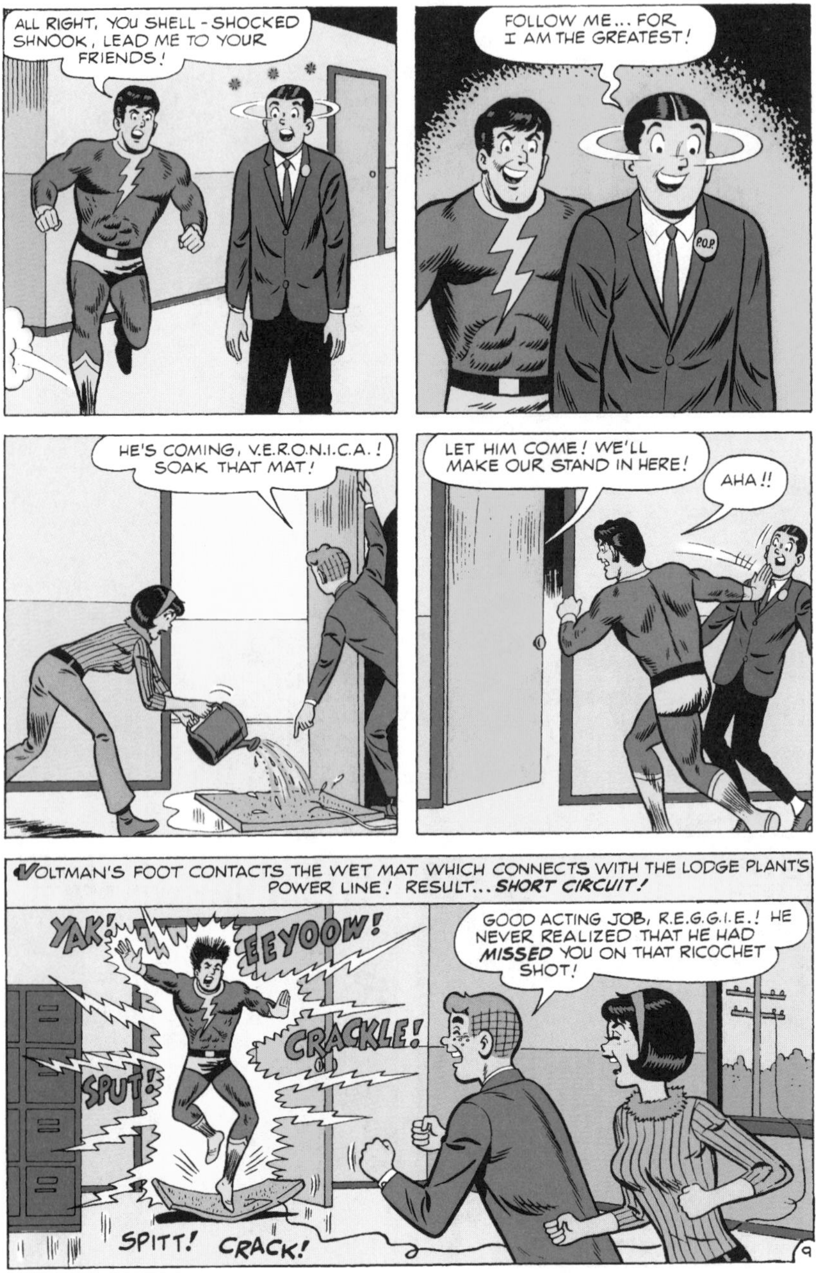

ALL RIGHT, YOU SHELL-SHOCKED SHNOOK, LEAD ME TO YOUR FRIENDS!
FOLLOW ME... FOR I AM THE GREATEST!
P.O.P.
HE'S COMING, V.E.R.O.N.I.C.A.! SOAK THAT MAT!
LET HIM COME! WE'LL MAKE OUR STAND IN HERE!
AHA!!
VOLTMAN'S FOOT CONTACTS THE WET MAT WHICH CONNECTS WITH THE LODGE PLANT'S POWER LINE! RESULT... SHORT CIRCUIT!
YAK!
EEYOOW!
GOOD ACTING JOB, R.E.G.G.I.E.! HE NEVER REALIZED THAT HE HAD MISSED YOU ON THAT RICOCHET SHOT!
CRACKLE!
SPUT!
SPITT!
CRACK!
9

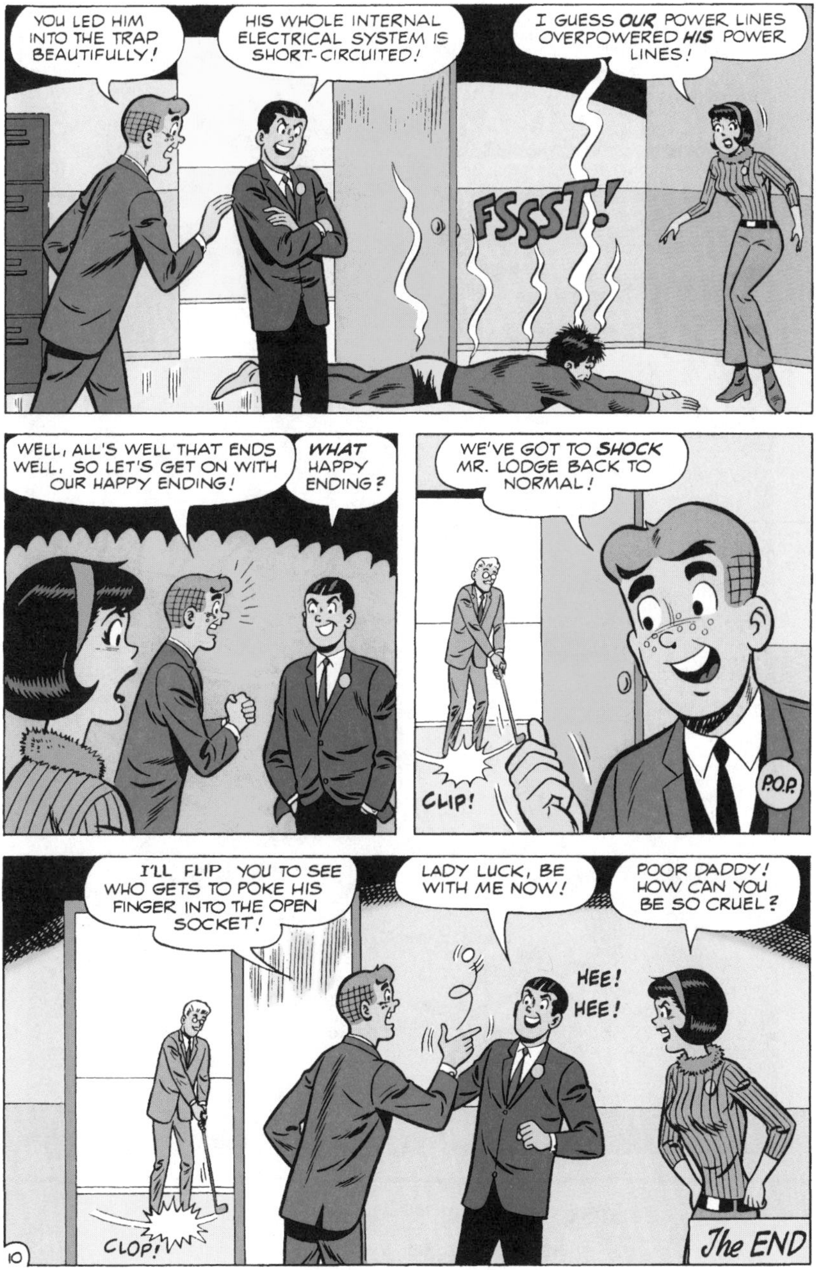
YOU LED HIM INTO THE TRAP BEAUTIFULLY!
HIS WHOLE INTERNAL ELECTRICAL SYSTEM IS SHORT-CIRCUITED!
I GUESS OUR POWER LINES OVERPOWERED HIS POWER LINES!
FSSST!
WELL, ALL'S WELL THAT ENDS WELL, SO LET'S GET ON WITH OUR HAPPY ENDING!
WHAT HAPPY ENDING?
WE'VE GOT TO SHOCK MR. LODGE BACK TO NORMAL!
CLIP!
P.O.P.
I'LL FLIP YOU TO SEE WHO GETS TO POKE HIS FINGER INTO THE OPEN SOCKET!
LADY LUCK, BE WITH ME NOW!
HEE! HEE!
POOR DADDY! HOW CAN YOU BE SO CRUEL?
CLOP!
10
The END

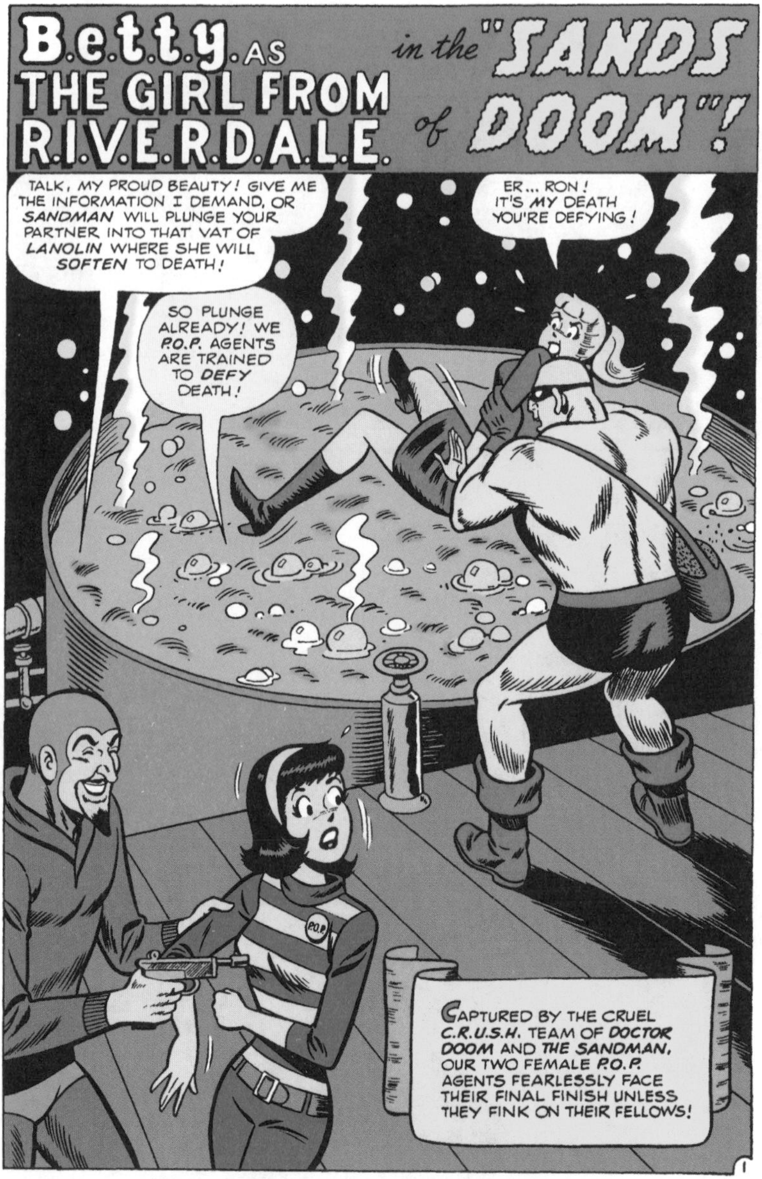
Betty AS THE GIRL FROM R.I.V.E.R.D.A.L.E. in the "SANDS of DOOM"!
TALK, MY PROUD BEAUTY! GIVE ME THE INFORMATION I DEMAND, OR SANDMAN WILL PLUNGE YOUR PARTNER INTO THAT VAT OF LANOLIN WHERE SHE WILL SOFTEN TO DEATH!
SO PLUNGE ALREADY! WE P.O.P. AGENTS ARE TRAINED TO DEFY DEATH!
ER... RON! IT'S MY DEATH YOU'RE DEFYING!
P.O.P.
CAPTURED BY THE CRUEL C.R.U.S.H. TEAM OF DOCTOR DOOM AND THE SANDMAN, OUR TWO FEMALE P.O.P. AGENTS FEARLESSLY FACE THEIR FINAL FINISH UNLESS THEY FINK ON THEIR FELLOWS!
1

Story: Frank Doyle Pencils: Bob White
Inks & Letters: Jon D'Agostino

Originally printed in LIFE WITH ARCHIE #58, FEBRUARY 1967

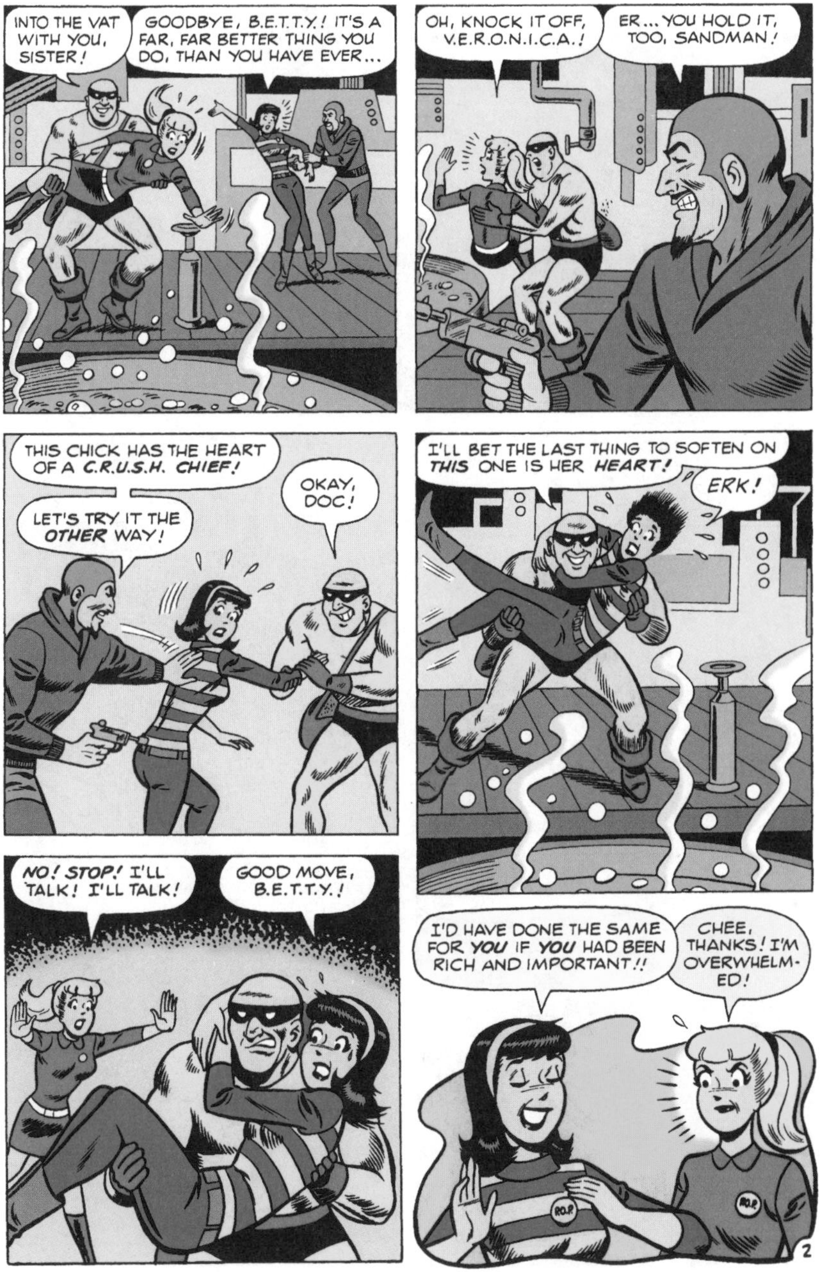
INTO THE VAT WITH YOU, SISTER!
GOODBYE, B.E.T.T.Y.! IT'S A FAR, FAR BETTER THING YOU DO, THAN YOU HAVE EVER...
OH, KNOCK IT OFF, V.E.R.O.N.I.C.A.!
ER... YOU HOLD IT, TOO, SANDMAN!
THIS CHICK HAS THE HEART OF A C.R.U.S.H. CHIEF!
LET'S TRY IT THE OTHER WAY!
OKAY, DOC!
I'LL BET THE LAST THING TO SOFTEN ON THIS ONE IS HER HEART!
ERK!
NO! STOP! I'LL TALK! I'LL TALK!
GOOD MOVE, B.E.T.T.Y.!
I'D HAVE DONE THE SAME FOR YOU IF YOU HAD BEEN RICH AND IMPORTANT!!
CHEE, THANKS! I'M OVERWHELM-ED!
2

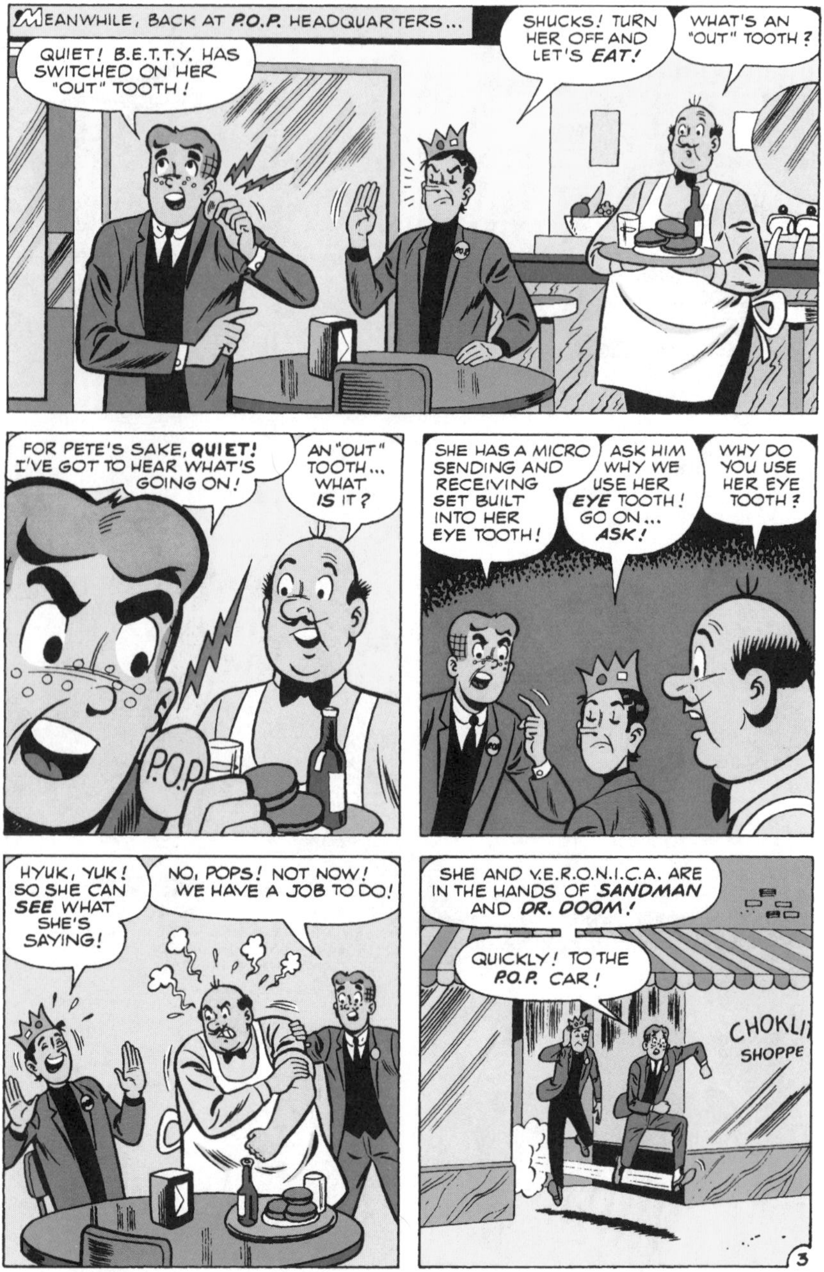
MEANWHILE, BACK AT P.O.P. HEADQUARTERS...
QUIET! B.E.T.T.Y. HAS SWITCHED ON HER "OUT" TOOTH!
SHUCKS! TURN HER OFF AND LET'S EAT!
WHAT'S AN "OUT" TOOTH?
FOR PETE'S SAKE, QUIET! I'VE GOT TO HEAR WHAT'S GOING ON!
AN "OUT" TOOTH... WHAT IS IT?
P.O.P
SHE HAS A MICRO SENDING AND RECEIVING SET BUILT INTO HER EYE TOOTH!
ASK HIM WHY WE USE HER EYE TOOTH! GO ON... ASK!
WHY DO YOU USE HER EYE TOOTH?
HYUK, YUK! SO SHE CAN SEE WHAT SHE'S SAYING!
NO, POPS! NOT NOW! WE HAVE A JOB TO DO!
SHE AND V.E.R.O.N.I.C.A. ARE IN THE HANDS OF SANDMAN AND DR. DOOM!
QUICKLY! TO THE P.O.P. CAR!
CHOKLIT SHOPPE
3

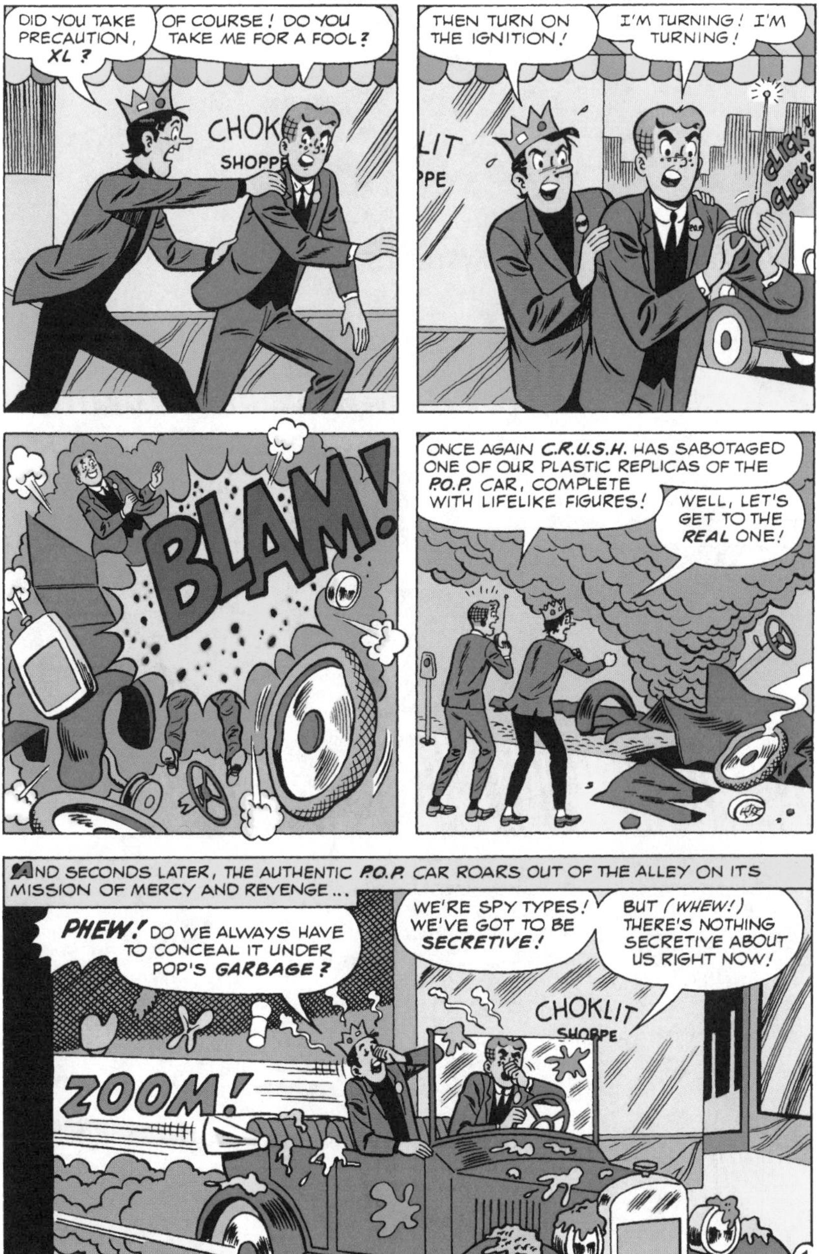
DID YOU TAKE PRECAUTION, XL ?
OF COURSE! DO YOU TAKE ME FOR A FOOL?
CHOK
SHOPPE
THEN TURN ON THE IGNITION!
I'M TURNING! I'M TURNING!
LIT
PPE
CLICK!
CLICK!
BLAM!
ONCE AGAIN C.R.U.S.H. HAS SABOTAGED ONE OF OUR PLASTIC REPLICAS OF THE P.O.P. CAR, COMPLETE WITH LIFELIKE FIGURES!
WELL, LET'S GET TO THE REAL ONE!
AND SECONDS LATER, THE AUTHENTIC P.O.P. CAR ROARS OUT OF THE ALLEY ON ITS MISSION OF MERCY AND REVENGE...
PHEW! DO WE ALWAYS HAVE TO CONCEAL IT UNDER POP'S GARBAGE?
WE'RE SPY TYPES! WE'VE GOT TO BE SECRETIVE!
BUT (WHEW!) THERE'S NOTHING SECRETIVE ABOUT US RIGHT NOW!
CHOKLIT
SHOPPE
ZOOM!
4

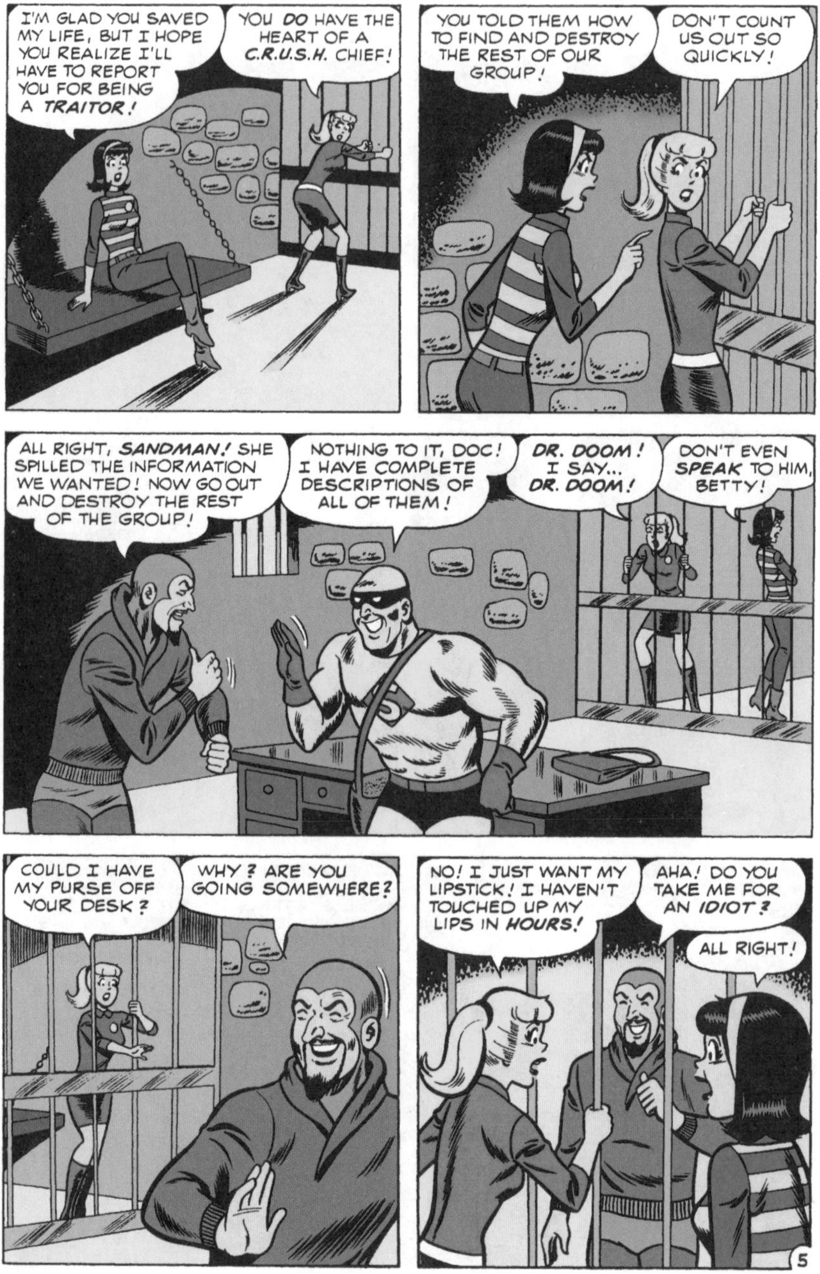
I'M GLAD YOU SAVED MY LIFE, BUT I HOPE YOU REALIZE I'LL HAVE TO REPORT YOU FOR BEING A TRAITOR!
YOU DO HAVE THE HEART OF A C.R.U.S.H. CHIEF!
YOU TOLD THEM HOW TO FIND AND DESTROY THE REST OF OUR GROUP!
DON'T COUNT US OUT SO QUICKLY!
ALL RIGHT, SANDMAN! SHE SPILLED THE INFORMATION WE WANTED! NOW GO OUT AND DESTROY THE REST OF THE GROUP!
NOTHING TO IT, DOC! I HAVE COMPLETE DESCRIPTIONS OF ALL OF THEM!
DR. DOOM! I SAY... DR. DOOM!
DON'T EVEN SPEAK TO HIM, BETTY!
COULD I HAVE MY PURSE OFF YOUR DESK?
WHY? ARE YOU GOING SOMEWHERE?
NO! I JUST WANT MY LIPSTICK! I HAVEN'T TOUCHED UP MY LIPS IN HOURS!
AHA! DO YOU TAKE ME FOR AN IDIOT?
ALL RIGHT!
5

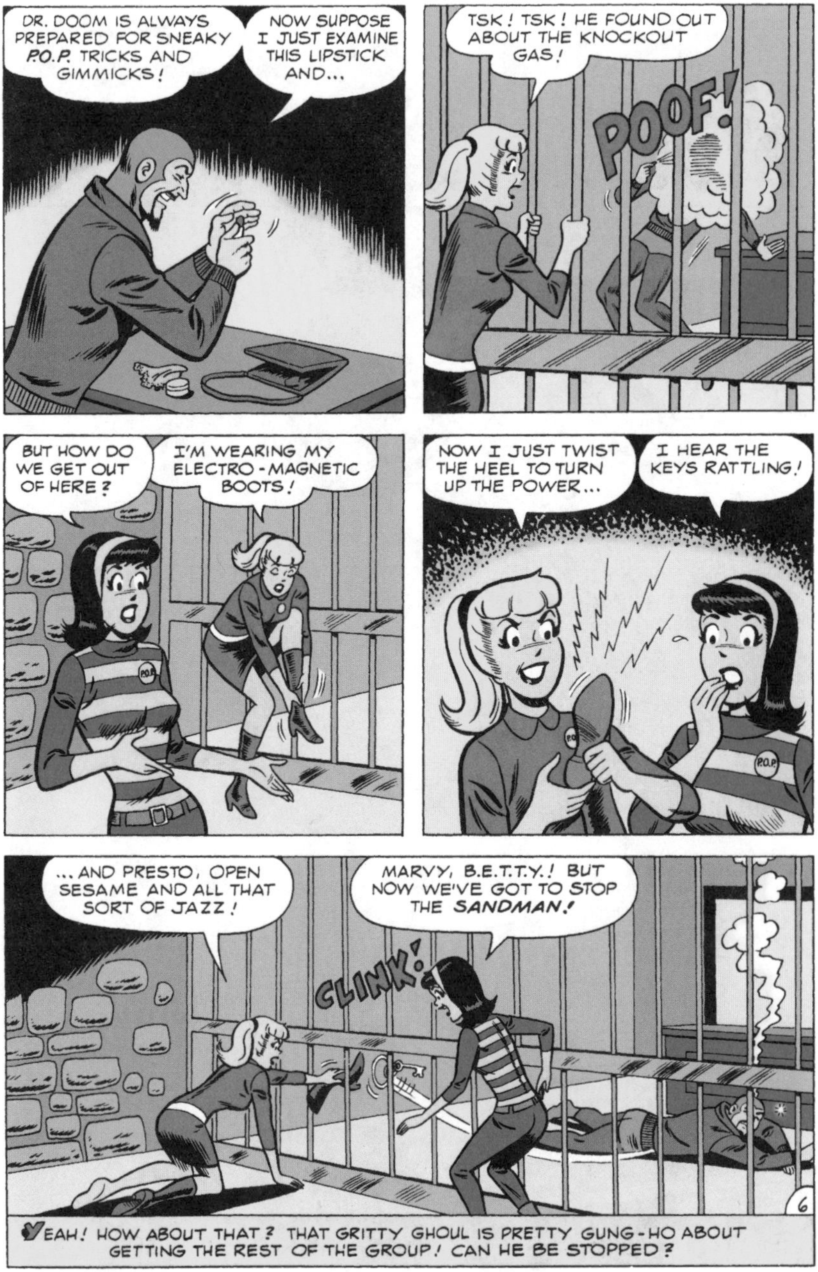
DR. DOOM IS ALWAYS PREPARED FOR SNEAKY P.O.P. TRICKS AND GIMMICKS!
NOW SUPPOSE I JUST EXAMINE THIS LIPSTICK AND...
TSK! TSK! HE FOUND OUT ABOUT THE KNOCKOUT GAS!
POOF!
BUT HOW DO WE GET OUT OF HERE?
I'M WEARING MY ELECTRO-MAGNETIC BOOTS!
P.O.P.
NOW I JUST TWIST THE HEEL TO TURN UP THE POWER...
I HEAR THE KEYS RATTLING!
P.O.P.
...AND PRESTO, OPEN SESAME AND ALL THAT SORT OF JAZZ!
MARVY, B.E.T.T.Y.! BUT NOW WE'VE GOT TO STOP THE SANDMAN!
CLINK!
6
YEAH! HOW ABOUT THAT? THAT GRITTY GHOUL IS PRETTY GUNG-HO ABOUT GETTING THE REST OF THE GROUP! CAN HE BE STOPPED?

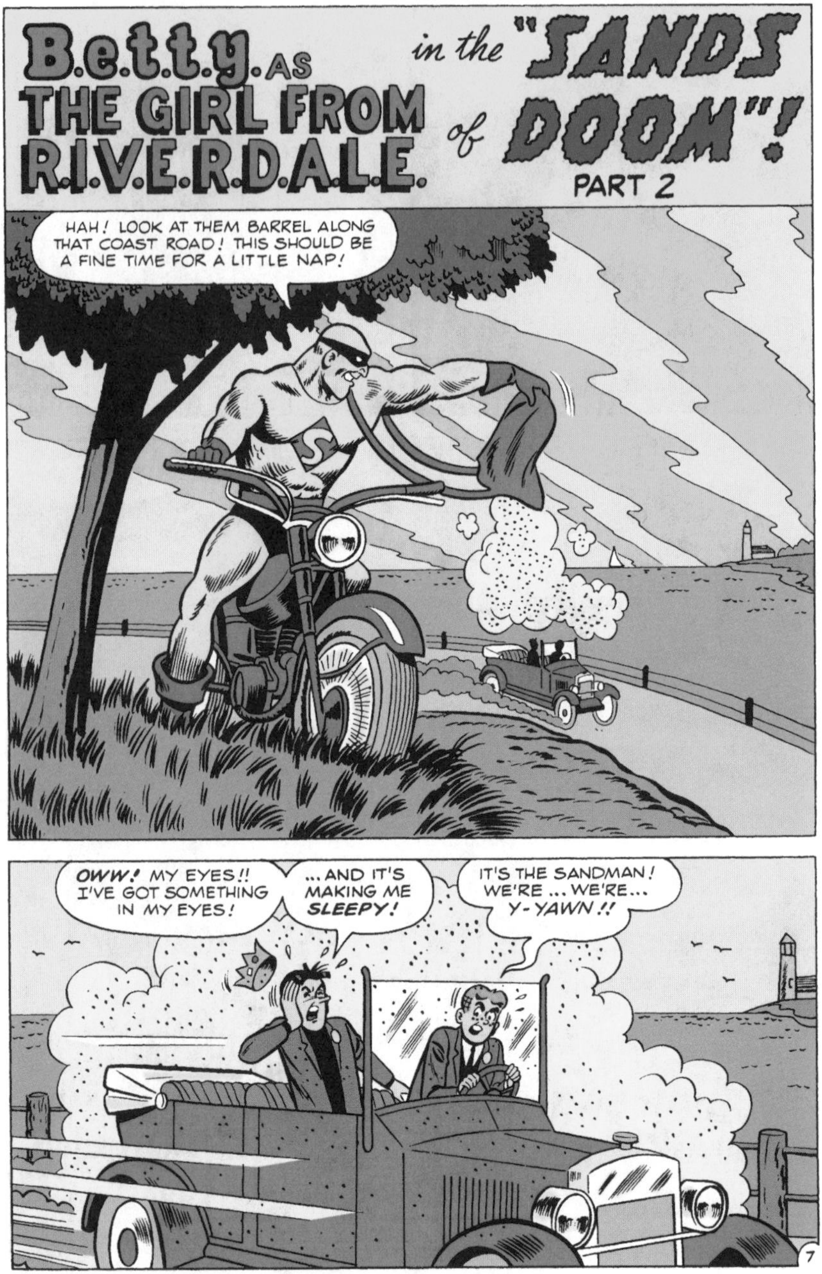
B.e.t.t.y. AS THE GIRL FROM R.I.V.E.R.D.A.L.E. in the "SANDS of DOOM"!
PART 2
HAH! LOOK AT THEM BARREL ALONG THAT COAST ROAD! THIS SHOULD BE A FINE TIME FOR A LITTLE NAP!
OWW! MY EYES!! I'VE GOT SOMETHING IN MY EYES!
...AND IT'S MAKING ME SLEEPY!
IT'S THE SANDMAN! WE'RE ... WE'RE... Y-YAWN!!
7

...AND OVER THE CLIFF PLUNGES THE SPEEDING *P.O.P.* CAR WITH ITS SLEEPING OCCUPANTS...

SNORE!
ZZZZZ!
BROK!
SNORE!

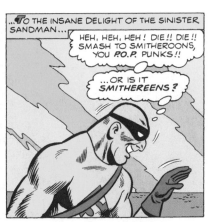

...TO THE INSANE DELIGHT OF THE SINISTER SANDMAN...

HEH, HEH, HEH! DIE!! DIE!! SMASH TO SMITHEROONS, YOU *P.O.P.* PUNKS!!

...OR IS IT *SMITHEREENS?*

BUT LEAVE IT TO THE GIRL FROM R.I.V.E.R.D.A.L.E. TO BE WHERE THE ACTION IS...

OH, NO! THEY'RE ASLEEP! A.R.C.H.I.E. CAN'T WORK HIS GLIDER CONTROLS!

QUICKLY, V.E.R.O.N.I.C.A., GIVE ME YOUR *P.O.P.* BUTTON!

HURRY, B.E.T.T.Y.! HURRY!

JUST LET ME CLIP OUR TWO BUTTONS TOGETHER!

...AND WE HAVE A REMOTE CONTROL FOR THE *P.O.P.* CAR!

NOW! DO IT NOW!

THERE! I'VE ACTIVATED THE STABILIZING AILERONS!

LET'S HOPE IT'S NOT TOO LATE!!

8

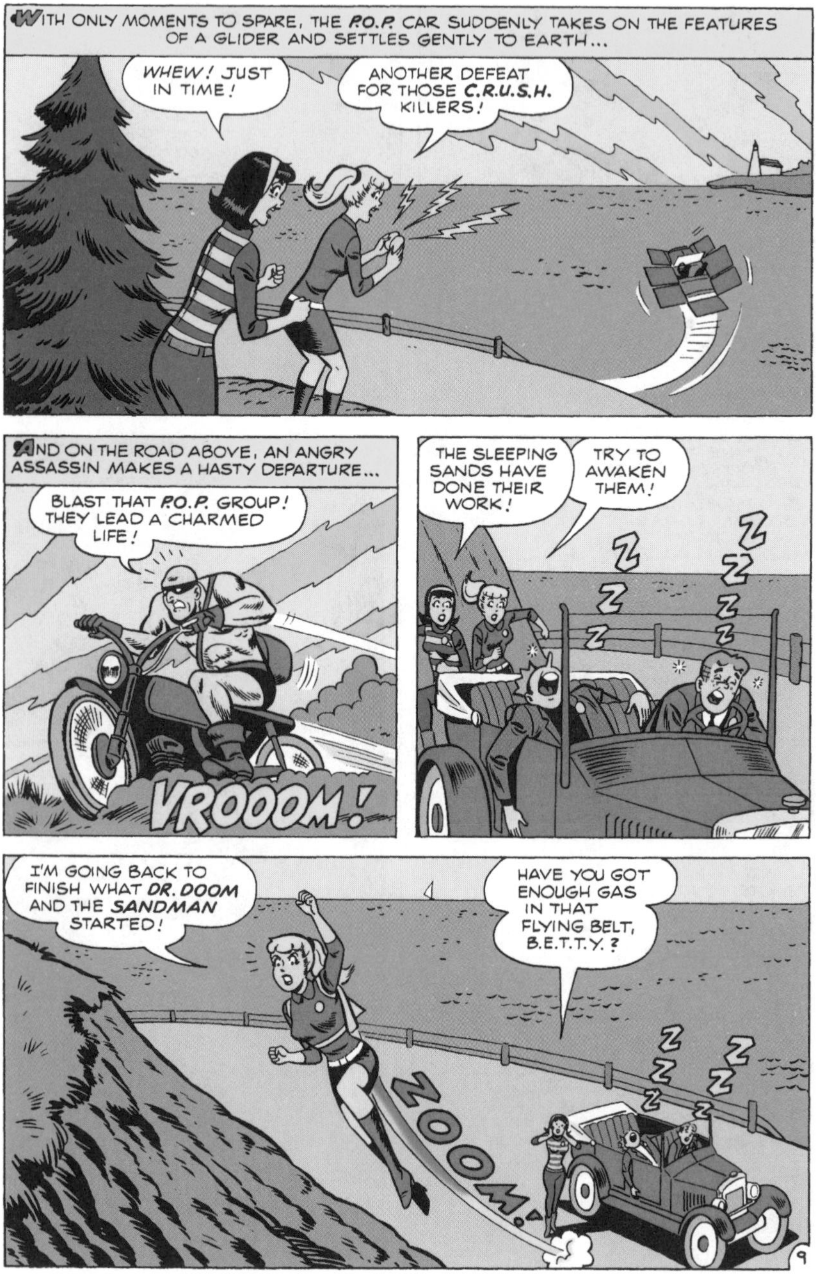
WITH ONLY MOMENTS TO SPARE, THE P.O.P. CAR SUDDENLY TAKES ON THE FEATURES OF A GLIDER AND SETTLES GENTLY TO EARTH...
WHEW! JUST IN TIME!
ANOTHER DEFEAT FOR THOSE C.R.U.S.H. KILLERS!
AND ON THE ROAD ABOVE, AN ANGRY ASSASSIN MAKES A HASTY DEPARTURE...
BLAST THAT P.O.P. GROUP! THEY LEAD A CHARMED LIFE!
VROOOM!
THE SLEEPING SANDS HAVE DONE THEIR WORK!
TRY TO AWAKEN THEM!
I'M GOING BACK TO FINISH WHAT DR. DOOM AND THE SANDMAN STARTED!
HAVE YOU GOT ENOUGH GAS IN THAT FLYING BELT, B.E.T.T.Y.?
ZOOM!
9

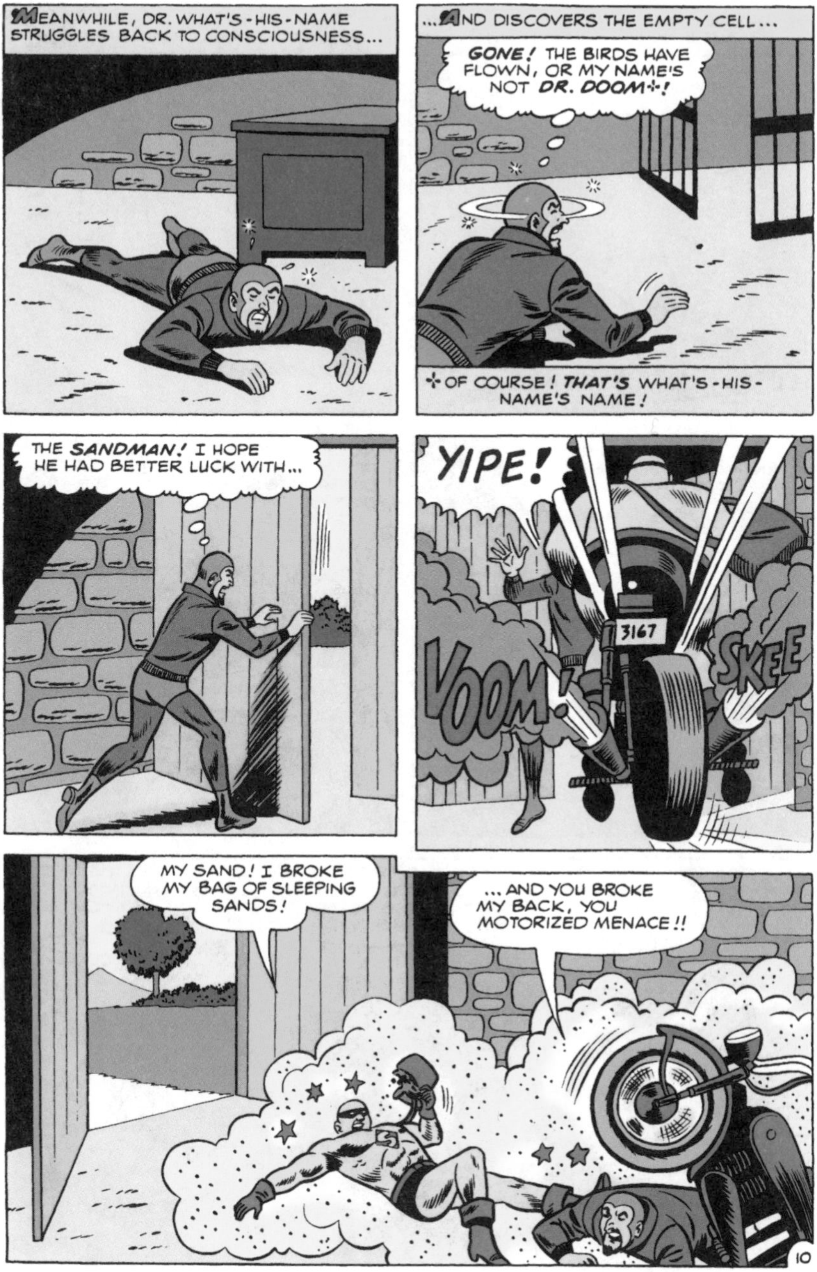
MEANWHILE, DR. WHAT'S-HIS-NAME STRUGGLES BACK TO CONSCIOUSNESS...
...AND DISCOVERS THE EMPTY CELL...
GONE! THE BIRDS HAVE FLOWN, OR MY NAME'S NOT DR. DOOM✣!
✣OF COURSE! THAT'S WHAT'S-HIS-NAME'S NAME!
THE SANDMAN! I HOPE HE HAD BETTER LUCK WITH...
YIPE!
3167
VOOM!
SKEE
MY SAND! I BROKE MY BAG OF SLEEPING SANDS!
...AND YOU BROKE MY BACK, YOU MOTORIZED MENACE!!
10

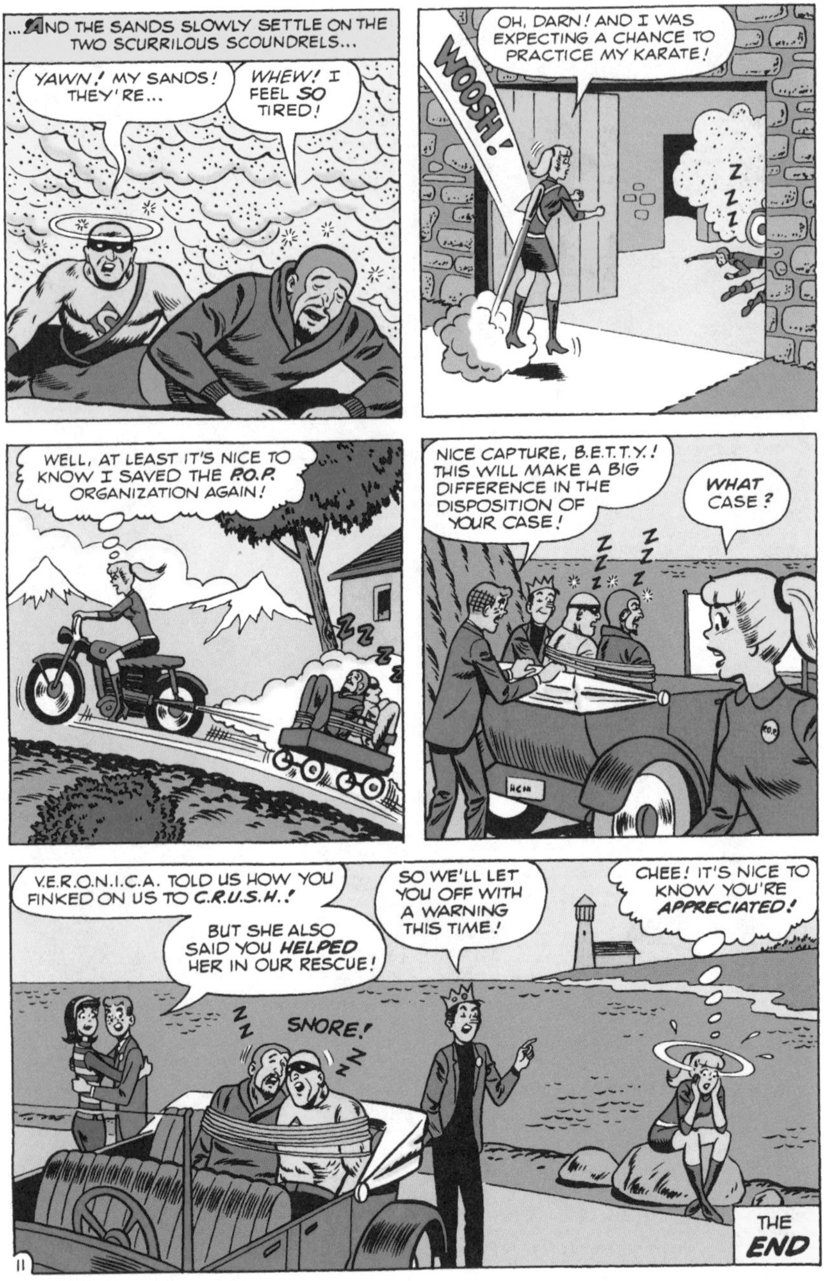
...AND THE SANDS SLOWLY SETTLE ON THE TWO SCURRILOUS SCOUNDRELS...
YAWN! MY SANDS! THEY'RE...
WHEW! I FEEL SO TIRED!
OH, DARN! AND I WAS EXPECTING A CHANCE TO PRACTICE MY KARATE!
WOOSH!
Z Z Z
WELL, AT LEAST IT'S NICE TO KNOW I SAVED THE P.O.P. ORGANIZATION AGAIN!
Z Z Z
NICE CAPTURE, B.E.T.T.Y.! THIS WILL MAKE A BIG DIFFERENCE IN THE DISPOSITION OF YOUR CASE!
WHAT CASE?
Z Z Z
Z Z Z
V.E.R.O.N.I.C.A. TOLD US HOW YOU FINKED ON US TO C.R.U.S.H.!
BUT SHE ALSO SAID YOU HELPED HER IN OUR RESCUE!
SO WE'LL LET YOU OFF WITH A WARNING THIS TIME!
CHEE! IT'S NICE TO KNOW YOU'RE APPRECIATED!
Z Z
SNORE!
Z Z
11
THE END

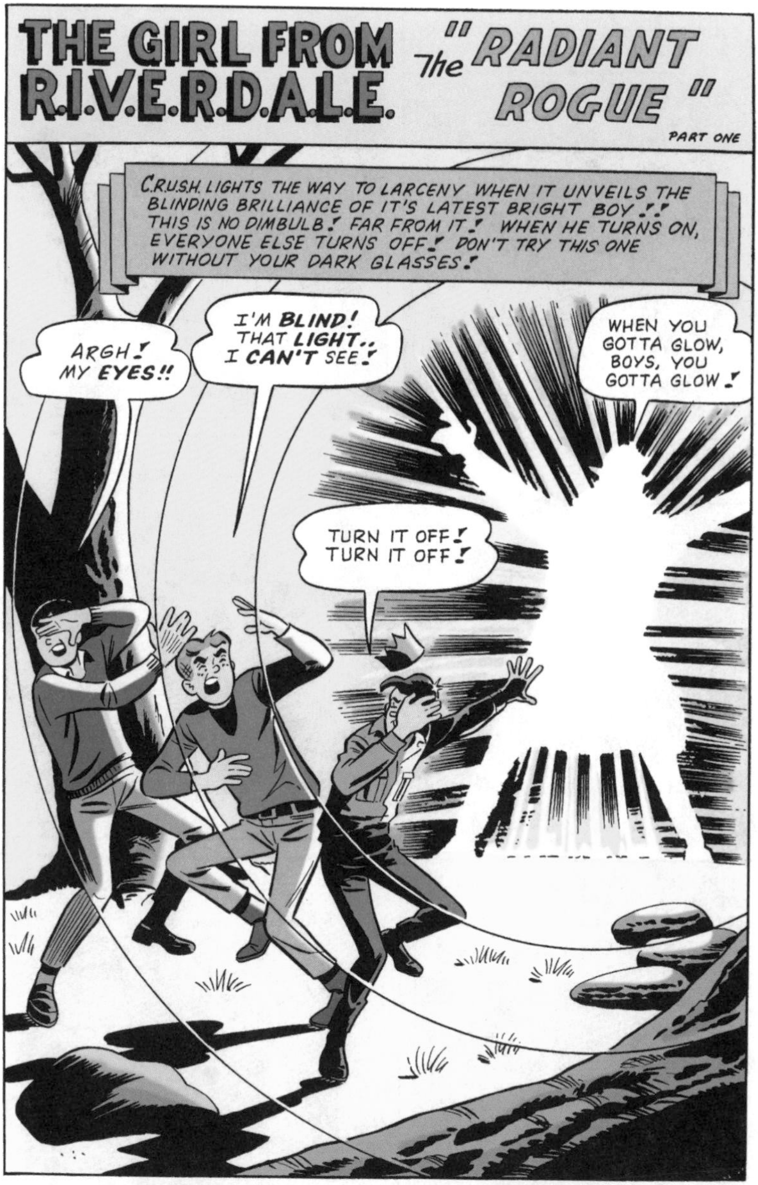
THE GIRL FROM R.I.V.E.R.D.A.L.E.
The "RADIANT ROGUE"
PART ONE
C.R.U.S.H. LIGHTS THE WAY TO LARCENY WHEN IT UNVEILS THE BLINDING BRILLIANCE OF IT'S LATEST BRIGHT BOY !!! THIS IS NO DIMBULB! FAR FROM IT! WHEN HE TURNS ON, EVERYONE ELSE TURNS OFF! DON'T TRY THIS ONE WITHOUT YOUR DARK GLASSES!
ARGH! MY EYES!!
I'M BLIND! THAT LIGHT.. I CAN'T SEE!
WHEN YOU GOTTA GLOW, BOYS, YOU GOTTA GLOW!
TURN IT OFF! TURN IT OFF!

Story: Frank Doyle Pencils: Dan DeCarlo
Inks & Letters: Vince DeCarlo

Originally printed in BETTY & ME #6, FEBRUARY 1967

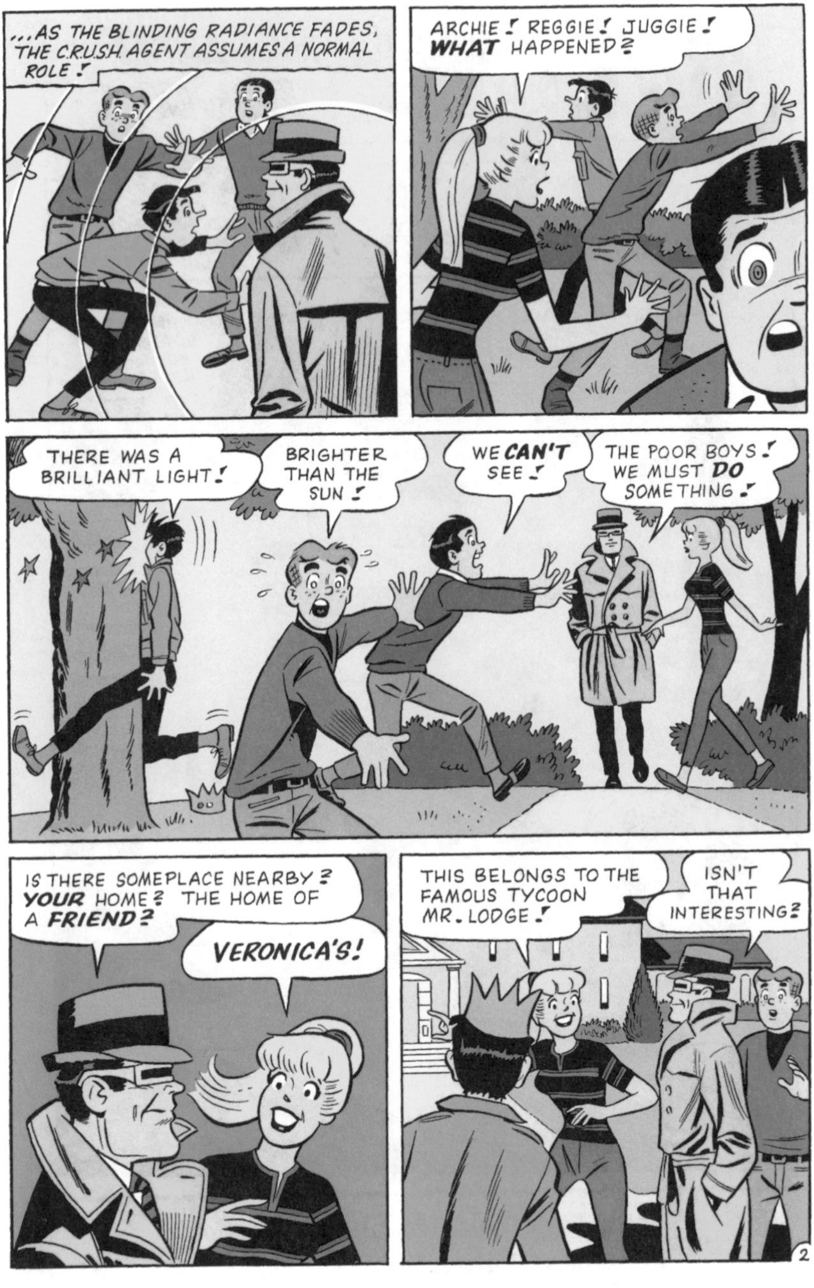
...AS THE BLINDING RADIANCE FADES, THE C.R.U.S.H. AGENT ASSUMES A NORMAL ROLE!
ARCHIE! REGGIE! JUGGIE! WHAT HAPPENED?
THERE WAS A BRILLIANT LIGHT!
BRIGHTER THAN THE SUN!
WE CAN'T SEE!
THE POOR BOYS! WE MUST DO SOMETHING!
IS THERE SOMEPLACE NEARBY? YOUR HOME? THE HOME OF A FRIEND?
VERONICA'S!
THIS BELONGS TO THE FAMOUS TYCOON MR. LODGE!
ISN'T THAT INTERESTING?
2

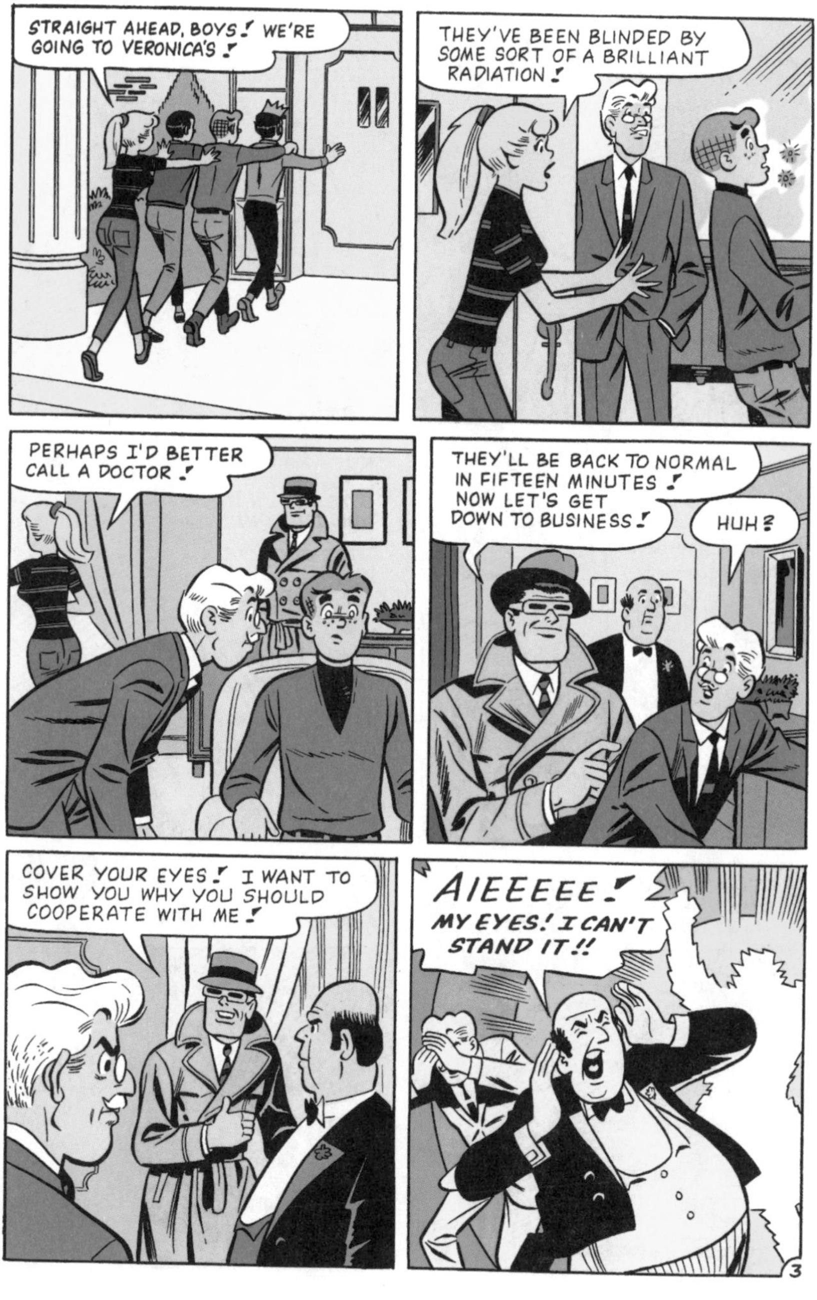
STRAIGHT AHEAD, BOYS! WE'RE GOING TO VERONICA'S!
THEY'VE BEEN BLINDED BY SOME SORT OF A BRILLIANT RADIATION!
PERHAPS I'D BETTER CALL A DOCTOR!
THEY'LL BE BACK TO NORMAL IN FIFTEEN MINUTES! NOW LET'S GET DOWN TO BUSINESS!
HUH?
COVER YOUR EYES! I WANT TO SHOW YOU WHY YOU SHOULD COOPERATE WITH ME!
AIEEEEE!
MY EYES! I CAN'T STAND IT!!
3

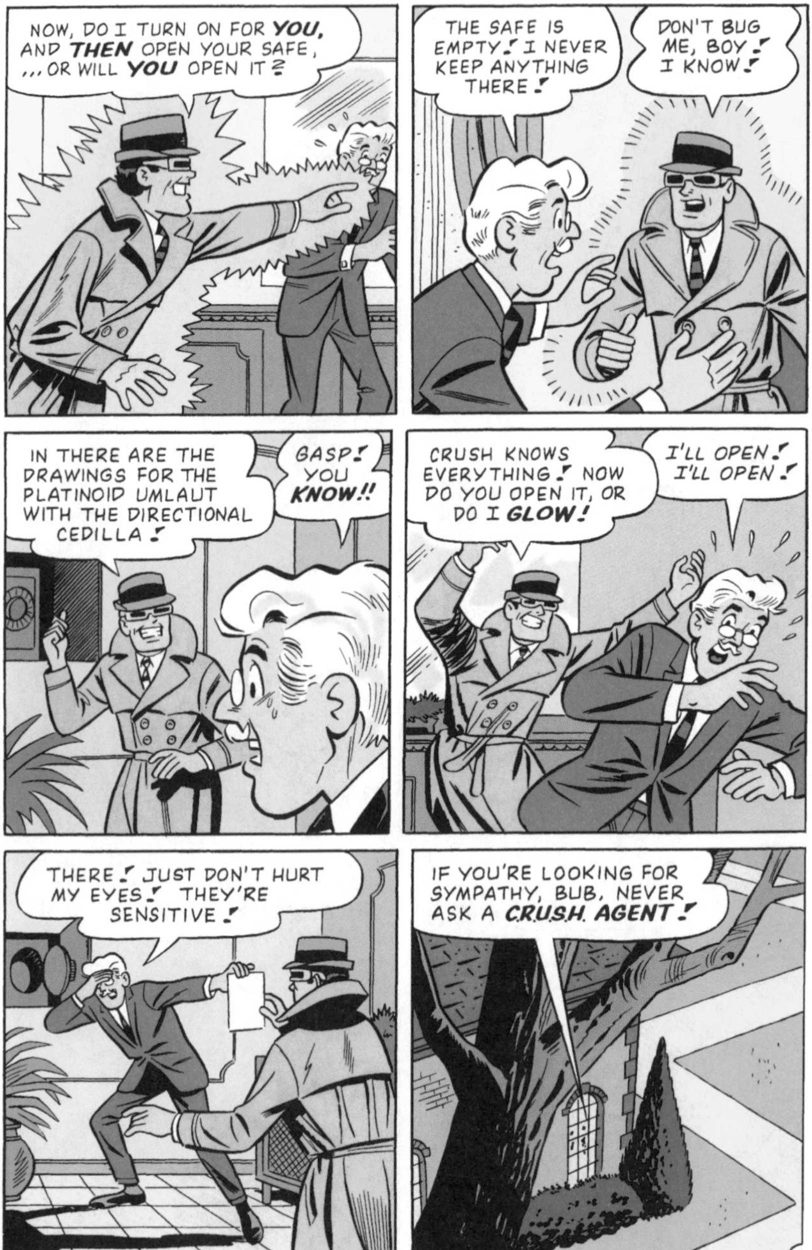
NOW, DO I TURN ON FOR YOU, AND THEN OPEN YOUR SAFE, ... OR WILL YOU OPEN IT?
THE SAFE IS EMPTY! I NEVER KEEP ANYTHING THERE!
DON'T BUG ME, BOY! I KNOW!
IN THERE ARE THE DRAWINGS FOR THE PLATINOID UMLAUT WITH THE DIRECTIONAL CEDILLA!
GASP! YOU KNOW!!
CRUSH KNOWS EVERYTHING! NOW DO YOU OPEN IT, OR DO I GLOW!
I'LL OPEN! I'LL OPEN!
THERE! JUST DON'T HURT MY EYES! THEY'RE SENSITIVE!
IF YOU'RE LOOKING FOR SYMPATHY, BUB, NEVER ASK A C.R.U.S.H. AGENT!
4

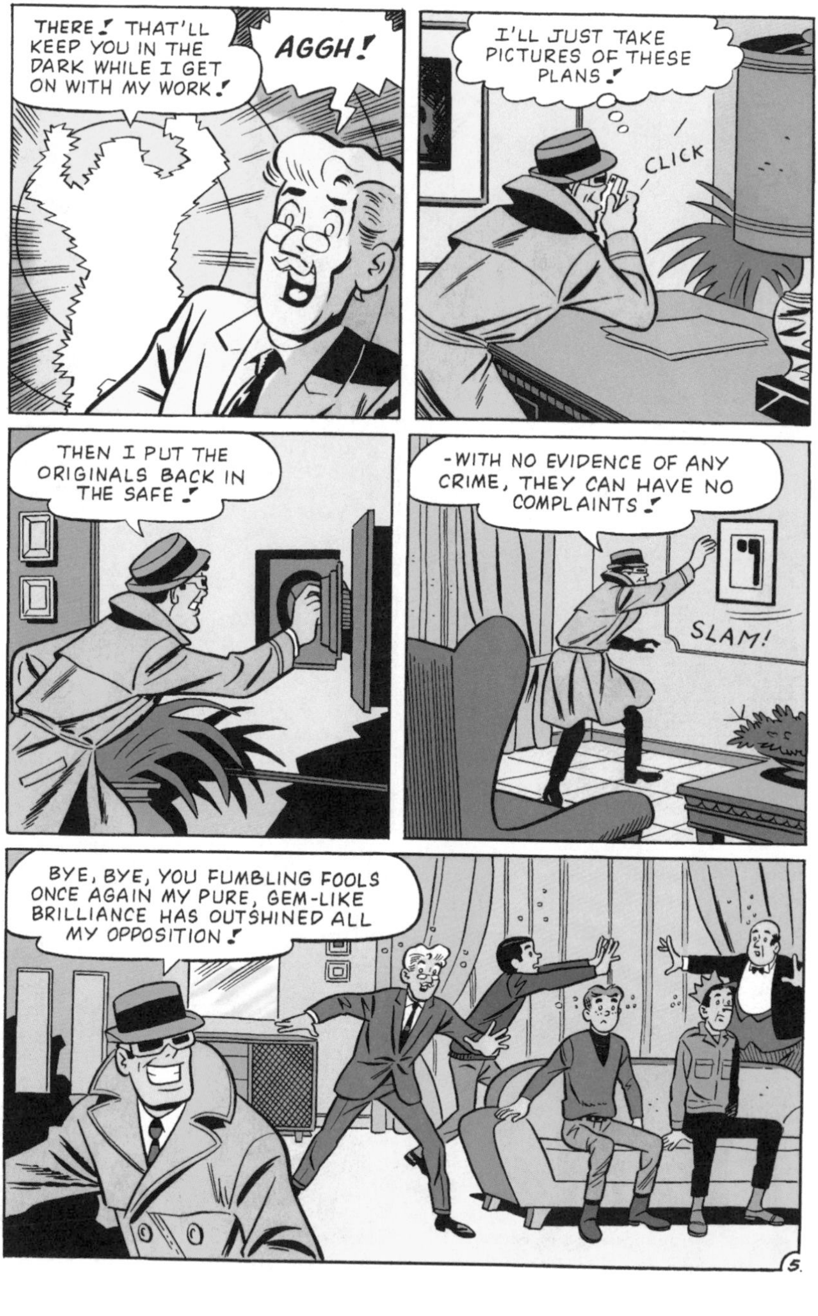
THERE! THAT'LL KEEP YOU IN THE DARK WHILE I GET ON WITH MY WORK!
AGGH!
I'LL JUST TAKE PICTURES OF THESE PLANS!
CLICK
THEN I PUT THE ORIGINALS BACK IN THE SAFE!
-WITH NO EVIDENCE OF ANY CRIME, THEY CAN HAVE NO COMPLAINTS!
SLAM!
BYE, BYE, YOU FUMBLING FOOLS ONCE AGAIN MY PURE, GEM-LIKE BRILLIANCE HAS OUTSHINED ALL MY OPPOSITION!
5.

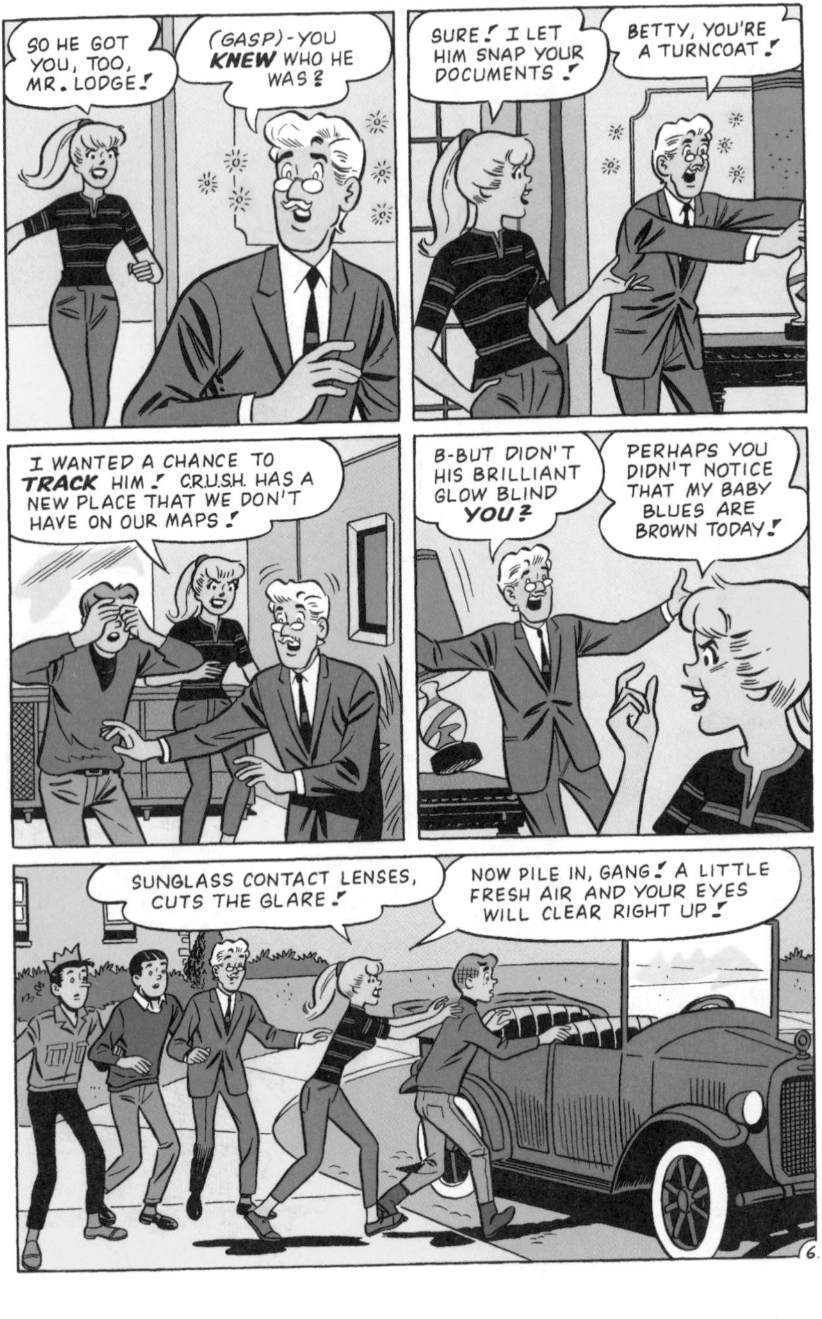
SO HE GOT YOU, TOO, MR. LODGE!
(GASP)-YOU **KNEW** WHO HE WAS?
SURE! I LET HIM SNAP YOUR DOCUMENTS!
BETTY, YOU'RE A TURNCOAT!
I WANTED A CHANCE TO **TRACK** HIM! C.R.U.S.H. HAS A NEW PLACE THAT WE DON'T HAVE ON OUR MAPS!
B-BUT DIDN'T HIS BRILLIANT GLOW BLIND **YOU**?
PERHAPS YOU DIDN'T NOTICE THAT MY BABY BLUES ARE BROWN TODAY!
SUNGLASS CONTACT LENSES, CUTS THE GLARE!
NOW PILE IN, GANG! A LITTLE FRESH AIR AND YOUR EYES WILL CLEAR RIGHT UP!
6.

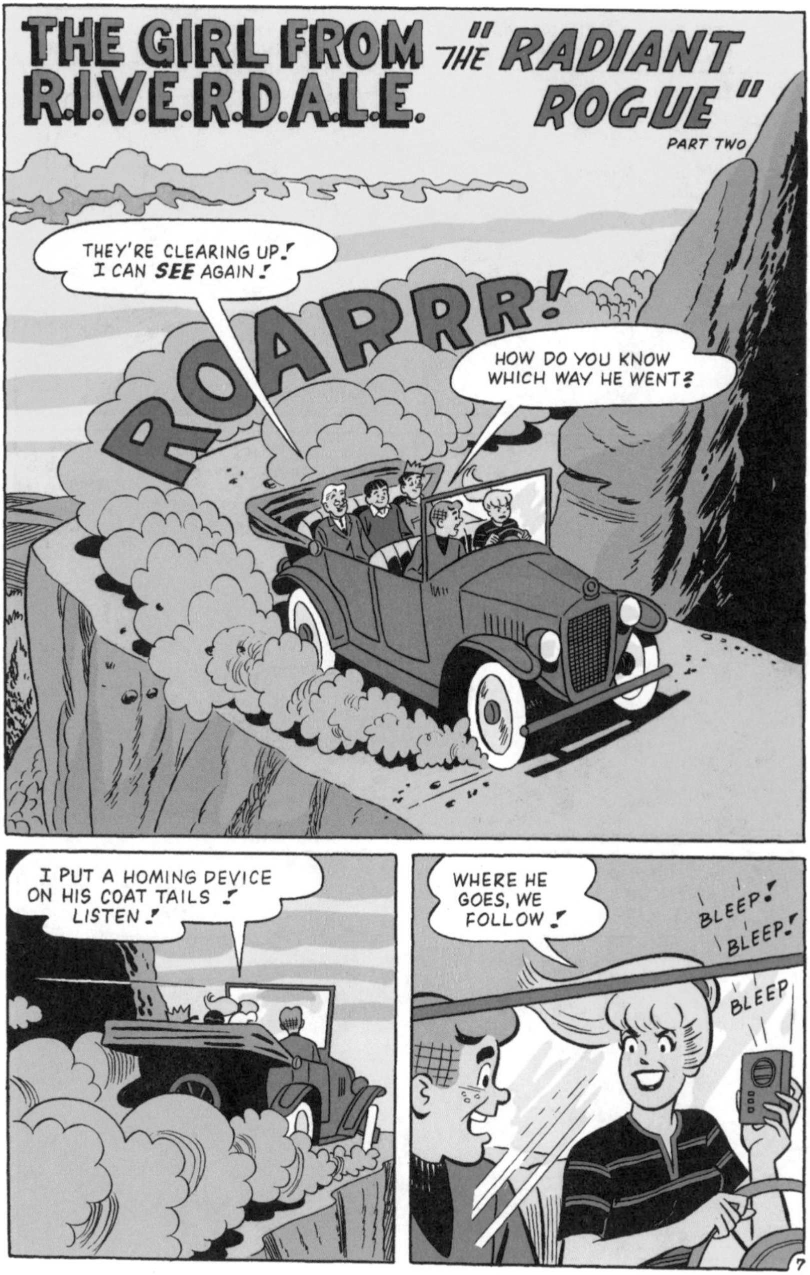
THE GIRL FROM R.I.V.E.R.D.A.L.E.
THE "RADIANT ROGUE"
PART TWO
THEY'RE CLEARING UP! I CAN SEE AGAIN!
ROARRR!
HOW DO YOU KNOW WHICH WAY HE WENT?
I PUT A HOMING DEVICE ON HIS COAT TAILS! LISTEN!
WHERE HE GOES, WE FOLLOW!
BLEEP! BLEEP! BLEEP
7

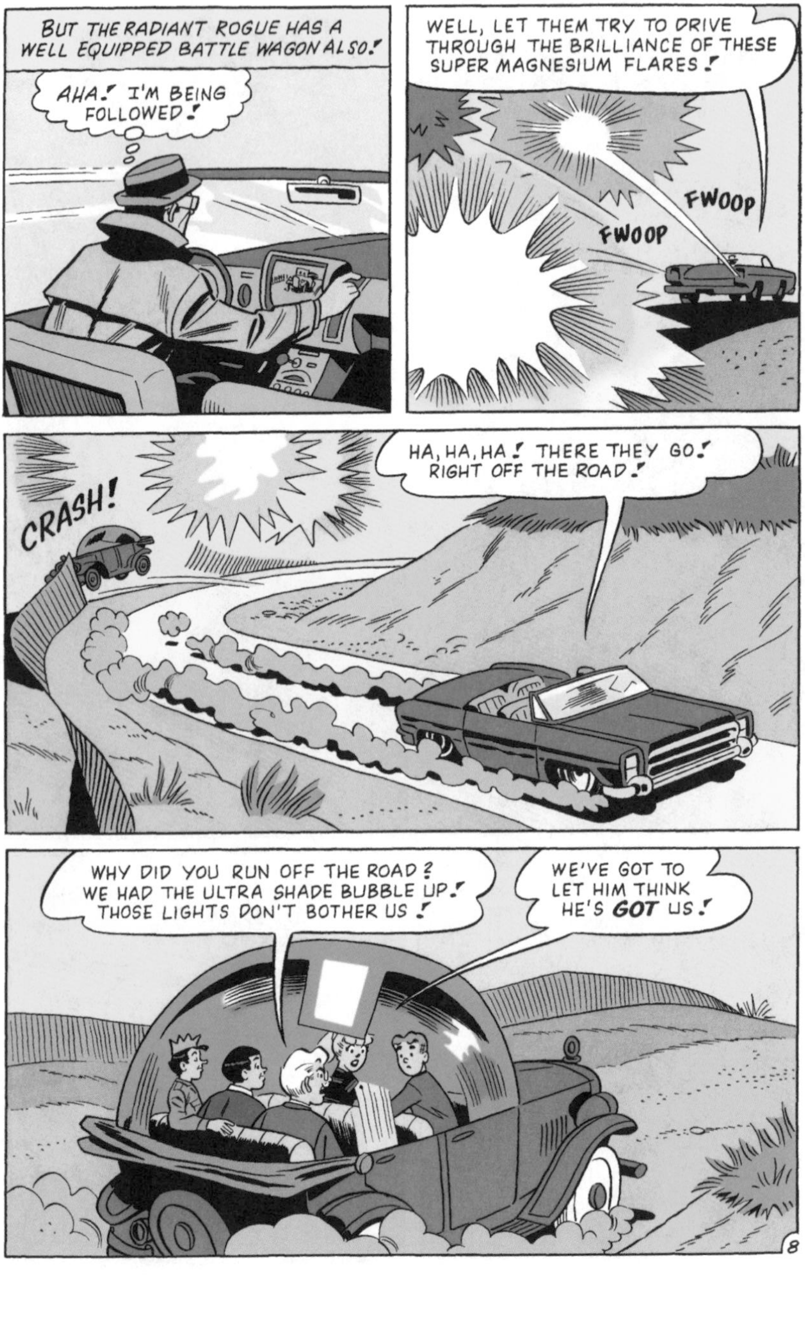
BUT THE RADIANT ROGUE HAS A WELL EQUIPPED BATTLE WAGON ALSO!
AHA! I'M BEING FOLLOWED!
WELL, LET THEM TRY TO DRIVE THROUGH THE BRILLIANCE OF THESE SUPER MAGNESIUM FLARES!
FWOOP
FWOOP
CRASH!
HA, HA, HA! THERE THEY GO! RIGHT OFF THE ROAD!
WHY DID YOU RUN OFF THE ROAD? WE HAD THE ULTRA SHADE BUBBLE UP! THOSE LIGHTS DON'T BOTHER US!
WE'VE GOT TO LET HIM THINK HE'S **GOT** US!
8

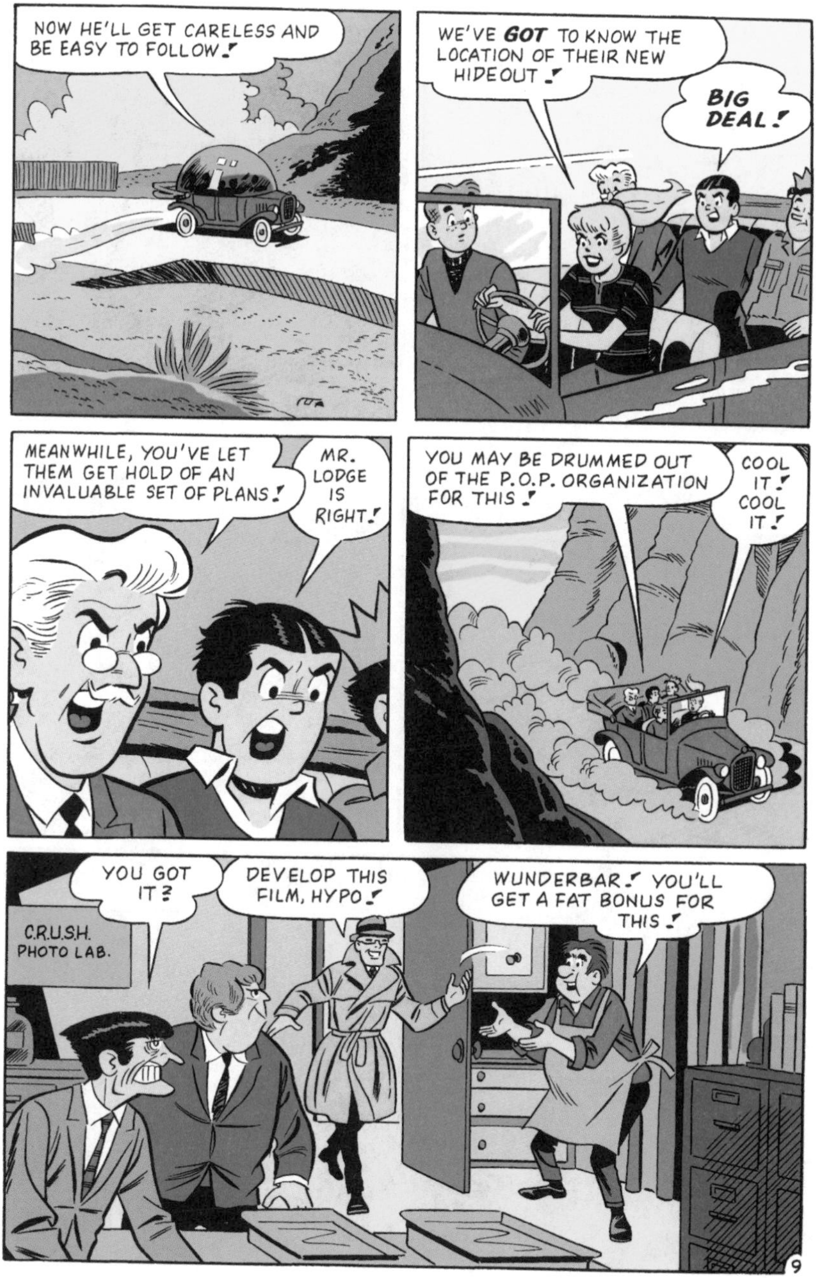
NOW HE'LL GET CARELESS AND BE EASY TO FOLLOW!
WE'VE GOT TO KNOW THE LOCATION OF THEIR NEW HIDEOUT!
BIG DEAL!
MEANWHILE, YOU'VE LET THEM GET HOLD OF AN INVALUABLE SET OF PLANS!
MR. LODGE IS RIGHT!
YOU MAY BE DRUMMED OUT OF THE P.O.P. ORGANIZATION FOR THIS!
COOL IT! COOL IT!
YOU GOT IT?
DEVELOP THIS FILM, HYPO!
WUNDERBAR! YOU'LL GET A FAT BONUS FOR THIS!
C.R.U.S.H. PHOTO LAB.
9

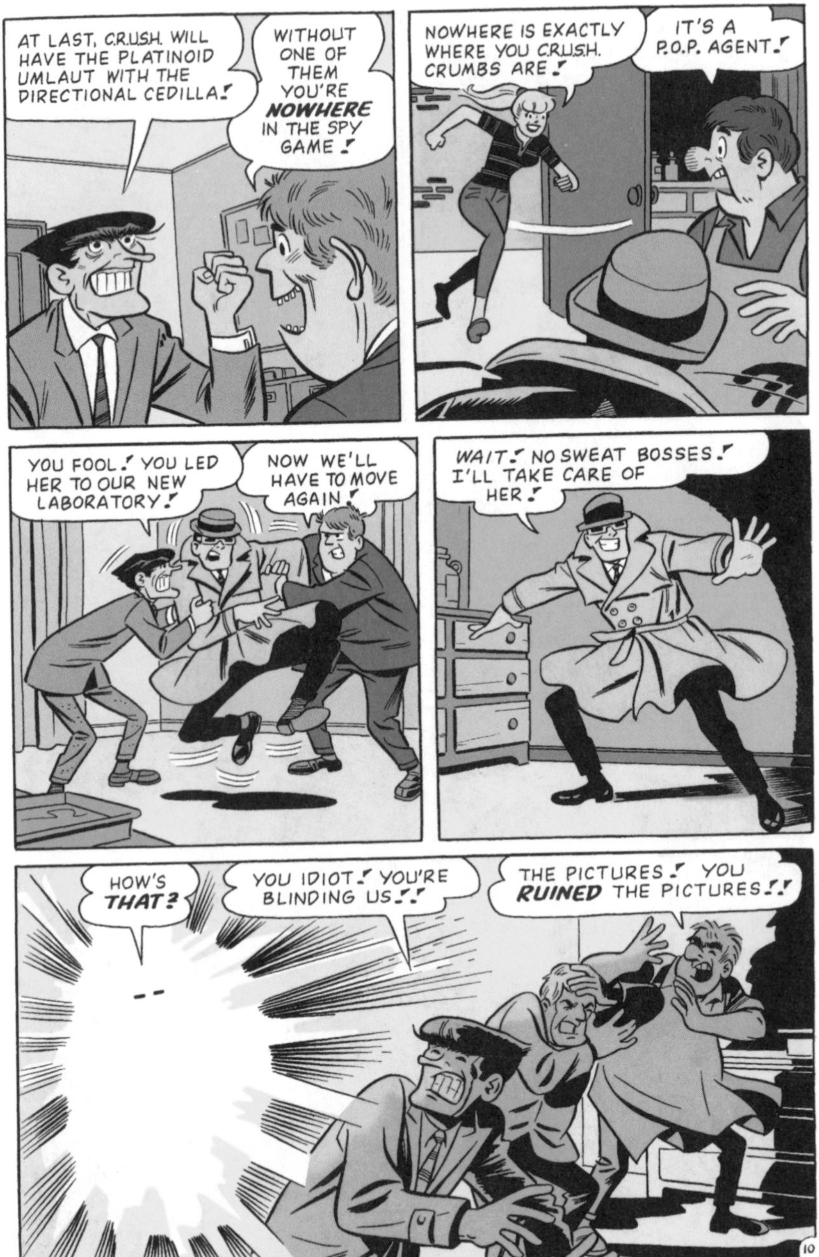
AT LAST, C.R.U.S.H. WILL HAVE THE PLATINOID UMLAUT WITH THE DIRECTIONAL CEDILLA!
WITHOUT ONE OF THEM YOU'RE **NOWHERE** IN THE SPY GAME!
NOWHERE IS EXACTLY WHERE YOU C.R.U.S.H. CRUMBS ARE!
IT'S A P.O.P. AGENT!
YOU FOOL! YOU LED HER TO OUR NEW LABORATORY!
NOW WE'LL HAVE TO MOVE AGAIN!
WAIT! NO SWEAT BOSSES! I'LL TAKE CARE OF HER!
HOW'S ***THAT?***
YOU IDIOT! YOU'RE BLINDING US!!
THE PICTURES! YOU ***RUINED*** THE PICTURES!!
10

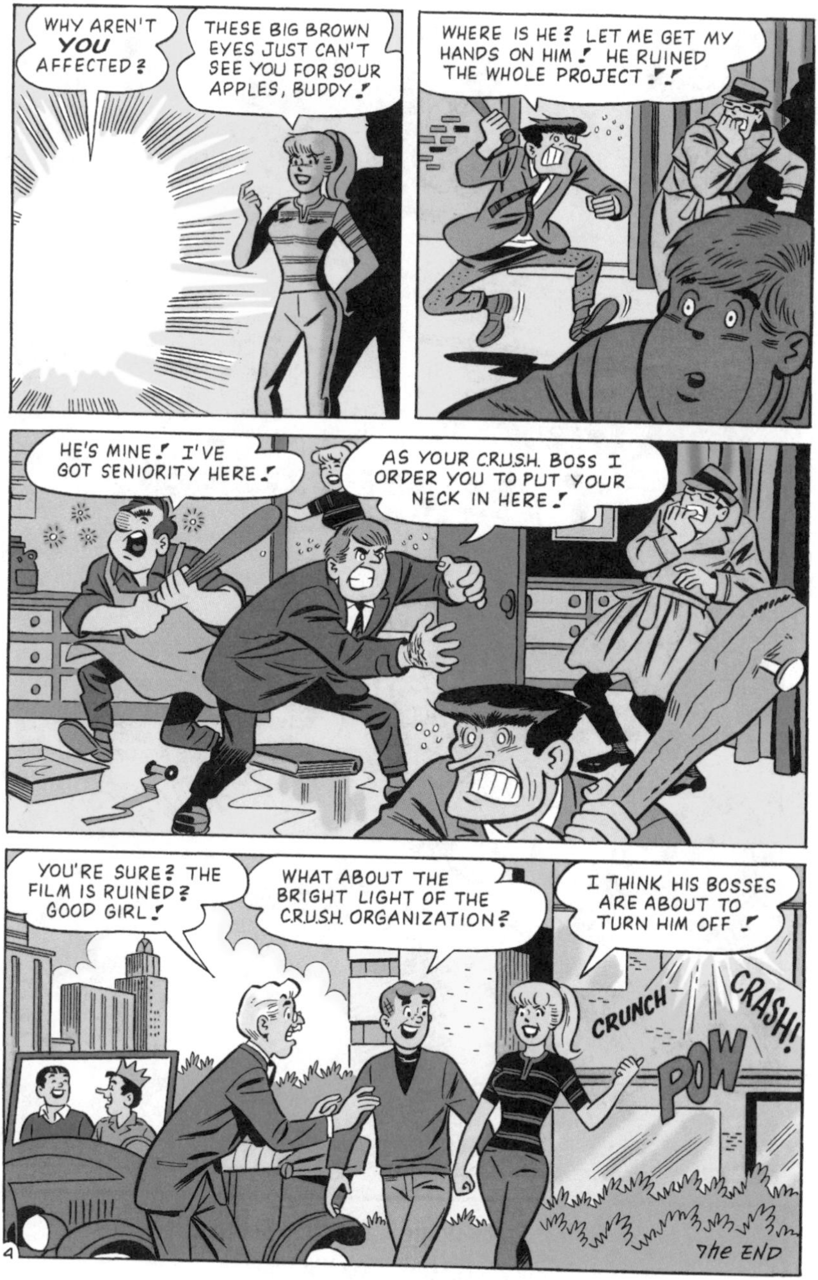
WHY AREN'T YOU AFFECTED?
THESE BIG BROWN EYES JUST CAN'T SEE YOU FOR SOUR APPLES, BUDDY!
WHERE IS HE? LET ME GET MY HANDS ON HIM! HE RUINED THE WHOLE PROJECT!!
HE'S MINE! I'VE GOT SENIORITY HERE!
AS YOUR C.R.U.S.H. BOSS I ORDER YOU TO PUT YOUR NECK IN HERE!
YOU'RE SURE? THE FILM IS RUINED? GOOD GIRL!
WHAT ABOUT THE BRIGHT LIGHT OF THE C.R.U.S.H. ORGANIZATION?
I THINK HIS BOSSES ARE ABOUT TO TURN HIM OFF!
CRUNCH
CRASH!
POW
THE END

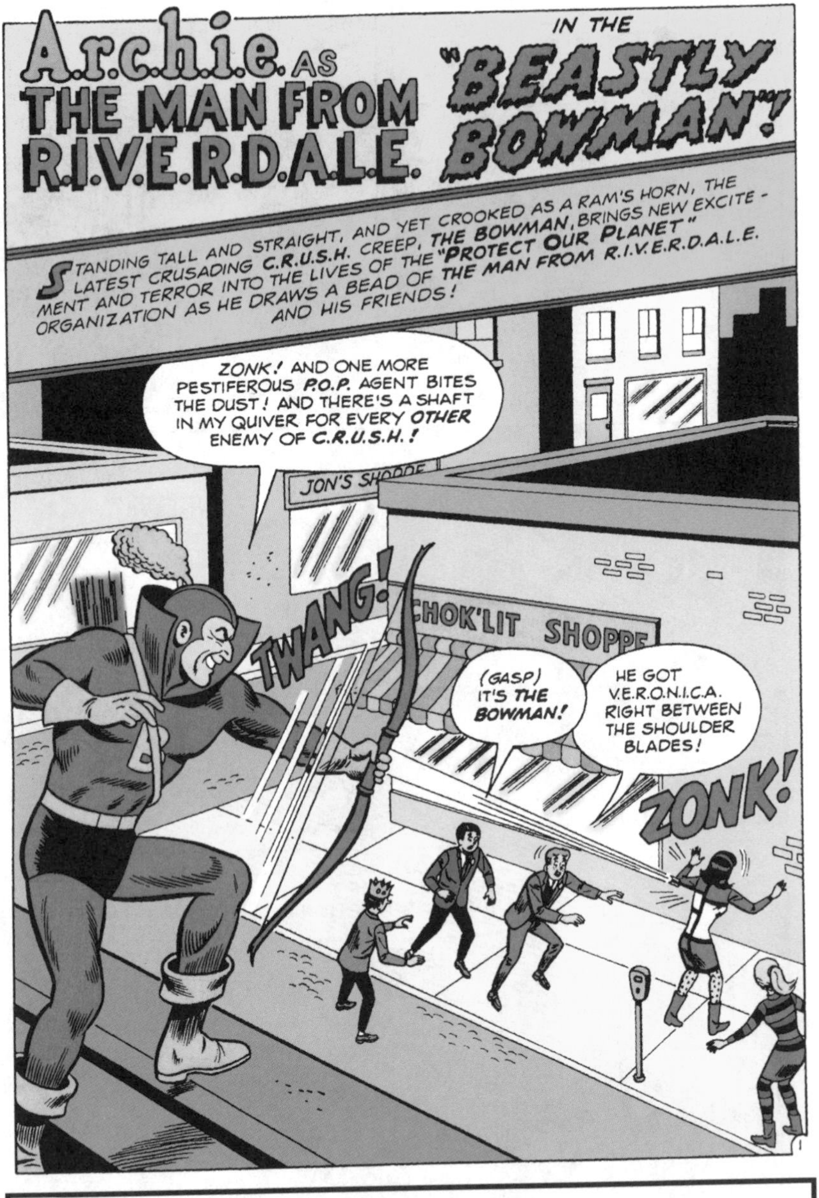
Archie AS THE MAN FROM R.I.V.E.R.D.A.L.E.
IN THE "BEASTLY BOWMAN"!
STANDING TALL AND STRAIGHT, AND YET CROOKED AS A RAM'S HORN, THE LATEST CRUSADING C.R.U.S.H. CREEP, THE BOWMAN, BRINGS NEW EXCITEMENT AND TERROR INTO THE LIVES OF THE "PROTECT OUR PLANET" ORGANIZATION AS HE DRAWS A BEAD OF THE MAN FROM R.I.V.E.R.D.A.L.E. AND HIS FRIENDS!
ZONK! AND ONE MORE PESTIFEROUS P.O.P. AGENT BITES THE DUST! AND THERE'S A SHAFT IN MY QUIVER FOR EVERY OTHER ENEMY OF C.R.U.S.H.!
TWANG!
CHOK'LIT SHOPPE
(GASP) IT'S THE BOWMAN!
HE GOT V.E.R.O.N.I.C.A. RIGHT BETWEEN THE SHOULDER BLADES!
ZONK!

Story: Frank Doyle Pencils: Bob White
Inks & Letters: Jon D'Agostino

Originally printed in LIFE WITH ARCHIE #59, MARCH 1967

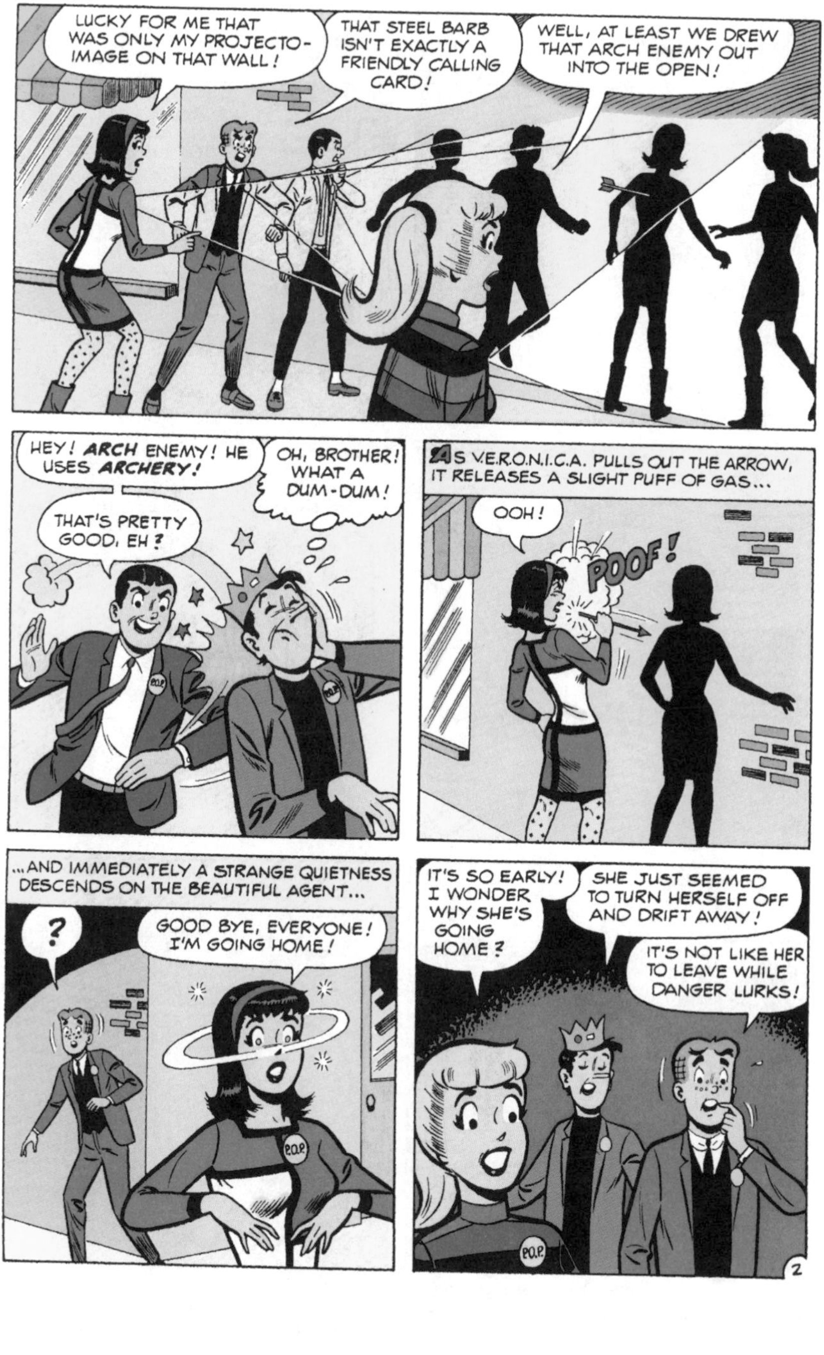
LUCKY FOR ME THAT WAS ONLY MY PROJECTO-IMAGE ON THAT WALL!
THAT STEEL BARB ISN'T EXACTLY A FRIENDLY CALLING CARD!
WELL, AT LEAST WE DREW THAT ARCH ENEMY OUT INTO THE OPEN!
HEY! ARCH ENEMY! HE USES ARCHERY!
THAT'S PRETTY GOOD, EH?
OH, BROTHER! WHAT A DUM-DUM!
AS V.E.R.O.N.I.C.A. PULLS OUT THE ARROW, IT RELEASES A SLIGHT PUFF OF GAS...
OOH!
POOF!
...AND IMMEDIATELY A STRANGE QUIETNESS DESCENDS ON THE BEAUTIFUL AGENT...
?
GOOD BYE, EVERYONE! I'M GOING HOME!
IT'S SO EARLY! I WONDER WHY SHE'S GOING HOME?
SHE JUST SEEMED TO TURN HERSELF OFF AND DRIFT AWAY!
IT'S NOT LIKE HER TO LEAVE WHILE DANGER LURKS!
2

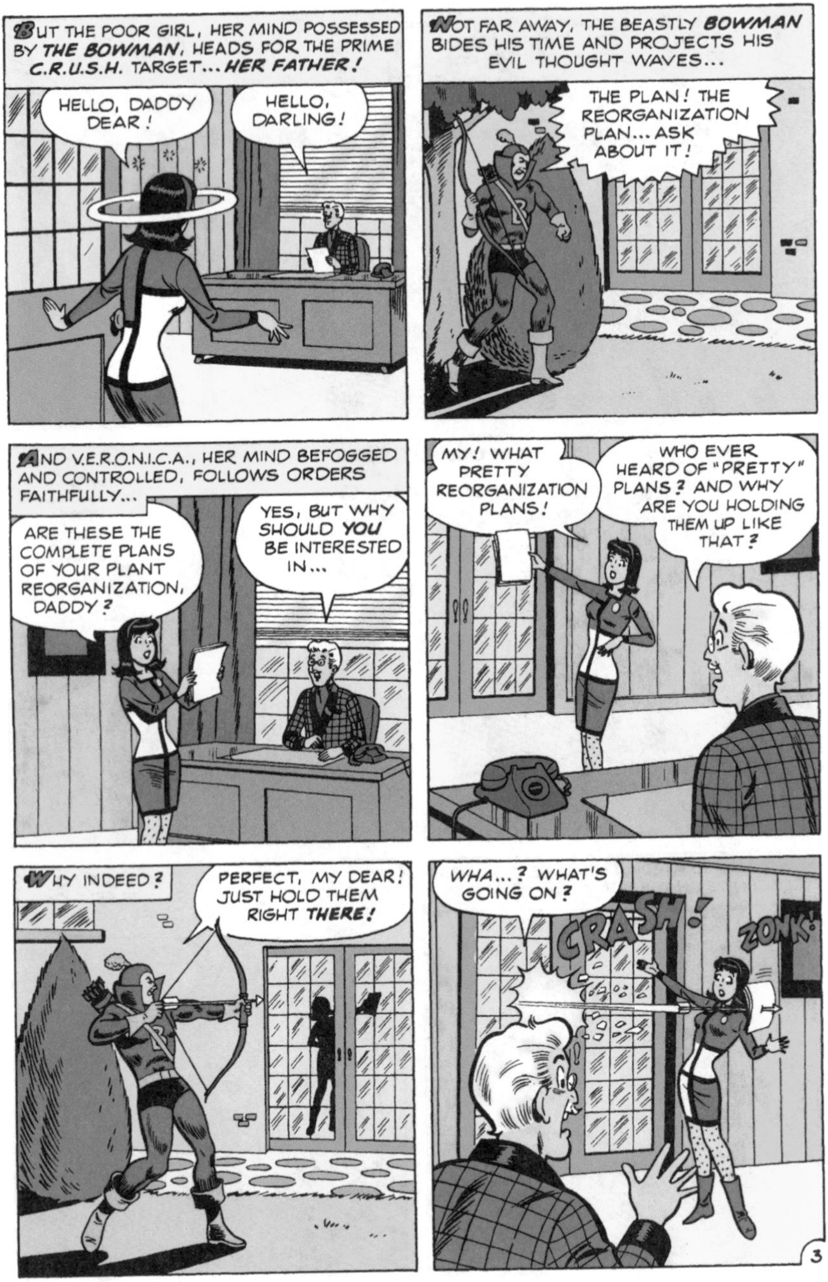
BUT THE POOR GIRL, HER MIND POSSESSED BY THE BOWMAN, HEADS FOR THE PRIME C.R.U.S.H. TARGET... HER FATHER!
HELLO, DADDY DEAR!
HELLO, DARLING!
NOT FAR AWAY, THE BEASTLY BOWMAN BIDES HIS TIME AND PROJECTS HIS EVIL THOUGHT WAVES...
THE PLAN! THE REORGANIZATION PLAN... ASK ABOUT IT!
AND V.E.R.O.N.I.C.A., HER MIND BEFOGGED AND CONTROLLED, FOLLOWS ORDERS FAITHFULLY...
ARE THESE THE COMPLETE PLANS OF YOUR PLANT REORGANIZATION, DADDY?
YES, BUT WHY SHOULD YOU BE INTERESTED IN...
MY! WHAT PRETTY REORGANIZATION PLANS!
WHO EVER HEARD OF "PRETTY" PLANS? AND WHY ARE YOU HOLDING THEM UP LIKE THAT?
WHY INDEED?
PERFECT, MY DEAR! JUST HOLD THEM RIGHT THERE!
WHA...? WHAT'S GOING ON?
CRASH!
ZONK!
3

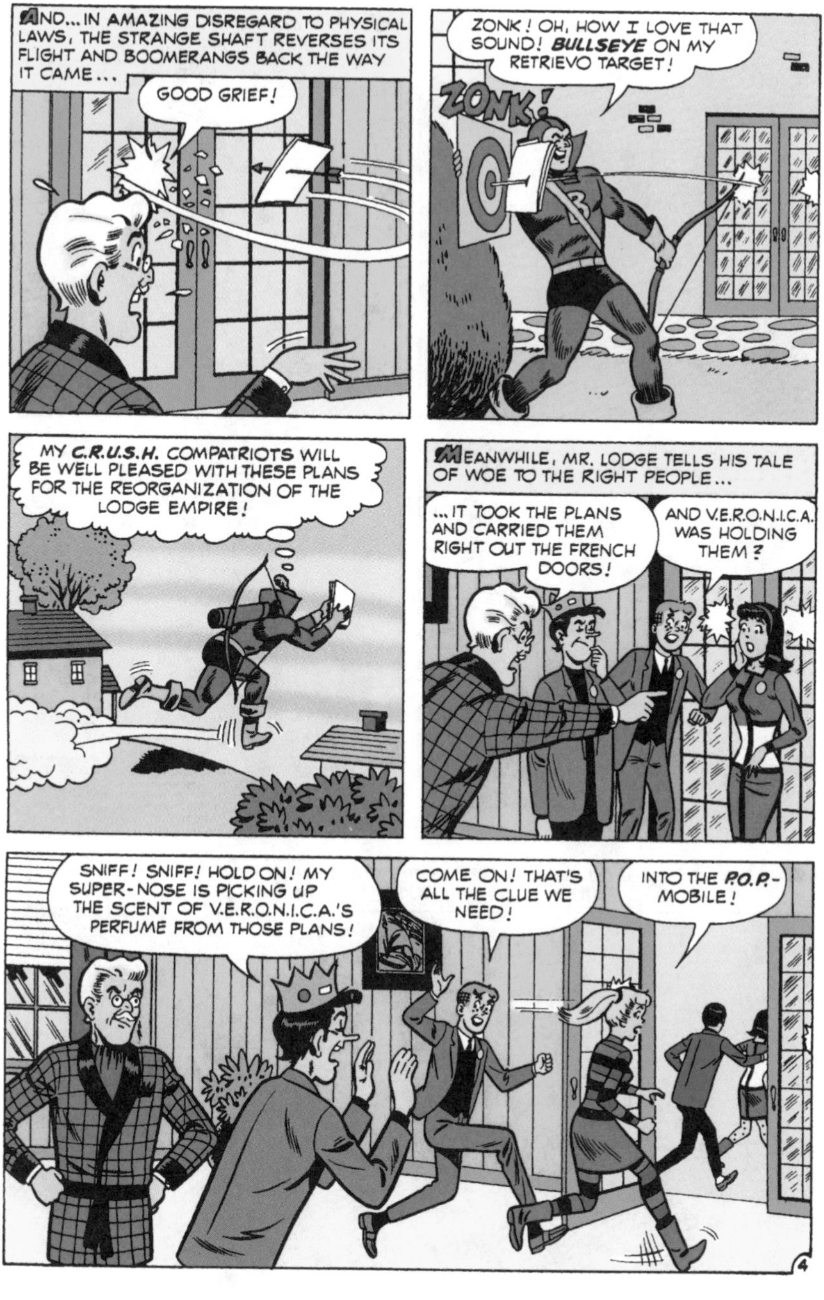
AND... IN AMAZING DISREGARD TO PHYSICAL LAWS, THE STRANGE SHAFT REVERSES ITS FLIGHT AND BOOMERANGS BACK THE WAY IT CAME...
GOOD GRIEF!
ZONK! OH, HOW I LOVE THAT SOUND! BULLSEYE ON MY RETRIEVO TARGET!
ZONK!
MY C.R.U.S.H. COMPATRIOTS WILL BE WELL PLEASED WITH THESE PLANS FOR THE REORGANIZATION OF THE LODGE EMPIRE!
MEANWHILE, MR. LODGE TELLS HIS TALE OF WOE TO THE RIGHT PEOPLE...
...IT TOOK THE PLANS AND CARRIED THEM RIGHT OUT THE FRENCH DOORS!
AND V.E.R.O.N.I.C.A. WAS HOLDING THEM?
SNIFF! SNIFF! HOLD ON! MY SUPER-NOSE IS PICKING UP THE SCENT OF V.E.R.O.N.I.C.A.'S PERFUME FROM THOSE PLANS!
COME ON! THAT'S ALL THE CLUE WE NEED!
INTO THE P.O.P.-MOBILE!
4

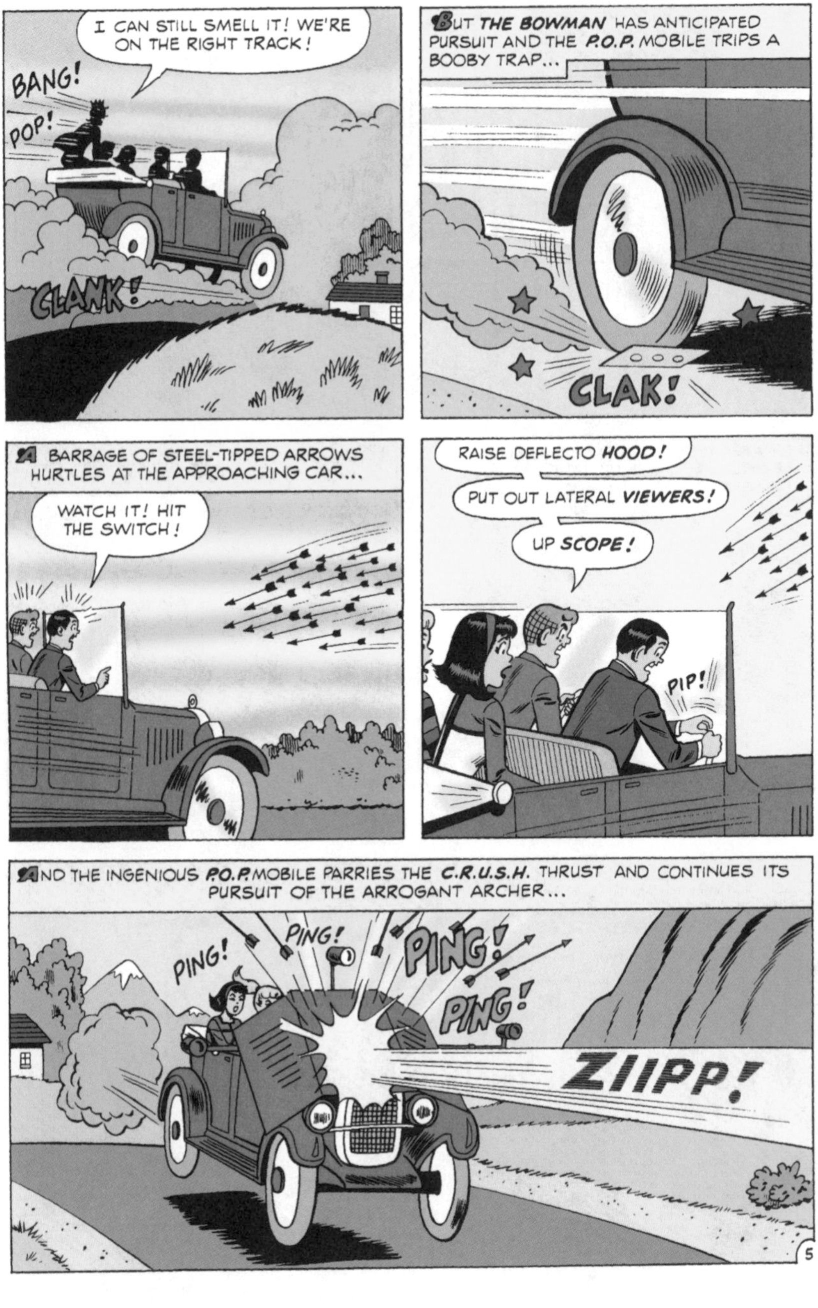
I CAN STILL SMELL IT! WE'RE ON THE RIGHT TRACK!
BANG!
POP!
CLANK!
BUT THE BOWMAN HAS ANTICIPATED PURSUIT AND THE P.O.P. MOBILE TRIPS A BOOBY TRAP...
CLAK!
A BARRAGE OF STEEL-TIPPED ARROWS HURTLES AT THE APPROACHING CAR...
WATCH IT! HIT THE SWITCH!
RAISE DEFLECTO HOOD!
PUT OUT LATERAL VIEWERS!
UP SCOPE!
PIP!
AND THE INGENIOUS P.O.P. MOBILE PARRIES THE C.R.U.S.H. THRUST AND CONTINUES ITS PURSUIT OF THE ARROGANT ARCHER...
PING!
PING!
PING!
PING!
ZIIPP!
5

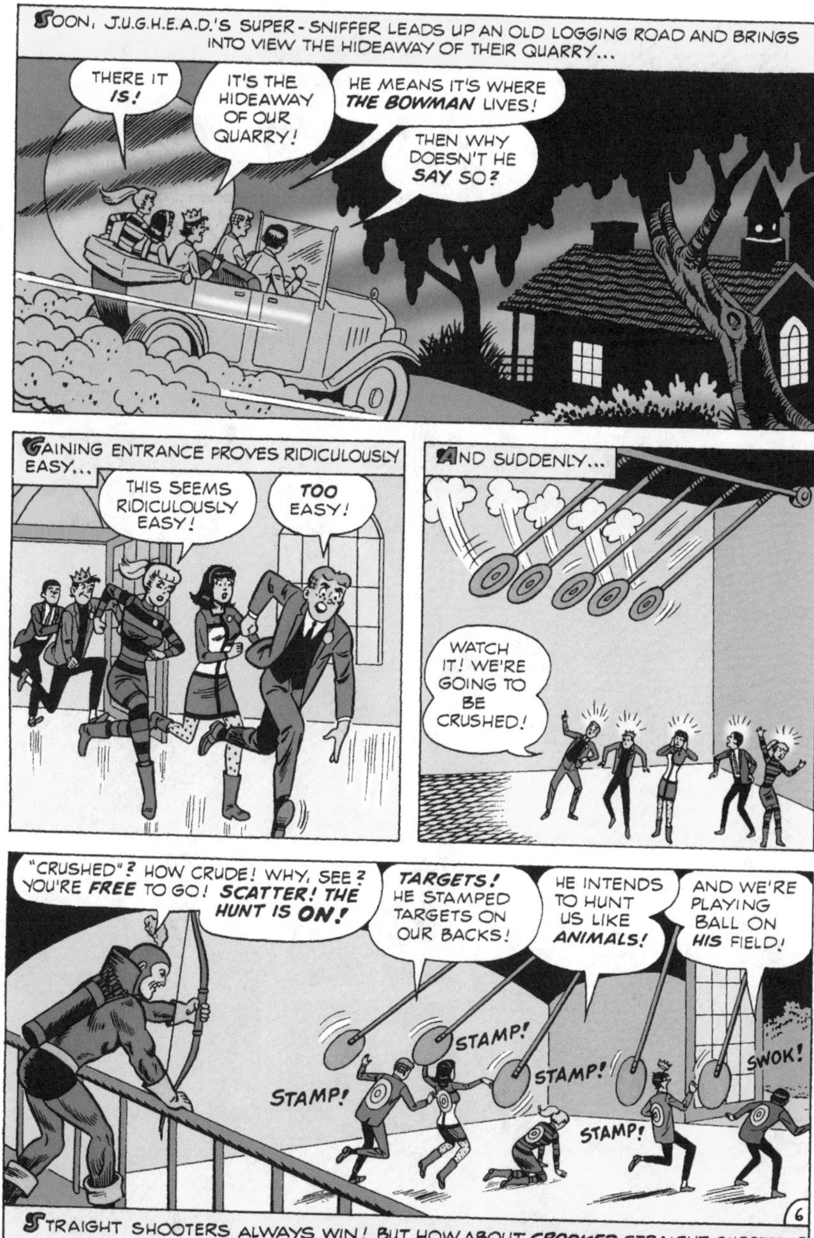
SOON, J.U.G.H.E.A.D.'S SUPER-SNIFFER LEADS UP AN OLD LOGGING ROAD AND BRINGS INTO VIEW THE HIDEAWAY OF THEIR QUARRY...
THERE IT IS!
IT'S THE HIDEAWAY OF OUR QUARRY!
HE MEANS IT'S WHERE THE BOWMAN LIVES!
THEN WHY DOESN'T HE SAY SO?
GAINING ENTRANCE PROVES RIDICULOUSLY EASY...
THIS SEEMS RIDICULOUSLY EASY!
TOO EASY!
AND SUDDENLY...
WATCH IT! WE'RE GOING TO BE CRUSHED!
"CRUSHED"? HOW CRUDE! WHY, SEE? YOU'RE FREE TO GO! SCATTER! THE HUNT IS ON!
TARGETS! HE STAMPED TARGETS ON OUR BACKS!
HE INTENDS TO HUNT US LIKE ANIMALS!
AND WE'RE PLAYING BALL ON HIS FIELD!
STAMP!
STAMP!
STAMP!
STAMP!
SWOK!
6
STRAIGHT SHOOTERS ALWAYS WIN! BUT HOW ABOUT CROOKED STRAIGHT SHOOTERS? TALLY HO AND AWAY! LET'S JOIN THE HUNT!

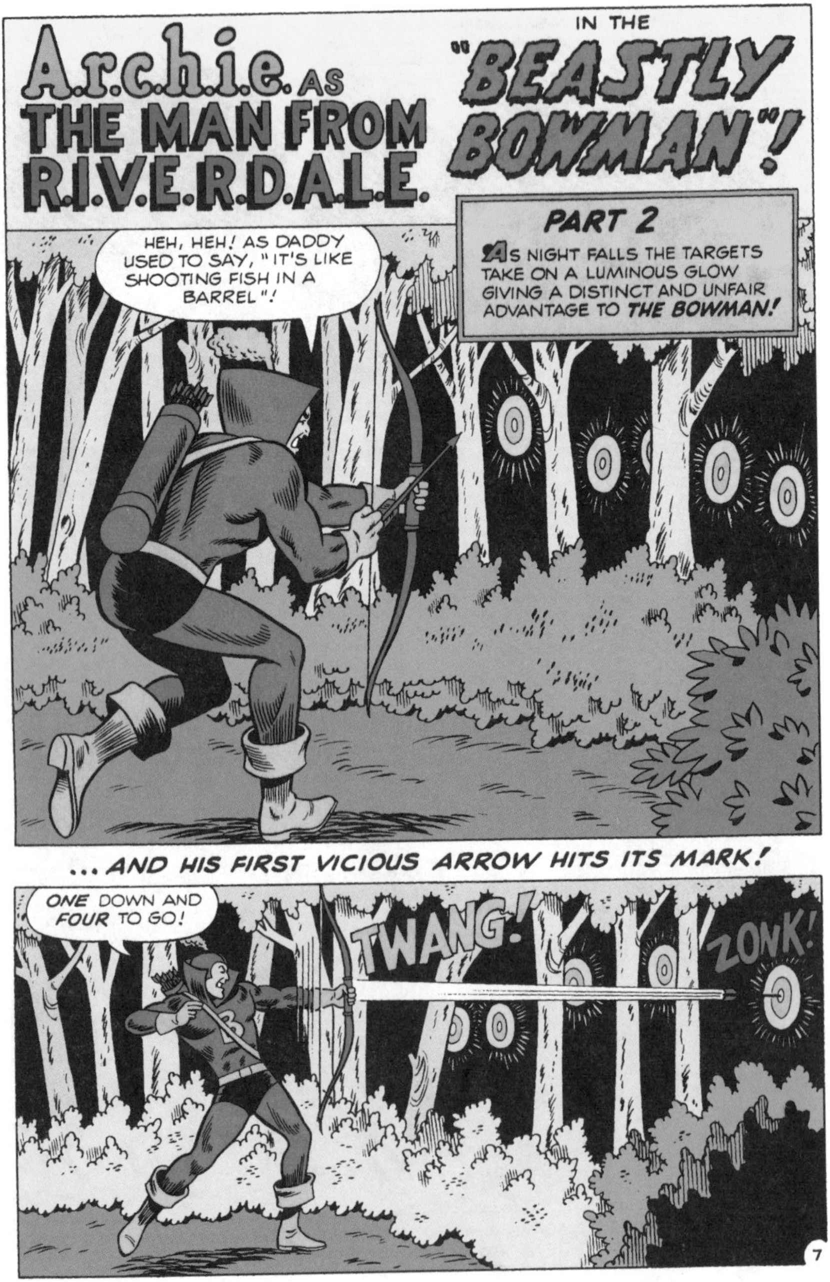
Archie as
THE MAN FROM R.I.V.E.R.D.A.L.E.
IN THE "BEASTLY BOWMAN"!
PART 2
AS NIGHT FALLS THE TARGETS TAKE ON A LUMINOUS GLOW GIVING A DISTINCT AND UNFAIR ADVANTAGE TO THE BOWMAN!
HEH, HEH! AS DADDY USED TO SAY, "IT'S LIKE SHOOTING FISH IN A BARREL"!
...AND HIS FIRST VICIOUS ARROW HITS ITS MARK!
ONE DOWN AND FOUR TO GO!
TWANG!
ZONK!
7

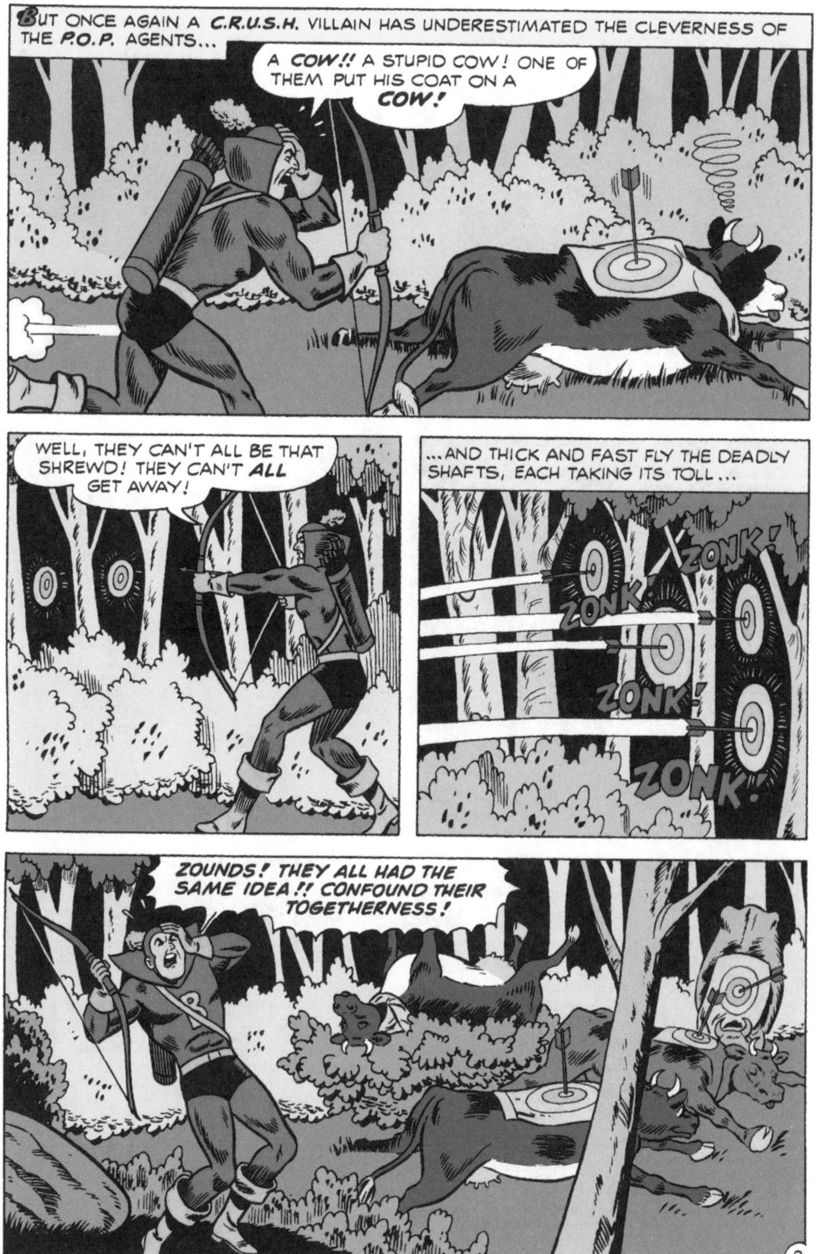
BUT ONCE AGAIN A C.R.U.S.H. VILLAIN HAS UNDERESTIMATED THE CLEVERNESS OF THE P.O.P. AGENTS...
A COW!! A STUPID COW! ONE OF THEM PUT HIS COAT ON A COW!
WELL, THEY CAN'T ALL BE THAT SHREWD! THEY CAN'T ALL GET AWAY!
...AND THICK AND FAST FLY THE DEADLY SHAFTS, EACH TAKING ITS TOLL...
ZONK!
ZONK!
ZONK!
ZONK!
ZOUNDS! THEY ALL HAD THE SAME IDEA!! CONFOUND THEIR TOGETHERNESS!
8

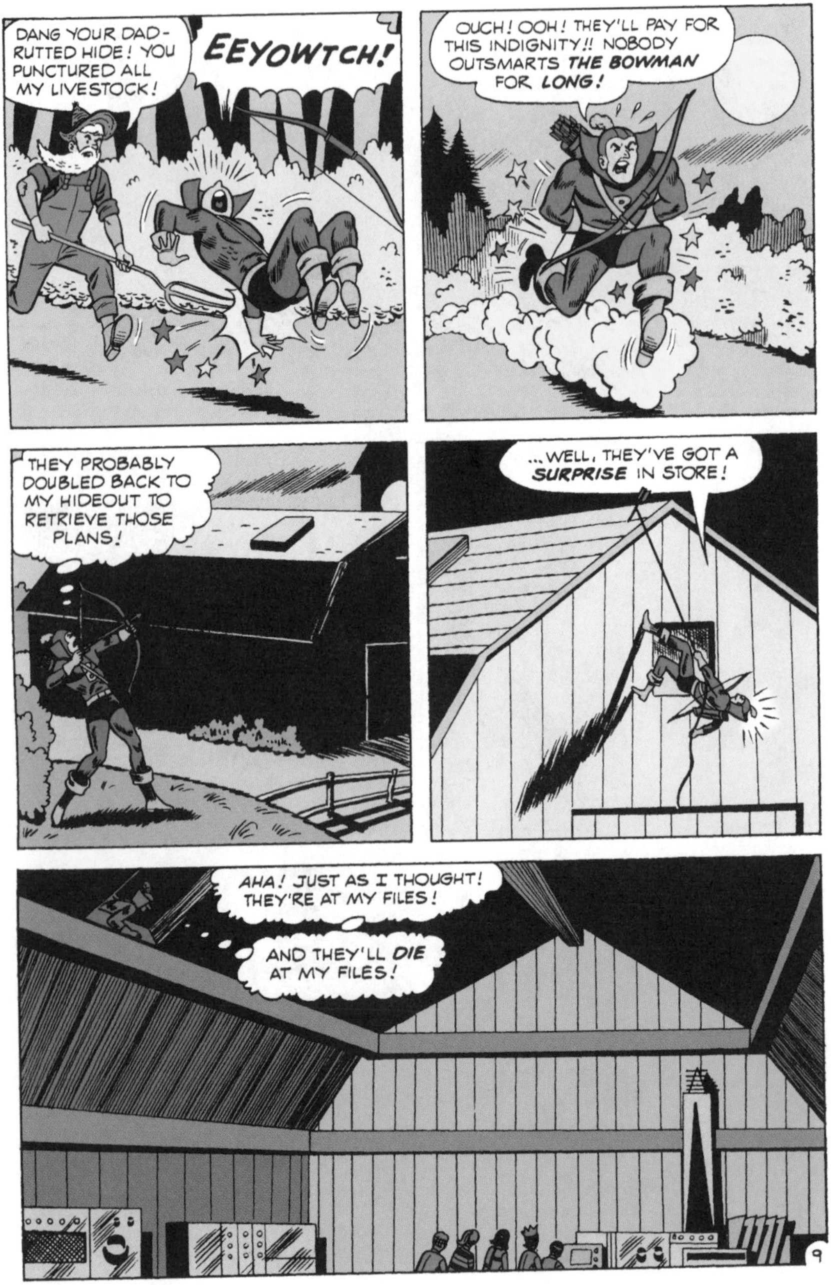
DANG YOUR DAD-RUTTED HIDE! YOU PUNCTURED ALL MY LIVESTOCK!
EEYOWTCH!
OUCH! OOH! THEY'LL PAY FOR THIS INDIGNITY!! NOBODY OUTSMARTS THE BOWMAN FOR LONG!
THEY PROBABLY DOUBLED BACK TO MY HIDEOUT TO RETRIEVE THOSE PLANS!
...WELL, THEY'VE GOT A SURPRISE IN STORE!
AHA! JUST AS I THOUGHT! THEY'RE AT MY FILES!
AND THEY'LL DIE AT MY FILES!
9

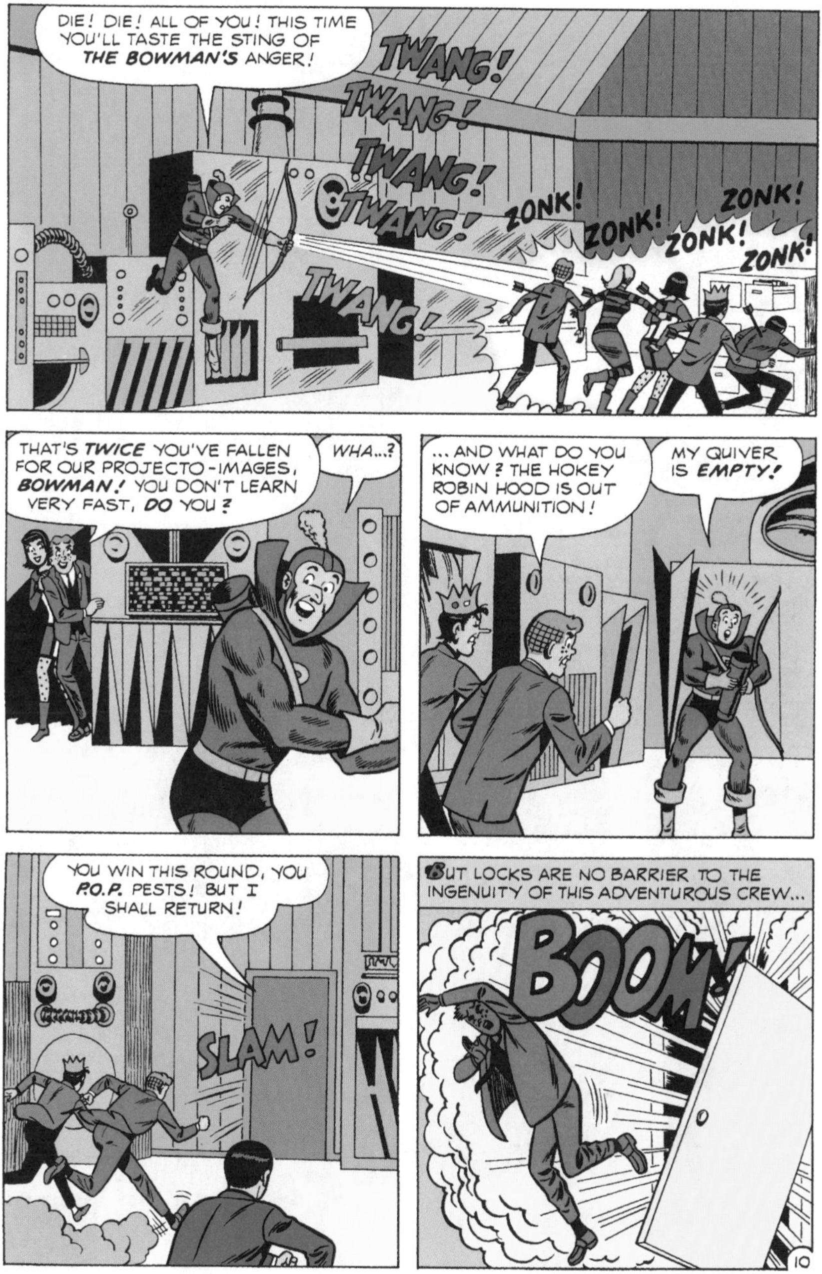
DIE! DIE! ALL OF YOU! THIS TIME YOU'LL TASTE THE STING OF THE BOWMAN'S ANGER!
TWANG! TWANG! TWANG! TWANG! TWANG!
ZONK! ZONK! ZONK! ZONK! ZONK!
THAT'S TWICE YOU'VE FALLEN FOR OUR PROJECTO-IMAGES, BOWMAN! YOU DON'T LEARN VERY FAST, DO YOU?
WHA...?
... AND WHAT DO YOU KNOW? THE HOKEY ROBIN HOOD IS OUT OF AMMUNITION!
MY QUIVER IS EMPTY!
YOU WIN THIS ROUND, YOU P.O.P. PESTS! BUT I SHALL RETURN!
SLAM!
BUT LOCKS ARE NO BARRIER TO THE INGENUITY OF THIS ADVENTUROUS CREW...
BOOM!
10

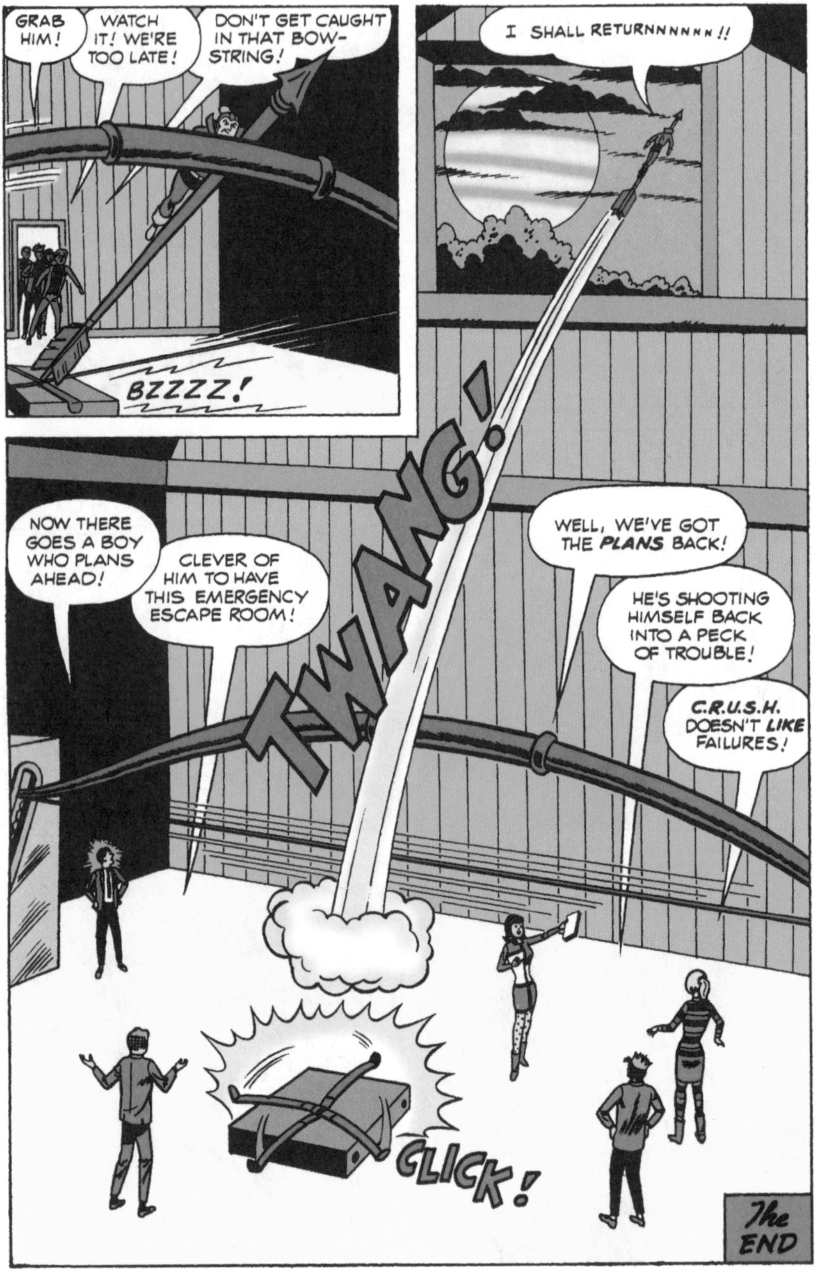
GRAB HIM!
WATCH IT! WE'RE TOO LATE!
DON'T GET CAUGHT IN THAT BOW-STRING!
BZZZZ!
I SHALL RETURNNNNNNN!!
TWANG!
NOW THERE GOES A BOY WHO PLANS AHEAD!
CLEVER OF HIM TO HAVE THIS EMERGENCY ESCAPE ROOM!
WELL, WE'VE GOT THE PLANS BACK!
HE'S SHOOTING HIMSELF BACK INTO A PECK OF TROUBLE!
C.R.U.S.H. DOESN'T LIKE FAILURES!
CLICK!
The END